THE BLACK SCORPION
PILOT

THE BLACK SCORPION PILOT

A Ford Stevens Military-Aviation Thriller

Book 2

LAWRENCE A. COLBY

MACH278

The Black Scorpion Pilot: A Ford Stevens Military-Aviation Thriller (Book 2)

© 2018 Lawrence A. Colby
Mach278 LLC Books
Dulles, Virginia, USA

http://www.ColbyAviationThrillers.com

Book and cover design by Ivan Zanchetta Design
Library of Congress Cataloging in Publication Data
The Black Scorpion Pilot: A Ford Stevens Military-Aviation Thriller (Book 2) by Lawrence A. Colby

ISBN-13: 9781541285835
ISBN-10: 1541285832

1. Stevens, Ford (Fictitious Character)—Military Thriller—fiction 2. Aviation—fiction
3. Armed Services—United States—Fiction 4. Military—United States I. Colby, Lawrence A.
II. The Black Scorpion Pilot. III. A Ford Stevens Military-Aviation Thriller (Book 2)

For my family, who said it could be done

A portion of the proceeds from The Ford Stevens Military-Aviation Thriller Series *will go to these two great veteran organizations:*

Team Rubicon Global
www.teamrubiconglobal.org

Team Rubicon Global provides veterans around the world with opportunities to serve others in the wake of disasters. Learn how you can support our efforts to build a global veteran community that provides assistance to disaster victims.

The Headstrong Project
http://getheadstrong.org/

Headstrong Project is a nonprofit partnered with Weill Cornell Medical Center to fund and develop comprehensive mental healthcare programs to treat Iraq and Afghanistan veterans free of cost, stigma, and bureaucracy.

PUBLISHER'S NOTE

All members, former members, and employees of the Department of Defense (DoD) are required to submit their writings for prepublication review. The prepublication review is the process to determine that information proposed for public release contains no protected information, is consistent with established Department of Defense policies, and conforms to standards as determined by the department leadership.

Author Lawrence A. Colby, whose career for DoD entailed real-world operations, abided by the policy. His manuscript was reviewed by defense officials in Washington, DC, and returned to him after an *in-depth and extensive seventeen-month review*. All edits that DoD determined were necessary are complete. The book is aligned with DoD for fiction publication, and all comments related to national security matters have been changed without protest from the author. The review does not constitute endorsement of his books by the United States Department of Defense.

This book has been approved by formal process at the Defense Office of Prepublication and Security Review.

We thank you for your understanding and look forward to your enjoyment of this book.

*WE CANNOT CHOOSE OUR EXTERNAL CIRCUM-
STANCES, BUT WE CAN ALWAYS CHOOSE HOW
WE RESPOND TO THEM.*

—EPICTETUS, AD 50–135

GLOBAL SMARTPHONE FACTS

Number of smartphone users worldwide:
2014—1.57 billion
2017—2.32 billion
2020—5.0 billion

Number of smartphone users in the United States:
2014—171 million
2017—225 million (100 million use the iPhone)
2020—285 million

Population of China: 1.37 billion

Connected to the internet: 688 million, more than half; more than 90 percent of users access the web by a smartphone

Largest group: College students and citizens under the age of nineteen

Activated smartphones in China: 780 million+, a penetration rate of about 59 percent of the population

Brand: iPhones account for 16.8 percent of those smartphones

China has more iPhones than any other country in the world.

TABLE OF CONTENTS

LIST OF MAIN CHARACTERS

Michelle Boyd
Missile Analyst, Defense Intelligence Agency, Washington, DC

Calvin Burns
Principal Deputy Director, Defense Intelligence Agency, Washington, DC

He Chen
Lieutenant General, People's Liberation Army Air Force, China

Jason Cohen
Executive Assistant to Deputy Director Calvin Burns, DIA

Robert Dooley
Intelligence Officer, Defense Intelligence Agency, Washington, DC

Jeanie Heller
Cyber Analyst, Department of the Air Force, Washington, DC

Dai Jian
Captain, People's Liberation Army Air Force, China

Chung Kang
Captain, People's Liberation Army Air Force, China

Bai Keung
First Lieutenant, People's Liberation Army Air Force, China, Aide-de-Camp

Mike Klubb
Missile Analyst, Defense Intelligence Agency, Washington, DC

Wu Lee
Pilot, Captain, People's Liberation Army Air Force, China

Emily Livingston
Economist, International Monetary Fund, UK Citizen

Michael Miller
Woodloch Pines Resort, Social Staff, and Resident of Hawley, Pennsylvania

Lance Monterey
US Consulate Officer, US State Department, India

Tiffany "Pinky" Pinkerton
Captain, US Air Force, B-1B Lancer Copilot, Ellsworth AFB, Rapid City, South Dakota

Samuel Price
Secretary of Defense, Pentagon, Washington, DC

Ravi Rahul
Group Captain, Indian Air Force

Mark Savona
China Aircraft Analyst, Defense Intelligence Agency, Washington, DC

Ford Stevens
Captain, US Air Force, B-1B Lancer Pilot, Ellsworth AFB, Rapid City, South Dakota

Zeke Ziehmann
Colonel, US Air Force, Diego Garcia B-2 Spirit Detachment Commander

PROLOGUE

Present Day
Defense Intelligence Agency Headquarters, Washington, DC

The deputy director of the Defense Intelligence Agency sat at his desk reviewing the morning *Early Bird News* when his assistant, Jason Cohen, knocked on the door.

Though hesitant to bother the boss first thing in the morning, the young man spoke first. "Morning, Mr. Burns. We got a bit of a problem right outta the gate," he said.

"What is it, Jason?" said Deputy Director Calvin Burns, looking above his cheater glasses on the edge of his nose. "Sorry, I should have said good morning to you. Yes, Jason, good morning."

Jason was still cordial. "A few months ago, you had me bring up to your office a missile analyst from downstairs. Employee named Mike Klubb."

"Hmm."

"Do you remember him?"

"Absolutely. Yup. Why do you ask?"

"Well, Mr. Burns. He's here. Says it's urgent. Something he has to talk to you about, a problem from the past. He won't talk to me about it, says I don't have a need to know. Clearance thing. Says he'll only talk to you. Said you would understand?"

Calvin sat back in his leather chair, rubbed his chin, and thought of Mike. *Why would he come back here?* the deputy thought. "Here? In the waiting room?"

The deputy looked at the wall of red digital clocks that told world time zones lining his office.

"Yes," Jason answered.

"OK, send him in," Burns instructed.

Mike Klubb walked in, more like rolled in, looking like he'd gained another few pounds since the last time the deputy saw him. His disheveled, white, collared shirt was untucked a bit in the rear, his black necktie was a wee bit too short, and his scuffed brown leather shoes had apparently never seen polish. "Hi, hello, Mr. Deputy Burns, sir."

"Hello, Mike. How are you? What brings you back up this way?" asked the deputy, coming around from his desk to greet him.

Mike was a missile analyst at the Defense Intelligence Agency, the DIA, working out of the headquarters on Bolling Air Force Base in Washington. He was a typical government bureaucrat, always keeping an eye on the clock and counting down the time until he could leave for the day. So many of the government employees were very talented, educated, and dedicated to the mission at DIA, but Mike broke the mold. He entered the facility at 6:00 a.m. sharp, walking like a zombie from the parking lot each morning, just staring at the ground, and never looked anyone in the eye. Before leaving each day for home at exactly 2:30 p.m., he always made sure to bring home the black lunch box his wife packed for him. Mike only put in the minimum effort for what was necessary to keep his job, sometimes doing what was asked, but never more. He gave other solid, hardworking government employees a bad name.

His last run-in with the deputy was inside the DIA auditorium when Mike and his team started to look into Chinese missiles a few months ago. The indications were detected by the Space Based Infrared System satellites, the SBIRS, which orbited the earth at some twenty-two thousand miles, watching from afar. SBIRS was used for missile defense and battle space awareness.

During the auditorium brief, analyst Mark Savona showed up uninvited and confronted Mike, leading to a nasty public argument. The deputy was forced to weigh in on the revolting confrontation and eventually told Mike to stop looking into the Chinese missile situation. A short week later, the deputy called Mike up to his office, shared that the Chinese event was highly classified, and gave him a personal gold and blue Deputy Director of DIA Challenge Coin to go away. Mike has it displayed on the fireplace mantle at home.

"Sir, we have more of your missiles over China," Mike explained.

"Missiles? I don't understand."

Talking quickly, Mike continued. "Sir, last time we met in the auditorium, it was because the SBIRS team out of Buckley Air Force Base detected missiles over China—the infrared ones that the Air Force monitors. We...we thought it was maybe another Chinese ICBM test. You brought me up here and told me to stop looking into it. It was going to be compartmented, and I never heard or talked about it again. Until now."

Calvin stood and stared at Klubb in disbelief. Calvin turned his head sideways in thought. "Really? Tell me more."

More nervous, Mike pressed on as asked. "We detected, or rather Buckley detected, eighteen flashes between last Thursday and today. It looks like another large ICBM, but...nobody has figured it out. The signature that is. But I remember this specific signature. The computer doesn't know it, but I do."

Calvin turned his head sideways in thought. Squinted his eyes a bit, and kept staring.

Located at Buckley AFB and housed in a humongous Satellite Operations Center facility, was the US Air Force's 460th Space Wing. The airmen from the wing controlled and watched the country's SBIRS, as well as the older system, the Defense Support Program, known as DSP. The group of hundreds of service members in active, Reserve and Air National Guard units watched the earth, giving decision makers the information as it came in. Their clients could be intelligence community agencies, the Pentagon, Department of Homeland Security, the military Combatant Commanders, and even the National Security Council.

Using the best poker face he could scrounge up, Calvin turned to look at the wall, then back at Mike while biting his bottom lip. "Very interesting, Mike. Thank you. Perhaps, if it's not too much trouble, could you send me what you have? Would that be all right? And, Mike, it doesn't require your team, just you; quietly bring it up here or send it to me on secure email. I'd be interested in seeing what you've got," asked the deputy. *What did this guy see?*

Mike instantly turned into a frenzy of activity, without ever moving from his original standing position. Talking even faster, he answered, "Oh, right away, sir. I've got everything. Everything from last week and from last night. I was having my morning hot chocolate that my wife makes for me every morning and, I…"

"Mike. Mike. Terrific. Take it easy," the deputy told him, moving his palms in a downward motion to keep him calm. "Just bring it on up. Yes? Good?"

"Yes, yes, sir. Will be right back. Thank you, Deputy Burns," Mike answered, as he massaged his hands together into a sweaty ball. Klubb turned around and banged his shin on the glass coffee table, backed up awkwardly, and left the room.

Deputy Burns could not believe what he just heard. He walked over to his couch and sat down, placing his forearms like he was sitting on the toilet. Leaning back, he stared out into the air for a few long seconds. He let out a sigh. *I'm retiring in a month*, he said to himself.

"Jason!"

Jason came hurriedly into the office. "Yes?"

"Get Mark Savona's ass up here ASAP. I don't care where he is on this earth; he needs to get his butt in here. We got issues. ASAP."

Jason took off on his mission to find Mark Savona from the Chinese Aircraft Directorate, while Calvin leaned over on his couch and placed his face into his hands. He rubbed his nose and eyes after taking off his glasses. Calvin stood up and folded his arms to think, reflecting that he thought he had seen everything in his intelligence officer career, from the Cold War to Gulf War I to Iraq and Afghanistan. Now this.

Even stealing the Chinese stealth bomber Devil Dragon from a few months ago was a career highlight. Just this past Tuesday, DIA and the US Navy had just finished the crane operation at Graham Island, Canada, about a thousand miles northwest of Vancouver. Devil Dragon was drained of the few last drops of fuel remaining, sawed and weld cut into specific pieces, packed in large nondescript crates, and loaded onto a commercial ship from the island to the mainland. Devil Dragon was then hauled via tractor trailer to Tonopah, Nevada. This latest news, though, topped everything for him. Burns was nearly speechless, bordering on shock.

Christ almighty…I just can't believe this. A month before retirement. The goddamn Chinese had two stealth bombers built. We stole one…and now they're test flying the other.

PART 1

CALLING

Coco Cay Island, Bahamas

D IA Analyst Mark Savona didn't have a problem in the world since setting sail on a Royal Caribbean cruise ship to the Bahamas. He and girlfriend, Jeanie Heller, were enjoying their third day at sea onboard the cruise ship *Majesty of the Seas*, taking in the sun and drinking the days and nights away.

Jeanie, who was one of the wildest girlfriends Mark ever had, was sporting a black string bikini and moved gracefully to the live Jimmy Buffet–themed band. Never at a loss for a drink, she sipped her red-colored Bahama Mama drink on the pool deck with a cute, youthful smile. Mark was already on his fourth drink, bare chested, and sporting a purple plaid swimsuit with flip-flops. Showing his forty-year-old body with love handles, Mark ran his hands through his long brown wet hair, slicked back from a dip in the swimming pool. He glanced around the pool deck behind mirrored sunglasses, giving a toothy grin, and wearing a freshly trimmed goatee.

Displaying a glowing tan and long, wet blond hair, Jeanie was receiving more than her share of glances from men on the ship. Only about 115 pounds, she was a pretty little thing, and it did not take much alcohol for her to dance like a wild lady onboard the ship.

"Mark, that ship announcement was for you, baby," rubbing her hand on his hairy chest.

"No one even knows we are down in the islands, sugar. We're just out here, away from that rat race. No problems."

Seconds later, an announcement came again, this time from the social director on board the ship, who was going through the lineup of the coming activities while in-port at Coco Cay Island. On the back end of the announcement was another search for a passenger named Mark Savona.

"Passenger Mark Savona, passenger Mark Savona, please dial 777 for the front desk. You have an urgent message. Mark Savona, dial 777. Thank you, and enjoy our beautiful weather at Coco Cay Island! We are looking forward to seeing you tonight at the captain's dinner!"

"Shit. You're right, Jeanie."

Mark's sixth sense kicked in, and it wasn't good. Almost no one knew he was on the cruise ship. At work, only the human resources computer database knew that he was away on a cruise and out of the country. Whoever wanted him had done their homework. They would have had to track him down out of all the world's cruise lines, then all the Royal Caribbean ships sailing at this very moment, then obtain the ship's phone number, then drill down to find him. *This has DIA Operations written all over it.*

"Go make your call, baby. I'll be right here," Jeanie said, giving him a wink. She eased down into the hot tub and looked over to check on the band.

Since Mark was a few drinks in, he thought about not calling and decided to blow it off. Slipping from the ledge of the hot tub, he entered the water to join Jeanie, and looked across the pool deck at the crowd. A big smile came across his face.

"No way, Jeanie. Staying right here with you, honey. You think I want to leave you alone so I can make a work call?" Mark placed his trademark Washington Nationals baseball cap backward and leaned back with his arms spread on the outside of the tub.

Jeanie laughed while stroking his arm, and they watched the surfing videos play on the pool deck's gigantic screen. The band was taking a break, and the Caribbean music was being piped in over the ship's loudspeakers.

"Ladies and Gentlemen, may I have your attention please. Passenger Mark Savona, Mark Savona, please dial 777 to speak to the front desk. Thank you."

"Well, persistent little buggers, aren't they? Three announcements," Jeanie said, turning to frown at Mark.

Mark looked at the pool full of passengers having a fun time, getting ready for the belly flop contest, and then glanced over at the bar. He then turned to look at Jeanie, and the expression on his face was priceless. "Jeanie, if I make this call, I can almost guarantee the result will be work related," as he ran his hand through his long hair. "Should I make it? Should I make the call?"

"Dude, just go," she replied. "You know you won't relax until you do."

Mark got out of the hot tub, grabbed the famous Royal Caribbean green pool deck towel, and quickly dried himself off. He went through the automatic doors that sensed him coming, and walked over to the house phone on the wall to dial. Mark turned to get one last glance at Jeanie, who was still getting stares from all the plump, older men and their larger wives. He chuckled to himself.

"Hello, this is Catapang from the Philippines. May I help you?"

"Hello, Catapang. This is passenger Mark Savona. I understand from the announcements that you've asked me to dial the front desk?"

"Oh, yes, sir. Mr. Savona, we've got a message, an urgent one: you need to dial immediately to this phone number. Please allow me to pass it. The number is 202-555-1212. And ask for Jason," Catapang told him.

Holy crap, Mark thought. "Are you for real? That's my work number. My work is calling me?" Mark asked.

"I guess so, sir. Actually, they have called a number of times. Very persistent."

"OK, thank you for the message."

Mark hung up and was stunned. Here he was, barely away from the office for a few days, and the deputy director's right-hand man was calling him on a cruise ship in the middle of the Caribbean. "Goddamn it. The damn Devil Dragon is already in Nevada. What does he need now?" Mark quietly and angrily said under his breath.

He made his way back to his oceanfront state room, walked out onto the balcony overlooking the beautiful, clear green water, and ensured the Peanut App on his smartphone was working. The Peanut App automatically encrypted his phone for secure voice, ensuring no one else could hear their call. It displayed a traffic light icon on the screen showing it was connected and turned green when it was secure. Since they were just offshore, his phone picked up the AT&T International cell tower at Coco Cay Island, Bahamas. Mark's anger was growing.

User privacy and messaging apps were becoming increasingly significant for both government and civilians alike. While the Peanut App was totally encrypted with all conceivable security applications, some commercial ones were thought to have encryption, but in actuality, did not. As an example, some programs used end-to-end encryption, such as Facebook's What's App, Apple's iMessage, and Signal's Open Whisper Systems. What was not encrypted were Google Hangouts, Snapchat, Skype, and WeChat. As the DIA knew all too well, commercial encryption methods could always be cracked, so designing their own Peanut App was the right move.

Mark Savona was DIA Deputy Director Calvin Burns's go-to man and an expert on Chinese fighter and bomber aircraft. A graduate of Johns Hopkins University in Baltimore, he earned an undergraduate degree in aeronautical engineering and a master's degree in international relations. He previously worked for five years with Pixar Animation Studios in San Francisco, California, but always had a curious eye on Washington. While most of his coworkers were reading *Variety*, the entertainment trade journal, he was reading *Foreign Affairs*. He continued to be attracted to DIA after seeing an ad in the back of the periodical.

A robust scotch drinker, card player, fan of fantasy football, and avid follower of the Washington Nationals, Mark had life tackled. His girlfriend wasn't too bad on the eyes either.

Mark was also very unusual. One look at him and you'd never know he worked at DIA or conducted covert business for the intelligence community. He looked more like a roadie for a rock band. Mark had long hair in a ponytail, sometimes a manbun, a few tattoos, sometimes an earring, and usually very, non-business-looking clothes.

He'd been known to wear Hawaiian shirts with nonmatching pants, no socks with funky shoes, shorts, and a tee shirt, and even one time, a cowboy hat...to work. When he wore ties, a rare occasion, they clashed in the most awful way. Although a top employee for being a producer, he had caused a number of human resource issues due to cursing or speaking his mind as needed.

By this time, the live band had started again on the pool deck, and it was quite loud from the room balcony. Mike dialed.

"Jason, this is Mark Savona. I received…"

"Mark! How are you?"

"Look, I'm fine. I can't believe you're calling me. I'm on a cruise ship in the…"

"Mark, what is that music I'm hearing? It's louder than hell. Sounds like reggae."

"No kidding, dummy. I'm on vacation. I'm on a cruise ship down in the Caribbean with my girlfriend. How come you're calling me? What the hell is going on that you have to interrupt me and my umbrella drinks?"

"We got a hot one. An item that the deputy wants to talk to you about. Some type of problem. Time sensitive."

"Oh, come on, Jason, I'm half in the bag. Can't it wait?"

"Nope, he wants to talk to you. Right now. I'm going to put him on. He told me to contact you anywhere you were on earth. I found you from your leave paperwork and the Operations Center downstairs told me where you were."

Oh, that's just great. I'm never gonna tell them again, he thought. "OK. Put the old man on."

"One moment please," Jason replied, laughing.

"It's not fucking funny, Jason. Hurry up, shit for brains."

About a minute went by as quirky jazz music played while he was on hold. *This music is awful*, Mark said under his breath.

"Hello, Mark? Is that you with that ruckus of music in the background?" Calvin said to Mark, then covered the phone with his hand. "Jason, is this freaking call secure?"

"Yes, sir!" Jason answered loudly from the outer office.

"Hello, Mr. Burns, Mark Savona here. Yes, it's me. I've been drinking, so be warned. I'm on a cruise ship. Caribbean."

"Don't worry, Mark, I know where you are. I've also had a few drinks in my day as well, too. Look, Mark, I really hate to do this, but I need to get you back here. Right away."

Mark looked out at the white Royal Caribbean shuttle boat that was ferrying ship passengers between the island and his ship. All sorts of overweight passengers with bellies hanging over their swimsuits were spotted. Some had horrible sunburns. "No, I'm on vacation with my girlfriend. I'm out at sea." He looked out at the island at all the new water slides.

"Yes, I understand, but sorry, Mark. I need you back here. You'll be docked tomorrow morning, in, let me see here…in Nassau. I'll send the jet down to get you at, let me see here on the paperwork…" The deputy shuffled around the folders on his desk.

Mark rolled his eyes, then closed them, letting out a sigh.

"Jason arranged for you to fly home from the Lynden Pindling International Airport. It's the Nassau Airport. An Andrews jet, a C-20, a Gulfstream III. I have your itinerary."

Years ago, Deputy Burns recognized Mark for his superb talent and recruited him to DIA. Mark may have read the ads in *Foreign Affairs*, but Calvin was the one who sealed the deal. Calvin knew Mark was the opposite of a yes-man and respected his antiestablishment attitude. He talked back to anyone, and Calvin thought Mark was the definition of peculiar, but in a good way. The deputy treasured the way he looked at problems and valued his diversity—both diversity of thought and action. Once in entertainment, and now in intelligence, Mark was *the* expert on Chinese aircraft.

"Sir…for real? What's so important that I need to fly back from paradise for? Did I mention I'm out on a cruise ship? Dancing? I have a young, tanned girl in a bikini waiting for me about two hundred feet away in a hot tub. Can't this wait?"

"No, Mark, something has turned up. Again, I'm sorry."

"Not coming. No. Not coming," Mark told him. Mark was fired up and wasn't shy about engaging the number-two man of the agency.

"Mark. I need you."

"Warm breezes. Bikinis. Red drinks. No," Mark replied.

"Mark."

"Nope, not an option. Not even thinking about it and not calling you back," Mark said as calmly as he could, and hung up.

PART 2

ROUTINE

Rushmore VFW Post 1273, Rapid City, South Dakota

Established in 1932, Rushmore Veterans of Foreign Wars Post 1273 on Main Street in Rapid City was open to the public and made available to support veterans in the community. The hall, usually reserved for special dinners, weddings, and banquets, was complete with a kitchen, bar, and billiard tables, and the perfect spot for tonight's squadron party.

Most of the aircrew from the B-1 flying squadron attached to the 28th Bomb Wing were present. Ellsworth Air Force Base, which was home to the largest B-1 Bomber combat wing in the US Air Force, had rented the hall tonight for their annual Kangaroo Court ceremony and party. While the wing had a total of twenty-seven aircraft and more than 3,800 military and civilian members, tonight's squadron aircrew was much smaller in size, and they were acting more like a fraternity at a college tonight than a robust group of professional pilots, navigators, and weapons-systems officers. There were also some visiting aircrew who flew in for the festivities.

Tonight's Kangaroo Court consisted of fifty-four aircrew, drinking heavily, partying hard, and carrying on with billiards, crud tournaments (full-contact pushing and shoving billiards without cue sticks), and beer pong. The Kangaroo Court was an unstructured and humorous ceremony, somewhat steeped in folklore and secretive ceremony, and was used to give new aircrew their permanent nicknames known as call signs. Some call signs could be related to unique last names, some were based upon dingy looks, while others could be based upon something silly that they did inside or outside the cockpit.

Call signs stuck with pilots for nearly all of their careers, even into general and flag officer rank. One of the worst things a guy or gal could do was complain about theirs, or ask that it be changed, because you never knew what it could become. The court could also decide that your new name was worse than the one you currently had. Rule of thumb was to be happy with whatever name you earned. Scab, Redneck, Toad, Ugly, Dirt Ball, Puke, or Virus—just be happy with your name.

Over the public address system in the hall was someone clearing his throat, then a non-professional-sounding announcement. "Ladies and gentlemen, may I have your attention please? Time to take your seats. Sit down. The court will begin soon," announced one of the young lieutenants, laughing.

The pilots were standing around, talking and drinking, in addition to playing darts and other games, and eventually made their way over to some bar and banquet tables to have a seat. The tables all faced a small, elevated stage that held a rectangular table with seats.

"Oh, this is gonna be good," said Padre, a visiting Marine Corps pilot from Camp Pendleton.

"Yeah, Padre. Maybe we'll give you a new call sign, like Nail-Polish, Hairspray, or even Glamour. Maybe Legwarmers. You take too long to shower and get ready. Like a girl," replied Lefty, chuckling, a fellow marine pilot.

"Lefty, listen to me, you rookie. I dare you to attempt changing it. Remember, payback is a bitch. You attempt to change mine and you can guarantee you new call sign is going to be…Catfish."

"Stop it. That's stupid. What kind of name is that?" asked Lefty.

Padre smiled. "Bottom Feeder."

Lefty kept his mouth shut and nodded.

Without a warning, the lights went out in the room. Near total blackness for a moment, then a spotlight normally used to illuminate a bride and groom entering the banquet hall came on and focused on the entrance to the room.

The PA speaker system came alive again, and you could hear guys fumbling around with the microphone. The crowd started to really come alive.

On the right side of the room along the wall of light switches, one of the lieutenants pressed play on his smartphone, held it up to the microphone, and out of the banquet hall's speakers came a song usually reserved for boxing matches. The crowd immediately jumped up and started yelling, whistling, catcalling, and standing on chairs. It went from a low roar to near chaos in a nanosecond. Someone overturned a table, and everything on it shot across the room. Others were throwing beer cans and cups at the stage. Someone else threw a chair across the dance floor, and it made a loud crash sound when it slammed into the wall. The laughing and noise were uncontrollable. The party had indeed started.

The spotlight still moved about the room now, then stopped at the main doorway for a moment, and back around wildly. After a few more moments, the light stopped at the doorway, and in walked four pilots from the squadron wearing dark business suits and sunglasses, playfully looking and acting like "Secret Service agents." They escorted someone, but it was difficult to detect who it was at first glance. Aircrew strained to see who it was, while others stood up on chairs and tables attempting to see.

The person in the middle of their grand entrance was wearing a complete Hawaiian brown-grass skirt, green-leaf headband, and red chest paint. The theatrical parade stopped walking so the pilot in the grass skirt could wave his hand, twisting it from side to side, moving it like he was the queen of England. The crowd loved it, and the pilots were as rowdy as New Year's Eve at midnight in Times Square. It was a male pilot wearing a girl's Hawaiian grass skirt.

The room started chanting slowly his name, "Big Kah-Huna."

"BIG...KAHUNA. BIG...KAHUNA. BIG...KAHUNA." The chanting increased in tempo. Two ceiling tiles slammed down from above after visiting pilots Sonny, Delta, and Chachi threw pool cues at each other, ending up hitting the ceiling instead.

The Big Kahuna and escorts made their way to the makeshift stage slowly, to the delight of the room, and stood in front of a white-tableclothed table.

The spotlight was steady on all of them now. The volume of noise was off the charts.

The pilot wearing the skirt, the Big Kahuna, picked up his wooden mallet and banged it on the table, attempting to settle the crowd. *This guy has a wooden mallet?* Lefty thought. It was the kind of mallet used by a judge on a legal bench.

"Settle down! Settle down!" yelled the Big Kahuna, taking a swig of some Colorado-brand whiskey.

More empty cans and cups were thrown around, and laughing echoes through every inch of the room. Bar owner Dave Duma poured another round of beer from Gideon's Brewery, while the guys were having the time of their lives.

Padre leaned over to one of the pilots from the 28th Wing. "Hey, who is your Great Kahuna? Rather, Big Kahuna? Who is this guy?"

The squadron pilot narrowed his eyes, then realized Padre was a guest visiting from outside the unit.

Laughing and throwing another empty beer can up at the stage, "Hey man, that's Captain Ford Stevens."

Coco Cay Island, Bahamas
Mark let out a long breath, looking down at the iron balcony on the cruise ship. He listened quietly to the cover band play his favorite music artist, Jimmy Buffet, up top on the deck, and continued to glance out at the clear water over at Coco Cay. He counted to five, then redialed to Jason back at DIA Headquarters and was immediately connected to Calvin Burns. Mark let out the longest sigh known to man. "Huff. Well, what is it? What is the problem?"

Silence filled the air between the two, Calvin having let it go for drama purposes, knowing Mark would call back. "It's from our last mission together. Something...something has turned up," replied the deputy.

"What do you mean *something has turned up?*"

"Something has turned up. I need you. Highest priority."

Mark looked up at the rust on the white balcony above his, then out at the new pier onto Coco Cay. "Well, I'm not coming back. This is *my* vacation. Upstairs there is a...a...a pool deck. And a live band. There's a goddamn magician tonight in the theater. And gambling. And lobsters. And in that hot tub is a half-naked, hundred-pound hottie waiting for me. Call Robert or someone else on the…"

"Mark. Mark!" Calvin yelled. "Listen up. We have more indications, OK? More satellite stuff like Devil Dragon. Just like last time."

Mark didn't say a word, squinted his eyes, and let the deputy's words sink in. *No kidding. More satellite indications?* Mark said to himself. This was heavy. Mark didn't have a clue what it really meant as an aircraft analyst and wasn't anywhere close to an expert on satellites. Actually, he sometimes laughed at what he referred to as "space junk" because he didn't understand it. What he did know, though, was that it was important to his boss. Not long ago, similar circumstances led to Air Force Reserve pilot Captain Ford Stevens and Chinese Air Force pilot Captain Wu Lee stealing Devil Dragon right out of China and onto the deck of the USS *Abraham Lincoln.* "Wow. More warnings?" he said quietly to Calvin.

"Yup," came the reply as Calvin slowly nodded his head up and down. Another five seconds of silence.

"I'm on my way," replied Mark as he ended the call on his smartphone.

"Hook, line, and sinker! Get the band back together!" Deputy Burns said loudly after hanging up the phone. Then he yelled from his office, "Hey, Jason, get me the chief of Air Force Reserve on the phone!"

A few seconds later, Jason came into the office. "Right away, sir. Topic?"

"Just tell her aide one name: Captain Ford Stevens. But I need to talk to her, too."

Mark looked out at the beautiful clear water, then out at the golden sand beach a few hundred yards from the ship, then out to the large yellow balloon. He looked down at his phone to ensure the call was disconnected, then back out at the billion-dollar view. Mark sat for a moment staring quietly, biting his cheek, then shook his head slowly from side to side slowly.

"*Motherfucker. They had two jets.*"

US Consulate, Chengdu, China

The excess display of antennas on top of the US consulate were in a variety of sizes and colors, and even rusty, and extended in all sorts of directions. To the casual observer, it looked like a porcupine. Some were for standard cell tower connections, while others were for the US Marine security guard detail, but one set of them was special. This set of acoustical signature antennas was, well, unusual.

Based upon recent history, this antenna system had recorded some very unique sounds. Not too long ago, the exclusive acoustical mark of the H-18 Devil Dragon were her four very dynamic engines, and was, in fact, previously recorded by these very same antennas. The signatures were retained and recorded in a database, and at the time the Devil Dragon was flying, DIA had no idea what the cavernous grumble was far off in the countryside. So DIA kept the sound on file, just in case. Furthermore, if another signature was detected, DIA analysts could then take a look for comparison. Through analysis when required, perhaps the analysts could determine what they had if a strange recording was detected.

This antenna system, also found on top of many US government buildings domestically and internationally, could detect and record everything from rocket launches to aircraft to gunshots. The system detection worked with several supportive acoustic sensors throughout a city or multiple cities to create a widespread coverage area. The range could be quite large, stretching to many, many miles across a country. Analysts could look and listen to audio software that identified the unique signatures in real time. If an analyst compared a sample to other collection evidence, like radar, radio emissions, and video, one could build quite a picture of an event, similar to a journalist at a newspaper.

Chris Sans, the lead DIA officer at the US consulate in Chengdu, saw the raw reports of the recordings, but did not know what they were. He was used to seeing news of random gunfire in the neighborhood, and then the computer software program would determine what the sound was, from airplanes to gunfire to a trash truck. This recent sound, though, was different, and he ensured that he would enter it into the database for Washington analysts to take a look. It sounded eerily familiar, but since Chris was not an analyst, he figured he'd let the experts do the thinking on this one.

Chris generated an email along with the sound file and sent it to the Asia section of DIA, knowing the China Aircraft team would see it. Manned by Mark Savona, Robert Dooley, and Emily Livingston, they were the experts that could help troubleshoot what it was. It also was convenient that they

THE BLACK SCORPION PILOT

helped poach the Devil Dragon, too. He included the location of the sound, length of the sound, direction traveling, incident history, and pattern analysis from the software program.

Chris also looked into another software program before hitting send. Checking an antenna system that scanned the horizon westbound, he collected electronic signatures and emissions for analysis. This antenna system detected the distinctive signatures of electronic emissions, such as smartphones and cell phones and wearable fitness trackers, which would normally be an average find to DIA.

Today, though, these were no ordinary cell phones and fitness trackers, as the ones he found were detected up in the air—airborne. If it were a passenger aircraft, he'd have a whole multitude of fitness trackers, giving away that it was a commercial jet. This Bluetooth electronic hit only had two fitness tracker detections.

I remember Mark Savona talking about this with Wu Lee, he silently said to himself. *Strange.*

Wearable devices, like smart watches and fitness trackers, emit Bluetooth electronic signals to constantly chat with smartphones, passing information back and forth. Sometimes that data is encrypted so hackers cannot listen in, but DIA could. Not only could DIA analysts comprehend the communications between the two devices, DIA could detect the MAC, or media access control, address. This MAC is the unique pattern with which the device communicates, and DIA was able to track and follow someone as he or she moved from place to place.

Chris, a former Marine, was heavily involved in recently helping Chinese Air Force Captain Wu Lee with stealing Devil Dragon and putting her into the hands of the United States. Before Lee passed of cancer, he helped deliver one of the most advanced stealth bombers the world had ever seen to America. But Chris's experience level was remarkable for someone in his early forties, and he took great pride in being referred to as one of the Three Horsemen as the Consulate. The other two Horsemen were the CIA officer present in China, and the legal attaché FBI Special Agent.

These acoustical sounds are somewhat familiar. They are so similar...could it be? he thought, as he hit send on the email.

Rushmore VFW Post 1273, Rapid City, South Dakota

Air Force Reserve Captain Ford Stevens, acting as the Big Kahuna, walked around the table as the music lowered, and he took his seat in a high-backed, fancy, brown wooden chair. The chair had intricate carvings and designs at the top, which reached about five feet in height. The gold seat cushion had elaborate fabric glued to the edges, as well as a few feet of shiny rope, making it look over-the-top gaudy. The lieutenants had decorated it to look like a throne, and it was apparent a lot of thought and time went into this elegant-looking chair.

Ford opened a sophisticated scroll that opened up from the bottom and top, expanding it vertically in front of him. He looked down at the names of call signs previously provided by the squadron pilots. Some on the list were absolutely hysterical: "Spot" was because one pilot had a deep scar on his cheek, "Sarge" was nominated to be Sarge because he was a prior federal law enforcement sergeant, and this year they had a "Mumbles" because a young lieutenant seemed to talk in a strange foreign language when he drank. Of course, Ford was in full theatrical mode, holding the scroll like he was a Supreme Court justice. He glanced around the scroll to look at the victims who needed call signs and laughed out loud.

One of the bogus "Secret Service agents" stood up and talked into his wrist, while placing his other hand on his earpiece. More laughing came from the crowd. It definitely looked like a joke, but the agent leaned over to Ford and said something into his ear. Ford's smile went to a frown rapidly.

"Seems we have a problem before the party can even get started. Sorry, guys. The Rapid City Police Department is here to shut us down for being too loud. They have received some complaints from out in the neighborhood," explained the Big Kahuna, while holding the silver microphone.

Just as he finished making the announcement, two uniformed police officers came into the room, to the shouting and booing of the crowd. The aircrew were visibly disappointed and mad and could not believe this was happening. The ceremony had just started, and the new pilots never had a chance to be awarded their call signs. The pilots didn't throw anything directly at the police, but they sure came close to hitting them.

"Hello, officers," Ford said, addressing the two police officers using the microphone.

The pretty female officer leaned over to the microphone in Ford's hand. "Are you Ford Stevens?" she asked.

Ford saw her long red fingernails, but was shocked she knew him by sight. *How does this cop know my name?*

She rapidly took the microphone out of his hands, and asked in a sexy voice for the whole room to hear. "Are you the…*Ford Stevens*…that is getting engaged soon? Come here, big boy!" The room was in an uproar now, with the guys yelling at the top of their lungs.

One of the lieutenants pressed play on his phone again, and industrial dance music blared over the VFW hall speakers. Three elderly World War II vets peeked into the banquet hall from the kitchen now, smiling from ear to ear.

Being the informal leader of the squadron was as informal as it got, but it was indeed a powerful position. Although military command and control was in full force from a formality structure, the captains and lieutenants ran the day-to-day operations of the unit. Informally, they could elevate someone who needed help, assist a promotion for someone by providing opportunities, or ground a pilot from flying because of something negative they were doing inside or outside the cockpit. The brotherhood was strong and powerful, and the Big Kahuna ran the squadron.

"These are no regular cops," Ford said laughing, figuring out what was about to happen.

Impersonating a police officer, the female entertainer began her hired dance for Ford. The other costumed police officer stepped aside and let the female cop do her thing. The lieutenants in the squadron had struck at Ford first before he could get them with their call signs.

Score: lieutenants,1; captains, 0.

Next Afternoon, Mountain Home Range Complex, Saylor Creek Bombing and Training Range, Idaho

Ford Stevens, thirty-one years old, was no longer hungover from the night before, but he sure was tired from the party. His drinking these days seemed to increase instead of decrease, but it did not affect his flying or his job.

"I want to come right a bit, copilot. Check that I'm clear," asked Ford from the left seat of his B-1B Lancer, also known among aviation enthusiasts as the B-ONE, OR BONE.

"Yeah, you're clear; come right," replied copilot Pinky Pinkerton, as she looked out the right window.

Ford and his crew were flying a low-level training route through the mountains and valleys of southern Idaho near Mountain Home Air Force Base. Although Ford was from the 28th Bomb Wing in South Dakota, it was a routine mission to practice conventional air-to-ground flying missions just a few states to the west.

Handsome, experienced, witty, and one of the best pilots the Air Force Reserve had, Ford was an exceptional officer and pilot. He was a full-time Air Force Reservist working in an active-duty squadron, making this his full-time job. After World War II, President Truman formed the Air Force Reserve military organization. Today, Air Force Reserve flies about 20 percent of the regular Air Force's work—not only the traditional flying that most Americans think of, but space and cyber, too. After the University of Notre Dame and Air Force ROTC, Ford started out as a second lieutenant in the air force and later was able to transfer to the Air Force Reserve team.

Air Force Reserve was looking beyond the traditional C-130 and A-10 roles from years past, and entering the heavy bomber business. With eyes on the new Air Force B-21 Raider stealth bomber coming to inventory, Air Force Reserve wanted a piece of the action. The current relationship that Ford was part of with his B-1 unit was no coincidence, as the Air Force Reserve was looking for the mission to stay for the long term. Not only was Air Force Reserve involved with the BONE and B-52 associations at places like Dyess Air Force Base, they were also part of cyber-warfare, intelligence, surveillance, and reconnaissance missions. The Reserves were also tackling new airframes, such as the F-22 Raptor, F-35 Lighting II, and KC-46 Pegasus. The manpower, experience, and ability to train faster than the active-component air force were special to the Reserve Force.

Ford's special achievement that nearly no one in Air Force Reserve knew about was his recent highly classified mission in stealing Devil Dragon out of China. Just a few short months ago, he used a wing suit to jump out the back of a modified Gulfstream 650ER business jet and clandestinely insert himself into a Chinese airport. His covert mission was to link up with his best friend, Chinese Air Force test pilot Wu Lee, and co-steal the newly built jet. His mission was a successful one, but one that he could never talk about openly. The Devil Dragon stealth bomber mission was so secretive that only the team involved in the mission could chat about it, and even then, only at appropriate locations.

Because Ford could not talk about it with anyone, he held a lot of his emotions and feelings inside. This was unfortunate because military units prided themselves on talking, even boasting, about certain high-risk missions. It was their culture. Not this one, though. The mission was not only sensitive but extremely dangerous, and it resulted in the loss of his boyhood friend Wu. To make matters worse, Ford's circle of trust was not at Ellsworth Air Force Base, where he lived and flew, but in Washington, DC.

After routine flights and missions, like the one he was on right now, Ford was normally able to talk with his squadron buddies over a drink or three. As a result of Ford bottling up his feelings, he seemed to turn to alcohol lately as a way of self-medicating.

Zooming along on the "Victor" route, or Visual Flight Rules-Visual Military Training Route, an invisible highway in the sky, they zoomed through the mountains in their B-1B bomber. Flying a nap-of-the-earth route only a few hundred feet above the ground, they yanked and banked the jet in an attempt to sneak up upon a simulated target. Using Global Positioning System (GPS) guidance, an internal guidance system (INS), and an APQ-164 air-to-ground radar, in addition to the navigator telling him the checkpoints, Ford and the crew were responsible for getting the jet from one checkpoint to another, plus or minus five seconds.

"Looking good, pilot. Keep it coming," one of the navigators announced over the intercom.

The air-to-ground radar provided the jet with a Monopulse Ground Map for all-weather navigation. The system also provided them an all-weather Terrain Following and Terrain Avoidance capability, in addition to high resolution Synthetic Aperture Radar for navigation and targeting nuclear and conventional weapons. The B-1B Lancer navigators could also use a two-axis, electrically scanned, phased-array antenna, a programmable signal processor, a radar receiver transmitter, a dual-mode transmitter, and a video signal processor to attack targets. All this technical stuff helped them get to where they needed to go.

"How we doing on timing?" Ford asked.

"Good; spot on. Next checkpoint in ten seconds. Get ready to come left to heading 279 degrees," answered the navigator.

They were conducting a bombing run to infiltrate a fictional country, dropping conventional weapons, also known as traditional bombs. Ordnance being dropped today were twenty GBU-31 Joint Direct Attack Munitions, known as JDAMs, and if the mission were real, the target would hopefully never know they were coming. The JDAM also had a guidance kit option that converted traditional unguided, dummy bombs into all-weather smart bombs. The B-1B's JDAM bombs were guided by an inertial guidance system that connected to a receiver, giving them a range of about fifteen miles. Today's JDAMs were five hundred pounds each.

"Pilot, navigator, come left heading to 279 degrees...in three...two... one...now. Thirty-four seconds until drop. Target will be at twelve o'clock, vehicles and buildings in the open," the navigator briefed.

"Pilot has it in sight, targets in sight," Ford replied. "What airspeed?"

"You should be at 330 knots," said the navigator.

"Roger, 330."

They continued to fly the B-1B Lancer by pushing the throttles up a bit more as Ford yanked the stick back to adjust the nose up another few degrees, then pushed forward and nose-dove toward the ground.

"Navigator, pilot, are we good with the lineup?" Ford asked.

"Yes, continue."

"We ready to release?" asked Ford.

"Yes, you're clear, pilot. Wings level," replied the navigator. "Prepare to drop...in three...two...one. Wings level, cleared hot! Drop!"

BOOP. An electronic sound went out over the frequency, telling all listening that live ammunition was being used.

BOOOOOOMMMMMM! The bombs had come out from beneath the large jet and impacted the targets precisely where they were supposed to go. There was a loud explosion, and a red-and-orange fireball shot hundreds of feet into the air, while a pressure wave extended out in all directions. Anything in the vicinity of the target would have been instantly vaporized.

They zoomed across the earth away from the drop zone, and the on-board computer calculated the impacts, determining a bomb-damage assessment, known as a BDA.

"Pulling off target! Shacked it!" Ford happily announced, moving the throttles forward to rapidly build up airspeed. Navigating out of the mountains using the terrain to mask and hide themselves from surface-to-air missiles and enemy radar, they snuck out of the Saylor Creek Range.

As they pulled off the target, Pinky was able to look out the window on her right side of the aircraft. She saw the plume of gray-and-black smoke rise into the air.

The aircrew executed the proper checklists to get out of the simulated combat environment and were busy moving switches around in the cockpit to ensure safety. Ford pulled the jet up and out of the low-level route, as Pinky contacted the range controllers on the radio to exit the Mountain Home Range.

"Range control, SLAM ONE transmitting on 342 decimal 5, exiting Romeo-3202 at 1612 Zulu, mission complete," Pinky announced on the UHF radio frequency.

"Roger, SLAM ONE. Have you off the range. Contact Center on 122 decimal 5. Good day," replied Range Control.

Pinky switched up the radios and gave a thumbs-up to Ford.

"Thanks, Pinky. Hey, Nav...how'd we do?" asked Ford.

"Spot on, Ford. BDA...targets destroyed," replied the navigator.

"Fantastic to hear, thank you. Superb job, everyone. Solid. Hey, let's go up and grab some gas and head over to Beale for lunch and..."

"Wait a sec. Hold up. Not so fast, Ford. Just received a secure text message for us to RTB," the navigator interrupted.

"RTB? *Return to base?* Why? Are we being recalled?" Ford asked.

"Yeah. Message says RTB. Says nonemergency, but they want us to come home."

Ford thought about it for a moment. That usually meant someone was in trouble, or an aircraft maintenance issue that the maintenance department didn't discover until after the jet was airborne. Either way, it wasn't good.

"Huh. Anyone here do something at last night's Kangaroo Court, or afterward at a bar, that I need to know about? Any issues with our weapons deploying?" Ford asked the crew. Everyone had replied back with "No."

"Well, crew, let's get some gas and head home then. Pinky, take us up to the 717-9A refueling track for some juice. We'll get some fuel and then head for home."

What the hell are we getting called back for? This can't be good, Ford thought.

PART 3

REUNION

DIA Headquarters, Washington, DC

The Chinese Aircraft Team at DIA Headquarters shared the Joint Base Anacostia-Bolling real estate in Washington, DC, with a variety of other tenants. Years ago, the base was the home to an assortment of aircraft on runways near the Potomac and Anacostia Rivers, which separated downtown Washington from the military facility. Today, the land hosted the helicopters for the president of the United States, the Air Force District of Washington offices, the White House Communications Agency, and the DIA.

Emily Livingston, the MI6 representative from the United Kingdom, was assigned to the DIA Chinese Aircraft Team as a liaison. Petite, attractive, sporting long blond hair, and influential, Emily was trained as an expert in human intelligence and could collect information on nearly anything on anybody. Especially when it came to men, because many men *loved* to talk to a gorgeous, fit blonde with a British accent.

Although she fancied Air Force Reserve Captain Ford Stevens, Emily was well aware of her professional abilities, common sense, and clever academic degrees, but also of her beauty. In her career, she had used her attractiveness powers to her advantage regularly. As a career operations officer, it had helped on occasion to wear a low-cut blouse here, a miniskirt there, and some perfume, and men sang like canaries about a glut of items. Using both her brains and her loveliness, she was an influential and skilled team player to both the UK and America.

Eastern Europeans were especially attracted to her. A few years before, Emily was in Crete, Greece, assigned to a counterintelligence mission at the US Naval Support Activity in Souda Bay. The mission was hatched after gate guards noticed an increase in vehicle drive-bys whenever the British Air Force Maritime Patrol Aircraft were flying in. Between the US Naval Criminal Investigative Service and MI6, this was determined to be some strange behavior.

Precisely when the Nimrod MRA4, a maritime patrol and attack aircraft was being flight tested from the UK to Greece, the same vehicles would develop a pattern and circle the perimeter of the base. The Nimrod, initially designed and flown to replace the Hawker Siddeley Nimrod MR2, was new, and, of course, of interest to other countries. These other countries were attracted to the significantly improved aircraft, especially since they had been upgraded with more efficient Rolls-Royce BR700 turbofan jet engines installed. Flying from the UK down to Greece allowed some reasonable flight testing for the aircraft for distance and over water. A foreign country would have enjoyed getting their hands on the new detection systems, too, as well as the additional weapon systems for antisubmarine warfare. Because of these special military parameters and upgrades, and the strange vehicles and behavior, Emily got the call for a mission.

The decision to get Emily involved on this specific case was a simple one. Simple, because she was easy on the eyes. By drinking and dancing at night clubs in the waterfront city of Chania on the island of Crete, she was able to mingle with a variety of suspected international men seen at the base's gate and fence line. She could collect information and intelligence by pretending to be attracted to them. All Emily had to do was smile and talk. By leading them on, they talked and drank and talked, more often than not about what they were doing in Crete and with whom. When it was time to go home at the end of the night, and the men thought they were getting lucky, she would excuse herself from the bar and head to the ladies' room. Instead of using the bathroom, she would exit the premises through the back door, departing with the information she and the MI6 team needed. It was a classic "honeypot" move, famous since the beginning of recorded time thousands of years ago.

Only a short three months ago, Ford thought Emily worked in finance at the International Monetary Fund and previously the World Bank. It was her cover story, the public persona that allowed her to move freely throughout the world conducting business for MI6 while maintaining a low profile. Emily's training made her an excellent collector of information. She had perseverance, had tremendous patience and tact, was creditable in her work, and could adapt to nearly any situation.

The condition that unfolded recently was when Ford was brought to DIA Headquarters unannounced for a video teleconference and coincidentally ran into Emily. Her hand was forced to fully reveal her intelligence background, and while Ford understood, their relationship was slightly strained for a bit. Ford was bothered at the deception and questioned her honesty but comprehended the nature of her work. In the back of her mind, she would love to marry Ford Stevens at their earliest possible convenience, but knew he was not ready to settle down just yet.

Concerning Emily lately was Ford's newest habit of drinking. His latest choice of alcohol was whiskey, and it only started after he came home from burying Wu Lee. Ford was on a brown bottle kick, or sometimes it was something West Whiskey, or even the white-and-blue label kind, but no matter what brand, she noticed the drinking had increased.

Many times, Ford called it whiskey tasting, consumed with single-malt at times, high-end brands at thirty dollars a glass during others. He liked the colored labels ranging from white and blue to gold, and glass bottles of all shapes and colors lined up behind a bar, and he would simply order them with just a splash of water or ginger ale. His favorite was when they were lined up behind a bar on multiple shelves with a white light as a background, enabling him to see all the liquid colors. What he actually laughed out loud about were the descriptions in magazines, such as "round and buttery with almond" and "signature rich sherry accented with citrus," or his favorite: "soft, gentle peat, but thick with floral and sweet chestnuts." *What the heck does that mean? Don't care about the description or age, just pour it already.*

Because Ford rarely talked about the secret mission, even with Emily, she knew he was harboring the stress of the event inside. Ford seemed to be turning to drinking daily and had all the classic signs of some type of post-traumatic stress. His drinking, combined with the recent loss of Wu due to terminal pancreatic cancer, was a deadly combination.

Also, on the team was another crucial member, Robert Dooley, a DIA intelligence officer and expert in operations. Robert, a deep-voiced man of few words, was also focused on the human collection of information from other countries. Robert liked being outside in the elements, conducting hands-on kinetic operations rather than being stuck indoors in an office environment and sitting in meetings.

If a real-world mission needed, for example, a specific eighteen-wheeler truck, he obtained the team a truck. If a mission needed a listening device in Rio, a white three-ring binder prop in Rome, a Manhattan-style pizza box, a Maine lobster tail in Paris, or a Bertram 35 Yacht positioned off Ireland, he could get them all. Because Robert was a classic stoic, he rarely smiled but always dug down hard into his work and came through for the team.

Born in Rochester, New York, but raised in North Padre Island, Texas, he was all about Syracuse sports and the University of Texas Longhorns. A veteran soldier of the army, he joined the DIA team from the Signal Corps. Robert was a principal teammate and was relied upon by Calvin Burns, Mark Savona, and Emily Livingston to make things happen.

The phone rang in the DIA China Desk area, and Emily walked over to Mark's phone to answer it. "Hello, this is Emily," she said with her British accent. It sounded like "Hah-low, this is Emm-a-Lee."

"Emily, morning. This is Jason from Calvin Burns's office. Mr. Burns would like to talk with you and the team at eleven thirty this morning. Your conference rooms. He has Savona coming back from leave, and Captain Stevens is on his way in from out west."

"Geez. For what? Mark is down on a cruise, on a…on a Royal Caribbean ship water slide near some tropical island. And Ford is flying training missions at Ellsworth."

"Yeah, we know. Something has come in, and it's hot. Needs to talk to the team this morning."

Sigh. "All right, Jason. Robert and I will be up there," Emily said, then hung up the phone. "Bollocks. What in the bloody hell does he have that's apparently so hot?"

Robert was sitting at his cubicle and typing away on his computer and could hear Emily talking to Jason. He couldn't help but overhear and decided to engage to see what was going on. "What is it, Emily?"

"You'll never believe this. Bugger," as she paused. She stared off into space, thinking about Ford coming in, checking on her fingernails. Emily was both excited and surprised. She was not sure what Calvin Burns had in store for them, but she would be able to see Ford again. *Ford!* Emily thought to herself.

"Helloooo? Emily? Are you there? What was the call about?" Robert asked.

"That was Jason ringing. Mr. Burns wants to meet with all of us later this morning. Eleven thirty. Two personnel movements are afoot. Mark was called back from the Caribbean, and Ford is inbound here to DC."

"Yeah, Mark *and* Ford? Mark must be furious! Whoo wee," Robert said laughing.

"You're not kidding. Stay away from him when he gets here."

Robert was instantaneously in thought and was rolling through his options. *What did Mr. Burns want with Ford? I can understand Mark, but both of them?* It was very rare to be recalled back from leave, especially from a cruise ship vacation. Robert interpreted that it must be something big—so big that you needed the entire China Aviation Team together, including the air force pilot. *The only one* who has ever flown a secret Chinese stealth bomber.

"Ford is coming!" she said happily, clapping her hands like a small girl in a school yard.

Robert, ever stoic and expressionless, looked at Emily.

"Emily. Why? What would Ford get called here for? That's pretty atypical. You know, pretty odd," Robert offered. "If he was getting another achievement award, something administrative, it would be handled by the air force. He's a pilot, out doing pilot stuff. You know, flying." Robert nodded a bit. "I hate to say this, but there is only one reason he is coming back. And there is only one reason that Mark would get recalled off a cruise ship."

Emily did not know how to take it at first and ran through a few items in her head. Nothing immediately came to mind. "What reason? What reason, Robert?" Emily asked. "I don't understand." She thought about it, and it still wasn't clicking. She had no clue why they would be recalled. She turned her head sideways in thought.

"Emily. Come on," Robert said in his low but deep voice. "You know."

The both stood staring at each other. The other office people moving and talking in the background were the only sounds around. No one else was in their meeting spaces. A pin could drop, and it would have been heard like a boulder down a hill. They looked into each other's eyes like a contest as the seconds went by.

Emily pulled her head back and raised her eyebrows toward the ceiling. "OMG," she blurted out. The idea just hit her. "No kidding? Bloody hell!"

"Yes," Robert replied, sitting down in his chair and sliding back to his cubicle with some excitement. Emily followed right behind him, leaning over his shoulder to stare at the computer screen.

"Shite! No way! Check the intel updates and see what we have. Wow." Emily had figured it out. "China. China is flying again. I just know it. Wu was right. Could be dodgy intel, but...that plonker General Chen has more aircraft," announced Emily with some emotion.

"I agree," answered Robert, sporting a rare smile, as they both dove into the computers to search for data to validate what they were thinking. They ran a search through the mounds of data, and it was like they were looking for a needle in a haystack.

Two words kept coming back, being repeated in their search, but had no context—not associated to anything they knew of just yet, but they could be important. The words "Black" and "Scorpion" were being highlighted.

"What's this 'Black Scorpion' word trend? Keeps coming up. Repeating," Robert asked Emily, not expecting a reply. "You ever hear of those words?"

She thought for a jiffy, and then it hit her. "Bollocks. Didn't Wu mention that? Is that the name of the second aircraft? Check what we have from the Devil Dragon debrief, yes?"

"No country trains only a few pilots. I bet they have a whole crop of smart pilots ready to go. Damn. Why didn't we think of that earlier?" Robert asked, not expecting an answer.

Emily and Robert turned from looking at the screen to face each other with big smiles, and simultaneously said the same name, the now-famous hothead Chinese air force lieutenant general that led their stealth program: "Chen."

Someplace over the East China Sea

The U-2 Dragon Lady high-altitude reconnaissance aircraft was conducting a mission out of Guam this morning, assigned by US Indo-Pacific Command (known as INDOPACOM), with its pilot wearing his orange astronaut pressure suit and fully enclosed helmet out of an abundance of safety. The pilot inside had worked his way up the career ladder at i3, the company that held the contract with NASA and the air force for the U-2. Pilot Bobby Anton, a former navy F-14D Tomcat pilot, was originally hired for the C-20 and DC-8 pilot positions, but quickly fell in love with the Dragon Lady and loved being a civilian contract pilot. He first started out helping the U-2 team as a chase car driver, then racked up enough qualified flight hours and trustworthiness to get into the U-2 pilot training program. Before he knew it, he was flying missions all over earth, including today over the Sea of Japan at seventy thousand feet with his radar and lenses to the west toward China.

To climb up to these impressive altitudes, aeronautical engineers in the 1950s had to create something special from just pencils and paper, old-school sheet metal, rivets, and slide rules. The engineers would eventually design one of the most fantastic aircraft ever flown, one that would resemble a glider with thin wings and a jet engine that could get her up to altitude. It couldn't be too weighty, though, because then the pilots could not get her airborne. It had to be just the right weight so she could rise high in the sky, above most aircraft, and out of reach of enemy surface-to-air missiles. It had to go and do what not that many pilots go and do: conduct high-altitude photography.

Luckily for pilot Bobby Anton, he had trained years ago down at Naval Air Station Pensacola, Florida, the birthplace of all naval aviators, and learned to fly around aircraft carriers for most of his career. Lucky, because the U-2 was one damn tough airplane to fly. Her long, skinny, straight wings were highly efficient and held all the fuel for long, twelve-hour missions. The flight controls were smooth and relaxed to manipulate up at altitude but required a power weight lifter to manhandle the controls during landing and taking off. Most modern aircraft had assistance from engine-powered hydraulics to move ailerons and elevator control surfaces, but in this bird, Bobby Anton only had his triceps and deltoid muscles. The winds for today's mission were calm enough to make him have confidence during takeoff, but wind that was not down the runway was a wind from hell. Crosswinds were a bear in this flying machine, and one wrong input with the flight controls and you scraped a wing tip. Or worse.

Anton's aircraft carrier career was an excellent breeding ground for flying her because the landing phase required intense concentration and just the right amount of skill to land safely, as it did on a moving carrier at sea. In fact, the combination of these skills was already used when pilots used to land U-2s on aircraft carriers! A controlled crash might better describe what he had to do to get her back on the ground. The two landing gear tires were under her main fuselage body, which was not that unusual. What was unusual to the eye were her removable wheeled sticks on the tip of each wing for takeoff, called pogoes which dropped from the aircraft upon leaving the ground. No other aircraft had this outlandish configuration. It was a sight to see on takeoff, as, when the jet lifted off the ground, the pogoes tumbled down the runway like a train wreck.

Anton had to delicately make his landing approach at 140 knots while listening intently on the radios, as he was focused like a laser with limited cockpit visibility to the front and sides. His ears were listening for a certain voice, and it wasn't for fellow aircraft and air-traffic controllers, but to his brother squadron pilot chasing behind him on the runway driving a Detroit muscle car. The pilot driving and racing behind him in a new Ford Mustang would give callouts, giving altitude calls— "five feet…four feet…three feet"—until touchdown landing. Anton would just yank it back to idle on the throttle, and smoothly stall her at only a foot above the runway or less. "Landing." That's old-school flying.

Today's mission required Anton to transmit live camera and video feeds to a variety of military and civilian organizations. The feeds, certainly encrypted, would hit the air force intelligence, surveillance, and reconnaissance squadrons for analysis. Osan Air Base in South Korea was closest. Sometimes Bobby had no clue as to the exact reason he was flying in location A or taking photos of location B, and this morning's mission in taking a peek in Asia was no different. This was built-in security, as the United States learned after the May 1, 1960 U-2 shoot-down of Francis Gary Powers over Soviet airspace. The historic incident was still fresh in the minds of the interagency, as this episode resulted in the cancellation of the Paris Summit. The less the pilot knew, the better off he and the United States were, especially if there was a mishap due to enemy fire or an onboard emergency.

The customers for today's mission included everyone from the DIA to the US Indo-Pacific Command to the US Air Force. One man's junk photo was another man's photo treasure. And this morning, this flight was no junk flight, as Bobby's images discovered something incredible.

DIA Headquarters, Washington, DC

"Hey, Em! Guess who?" said Ford, as he called over to Emily from across the office.

Ford was full of ego and humble pie at the same time, wrapped into a pilot's pilot, completely dedicated to flying for his country. Growing up all over the world and dreaming about becoming a pilot since his teenage years, he was one of those guys who did what he said he was going to do and accomplished his childhood dream.

With short brown hair and a big smile, and in excellent physical shape at five foot ten and 190 pounds, he was full of life. He was sensitive to others, all business when the time came, and dedicated to family, Emily, and his work. Ford loved the flying, the teamwork, and the pride of accomplishment.

A shriek echoed across the office as Ford grabbed Emily from behind. "Whoooo! Ford! Hello, love," Emily said excitedly, wrapping her arms about his tough, Notre Dame NCAA college football body.

He was dressed in his olive-green flight suit, sporting zippers for pockets all over the place, and colored, embroidered patches that covered his chest and shoulders. His maroon and gray patch said "Blackhills" along with a silhouette of a B-1, which was his largest and brightest patch. Emily also noticed he stunk of alcohol again and figured he must have had some drinks on the way in from the airport.

"Hmmm. I've missed you," Ford told her as he picked her up and twirled her about a bit. He spoke quietly so he could whisper in her ear. "You smell wonderful, Emmy." Ford gave her a kiss. They were a couple in love, and any stranger who was to glance at this reuniting would see the look they gave each other. The love was in both of their eyes.

Robert stood up from his cubicle to say hello to Ford, as they knew each other well from the recent Devil Dragon mission. Robert handled the delicate task of ensuring a Gulfstream 650ER that they had borrowed for a mission was modified with a special exit ramp. The ramp, lowering and raising like the back door on a C-130 Hercules, allowed Ford to parachute out over China to steal Devil Dragon. This custom ramp was designed and fabricated by Gulfstream Airspace of Savannah, Georgia, and the airplane was borrowed from Corning, Incorporated, of Corning, New York. To say that both companies were a friend of the DIA was putting it lightly.

"What's up, brother?" Ford said to Robert, hugging him. "You doing OK, man?"

"Awesome to see you again, Ford," replied Robert. "Welcome back. Yeah, all good here. All good."

"Thanks. Great to be back," Ford said, glancing around the office space. "Where is our good, uncanny, eccentric friend, Mark Savona? Is he out doing a yoga class or parkour somewhere?"

Ford certainly knew Mark from Devil Dragon, too, as he was their leader on the operation. He and Ford had a terrific relationship, and they were both fond of each other. Mark, being a bit older, routinely called Ford "kid."

Robert smiled. "Ha! Ford! Well, he was on a cruise with some new girlfriend down in the Caribbean. Burns called him back. Sent a military jet out of Andrews to get him. Jason arranged for both of you to get back here."

"No joke? All I got was a notice from headquarters air force reserve to show up here as soon as possible. Wait, Mark was vacationing with a *girl*?" Ford said jokingly, as if it was a surprise he had a girlfriend.

From across the room came a loud voice familiar to all in the China Desk area. It was Mark Savona. "Anything else you fuckers want to say while I'm standing right here? Yes, with a girl! Well? What the hell is going on? I got called back to the office…only to see your ugly mugs?" He was smiling, making his presence known as he walked in.

"Mark!" they all said, welcoming him back from his short trip. He was, of course, kidding with the bitter attitude, and gave hugs to everyone. In signature fashion, he was wearing a Hawaiian print shirt, nonmatching patterned cargo shorts, and tan sandals, all in a professional office environment. In many ways, Mark did not give a crap about the Washington bureaucracy, with their starched white shirts and blue suits, which was what made him so unique. Wearing the opposite of what was expected was Mark's way of rebelling. This, along with disagreeing with senior leaders and sharing his opinion no matter who it was in the chain of command, was his calling card.

Mark continued to smile. "Thanks everyone. Yeah, I'm back, too. Painful to leave early, believe me. So, Old Man Burns and I had a short call. Got up here as quick as I could. He said we had more *satellite indications*? That's the reason I am back here," Mark told them. "What the hell is going on? What are the details?"

"Understand, Boss, Emily and I have been looking into it on our own without official tasking from Burns just yet. We found a whole host of interesting things coming in over the past few hours. We need to show you before we see Mr. Burns at eleven thirty." Robert rotated in his seat to glance at the wall clocks. "That's only in an hour and a half or so. Why don't we hit our conference room, and Emily and I will show you what we've got?" Robert asked.

Robert and Emily had been digging around on the computer all morning, reading and reviewing data to see what they could find. They compared and searched as much as they could from 6:30 a.m., ranging from the *China Daily* newspaper to the flight feedback from surveillance aircraft. They even dug up some State Department cable traffic from the Asia region, just to see if there was some nugget that would help piece together a story. Now that they had a historical pattern from Devil Dragon, and owned her now, they knew to look for a few specific items.

The team walked down to their small conference room, which still looked as sloppy and unkempt as ever. The team didn't care because that was what made them click. Eating takeout at one in the morning, or having an Old Ox beer at lunch, or even watching *Harry Potter* movies together to take a break from challenging problems was the special fuel that bonded them.

"Ford, could you lean over there, kid, and lower the screen for us?" Mark asked.

Robert and Emily had already put together a short slide show that demonstrated all the facts they had accumulated already. Their reach was worldwide, and since they had a certain location and aircraft in mind, they could focus their research efforts in one area: China.

"Robert, kick this off. We don't have much time before we see the Old Fella," Mark asked, aware of the time.

"Yep. Bottom line, Mark and Ford, is that we have us another aircraft. A second jet. We think we have another Devil Dragon–type stealth bird."

"We do? Holy shit," Ford said in disbelief.

This news really caught Ford by surprise, and he let out a long sigh. The physical and emotional scar tissue had just barely healed from the last mission, to include burying Wu in Section 60 over at Arlington National Cemetery. Under the fictional name of Captain Wilson Leonardo, US Air Force, was Wu Lee, lying in peace. Although Ford flew Devil Dragon to the carrier, the DIA arranged for it to be delivered to the United States, specifically Nevada. And he hadn't stopped thinking about it since.

Ford's thoughts raced around, as well as his feelings. He was instantaneously excited with this recent news, yet continued to suffer at the same time. Thinking about the emptiness inside and the loss of a true friend he'd known since he was a child, Ford hadn't really recovered yet. And probably never would. Now, a second jet was being discussed, and it really caught him off guard.

Robert continued. "Do you remember when Wu was talking about how he was selected as the number-one pilot out of a few pilot candidates for Devil Dragon? Other pilots were selected as well, but Wu said he was the one chosen for Devil Dragon because of his test pilot experience. We never really followed up on it because we were focused on grabbing the jet. Now that we have time to think about his comments and read all our info on Operation WHIRLPOOL, we have a real pattern now. If you think for a moment, why would General Chen train more than just Lee, unless there were additional aircraft built besides Devil Dragon?"

Lieutenant General He Chen of the People's Liberation Army Air Force, the PLAAF, ran the stealth bomber program in China and was Captain Wu Lee's boss. Chen was an arrogant three-star general and pilot who was personally responsible for the building and test flying of China's secret program, of which not many in the Chinese Communist Party or the military knew about. Chen lifted the blueprints from a US defense contractor using cyber methods and modified the jet a bit, and the result was Devil Dragon. Wu had previously shared some significant things about Chen, especially his fiery temper, excessive drinking, and micromanager tendencies.

Many of the Chinese generals drank a rice-based drink called baijiu. This baijiu, also known as Chinese vodka, was Chen's daily drink of choice. Wu had a hatred for Chen, mentioning more than one time of Chen's sloppy drinking and staggering during all times of the day and night, his irritability, his aggressiveness for wanting a fourth star, and his ability to easily walk all over subordinates below him. Based upon what the DIA team knew about Chen and his personality style, there was no question that after losing Devil Dragon, Chen could easily have more aircraft.

Ford rubbed his chin with his hand as his arms were folded. "No shit. Yeah, that's right! Remember Mr. Burns was pressing him on that video teleconference about Devil Dragon engine performance, and Wu said he wasn't sure about the future plans? Chen was looking at a Mach 6 aircraft for the future. Devil Dragon had two standard turbofan jets and two ramjets, and Wu told us Chen was looking into future scramjet technology."

A standard afterburning turbofan engine came in all shapes and sizes. The formula for flight was basic: throw in some air and fuel, compress it, light it, and you zoomed off. A ramjet, on the other hand, was no conventional jet engine. While it still sucked in air through air intakes, it used the forward motion of the two standard engines to get air down the ramjet engines. That forward motion to compress the incoming air without an axial compressor was the special Chinese engineering magic, and no US war bird aircraft had this configuration.

Ford's mind was wandering all over the place now, considering if this new jet had the scramjet technology. If it was a similar setup and design, the new jet engines couldn't produce thrust at zero airspeed. They would need two types of engines on the same airframe again. The Devil Dragon required an assisted takeoff from her two standard afterburning turbofan jet engines, and then once they had some forward motion and had some airspeed, the ramjets took over to kick in the required speed. Wu discussed supersonic speeds approaching Mach 5, and the smartphone aircraft performance records the DIA just grabbed proved this, but Chen pulling off speeds of Mach 6, or close to 4,600 miles per hour, would be incredible. In this modern era, it would also be valid and believable.

Aviation reports of strange sonic booms had been told for years over Southern California, and speeds like this seemed made up at first glance, but they were not. Seismograph data had previously determined speeds past Mach 5. Mach 6 was also being discussed publicly by Lockheed Martin in their SR-72 aircraft, the son of the mighty SR-71 Blackbird.

When a November 1, 2013, *Aviation Week and Space Technology* article came out on this same subject, so many people went to their website that the server crashed. In addition, just a few short months ago, Lockheed's CEO stated that the company was close to a high-tech innovation that would allow its conceptual SR-72 hypersonic plane to reach Mach 6. A hypersonic demonstrator aircraft the size of an F-22 stealth fighter could be built for less than $1 billion.

Lockheed was also into building their low-boom demonstrator for a supersonic business jet and airliner. Named the Quiet Supersonic Technology aircraft, or QueSST, the 120-seat jet was advanced technology. The C606 test aircraft, at ninety-four feet long and twenty-nine feet wide, was already planned out, down to sonic boom decibel sound tests. In addition to Lockheed, the Hikari Consortium, a group of European and Japanese companies, were also building their Lapcat jet. Skunkworks and Hikari were busy, but so were the Chinese.

Mark looked down at the table, adjusted his manbun, and adjusted the sleeve on his Washington Capitals hockey jersey, which was hidden under his Hawaiian shirt. It didn't match, and it looked awful. "Fellas, I do remember all that. But we had no hard evidence from Wu on Mach 6, just conversation. Do the reports mean anything? Meaning, are they backed up by other info?"

Emily sat up a bit and cleared her throat. "Yes, Mark, we do. They do mean something. We have very recent data from this morning that just came in. The satellites picked up stuff we recognize from Devil Dragon. They are extremely similar. Robert and I think it's the new aircraft out for flight test. We're seeing the same pattern as last time, but the temperatures are a bit hotter. Computers did not pick it up at first because it wasn't an exact match."

Mark listened intensely. "Go ahead. Keep going."

Robert knew his slides were next. "The satellites tipped us off to check other sources, so we started with the US embassy and consulates. There was no news from the US embassy in Beijing. But we do have audio recordings of distant sounds, now identified as an aircraft, off the US consulate in Chengdu. Our good friend, Chris Sans, sent in some exceptional audio recordings that don't sound like much, but when they were run through the software were very close to Devil Dragon's signature."

"OK. Pretty good sign." Mark nodded in agreement. "How do we know it's an aircraft and not some other machine or factory somewhere at the same audio frequency and length?" Mark asked, wanting to ensure the data was valid.

Robert shook his head in agreement. "Well. This is the triangulation microphone package, Mark. It is normally used to track gunfire on the ground. You know, from, for example, the Pentagon or the White House, or even at a football stadium. This is the commercial, off-the-shelf tech State Department uses. We can accurately pinpoint the sound, and from the speed and direction, it's no ground sound. In addition, in addition," as he raised his index finger, "we have, believe it or not, EMI."

"EMI? *What?* Electromagnetic interference? From the jet? Again?" Ford questioned, thinking that the jet had to have some type of filter to protect its signature. "How the hell did you capture that?"

EMI was the interference of an electronic device when it was physically close to an electromagnetic field in the same radio frequency spectrum as another. It can also be something as a simple signal from one device to another. White noise static on an FM radio is EMI.

"Yes, Ford," Robert showed him on the screen. "Check this out. We detected it from the roof of the consulate. Again, Chris Sans as the source—two smartphones at altitude that match the same location as the sound, as well as two fitness trackers. Emily and I were still running the data down when you guys walked in, but if you combine the flashes, the sound, EMI, and this one additional item we'll tell you about next, we have something brewing."

Emily warmly peeked over at Ford while Robert was talking. Emily had been dating Ford for some years, and she was familiar with his facial expressions, detecting something was amiss. She didn't say anything to him, but made a mental note to do so later.

She stood from her seat at the small table and walked toward the screen. "Robert and I are waiting for the fitness tracker cross check and the rest of the cell phone data to come back from the search, but we did some other homework. We do have some initial cell data that is most interesting, but there is something else we need to show you first. We reviewed the last feed from the 6th Intelligence Squadron out of Osan Air Base in Korea. Yesterday morning, a U-2 Dragon Lady was on her Indo-Pacific Command routine run, and discovered this gem," Emily said, putting an image on the screen.

Everyone stared at the screen.

"What the hell is that?" asked Mark, looking at the screen and pointing.

"Let me zoom in a bit for you on these next few slides," she told the team, secretly beaming with pride that she and Robert had found it. Emily flipped through the PowerPoint, and the images from the U-2 became clearer and clearer, and the details were coming into view.

"Whooooaaaa. Where is this?" asked Ford.

"Looks wonky, eh, blokes? This is Guiyang, China, in Guizhou, at the airport. A commercial airport."

Ford knew some cities in China from living there for years, plus could read and speak Mandarin, but had no clue as to where this was on a map.

He was thinking of where it might be located, but he was not familiar with anything in Guizhou.

The room was still silent as Emily zoomed in as far as she could. The image was now pretty clear, and if you had never seen one of these on the screen, you'd miss it.

"What is that? I can't really make it out. Is that an aircraft hangar?" Mark asked.

"Abso-bloody-lutely. Standard aircraft hangar, sitting on their tarmac. Those are nearly closed doors on the hangar," Emily replied.

"Sooo…what is that sticking out? Sticking out of the hangar doors there? On top—that black object?" Ford asked. Ford thought it looked familiar but wasn't sure.

"That, my friends, is the tail of our latest problem. Correction, our latest challenge. That black object is the rear of a jet. The jet is now known, from this point forward as…"

"As what? Come on, Emily," Mark said, getting impatient.

"Black Scorpion."

"Another jet!" Ford exclaimed. "Black Scorpion?"

"Another jet seems about right. Wait. Black Scorpion is her name?" Mark said out loud, seeing the back of the black jet for the first time with his own eyes. Mark looked at the screen and thought of the factual data presented. "How the hell do you know the name already?" tapping his pen on his yellow legal pad.

Robert nodded. "The names 'Black' and 'Scorpion' kept repeating in the reports, and we cross-checked the Devil Dragon engine data from Wu's app. Seems there was another empty set of lines for engine data, for a second aircraft."

"Holy crap. OK, OK, calm down everyone. We have work to do. We have on our hands"—he paused briefly—"one hell of a world-class shit show."

Emily nodded her head and smiled, winking at Ford.

"Who else knows about this?" Mark asked, realizing the magnitude of what they were discovering.

PART 4

REPORT

Jinghong, Xishuangbanna Airport, Yunnan, China

Two Chinese girls in their late twenties left Lieutenant General He Chen's portable airfield Airstream trailer after spending the night. Chen woke up with his standard baijiu headache and stumbled about his small bedroom wearing only his plain white boxer shorts, large potbelly hanging out and over the waist band. He looked at the wall clock and saw he had plenty of time to get cleaned up and over to the hangar.

Chen was scheduled to fly a two-seat Su-35 Flanker fighter chase plane later this evening to follow Black Scorpion during a portion of her flight test card. Russia recently supplied China with twenty-four multirole Su-35 fighters at the cost of $83 million each. The Su-35, codenamed Flanker by NATO, was a fourth generation plus high-end fighter and provided an improved addition to their air force–modernization plan.

Chen got into the hangar spaces and went directly to his first-floor temporary office. Along the way, he passed a bunch of maintenance technicians, who greeted him, and as usual, he ignored them. His office connected to the wide, open hangar space where aircraft were parked and worked on.

Freshly printed and placed on his desk this morning was the new, internally published report of the Devil Dragon mishap, which were the facts and analysis of the limited wreckage found, along with autopsy information on the two pilots. He sat down at his metal desk to read the report, which was written by one of the other test pilots on his staff. Chen knew if he had others outside the stealth program do a mishap investigation, the amount of people who knew of the program would get out of hand. This Black Scorpion jet, along with Devil Dragon, was still a guarded secret from most of the rest of China's military. Plus, the info contained here could interfere with his promotion potential, so it was as close hold as possible.

Chen scanned the executive summary in the front of the report. The spiral-bound paperwork titled "MISHAP INVESTIGATION: *DEVIL DRAGON*" looked to be about half an inch thick. The summary mentioned that no aircraft parts were found on the water's surface, and that only the bodies, aircraft wiring, and some paper aviation charts were located. The publication said, "Due to the high speed and impact of the aircraft on the surface of the water, there was no wreckage and no survivors. The bodies were unrecognizable due to the impact and post-crash fire. The pilots, both captains, were aircraft test pilot Wu Lee, 30, and copilot Liu Nie, 32."

What Chen did not know was that the DIA team had obtained two decoy bodies from the Tokyo Police Department via the Federal Bureau of Investigation and airdropped them into the intercoastal waterway in the Yellow Sea. DIA dressed them up in ragged and burned-out flight suits, and even placed a decoy wallet in one of the pockets. The bodies were found, as hoped and predicted, by a Malaysian commercial ship and picked up along with the maps.

Asian Cargo Carriers Unlimited of Kuala Lumpur owned and operated chemical tankers and offshore support vessels for oil majors operating within the Arabian Gulf and Asia Pacific region. On a routine route ferrying high-speed diesel oil to Myanmar, the Singapore-based tanker *Sweet Island Breezes* made the discovery. No large debris was found because the US C-130 that did the airdrop mission didn't drop any.

This old smoke-and-mirrors ploy by Mark Savona was actually historically based. Named OPERATION MINCEMEAT, the original deception was envisioned to mask the 1943 Allied invasion of Sicily during World War II, and it was successful. Mark generated the airdrop idea, and to date, his plan worked.

Chen turned the page of the executive summary and was growing anxious as he kept reading. He wanted to know what the cause of the mishap was. Scanning, scanning. *Where was it?* Chen grunted to himself, alone at his desk.

He then read the first sentence out loud, his words drifting as he read more, setting off his trademark temper. "Hypoxia, caused by lack of oxygen, and additional psychological events experienced by the crew members at high altitude, most likely caused both crew members to become dizzy and confused. Both were of dangerous states of mind when flying at enormously fast speeds at high altitude. The emergency oxygen supply, most likely, was never turned on and used. The emergency oxygen supply, in most cases, may help a tired or run-down pilot, but only lasts about ten minutes. That is not enough to descend down from the Devil Dragon's extremely high altitude and land safely. PLAAF has recorded 366 oxygen incidents for fighters from 2010 to present day, and the oxygen problems with the primary contractors are well known in the community. None of the episodes have resulted in loss or damage of an aircraft prior to Devil Dragon."

Chen made a face that would make a baby cry. "Bullshit! No! No! Why my aircraft?" Chen yelled at the top of his lungs, throwing the binder to the other side of his office, hitting a table. His water heater for tea hit the floor, shattering the glass pot all over the office walls. Chen's temper was boiling.

Chen rapidly got out of his chair and threw the door open into the hangar, making a loud bang of metal slamming into metal and echoing across the hangar. Facing him was Black Scorpion, tucked in the hangar with a whole host of people prepping her for flight. Engine maintainers, used to working on the Su-35 Saturn 117S engines, were tending to the advanced turbofans, while avionics folks were on top adjusting satellite navigation antennas. Others were standing looking at laptops connected to the jet and leaning on large, movable tool boxes. Most everyone in the hangar glanced at Chen standing there, obviously enraged, and then quickly looked away.

"Engineering. Maintenance. Get in here!" he barked.

The chief engineer hurriedly came in, as well as the chief of maintenance. They stepped over the glass but had to stand in a puddle of tea.

"I just read about the cause of the Devil Dragon mishap. You two read this? What are we doing to ensure this does not happen to Black Scorpion?"

The chief engineer stood there considering what words to use to explain to an angered Chen. "General, we do not know of an oxygen malfunction on board. We are not aware of a problem on these two models because the devices we normally use to monitor are not installed inside their airframes but are only for use on the ground, in computers. We don't know if a system is giving too much oxygen, too little oxygen, perhaps a toxin, or even carbon monoxide."

Chen stared at the chief engineer and didn't say a word. He then looked directly at the eyes of the chief of maintenance.

"General, for us to monitor the breathing air would require us to design and install some complex monitors that are not currently available during flight. At the moment, they are only available on the ground. There is no safe or normal way to monitor the pilots' oxygen while airborne, but we may be able to…"

"Well, how about you make it available?" Chen asked them, but it was more like he told them. Both men nodded in agreement.

Chen was fuming because what really drove his motive was his fourth star, and he did not want his life goal to slip away for some skeptical oxygen problems. He selfishly couldn't give a crap about the loss of life but was only concerned about the aircraft itself. Chen wanted that jet staying healthy for the sake of competition against the Chinese navy, the fighter community in the Chinese air force, and the United States. Losing an aircraft like Devil Dragon was just the right amount of adverse information to sway the four-stars from promoting him. Although he was told he was clear of the blame because it was not disclosed publicly, he still took every precaution.

"What the hell are you two going to do about it?" Chen asked. "What are you going to do to ensure that we don't have any more mishaps?" He narrowed his eyes and crunched up his face, then pointed his finger at each man. Growling now, he stared. "Don't you realize what these jets mean to China?"

Both men were scared shitless and on the verge of peeing in their pants. The chief engineer wiped the beads of sweat off his bald forehead with his long-sleeved shirt.

"Yes, General. We have a list of measures that we are doing to improve the situation. We have an idea that might work. We can install new carbon monoxide scrubbers that can transmit live computer data back to us here in the hangar while Black Scorpion is flying. It may work. We also have molecular sieves to filter unnecessary nitrogen, in addition to new depressurization warning indicators," replied the chief engineer.

"And General, in maintenance, we have generated a postflight checklist for our maintainers to check the oxygen generators, the pressurization systems, and a scan for contaminants, environmental control systems, and any emergency oxygen usage." They were really covering their asses.

Chen was reassured that his team was on top of it and calmed down a bit while they gave him answers. Little did he know, though, that this new method of monitoring the carbon monoxide, this new scrubber they referred to, would be of interest to others outside of China. The maintenance department was not skilled in the art of operational security or counterintelligence, as maintenance was skilled in wrench turning and fixing aircraft that were broken. What went right over Chen's hangover and clouded head was that this transmission of data would be active and unencrypted. It would act like a bright tracking beacon in the night sky to anyone looking and listening.

"Approved. Get out."

DIA Headquarters, Washington, DC

The DIA team stood up and departed to head back to their cubicles so they could do some more research before their meeting with Mr. Burns. Emily and Ford stayed behind, finding a private place in a conference room to be alone and talk.

"How's my chap?" asked Emily, putting her arms around Ford. "You OK?"

"You could tell, huh?" Ford replied.

"Of course I could tell. Something is bothering you. Wu?"

"Hmm. Thanks, Em. Great to be back, and of course, see you. All this talk of Devil Dragon makes me think of him. I really miss him, ya know? You and I never really talked about it, but I was floored when toward the end, when we were holding his hand on the ship...before he passed, he said out loud to his mom and dad that he was coming."

"I remember. Emotional for all of us. Powerful," she said.

"He had not seen his father since he was a young kid. You know, grew up with just his mom. And his mother passed a few years ago. To say that he could see them and was coming to them...was upsetting. And stunning, really."

"I'm sure he's in a good place, love. Pancreatic cancer is devastating. Any cancer is. I'm happy he made it a few months for you and your dad to see him. Some people live only a few weeks after being told of their diagnosis. And we got to see him off."

Ford sat in silence, suffering and mourning. Ford, a man's man, a pilot's pilot, a rising star in the Air Force Reserve, was truly upset. Emily held him, his head close to her chest, comforting him in his delayed grief. They sat for a few minutes quietly, comfortably. Ford, tears coming down his face, eyes red, was as exposed as he ever had been.

"Thanks, Em. For being there."

A knock came on the door, and it opened. "Guys, you need to come back. You need to see what I found," Robert said, sticking his head in the room.

"What is it?" Ford.

"Come, you'll see."

PART 5

LASER

Jinghong, Xishuangbanna Airport, Yunnan, China

B lack Scorpion's flat-black color made her tough to see parked outside on the ramp in the dark sky. The maintenance crews were first taking care of the Su-35 on her start sequence, and the flight line was already loud. The Sukhoi Su-35 was really an upgraded derivative of the Su-27 Flanker jet, and on par with many United States fighter jet aircraft. The two-seater would be piloted today by Chen, along with another pilot, and launched early as to watch Black Scorpion do her magic from the air. An air-to-air rejoin was normal operations, but it wouldn't last long, as Black Scorpion's mission was to get to the weapons range and take care of business on the flight test schedule.

Chen was along to see the newly designed weapons demo tonight so he could witness events with his own eyes. Chen's first reason was for him to be able to explain it to the party's leadership when asked, and second, tonight was personal. Chen's sixth sense was always nagging about Wu Lee, that something just wasn't right before Lee and copilot Nie disappeared with their mishap. Flying alongside this jet tonight made Chen feel better.

The flight line rumbled with the start of the first of two outside engines on Black Scorpion, outboard engines numbers one and four, gulping air to make her body come alive. The air start from the ground start cart provided both electricity and air for the aircraft commander in the left seat to crank

44

them up. The turbine spun from the compressed air being forced in, and once the pilots introduced a spark and added fuel, she lit off. It made a profound, never-forget growl on the ground, just as Devil Dragon did, and both Chinese air force test pilots went through their start checklists.

Aircraft commander Captain Dai Jian, thirty-three years old, and copilot Captain Chung Kang, thirty-two years old, were both graduates of Stanford University, earning their bachelor's degrees in aeronautical engineering some eleven years ago. Their career paths matched nearly perfectly, both coming from Shenyang J-11 Flanker B+ squadrons before heading off to the Test Flying Academy of South Africa. Chen contacted them about a third of the way before graduation, telling them they were being assigned to a secret program, and to not discuss it with anyone.

Almost exactly as with Wu Lee, their flight test work in the Rafale, Mirage 2000 D/N, Typhoon, PAK FA T-50, and Socata TB 30 Epsilon provided them with good training flights before taking on the Black Scorpion mission. Both of them also flew with the Chinese Flight Test Establishment and Nanjing University of Aeronautics and Astronautics, allowing them to later on feverishly go through the flight test portion of the stealth aircraft parameters. They studied Devil Dragon's aerodynamic characteristics extensively, and in a short amount of time, they were already up to the weapons test phase on Black Scorpion. Chen loved that they were ahead of schedule.

As Wu and Liu had trouble initially in Devil Dragon's loads, flutter, stability, and control, so did Dai and Chung on this jet. The modifications to the airframe and wings settled her down in high-speed flight between certain airspeeds, and both current test pilots felt comfortable to enter the last phase of her flight test.

"We're clear all around. Radar is showing Chen's *Su-35* at twelve miles to the northwest. Let's taxi for takeoff," said Dai.

"Another day at the office. Cleared all around. Go," replied copilot Chung.

Dai and Chung taxied the jet for takeoff, rolling her out of the parking spot in front of the hangar into the dark. There were floodlights in the area on towers and on the roof of the hangar, but they were not turned on where they were parked. No Black Scorpion external lights from the jet were illuminated, either. They taxied in the black, using infrared lighting and night-vision goggles, and the only thing an observer on the ground would notice would be the unique, profound grumble of her engines.

They brought the jet down the taxiway, stopping short of the runway. Chung had his head down, sitting in the right co-pilot's seat, and was punching in their location in latitude and longitude to the onboard inertial navigation system before the satellites picked them up on GPS.

"Chung, brief us up for takeoff," ordered Dai.

"OK, Dai, we're at 21.973421 north, 100.76646 east. Airport identifier is ZPJH; set altimeter to 1,815 feet, or 553 meters."

"Roger, 1,815 feet on the altimeter."

"VHF Radio number one is tuned up to 130.0, but all commercial traffic is grounded during our window tonight. Concrete runway, length for runway one-six and three-four is 7,200 feet. RNAV Departure, good GPS satellites. Standard cockpit calls for the flight. It's about ten miles from the field. Takeoff airspeed calculated at 155 knots."

This wasn't your father's general aviation aircraft, manually tuning and identifying frequencies like the days of yesteryear with raw data coming from the surface of the earth. With the touch of a few buttons, the computers pulled up area navigation, or RNAV, on the jet. It knew exactly where they were on the earth at all times, as well as their destination.

"OK, thank you; 155 knots. Concur on the satellites," replied Dai. "Tonight's mission, just to confirm?"

"Airborne laser testing, Range AW-140, 220 miles northeast of here," replied copilot Chung.

"Concur."

PART 6

GHOSTS

DIA Headquarters, Washington, DC

The three of them walked over to the cubicles and looked at Robert's gigantic thirty-four-inch monitor. It was enormous and really brought images to life. It took up most of the second half of his desk, and looked to cost a fortune.

"That's a hell of a monitor. You could watch Amazon Prime on that thing," Ford sarcastically said. "My TV at home isn't that big."

"Quiet, Ford. Look at this," Robert told him.

"What are we looking at?" Emily asked.

Mark was over with them now, looking over Robert's shoulder.

"Are you familiar with the Ghost Army from World War II?" Robert asked.

"No...we're talking ghosts now?" Ford asked. "Like, haunted?"

Robert cleared his throat. "No, no. The Ghost Army was a US Army deception unit from the 23rd Headquarters Special Troops. They were a one-thousand-man organization that impersonated other US Army units to deceive Hitler. History books tell us that around D-Day until the end of the war, they conducted business all over Europe. They traveled with fake inflatable tanks, bogus sound trucks, and false radio transmissions. The Ghost Army put on a real Hollywood-style show. Complete theatrics...for battlefield deceptions. Artists were hired to make it look like an army, but there never really was one."

"OK. And? So why the history lesson here, Robert? Mr. Burns will be here soon," Mark said impatiently.

"Because that black tail in the hangar is a decoy," Robert announced.

"A decoy? Bloody hell! How do you know?" Emily excitedly asked.

"Our smartphones and fitness tracker data are finally in. Complete ones. The data shows they are currently way over here at the Xishuangbanna Airport in Yunnan, China," Robert explained, showing them on a digital map and image.

"I don't understand. Our U-2 image showed the tail out of a hangar in Guiyang, China, in Guizhou," Mark said.

"Maybe that's what Chen wants us to think. Here's why. The cell phone locations connected to the towers don't match the airport where that black tail was spotted. Actually, hundreds and hundreds of miles apart. So I looked at some more imagery from the U-2 flights, and searched the commercial imagery specifically for where the phones were currently located. I remembered that Wu told us they moved Devil Dragon every night to a new airport," Robert told them, pausing.

"Yes? Keep going," Mark said.

"Agree, keep going," said Deputy Director Calvin Burns upon his arrival to their cubicle office area. He said hello to all and encouraged them to keep talking.

"Hello, sir. Yes, well, Wu said that General Chen flew in his own business jet, a Dassault Falcon 8X. Look right here," Robert said as he pointed to his screen. "That's a Dassault Falcon 8X parked on the ramp at the Xishuangbanna Airport. And maintenance travelled in a Y-9, a…Shaanxi Y-9 aircraft, right? The medium-range transport aircraft? That's it parked right here, at the Xishuangbanna Airport," pointing to the other side of the ramp.

Calvin leaned in. "I'm impressed. I see you guys have been busy. So you have phones and fitness trackers of the two suspected pilots again, Chen's jet, and their maintenance bird, all at the Xishuangbanna Airport?" he asked, smiling.

Mark could hear in Calvin's tone that he was ready to ask about fifty more questions. This wasn't the first time Mark had worked with the deputy director of the agency, and he always worked to beat Burns at his own game, hoping to answer all the questions he may have before he got a chance to ask them—in other words, to anticipate his questions ahead of time.

"Actually, we have more data than that. Perhaps we could bring you in the conference room and share what we have so far?" Mark asked.

Calvin Coolidge Burns, the principal deputy director, was a career Defense Intelligence senior executive. If there was ever a senior executive in the civilian federal government with a picture-perfect level of emotional intelligence, it was Cal Burns. He had dedicated nearly his entire adult life to the military and DIA and was looking forward to retirement in only what seemed like a few days. Cal, born in Richmond, Virginia, was well respected by all. He was an undergraduate of the historically black Savannah State University, later earning an MBA degree from the Naval Postgraduate School. He had all the academic credentials to climb the career ladder.

His most treasured educational experience was The Power Lab up at Cape Cod, where he learned to see organizational systems as a whole. Learning about these systems in organizations helped him lead at DIA, making the crucial connections between bottoms and tops, or entry-level employees and senior leaders, as they were known at Power and Systems' Power Lab. It was here where Calvin learned also about using the middle-level leaders as conduits between the two. This was where Calvin derived his special leadership touch in running efficient organizations.

Calvin's wife convinced him to stay the remainder of this year, which he did, and then Devil Dragon came along. He led the Operation WHIRLPOOL mission for DIA, then was ready to call it a day and retire, until this latest gem of an issue arrived with a red bow.

"OK, conference room it is. Let's go," the deputy told them.

Mark led the way until Emily called him back, asking him if he had a minute. "Mark, I know you and Robert will kick this off, but we need to check the hourlies. You know he'll ask, and we never checked."

Mark thought about it for about a half second. "Good idea. That'll be the second question out of his mouth."

Takeoff and Inbound to Chinese Aircraft Test Range near Yunnan, China

As aircraft commander Dai Jian did one last scan of the instruments and pushed the throttles forward, and they taxied on the runway. He stopped just forward of the white numbers painted on the runway.

"Clear for takeoff," announced Chung.

Dai scanned inside again, then outside, and slid his feet off the brakes and pushed all four throttles forward. They were slammed back in their seats as the two main engines lurched them forward. Once they built up some airspeed, the two scram jets in the center of the fuselage, engines two and three, auto-ignited and came to life. Their heads were now pressed back in their headrests.

Chung spoke quickly. "That's a hell of a jolt. Speed looking good. All four engines in the green. Airspeed rapidly building. A hundred and twenty knots. Keep the throttles forward."

"OKaakkkay," Dai said, voice vibrating.

"Almost there...155 knots. V1. Rotate," said Chung quickly, eyeing the airspeed indicator.

There were no obstacles in front of them, such as power lines, trees, or terrain. The jet screamed into the night sky, sucking the cool spring air into her four massive engine air intakes. Her roar on takeoff had the maintenance crew outside of the hangar lined up to see her, feeling the physical vibration and tremble of her sound waves passing along the ground.

"Roger, gear up," Dai commanded Chung as he lifted the small wheeled landing gear handle on the right side of the cockpit. The cockpit was pretty wide, and the gear handle was far enough over to the right that it was nearly impossible for any pilot in the left seat to reach.

The high-tech cockpit was nearly a spitting image of Devil Dragon, with multiple colored glass screens in front of the pilots that displayed flight instruments, engine performance, and radar displays, among other indicators.

In between the two seats were four throttles, radios, navigation, flaps levers, and some autopilot dials. The cockpit also had a hatch on the floor, which opened to the ground near the nose landing gear. This was the same hinged hatch where Ford was engaged in hand-to-hand combat with Devil Dragon copilot Liu. Ford fought, and eventually threw, copilot Liu to his death during the final takeoff roll.

Lieutenant General He Chen, ever one to constantly steal ideas from the US defense community, continually scanned the cyber networks to see what other countries were doing in research and development. After the Chinese cyber sleuths unearthed the US Air Force B-21 Bomber plans and their new heads-up display, a HUD, he had one installed for Black Scorpion. One phone call to the Russians, to his friends over at Sukhoi, and a HUD was rapidly built for him by Komsomolsk-on-Amur Aircraft Production Association and integrated into her avionics systems.

The upgraded stealth technology on both Devil Dragon and Black Scorpion was remarkable, giving a radar return of a parakeet. Chen was constantly all over the contractor, ensuring every step was as detailed and precise, in addition to as secret, as possible.

As an example of Chen's obsessive-compulsiveness, he ensured that the Black Scorpion was the only version assembled in a certain section of the half-mile-long manufacturing facility. Once Black Scorpion was ready to leave the delicate production line, she was cautiously rolled into a windowless, multistory, two-hundred-thousand-square-foot aircraft final-finishes facility. Black Scorpion was parked in a paint bay, where laser-guided robots sprayed radar absorbing material on all her surfaces. This was a delicate, five-day process, ensuring everything was done properly.

"Let's climb up to flight level two hundred, level off, and get out the test cards and prepare," Dai announced.

As they were in the climb to twenty thousand feet, the maintenance and engineering chiefs were delighted to see the oxygen and carbon dioxide readings transmitting successfully to the laptops in the hangar. What they didn't notice was that the data streaming to the ground were on unencrypted frequencies. Looking at the laptop screens open and displayed on the portable hangar toolboxes, many technicians in the hangar were on the encrypted and password-protected Wi-Fi system, but the data flowing in was in the open.

"Pilots healthy. In the green," the chief of maintenance said, with just a small hint of pride, to the chief of engineering.

"Yes, yes. I see," the other responded, nodding his head. "This will keep Chen off our asses. That asshole."

Black Scorpion was pushing out and transmitting the data, as her combined engineering and maintenance team had designed, as if she were an AM radio station broadcasting out of Chicago, Illinois. The signal went from the aircraft, up to the satellite, and down to a receiver, then over Wi-Fi to their computers. To the Black Scorpion team, it worked perfectly. They had not a clue as to the implications of their actions.

Black Scorpion was inbound to the weapons range, nearly level at her planned altitude, and the flight crew could see the Su-35 visually on their night-vision goggles. Fluctuating between a third of a mile and two miles off their right wing, Black Scorpion's pilots double checked their onboard radar. Both jets were still blacked out to the naked eye, but lit up well with infrared lights for air-to air-safety. The Su-35 did the external radio calls for the airspace, contacting range control on the UHF frequency, but both cockpits knew only one aircraft would be conducting the show tonight.

Black Scorpion had two significant weapon-system additions that Devil Dragon did not have, ones that were still closely held secrets even to most people who knew about the stealth program. Devil Dragon was a distinct aircraft because of its speed and stealth capability, enabling it to fly long distances undetected at unbelievably amazing speeds, with the specific purpose of delivering both conventional and nuclear weapons.

What made Black Scorpion superior and different was her new weapons, certainly not known to most of China's military and political leadership, or any other country on earth. Her new systems would change warfare forever, as she carried a new airborne laser weapon and an electromagnetic pulse weapon. Both systems were virtually unheard of outside of initial test phases.

Chen was no dummy and was a well-informed student of history. He had read that US President Ronald Reagan had put together a commission some thirty years ago on electromagnetic pulses, and, as usual, Chen saw opportunity in it. The commission's report stated there would be major loss of life from a weapon like this: if you lost the US electric grid over a five-year span, two-thirds of the population would be dead due to social disruption and disease. Experts have warned members of Congress very recently that igniting a pulse like this could destroy 90 percent of the US's food supply and electrical grid, including phone lines and internet. To Chen, opportunity.

Because the United States' global national security environment caused it to continue demonstrating their attraction to nuclear weapons, China felt the need to always keep up the arms race. This Reagan report fueled the Great Power competition, and the US used nuclear weapons as an effective deterrence. It was also a bet against an ambiguous future; they used it as an insurance policy.

China was a unique nation when it came to nuclear technology, too. Since 1977, China had been interested in radiation weapons, but never deployed them. Their specialized nuclear weapons had a smaller blast with enhanced radiation, which made them the perfect tactical option. Then, in 1988, China tested them. But what was interesting to strategists was that China shelved the technology, meaning they built and tested the technology and weapon, but did not develop it for use. Was Black Scorpion a change to their national-security decision making? Was Black Scorpion an extension of their hypersonic glide vehicle system?

Chen's vision was for Black Scorpion to use her laser weapon for strategic close air support and long-range air-to-air interdiction, which was a crucial and important platform for a laser. Because Black Scorpion was larger than any fighter aircraft, she had the size, weight, and power to carry these two new weapon systems, making her a terrific platform for delivery. Of course, she was also nuclear capable.

The Chinese laser that Chen's team built was at least five years ahead of the United States', leveraged from the Defense Department's third off-set strategy, which the secretary of defense was publicly touting in America. Every defense publication, television talking head, industry lobbyist, and trade magazine, preached this now-famous third offset, yet to Chen, the

United States was all talk and no action on the subject. Certainly, the defense industry would be happy to take on the business, but Chen knew the industry needed the Defense Department money to develop it. This was where Chen took advantage of someone else's problem: the United States had just finished multiple wars, had a relatively new administration, and was stressed on funding and resources.

China, though, was smart about its development. In fact, development was an overstatement, because China really didn't develop it. The laser was inexpensive enough to manufacture after stealing the plans from the United States, and it was a very reasonable way to achieve weapon effects in combat. As any true strategist would know, the real secret sauce was that the aircraft never needed to reload physical ammunition.

The Chinese team was able to lift the technology from the Air Force Research Laboratory, a robbery of years of studies and learning from the mistakes of America. The larger study from the Naval Surface Warfare Center in Dahlgren, Virginia, was where much of the research associated with the laser weapon system was conducted. A close second was the US Navy, where in one easy phishing scam onboard the USS *Ponce*, all their studies were captured in one simple and quick evening.

A few years ago, Chen's cyber team pretended to be employees from a US-based defense contractor working with the navy. Over an email, they asked targeted sailors to send them their username and password, and unfortunately for the United States, some young and naive sailors did so. It was similar to the way the Russians were suspected to have infiltrated the Democratic National Committee computers, apparently affecting the US presidential election. Chen walked in through the open front door, and walked out with everything.

What Chen also loved about the Department of Defense was that they publicly broadcast their exercise assessments and systems tests. He adored that the department had four key categories of vulnerabilities published for all to read! Chen couldn't believe it when their director of operational test and evaluation wrote in a public release that they had "exposed or poorly managed credentials...that their IT systems were not configured to identified standards…that their systems were not patched for known vulnerabilities, and that their system/network services and trust relationships provided avenues for cyber compromise… [and these] were all areas they need to improve upon." How exciting! To Chen, this was a cyber invitation to come in and shop around and take what he wanted. He once boasted at a general officer symposium that it was like "taking candy from a baby."

"We're leveling off here, Dai. Want me to run the weapons checklist?" asked copilot Chung.

Dai was busy calculating his entry point into the range, which was larger than of the state of Rhode Island. For him to turn around the jet at nearly six hundred knots would take miles. It was important for them to enter the range at the correct location so as to not waste time.

"Yes, let's run it. I'll slow us down to 250 knots. Maintain twenty thousand feet, so we can squirt the laser. We need to stay in the range here," Dai said, pointing at the glass screen where the range had a box displayed on a moving map.

He reached his hand up to the autopilot in front of him and twisted a round, black dial for the altitude. He then moved his right hand to the throttles and set a power setting, which was reduced from the climb setting to cruise.

"All set, Chung. Go ahead with the checklists."

During the laser testing last week, Chen was impressed at the precision accuracy and its ability to pull off low collateral damage. It could easily hit buildings, communication nodes, and even power towers holding thick cables. He also liked that they could be used defensively against other aircraft or even enemy missiles. What Chen loved as a strategist was that Black Scorpion only required bursts of onboard electricity, which she could easily produce and handle to push out a beam. The laser power would be extracted from multiple batteries that stored the energy, and would be constantly recharged by Black Scorpion's powerful engines via invertors and generators.

"Checklists complete, Dai. Range is clear; no other aircraft around."

"Roger. State battery setting," Dai asked.

Chung looked at his array of numbers on gauges displayed in the cockpit. There were hundreds of switches, levers, screens, buttons, circuit breakers, and handles, and both pilots had to know where all of them where. It took Chung just a moment to locate the weapons section of the screen, then drill down to the laser battery power levels. "Fully charged, 100 percent."

"Got it. OK, we're ready to conduct mission. Speed, 250 knots. In the green range."

"Yes, OK. We are in position. I can see the target. If you are ready, I am ready. Target's in sight; my crosshairs are aligned on the display screen. Go ahead, pull the trigger, Dai."

From the left seat, Dai pulled the trigger with his right index finger on the control stick between his legs. The batteries, already charged from the magnets in the engine's generators, produced enough power to shoot the laser all night long. The electrical current flowed from the batteries through the miles of tin-plated copper conductor wires, covered with PVC insulation and a nylon jacket, hidden inside her fuselage body, and over to the electrical switch in the stick. By closing the circuit, this allowed the electrons and protons to travel to their destination in the laser turret in the nose.

"Trigger is pulled."

PART 7

OPTIONS

Over the Jeju Straight Waterway, South Korean Airspace

The unidentified air force aircraft was airborne, with her high-bypass turbofan engines pushing out thousands of pounds of thrust. She could fly unrefueled for long distances with a heavy takeoff weight and cruise pretty well, but the two pilots up front would not need to fly that long tonight.

The flight crew was busy doing their mission at thirty-four thousand feet mean sea level, heading southbound near the Jeju Straight. They used their GPS for navigation on airway Y711 to waypoint KIDOS, then over to waypoint TOLIS to the west, and their mission was scheduled for about six hours.

Over the UHF radio, a call was broadcast on the crew's black Bose-brand headsets. "HAMMER 88, Incheon Center."

The aircrew up front in the cockpit were from a US air base and were lost in conversation about music, movies, girls, and Major League Baseball, not paying a lick of attention to the radios. The night sky was bright with starlight, and there were no other aircraft that they could see. The lit ships way down below on the ocean surface stood out on the dark water, but they did not interfere with the argument taking place in the cockpit over the intercom.

"You are wrong, brother. No way. *Mall Cop* was a much better movie than…"

The radio broke into their conversation. "HAMMER 88, HAMMER 88, Incheon Center, how do you read?"

"Damn. We must have missed their call," the aircraft commander said, glancing down at the radios to ensure the volume was OK.

"HAMMER 88, come in," the center controller announced again, searching for the aircraft.

"HAMMER 88 here, go ahead center. Read you loud and clear."

"Copy, HAMMER 88. Thought I lost you for a second. Present position cleared direct to TOLIS; climb and maintain flight level 360."

"Roger, HAMMER 88 cleared direct to TOLIS, departing three-four-zero for three-six-zero."

Over the intercom: "Nah, I'm telling you, Gus, *The Big Lebowski* is number one. Way better. The cult-like following is epic…" The flight crew made the turn to the west, still well within the Korean airspace, and sipped on coffee. The pilots couldn't give a crap that radio calls were missed, and got back to the movie-ranking business.

In the rear of the jet sat a variety of talented airmen, conducting their airborne sweeps. As soon as the jet turned to the west, the sensors began tracking a single aircraft out on the horizon

"This is weird," said Airman First Class Jennifer Harris over the intercom to some of her crewmates.

"What is?" replied Sergeant Nate Thomas, a communications expert.

"Well, are you seeing what I'm seeing?" Jennifer announced.

"Yup, just got it now. I'm on it," Nate replied.

"Very unusual. I've not seen this before." She paused, then asked. "So. Hey. *How'd he do that?*" she said, staring at her avionics equipment.

"I don't know what to make of this. Some type of new aircraft?" Nate asked.

"From what I can tell. Never seen this before."

"Yup. He's moving from here to here," Nate replied after looking on his screens, giving Jennifer a nod with his head.

After hearing the chatter on the intercom between Jennifer and Nate, First Lieutenant Jake Greentree stood up and walked over to their consoles. "What do you guys have brewing?"

"Hi, Lieutenant. Um, we're both looking at something…unusual. He's about twenty thousand feet, in an oval pattern and holding. His behavior and flying is just…weird," Jennifer explained.

First Lieutenant Jake Greentree, US Air Force, was relatively new to the mission, and he, too, had not seen this before. It did not come up at school last year during his training, so he thought to ask one of the senior enlisted aircrew for help. He leaned over their shoulders and stood looking at the avionics. *What the hell is this?* he thought. Before Jake could approach anyone, over the headset came another aircrew member from another crew station console even further in the back of the jet.

"Hey, sir, Garner here, in the back. I'm following your conversation on that jet and have something to add to your weirdness."

"Go ahead; what do you have, Garner?" replied Jake.

"Martinez and I are following your jet, and it's nothing we've ever seen before either," Garner commented.

Garner and Martinez were some of the smartest aircrew guys Greentree knew, so it puzzled him even more. "Crazy. All right then…make some notes for later, and we'll send it to the boys in DC," Jake replied.

"Huh, I'll be damned," Jake said to himself quietly, just as astounded as the rest of the crew.

DIA Headquarters, Washington, DC

Emily was alone in her cubicle, scanning the world's incoming data from their collection runs. Using her Windows 10 software, she read and read, until she found her needle in a haystack. She turned and smiled, curious at what an aircrew had just written up from their flight. Emily looked at her watch, and saw the latest update was only minutes old, filed while airborne.

"Bollocks," Emily exclaimed. "This has got to be them. This must be Black Scorpion." She smiled.

She also took off the printer the cell phone data, which included the names of the cell phones' owners and all their apps. One app of interest was the aircraft engine and avionics performance figures, which she was familiar with from Devil Dragon. The Chinese had invented a smartphone app that communicated with the jet, downloading data from the aircraft to the phone.

This allowed the maintenance crews on the ground to analyze the performance upon landing, providing technical data for adjustments on the high-performing engines and avionics. It was also a treasure trove of information to DIA.

Emily took her pile of papers from the computer and walked down to the conference room, where her team was in full stride in briefing Mr. Burns. She passed a group of four uniformed military guys standing in the hallway, and they couldn't help but stare at the petite blonde in a short skirt and Steve Madden–brand leather heels. It was very non–politically correct to stare like they did, but nevertheless, they did it quietly. "Hello, boys. Good morning," she greeted them, looking befuddled carrying, in addition to her coffee, a stack of white printouts that looked like they were going to fly across the office.

"Hey Emily…" they responded, ogling. They also got a whiff of her Jo Malone perfume, the woodsy and sea salt version, which the men loved. Emily knocked on the door quietly with two knocks and walked in on the briefing wearing a slight smirk. She kind of liked that she still had the power to get glances.

"And, based upon everything we have talked about so far, from the satellite stuff to the recorded sounds to parked aircraft, more probable than not, the Chinese have another jet," Mark told the room, finishing up the brief.

"I haven't heard you brief if there were flights in the area," Calvin said, predictably.

Mark nodded over to Emily.

Emily lit up with a beautiful smile. "Cheerio. This is what we have so far. First, not sure if Mark or Robert told you, but we now know the aircraft is named Black Scorpion, which we think is their H-20 designation. We were getting raw data from some of those cell phones and, until very recently, only knew the aircraft name from their phones. Now that the algorithms and software have had some time to go through the phones and apps, we have the engine and avionics data."

"Black Scorpion, eh? Are the readings from this aircraft similar to Devil Dragon? What else did it say?" Calvin asked, with a mind full of additional questions. His wheels were turning now that there was a hill of evidence building.

Emily walked over to the front of the conference room. "First off, our two People's Liberation Army Air Force pilots are named Dai Jian and Chung Kang. Unknown backgrounds at the moment, but the owners of the phones not only have this encrypted engine app, but aviation navigation software for mission planning. Wu Lee had the same thing on his phone, so it's a match."

Ford was amazed at the similarities already, and he had only been here for a few hours. It was unfolding as it did before, and the more he sat there, the more he was eager to be involved. His mind was racing, wondering if he was going to get another go, another stealth bomber flight. *The only pilot to steal two bombers from China!* he thought. *There is no way Calvin Burns will let this go...this aircraft couldn't possibly remain in Chinese hands.*

Robert immediately typed the two pilot's names into Google and found their profiles on a social-networking site. "Well, so much for keeping a low profile. They are both on LinkedIn. Guys have pretty generic profiles on there, but...looks like they graduated from Stanford University together. School of Engineering...then...returned to China to work engineering jobs."

"We freaking educated these two pilots?" Calvin said, taking off his reading glasses and sliding them across the brown conference room table. "Really?" as he shook his head and placed his face into his hands. "This is just like how we strung up aircraft at the damn Wright-Patt Museum for the whole world to see...only to have the technology used against us. Goddamn it. When are we going to learn?"

Calvin was referring to the Wright-Patterson Air Force Base in Dayton, Ohio, where the US Air Force had on display many of their historical aircraft. Calvin's anger was because, through the years, General Chen used Ohio State University students with camera phones to take pictures of our U-2, F-117, B-2, and SR-71, which were all on open static display in the museum. The Smithsonian Institution Air and Space Museum at the Dulles Airport had a similar display. Both of these made Calvin furious because he felt we were giving our technology to the Chinese on a silver platter. It bothered him a tremendous amount.

Emily gave a nervous smile now and knew that his sensitivity was only temporary. "So, we should probably talk about the details of the items that just arrived. A bird off Korea."

Robert and Mark both leaned in to hear what Emily was going to say, while Ford looked at Robert and Mark. Ford thought their mannerisms were funny and considered their body language. It reminded him of a family dog that was ready to get a biscuit.

"Calm down, you two," Ford said, seeing an opportunity to bust their chops.

Emily continued. "The crew was first picking up some new and usual things, which just didn't add up."

"Hey, that matches Devil Dragon. She had the same profile," Ford said.

"It does? Huh. Same ops. I must have forgotten that. OK, please continue, Emily," Calvin commented.

Emily nodded in agreement. "A separate collection asset detected an anomaly on a routine night flight of an Su-35, a single ship in the same area. This info verified the cell phones I just briefed you on, and the author mentions that the actual cell phones were 'flying in formation' with, or alongside, this Su-35 over a bombing range. Range between invisible aircraft and Su-35 were from four to seven miles away from each other. No radar hits to any aircraft in the area except the 35."

Ford crunched his face up in amazement. "Invisible aircraft over a *bombing range*? Not just flight test? What...were they doing...over a bombing range?"

"Yes, Ford, I'm glad you asked. Underneath this 'phantom jet,' as the crew called it, carrying these two cell phones and transmitting all sorts of data, were ground explosions. But no weapons were detected as firing. No bombs were detected as being dropped. The traditional 'boop' sound was not heard on any frequencies by our asset."

As the only pilot in the room, Ford took on the role of subject-matter expert for this aspect of the aircraft. He was an airborne weapons expert, was skilled in both fighter and bomber aircraft, and previously did a joint tour with the navy as an F/A-18 Hornet pilot. To him, this was most unusual, because it meant the first few phases of flight test were complete. It meant the jet was stable and safe, and now you could fight with it.

Ford's expression changed to serious. "Can I see those printouts, Emily?" Ford asked with his hand out. Emily passed them to Mark, who peeked at them, then handed them to Ford. He read them line by line, taking a close look at the app data feed from the Black Scorpion to the phone.

"It continues in a unique line code of data, being transmitted up to a ChinaSat 2C satellite, then transmitted down to a ground antenna. The unencrypted data was aircrew oxygen and carbon dioxide usage levels."

Ford looked up, puzzled. "I don't recall that feature on Devil Dragon."

Emily nodded in agreement. She knew this was fresh material that did not have much analysis but figured it was worth talking about now since it was related to the matter at hand.

"Why then…would Chen want live feeds of oxygen usage of aircrew? That seems odd," Mark offered.

"I know, I know. Here's the kicker. This says they detected a downlink to Xishuangbanna Airport in Yunnan," Emily said, completing her presentation with all the information she had.

Robert laughed out loud. "Well, isn't that pretty? That's where our boy Chen is with his fancy business jet and the maintenance team in the Y-9."

Ford was already on his fourth page of data when he started to see some trends. Altitudes, airspeeds, and massive electrical drains on power. Generator levels. Unique readouts of volts and amps not previously seen on new, large-capacity batteries. And oxygen readings, too. *Something isn't right here,* he thought.

Calvin quietly looked at the screen and went through the slides again silently. "Let's quietly think this one through. I'd like to see some more information on what Chen wants to do with this aircraft. I've got plenty of additional questions, starting with if we should back-brief the director, or even the secretary of defense. Or higher. We are in no rush to…"

"I got it!" Ford yelled out.

"That's not quietly thinking through, Ford," Mark told him.

Ford was bursting with energy. "You quiet. Listen. Sir. Excuse me," he said, excitedly. "Two items. The F-22 Raptor and F/A-18 Hornet have had oxygen problems. You know, where the pilots did not get enough air through the mask, and it caused hypoxia. Pilots were getting light headed at altitude, some even passing out. It was causing mishaps…killing pilots. There was no way to record the oxygen breathing while the aircraft was airborne, but certainly they could see it once on the ground from maintenance. I'm willing to bet money Chen has a problem with oxygen. I'd also bet even more money that he thinks that's why the Devil Dragon went down."

Mark was impressed. "How? What do you mean?"

"In flying, you just don't install a device to begin transmitting oxygen levels unless it's a problem, a requirement. That equipment is excess weight, which offsets the four forces of flight. Plus, it gives the aircraft away. Very untactical."

"The what? What are the four forces of flight?" asked Mark.

"Well, rookie, they are lift, thrust, drag, and weight. Basic aerodynamics. Imagine an airplane hung in the air on a string. If it's too heavy, it comes down. It must produce enough thrust to project it through the air, to overcome the weight and drag. Wings do the aerodynamic magic by providing lift."

Ford got up out of his seat, then subtlety cleared his throat. "I bet Chen wanted to know why Wu crashed. We know he discovered the two bodies that Mark airdropped as a decoy. In aviation, pilots—and the entire aviation community, frankly—always do an investigation on the mishap. We have an entire academic program in aviation safety at the Naval Postgraduate School, and over at USC for this. I bet Chen thinks they ran out of oxygen, and the aircraft flew on autopilot while the pilots were passed out, until fuel starvation. Then, they impacted in the water at a high rate of speed."

"Well. That does seem pretty reasonable," Calvin said.

Robert raised his eyebrows. "What was your second point? You said you had two. A second item?"

"Yeah, yeah. These printouts from Emily here," Ford said as he pointed to them on the table. "They have strange readings on volts, amps, and batteries. Normally, aircraft only use a battery for starting the engines, and you mostly use a ground power cart when you start. Rarely a start off your own batteries. Once the bird is started, it uses onboard generators and invertors to power the avionics, like lights, radios, air conditioning—items like that. In fact, you can disconnect the battery after start, and the jet runs just fine. All about the generators at that point."

"Ford, why have powerful batteries like the ones you're seeing then?" Emily asked.

Ford paused. Ford was guessing on this next idea, but trusted everyone in the room. He'd already had multiple life-and-death experiences with them, was with the love of his life, Emily, and was going to step out on a limb with this next idea. *Do I say it? Damn it*, he thought, as he hesitated.

"Go ahead, Ford. We're family now," Calvin reassured him. "Give it some critical thinking." Calvin wanted to instill in his young team that it was OK to provide outlandish ideas, as everyone's opinion was important. He used a few techniques, teaching them to his team, which Mark knew from history. Calvin's big four on critical thinking were to value it and be open minded, to be alert to opportunities to make decisions and solve problems, and to accept missteps. Bottom line for them was to give your idea up, and it was OK to make a mistake.

"You would have a massive array of batteries like this…to…charge your laser weapon."

Mark started laughing. "What kind of idea is that? Oh, come on, Ford," Mark told him. "A laser? This isn't *Star Wars*."

Calvin shot Mark a death stare. "Mark, you come on. You've had your day of eccentric ideas, believe me. Let him finish," Calvin told Mark. Mark nodded.

"All right," Mark answered, sighing and cracking his knuckles. "This kid…" Mark loved busting his chops.

Ford took a deep breath. "Mr. Burns, lasers have been around since, what, 1960 or so? It's a device that emits light…you know, optical amplification. That's fifty-plus years for the world to work on something. Missile Defense Agency tried it on a Boeing 747, the navy tried it on surface ships. Even Special Operations Command on a C-130…the…whatever the name is…the Advanced Tactical Laser Program. Heck, we use it for pulling over speeders and mapping the earth with light. LIDAR. There are cops pulling people over right now for speeding on I-95," Ford said, pausing briefly. "We even use it for reading compact disks for music! All it is, is stimulated emission of electromagnetic radiation. And it will cut through a tank or a building like a warm knife through butter."

Everyone in the room stared at Ford.

"That's it? That's all you got?" Mark asked sarcastically, rubbing the tattoo on his forearm.

Ford paused. "Look. This aircraft has enough direct current with batteries to power a small fishing village in Minnesota. I am really having a hard time thinking of why, other than using it for generating enough power for a laser. We use lasers, and that's what the batteries are for. The evidence is right there. Put the baby to bed; I'm done. I rest my case."

Ford was spot-on in his assessment of lasers. Recent news becoming public in the press was of the US armed forces seeking a low-kilowatt laser, especially after figuring out in testing that it was inexpensive, effective, and accurate. It was more of a policy discussion at the Pentagon now, with lawyers determining where you could use it on the battlefield.

"Nice job, lawyer," Mark said, poking fun at Ford.

Calvin leaned forward, picked up his reading glasses again, and put them on the bridge of his nose. He sat in the chair with his arms folded, rubbing his chin. "So, we have a Chinese stealth bomber that can fly undetected anywhere they want at Mach whatever," waiving his hand around, "that delivers nukes, or...now...can deliver unlimited firepower with a newly developed laser weapon?"

"Yes, sir," Mark told him. "Seems like it." He adjusted his blue-and-white wrestling shoes, pulling the tongues up on each foot.

The room was disconcertingly quiet, and the team sat in thought. After a few seconds, Calvin Burns stood, followed by Mark and Robert. He grabbed his pen and pad, his eyeglass case, and made his way toward the conference room door.

"All right, all right. Definitely the director, and I'm leaning on telling the secretary. Mark, get me options," said the deputy as he left the room.

Shoreline of the Potomac River, Bolling Air Force Base, Washington, DC
Ford left the DIA Headquarters building and went for a run around the base, taking in some fresh air. He always carried his running gear with him when traveling because not only was it cost effective, but he could run anywhere.

He didn't need a gym to get in some exercise, which was not only good for keeping fit in the cockpit but allowed him to eat desserts. It helped him burn off the stress.

What also was helping him burn off the stress was turning to the drink, which according to Emily, was troublesome. Ever since his wild days at Notre Dame, he'd been fond of alcohol. At first beer, then liquor. *Maybe I do drink a lot now? Nope,* he said to himself. Since the loss of Wu, he had been suffering in silence in his own way.

Guys in the squadron knew he drank, because many of them were just like him. Ford did get drunk a lot lately, though. He did text and email drunk, as Emily accused him of. She had, in the recent past, found him lying on his bed naked, drooling. Sometimes he had one leg down on the floor, attempting to make the room stop spinning. Ford had also hidden his drinking from others, mostly out of embarrassment, particularly from nonpilots, who just would not understand, and especially this latest mission, which no one could ever fathom.

Professionals called someone with this condition a high-functioning alcoholic. At least 20 percent of alcoholics were high-functioning alcoholics, meaning they were successful in their personal and professional lives. Researchers had recently found that in America, the top 10 percent of alcoholics who drink, which was about 24 million people, consumed an average of sixty-one drinks a week. About 15 percent of these people consumed 75 percent of the alcohol domestically in the US. One or two drinks a day was healthy by many standards, resulting in reducing heart disease, diabetes, and stroke, but more than that and it was a medical issue. Alcohol overworked your liver and increased your blood pressure and chances of cancer, in addition to decreasing your immune system.

"What the hell is she talking about?" Ford said out loud, referring to Emily. He carefully reflected on his past few months. Ford was a responsible, productive military officer and pilot and showed up for work each day with vigor. He was an achiever. Ford was also in denial. *I don't have a problem.*

Experts on alcohol abuse say people can drink heavily, be professionals, and come from all walks of life. Ford's drinking increased to heavy drinking status over the past few months because he was easily having more than four drinks a day. Because Ford was blind to it, only Emily could see the signs. She saw in him that he needed alcohol to relax, that he sometimes drank alone and often, and that he was now denying his drinking. Ford had also gotten heated after Emily confronted him, adding yet another red flag to her informal list. His actions were causing concern to her, who loved him dearly. It was Ford's true ding in a perfect hero's armor.

Ford stopped at the Potomac River after putting in three miles, hit the stop button on his watch, and sat in the grass overlooking the water. The so-called white space on his schedule helped him think, and if done properly, his mind would solve the most difficult of problems for him in due time. His meditation routine, once laughed at by the other pilots in the squadron, was now catching on with others, and the quiet time helped him settle his mind. It also aided him with the fact that he had a job in which he faced death regularly, in peacetime or in war, because every time he took up an aircraft, or jumped out of one, he took great risk. The meditation helped him with self-discipline and focus.

His civilian peers from Notre Dame, now selling insurance, running numbers in finance, showing real estate, practicing medicine, or working in air-conditioned offices in places like Cary, Malibu, St. Louis, Orange County, Fairfax, or Grosse Pointe, would never comprehend his lifestyle. The Zen thinking, which Ford was attracted to, enabled him to move forward 100 percent once a decision was made. This aided Ford to push forward on difficult missions, not letting anything get in his way toward success.

To Ford, quieting the mind and emptying it freed him from the uncertainty and fear that could seep into the untrained pilot's mind. Ford was taught to consider all options before he acted, whether on the ground or in the air, but then once a decision was made, he pressed on. He was also aware that to someone who was using mindfulness, overthinking led to people being paralyzed thought-wise, and usually at the worst possible times. Ford thought that moving forward, curbing his ego, and pushing toward a mission with the smallest amount of thought and reflection produced mission success.

Some of his pilot buddies busted his chops when they saw Ford meditating. Ford usually responded with a humorous one-liner, but other squadron pilots eventually caught on to the idea, especially since it helped them deal with death and fear. The saying in one of his squadrons was "Train like you fly, fly like you train." To Ford, his mind could get seized by negativity before the fighting even began. He trained himself to not focus on his personal or professional problems or the criticism from others, or he would no longer be able to act unconventionally and autonomously. Meditation allowed Ford to face challenges with a positive attitude, attempting to overcome his weaknesses. Today, though, it helped him think through what Lieutenant General He Chen might be up to in China.

Ford let out a little laugh, finally understanding why Chen drank. *Most likely due to the stress,* Ford thought. *I get it, believe me. Wow. The loss of Wu and this past mission is really affecting me. Am I an alcoholic?* He was as torn as ever on this topic. *Nah.*

Sitting in the grass on the Potomac shore, Ford's mind drifted. He was now thinking though the history of US stealth aircraft, along with Chen's desire to have these types of stealth aircraft.

Ford was not serving in January 1991, but back then, ten F-117 Nighthawks were able to quietly penetrate Iraqi airspace at the start of Operation Desert Storm. No one saw them coming, especially the Iraqi radar controllers using old-school Soviet air-defense equipment. The Nighthawk, Devil Dragon, and now, it seemed, Black Scorpion were all designed to reflect radar returns away. Each of the aircraft were painted the same flat-black color, while their exhaust was discretely lost and diversified with cooler air. It was brilliant.

Each of the aircraft, for the most part, could be flown EMI free, too. If you shut down the electronic transmissions of the navigation data, radios, and even the radar and radar altimeters, it was like flying a World War I aircraft when radar didn't exist. *How many does Chen have? What's he up to?* Ford thought.

Ford looked across the water to the United Airlines 737-800 aircraft taking off to the south at Reagan National Airport, while a JetBlue Airbus A320 was getting ready to land, hugging the river. The commercial jets were loud, as the uninterrupted sound easily traversed across the one-mile distance to the airport's east. *Wait a minute...sound. Sonic booms and lasers. They can be detected and measured! Will have to make note of the idea for later...I need evidence to show Mark and the team.* The white space was helping him think.

Chen's desire for stealth was born from the days of Chinese general and military strategist Sun Tzu, where surprising one's enemy was always desired. Chen followed Sun Tzu's philosophy of "mystify, mislead, and surprise the enemy" to the letter. Stealth technology was right up his alley, thanks to the concept of low-observability physics and radar.

Radio Detection and Ranging, or Radar, sent out a radio frequency signal across the sky. Any radio frequency energy that reflected off an object toward the observer created a return. An Airbus A320 created quite a large return, or echo, while a Cherokee 140 private airplane created a smaller one. The Black Scorpion returned almost nothing. She was able to hide in the lower-frequency radars, taking advantage of the longer wavelengths. Black Scorpion's ability to use backscatter, or the reflection toward the emitting radar, was improved dramatically because of her angled surfaces. It was literally hiding in plain sight.

The father of stealth in America, William F. Bahret, figured out which structures on an aircraft mattered on the echo return. Metal skin like aluminum was important, as were curves of the wing, fuselage, and tail sections. What if you could hide engines and antennas inside an aircraft, one with straight edges that reduced its radar return? You know the rest as history. Lockheed built and test flew in 1978 an aircraft codenamed SENIOR TREND and HAVE BLUE, which morphed into the F-117 program. The fact that the United States used them successfully in January 1991 opened the front door for Chen.

Chen was obsessed as a young pilot and officer that another country such as the United States had this technology, and he wanted it. To have a radar cross section of a small bird was the ultimate weapon, and he would stop at nothing to get ahold of the blueprints so he could build them. Chen studied and studied the stealth and radar technology so that he would become the subject-matter expert one day.

Chen even located the 1999 Serbian report of the missile brigade that had shot down an F-117, aircraft call sign "VEGA 31," over Serbia. Using a Soviet P-18 SPOON REST D, an old school Very-High Frequency, or VHF early-warning radar, the Serbians could track and launch a SA-3 LOW

BLOW surface-to-air missile at the jet. Chen did his homework, and now the Americans were paying for it.

Ford was not aware of Chen's specific cyber capabilities, but Chen sure continued his laughter at the United States' attempts to defend themselves on the cyber front.

Just recently, the Department of Defense information technology budget request was over $38 billion, which included $6.8 billion for defense cyber operations. Chen found it most humorous because the US spent so much attempting to protect themselves, while human dynamics were always the downfall, not software or hardware. The Chinese were experts at reading open-source news, and knew from risk assessment articles that 74 percent of computer attacks came from careless employees. Chen knew there would never be enough money in their budget to deter him.

The United States was concerned not only about China, but also about the threat that came from Russia, North Korea, and Iran. The linking between technology and theft of intellectual property with American businesses for competitive advantage was strong, as well as the traditional military and intelligence activities. The internet of things was a real concern to administration officials, especially the critical infrastructure, which Chen adored. Power grids, energy systems, and large computer systems were a treat to him.

What gave Chen a rare smile was in penetrating the machine-to-machine sharing called STIX, or Structured Threat Information Expression, which was a means of disseminating the threat information. It acted as a report card for the Chinese, and told them which methods were or were not working. *How dumb can these Americans be?* he often asked himself.

Ford stood up in the grass, spread his legs wide, and began stretching out while listening to more commercial jets taking off. *We need to verify this jet exists, and then verify the laser. We need to get Black Scorpion, and bring her home.* Ford took a swig of whiskey and ginger ale, conveniently located in his water bottle.

Just then, Emily came up to him, complete in her running gear of a simple T-shirt, shorts, and running shoes. "Hello, mate. How was your run?"

"Hi. Good. Real good. Just wrapped up a few miles," he said as he looked out over the water, then to her. "Em, I've been doing some thinking."

Emily's mind and heart, spring-loaded to think it was about them and their long-distance dating or even their earlier chat about drinking, was immediately excited. She was sure he was thinking about their relationship, of course—the two of them long term—and perhaps would even discuss marriage. *This was it,* she thought. *Marriage, drinking, perhaps? Wait, is that alcohol I smell?* Alone, taking a break, with a beautiful view of the river. "Yes, Ford. Thinking about what?"

"I have an idea about the mission. Not sure if Mark would like it, but here's what I think," Ford said to her.

"Go ahead, love, what is it?" *Damn,* she thought privately and disapprovingly. *This is work related, not about him or us.*

"Well, the Missile Defense Agency has a special Gulfstream aircraft that can fly and detect wavelengths from afar while airborne. It has a large, usual protrusion on its roof, full of all sorts of technical gear."

Ford was right. The Missile Defense Agency did have a Gulfstream II-B business jet, called HALO-II. It was an airborne observatory that offered excellent aircraft performance and long flight endurance for their observation mission. The aircraft's ability to climb to a very high altitude, above obscuring clouds and atmosphere, provided onboard sensors with a clear view. The electronic optics and infrared sensors and radar sensors were installed in a pod located on top of the fuselage, which enabled a terrific look around and horizon-to-horizon elevation viewing. More great work from the Special Missions section at Gulfstream in Savannah.

"Not too bad for a pilot who doesn't know the intelligence community," said Emily, giving him a dig. It was completely lost on Ford.

"What if we got the State Department to invite this fancy agency to fly the jet into Mongolia, or even Burma? Call it a foreign-policy trip to support the government. This could be easily arranged. While there the aircraft can launch and get into a holding pattern until Black Scorpion launches. That way we could verify that there is a laser on board. The ideas that I mentioned about the batteries were just that, ideas. We have no validation of the laser energy yet."

Emily worked hard in her mind to not be negative. "Hmm, hmmm. I like that idea, Ford. I think we should talk to Mark about it when we get into work later." She paused and grabbed his hand. "By the way, love, why don't we talk about us? Pick up where we left off, maybe at dinner tonight, the two of us?"

"Yes. I'd like that. I was doing some thinking about us, too. We have been dating awhile. We know each other well, have met each other's families. And…I'm ready to commit my life to you. You and I are…" Ford started in, then stopped suddenly.

The timing couldn't be worse as Jason pulled up in his car alongside Ford and Emily. "Hey, Mr. Burns asked me to track you two down. Robert's been looking for you two. Need you to come back. Hot item. Get in."

Damn. All I wanted was a few minutes with him, Emily thought to herself.

Miller Residence, Hudson Street, Hawley, Pennsylvania

"Dad, Dad, what is this?" said Rex Miller, an energetic and excited ten-year-old boy, to his father, Michael.

Michael, on the Social Committee at a nearby Poconos Resort named Woodloch Pines, was all about family. Michael organized old-school fun backyard games in a resort-style atmosphere, ranging from potato sack races to trivia contests to a capstone event called the Family Olympics. Rated the number-one family resort in the United States by many travel organizations, the lakefront property had Michael to thank for guest fun.

"Well, Rex, that's the dial to tune in the frequency. This is an amateur radio. Also known as a ham radio. We can talk to people all around the world with this radio gear," replied Michael.

Sitting on their basement table pushed up against the cement foundation wall was their transceiver, connected to the home's electricity via a plug, complete with an antenna in the attic, a microphone, and a frequency logbook.

"This is cool, Dad. Tell me more. I want to talk to someone far away. Please?" an enthusiastic Rex asked.

"OK, OK. Hang on. I figured it was time to share with you my hobby. Let's see," Michael replied, tuning up his $150 starter radio.

The ham radio industry had boomed lately thanks to doomsday preppers and hobby fans around the world. It enabled nearly anyone with one of three licenses in the United States to communicate around the globe at nearly anytime. Easy entry to the hobby field allowed citizens to relay news and weather and communicate as far as one hundred miles away with a technician license, or across the earth with a general license.

"Rex, listen in. Put this headset on over your ears." Michael showed his son how to wear the headset, adjusting it to his ten-year-old head. "This is the Radio Society of Great Britain right now. They are located at the National Radio Centre in London. That's in England. Look over there at the wall map there and point that out for us."

"Wow. We can talk across the whole Atlantic Ocean with this radio?" a wide-eyed Rex asked.

Airspace around Xi'an Xianyang International Airport
There was no immediate reason for Chen to land his Su-35 at the same base as the Black Scorpion, so Chen returned to the Xishuangbanna Airport in Yunnan. The Black Scorpion crew, keeping operational security on their front burner, continued forward to their next scheduled location for the night at Xi'an Airport.

Copilot Chung Kang put his head down and punched in XXIA for the four-letter airport identifier code. It came up immediately on the display screen in between their seats in the Flight Management System database. He then verified the latitude/longitude at 34°26'49"N, 108°45'05"E, and punched in the key labeled "Direct." Direction lines that resembled Google Maps appeared on the flat-panel screens in front of them, from the aircraft icon to the destination. If they just flew the line or used autopilot, the aircraft would go direct to Xi'an Airport. It worked the same way as modern car navigation systems, plotting a route to an address.

Looking at the newly built runway on the cockpit display, Runway 05 Right, built in 2012 to handle the gigantic commercial Airbus 380, aircraft commander Dai was tempted to bring Black Scorpion in because of the fantastic 12,400-foot length. Unfortunately for them, they needed to park and hide Black Scorpion for the next twenty hours or so in the large white hangar at the end of Runway 05 Left, located on the other side of the airfield. Even though it was night and there were not many people around to see them, the risk was too great to taxi across such a distance. They would have to land on Runway 05 Left, the shorter of the two runways.

Kang slowed her down and ran the descent checklists up at altitude, ensuring the aircraft was safe since they just finished their weapon test. Dai made some notes on his kneeboard-size card with a pencil, with his head down inside the cockpit. He wrote some of the aircraft performance parameters and switch settings and copied the atmospheric conditions like outside air temperature and humidity, which engineering would care about. In order to adjust the laser for maximum firepower and lethality, a whole list of items would need to be fine-tuned.

Their next test tomorrow would be to take her down to the South China Sea, Woody Islands, to do a surface-to-air missile (SAM) battery test with some military radar equipment. Along the northwestern coast of the island were a deployment of these SAM units, along with a single HT-233 target engagement radar, supported by a target acquisition radar. Four pairs of vehicles carrying these missiles, known as transporter-erector-launchers were there, too, totaling thirty-two surface-to-air missiles. This was well publicized in the open international news, but Chen wanted to fly down there anyway.

Woody Island was located in the Spratly Islands, the oil- and gas-rich real estate claimed by multiple countries, which made headlines on a daily basis. The islands were located between Vietnam and the Philippines, while the actual boundaries were heated points of tension that had the potential to spark into a major conflict one day. The United Nations Convention on the Law of the Sea, which was a country's Exclusive Economic Zone, stated that it "shall not extend beyond two hundred nautical miles from the baselines from which the breadth of the territorial sea is measured." In the Exclusive Economic Zone, each country can use natural resources, fish, construct artificial islands, and lay undersea cable. China was pushing the limits, literally, politically and militarily.

Testing had been going on down there since 2005, and Chen recently had some J-11BH and J-H7 fighters sent down to warm up the military radar controllers. His vision of these deployments allowed ground crews to operate in conditions that looked like other areas of the world. Chen also deviously wanted to test military radar against Black Scorpion.

"Let's run the before-landing checklists," Dai commanded, and Chung gave a thumbs up as he turned the page in his pilot's checklist.

"OK, before-landing checklist. Seats and harnesses?" Chung said out loud.

"I'm lock—"

BAAAM! BAAAM! BOOMP!

The jet shuddered, and impacts to her external skin were felt inside the cockpit.

"What the hell was that?" Dai said over the intercom. "We hit something."

"*Whoa!* We just hit a flock of birds. Bird strike. Bird strike," Chung said.

"WHOOP. WHOOP. ENGINE NUMBER ONE FAILURE. ENGINE NUMBER ONE FAILURE," the Black Scorpion on-board flight computer, in a female voice, announced over the intercom of the aircraft issue.

"We sucked in a bird into engine number one. She's failed. Damn. Shut her down. Shut her down," Dai said.

The jet yawed to the left slightly because of the loss of power on that side. Since engine number one was on the left side of the aircraft, the right side produced more thrust at that instant and the jet over compensated. For a solid few moments, the aircraft's turn and bank indicator was not centered, and the small ball that demonstrated balanced flight was way off to the side. Not a good situation, as the aircraft was slicing sideways through the air and losing some altitude. Since Dai was flying manually, he stomped on the rudder pedal to balance the aircraft again. He also had the control stick banked to the right so he could maintain straight and level flight.

"Chung, verify I have my hand on throttle number one?" Dai asked.

"Yes, yes, number one. Confirmed."

The cockpit lights were already all lighting up because of the loss of oil and fuel pressure, generator power, and turbine speed. Hydraulics were shared by other engines, so assisted power to the flight controls were not affected. The aircraft's engine could easily be eating itself, literally spinning and disintegrating metal in the air and on fire. For all they knew, the jet could be shooting flames out the back and littering the countryside with aircraft fan blades and engine parts.

"WHOOP WHOOP. WHOOP WHOOP. EMERGENCY. EMERGENCY."

"Silence that damn thing already, Chung."

Dai moved his right hand on throttle one and pulled it back all the way, and then lifted it up and back. By doing that, he shut down the electrical connections to the engine, including the fuel pump, securing the engine completely. He adjusted the other throttles to make up for the loss of power on the left side of the aircraft. It was not a nightmare for a large multiengine aircraft to lose an engine, but it was a big deal to hit a bird and have it fail without knowing what type of damage it caused. Plenty of aircraft hit birds annually and most aircrews survived. In the United States alone, bird strikes caused $1.2 billion in damage to commercial aircraft each year.

"Engine is out, Dai. I know there is no way to tell from here, but I heard more than one thump hitting the jet. We may have taken a flock of birds to the fuselage...or even the left wing," Chung said.

"Understand. Let me do a few maneuvers here at altitude. I'm going to... slow her down, check the controllability. We're at a good landing gear and flaps speed, so let's lower the gear and see what we have," Dai replied.

Chung checked the airspeed indicator, and it read below 220 knots. He moved his hand up to lower the landing gear with the handle, waited a moment, then put the flaps at 50 percent. They flew the aircraft around at three thousand feet above ground level, and it flew fine. Ops normal.

"Put flaps to 100 percent," Dai commanded.

Chung put the flaps down, and the aircraft pitched as it normally did, but they had no issues either in that configuration. He banked left and right, no issues. Started a descent, and no issues.

"All right, let's clean her up. Gear and flaps up, and we'll take her down to 1,500 feet and get dirty down there."

Chung raised the gear and flaps, as Dai began the descent. He did a standard rate of descent of five hundred feet per minute, just to take it easy. Certainly, Black Scorpion was capable of diving at the deck with a purpose, but this wasn't the night for that.

The gear and flaps came down again normally as they got to 1,500 feet for a five-mile straight-in approach, and they worked themselves into the landing pattern without their lights on. They didn't talk to anyone on the aviation frequencies, and they did not show up on the approach controller's screens. The runway was dark, with no commercial air traffic on their on-board radar.

Their night-vision goggles, or NVGs, were in the infrared light spectrum and allowed them to see clear as day as they approached the airport on short final. The NVGs were optoelectronic devices that allowed images to be produced in levels of light approaching total darkness and showed in shades of green to the pilots. On the electromagnetic spectrum, infrared was 700nm to 1 mm on wavelength, and 430 THz to 300 GHz on the frequency range. Their Generation III devices attached to their helmets and moved on a hinge over their eyes, consisted of an imagine intensifier tube, telescopic lenses, and an infrared illuminator, and they easily allowed them to roll to a safe landing.

They came off the runway and taxied to the empty ramp where the advance maintenance crew was waiting for their arrival. The sound of the jet was more like a roar with a forceful grumble. It easily made your insides vibrate, and you not only saw the jet, but your whole body felt it. It was completely dark outside still, but even under the cover of darkness, Dai and Chung could see the excitement from the taxi director pointing at the left side of their aircraft.

"What's he pointing at?" Chung asked.

They shut down the remaining three engines using the checklists and sat in the seats doing all the usual post flight items. The hatch levers from below that allowed entry into the cockpit were noisy as the fully enclosed cockpit opened up to the outside world, fresh air flowing in. The maintenance crew climbed up the ladder from the ground and came up and into the jet. Dai also took a good look outside his left window, and saw a gathering of maintenance and engineering folks.

"Well, that's one hell of a family of birds you hit," a maintenance guy said as he stood in the cockpit.

"We figured. Sucked into the engine. We lost engine number one in the descent to land," Chung replied, casually.

"You did? Heck, I wasn't even talking about that. You have half a goose stuck in the middle of your left wing, and another open gash where the wing meets the fuselage…size of a large softball. I'm talking a hole this big," he said as he held his hands up. "Some severe damage from hitting a few birds, actually. You're lucky you didn't lose the entire aircraft. Damaged the exterior of the wing pretty good."

Both Dai and Chung looked at each other strangely, then unstrapped and got out of the jet to look. They saw the crowd of ground folks all holding flashlights up to the wing, who now looked at them instead of the aircraft, attempting to gauge their reaction.

Dai and Chung looked at the left wing themselves, then at each other. "Shèng shǐ," they said in unison, which was "holy shit" in Chinese.

The chief engineer came stomping over. "What the hell is this?" he said, waving his arms around, glaring at the two pilots. "Aw! Chen is going to be fuming," as he spit on the ground.

DIA Headquarters, Washington, DC

There was no one around, so Emily sat at her desk, and Ford pulled up a chair to look over her shoulder to read the screen. It was only a moment before the rest of the team showed up.

Mark stood in their cubicle space, while everyone else sat. Ford and Emily were present, as well as Robert. "Let's get started. Old Man Burns wants some speed on this and would like to meet again soon. This op will now be known as Operation SANDY BEACH and…"

"Why SANDY BEACH?" asked Ford, interrupting.

"Stop being a pain in the ass, kid. Let me continue."

"So, SANDY BEACH will consist of us doing a full scrub of all options to present to Mr. Burns. All ideas are on the table. He first wants a complete brief on the status of the Chinese air forces, so I'll contact one of the senior executives who runs China upstairs, and he can brief that. We'll take a look at the entire spectrum of data we have available on just our op and present the recommendation to him for decision."

"Well, there should only be one decision," Ford stated right out of the gate.

"We don't even have all the facts, Ford. We can't make a recommendation yet," said Robert.

"We have enough, Robert. Laser or not, we know the jet exists." *Most likely,* he silently thought. "Evidence is there. Chen and crew lifted, or stole, the technology from us. We know this for a fact. Wu confirmed it. Bottom line is we go get the jet."

Mark nodded. "Thank you, Ford. I do think we are in a good position again. I agree 100 percent we must do something, and I have an early plan in the works. We just don't know if they know that we are on to them. Let me start by going around the team here, starting with Robert. What items did you find since we last met? You have something hot?"

Robert sat up in his black, wheeled chair and cleared his throat. "So, the medical folks up at Fort Detrick discovered that there was a DNA request made for the two airdropped bodies we organized during the Devil Dragon heist. The request was made by Chen's military aide, First Lieutenant Bai Keung. What's particular about the request is that a military aide-de-camp really only does what his boss asks. That tells us Chen wants to verify the two airdropped decoy bodies are indeed the Devil Dragon pilots. It may have bought us some time, pulling this old-school World War II stunt, but in a matter of time, Chen will know some of the truth."

"Shite," Emily said, surprised. "That means we have to hurry. If he starts an investigation, we could get caught. We may have missed something along the way that Chen could discover."

Mark had his infamous yellow pad out, taking notes and scribbling all over it. He was daydreaming and thinking, really only having one ear on the conversation. He got like this when he was focused on an idea that he wanted to develop. "OK. Go ahead with your ideas. Continue."

Ford, Robert, and Emily all gave each other dirty looks, then laughed at Mark.

"Hello, Mark? You even here? We just got done talking." she said.

"Oh, sorry. Just thinking. Have an idea I've been working on with someone here at air force. Outside our team. I know we have more data to put together, but…" Mark said.

"But, what, *kid*? Let it roll," Ford said, using the nickname usually reserved for him. Ford was busting Mark's chops right back at him.

Mark's tone changed. "Well, if Chen knows or will know that our decoys are horse crap, he may react by protecting the jet more than normal. Wu said he was fuming, a micromanager...short tempered. So, I'm thinking that sending Ford back in...to steal her...is not an option."

"That's bullshit!" Ford said, standing. "I can do this, Mark. We already did it as a team once, and we can do it again. I don't know what the plan is yet...but we just did it successfully months ago, and there are no issues doing it a second time. Don't be an asshole, man." Heated, he sat down.

Mark put his hands up in a gentle wave. "Wait, Ford, wait. Hear me out. I do think we should retrieve the jet, like I said earlier. I do. I really do. But what if we...do it differently."

Just as Mark was getting ready to explain his thought, into the room came a young twentysomething tanned girl with long blond hair; she entered their cubicle area. She was definitely an intelligence community employee because she was wearing her badge around her neck on a lanyard, but she did not look like a typical government analyst.

"Hi, Mark," said Jeanie, Mark's girlfriend. They had last seen each other on the Royal Caribbean cruise ship off Coco Cay near Nassau.

Jeanie Heller, a native of Denver, Colorado, was part of the Cyber Security Analyst Division at the Department of the Air Force. With her work background in information technology, a University of Maryland master's degree in cybersecurity, and a high-end security clearance, she was worth her weight in gold to the air force. What also made her special was her experience, studying under the experts who did the damage assessment for the 2003 coordinated attacks on American computer systems, known as Titan Rain. With this experience, it enabled Jeanie to be a major player in other cyber program analysis, such as Agent.btz and Operation Aurora.

"Hey, Jeanie. Thanks for coming. Please, join us. Have a seat," Mark told her, giving her a hug and a hidden squeeze of her behind.

"Oh, brother," Emily said sarcastically, quietly and under her breath. Only Robert could hear her.

Mark wasn't sure with the recent outburst from Ford if the timing was right since time was not on their side. Mark previously decided that this was really the only time to bring Jeanie in, so he made it happen. "Team, this is Jeanie Heller. She's from Cyber over at air force. Can penetrate any IT system out there, track anything, crack anything, to include smartphones. Smart as a whip, and I invited her here." Mark did the introductions to the team. "Yes, this is the same Jeanie I was in the Caribbean with."

"For what reason? Why is she here, Mark?" Emily asked, defensive in nature.

"I'll explain. Ford, let's first get back to you. Hear me out. What I am saying is that I do want to get Black Scorpion. I want that aircraft as much as you," Mark explained. "What I am getting at is…maybe getting Black Scorpion does not require your physical presence for us to steal her."

Emily was puzzled, thinking about what he meant. Ford looked at Robert, then back at Mark. He adjusted himself in his seat, then pulled a pen out of his green flight suit pocket.

"You are going to convince, not one, but two Chinese military pilots we don't know, to *fly it to us*?" Ford said, with some dripping sarcasm, raising his eyebrows with disbelief.

"No, no, not necessarily," Mark answered.

"What then?" asked Robert.

"Remotely," answered Mark.

"Remotely? Christ almighty," Ford said loudly. "How the hell are you going to do that?"

Wearing tan sandals with bright-red nail polish, toe rings, and tight shorts—shorter than most human resources departments would ever normally allow—Jeanie put her hands on her hips. "That's where I come in."

Ford gave a big smile as he looked at her more closely this time. Emily gave him a stern look back.

Emily's Apartment, Arlington, Virginia

Emily and Ford sat on the couch, and she ran her hands through his hair and thought twice about bringing something up, but went ahead and did it. "Ford, another item I need to talk to you about. It's your…your drinking. This is uncomfortable for you, I understand. But you are drinking a tad much, just too much partying. To me, you've been plastered a lot over the past few months. Just pissed drunk. And the drunk texting, drunk emailing. Then there is your vomiting and hung-over, knackered state. You're in shambles. I'm…just concerned, love."

Ford, feeling irritated at her comments, was triggered. "Emily, I don't have a goddamn drinking problem. You have no idea how I feel. You have no idea what I had to do, what it took. I had to fucking wingsuit my ass in there after nearly being air dropped to the wrong airport. Then, I had to fight and kill someone. After escaping that nuisance, I had to land a foreign bomber that I've never flown before, with no tailhook and no fuel, onto a moving aircraft carrier. The only other airplane and pilot to do that in history was a Marine Corps C-130 some forty years ago…come on, Emily."

Ford pulled away from her arm.

Emily wasn't being brash, but caring. "Love, I'm not doubting your courage or anything. You're just vulnerable from a high-stress mission. Please let me help you."

"Fuck. Emily, I had to fight and kill a guy so I could takeoff in that goddamn thing. Jesus! And I don't appreciate your lecturing…"

Emily couldn't believe Ford was denying his drinking. *This is a giant issue,* she thought.

Above Xishuangbanna Airport, Yunnan

Chen was already on his fourth drink when his Aide came to his cabin in the Dassault Falcon 8X. Chen was half reading a binder that was informing him where the air inflatable decoy Black Scorpion was today, reading it was way up in Harbin, northeast China.

"General, you have a phone call from the chief of maintenance."

"No. No. I'll talk to him when I land," Chen replied, his attention focused on the girl in front of him, who was hidden from the aide's view. Chen had other things on his mind, and talking to someone on the phone wasn't important right now.

The Dassault Falcon 8X was a large-cabin, long-range, three-engine Pratt & Whitney business jet manufactured by Dassault Aviation. It was born from the Dassault Falcon 7X, with longer range built by engine upgrades, aerodynamic improvements, and an increase of fuel in the tanks. It was a beautiful aircraft by any standards.

Chen was considering the Gulfstream G280 if he was promoted but did enjoy this jet a lot. Knowing it could get him to the South China Sea islands, or Beijing, or Europe, while traveling in complete luxury, made him feel important. The two Chinese military pilots assigned to fly Chen were type-rated, able to fly the fully loaded jet of nineteen passengers nearly anywhere as needed. The eighty-foot length was long enough for Chen to have both an office and a bedroom, in addition to meeting spaces for subordinates or superiors. The empty weight of forty-one thousand pounds was light, but heavy enough so you didn't feel every bump in medium-chop turbulence. Her max speed of six hundred knots and distance legs of 6,450 miles was outstanding performance, too.

Chen landed at Xi'an Xianyang International Airport, satisfied from his flight in his private bedroom with the girl, and the pilots parked his jet on the near-empty ramp. The Dassault 8X taxied next to the maintenance Y-9 aircraft, but no one was there to greet him.

The copilot opened the door, and Chen shuffled his overweight, drunken body down the staircase in the golden morning sky. Upon stepping off the last step of the stairs to the tarmac, he stumbled and fell down hard. He put out his hands in front to catch himself, but it was too late. Chen slammed his hands on the ground, as well as his chin. He let out a low grunt, as his aide, Bai Keung, came running down the stairs to lend a hand.

"General, are you OK?" Lieutenant Keung asked.

"Get awaay. Get awaay. I'm fine," he yelled, in a complete drunken slur.

Chen staggered across the open tarmac, passed his portable trailer that was flown in for him previously, and went into the aircraft hangar where Black Scorpion was parked. He opened the door with a purpose, and it slammed open, bouncing off the large hangar doors.

WHAM!

The maintenance crews turned their heads to see a disheveled and bleeding general, and the men instantly stopped what they were doing for a quick stare. The chief of maintenance hurriedly came over to him with a roll of paper towels and asked him if he needed assistance.

"General, you are bleeding from your chin. Please allow me to help."

"Whatt are youuu looking attt?" Chen yelled to the maintainers, waving his arms around. They rapidly lost eye contact with him and went about their repair work again. The blood was dripping slowly off his chin and onto his uniform and floor.

The chief took the sheet of the paper towel and gave it to Chen for placement on his new wound. It was saturated in moments, telling Chen he probably needed stitches.

"What...what is the status of...of the...aircraft, Chief?" Chen asked him.

The chief of maintenance was nervous to answer the general because of his condition, including both the alcohol and the gash on his chin. There was no getting out of this one.

"Chief! I asked youuu."

"General, the pilots hit a flock of birds on the descent last evening. They fouled engine number one, resulting in a shutdown while airborne. Engine number one was destroyed. It requires an engine change, which will take us some time. They also hit multiple birds on the left wing, exposing both the wing spars and the bleed air used for deicing. Large hole. This also resulted in multiple cracks to the wing, which will also result in a delay."

Chen continued to sit in his drunken stupor, and the chief of maintenance wasn't sure if the general was comprehending what was happening. Chen's eyes were glazed over, but he still could drill his eyes into you, giving you fear that would last a lifetime. He looked at the chief.

"General? Do you..."

"I heard you. Show mee. Nowww," Chen said loudly, still slurring his words.

The chief of maintenance brought Chen from the right wing of the aircraft, around past the nose, and he stopped in front of the left wing. Chen followed right behind him. A maintenance team of eight men were busy working, and stopped to see their visitors. The chief waived his hand, telling the maintenance team to get away.

"No. No delays. No," Chen yelled out, looking at the eight-inch hole in the wing. It looked like someone had shot the aircraft with a Civil War cannon, wounding her.

The chief knew he was in no position to explain anything.

"Fix it. Fixxxx it now, Chieeff," Chen boomed in a fit of rage, then walked over to the small transportable red tool chest and leaned on it. "Now!" Chen leaned and pushed on the heavy toolbox to hold himself up, knocking it over. Hundreds of aircraft tools and spare parts that were perfectly lined up on display racks and drawers spilled on the white hangar floor, sliding far and wide, making a thunderous roar in the cavernous ceiling and echoing.

Chen shuffled his way back toward the doorway he entered, walking slower than his normal pace. He threw the bloody paper towel on the hangar deck, and the red blood stood out from the immaculate gloss white floor. It made a wet, squishy sound upon impact. No further words were spoken by anyone as Chen returned to his trailer to sleep off his drunkenness.

PART 8

HIJACK

Conference Room, DIA Headquarters, Washington, DC

"Jeanie, look, no offense, but Mark said you are a cyber expert. What does that have to do with aviation?" Ford asked, taking a little offense and showing some jealousy that someone new was joining the team.

"Well, Mr. Hot Shot Pilot," Jeanie said, noticing how attractive Ford was but stuffing it right back to him, "it has everything to do with it."

Mark detected the tempers of the team getting heated and suggested moving the meeting to their conference room. They agreed, and everyone walked down as a group, mostly in silence. Ford was really thinking that if Mark brought her into the fold, she must be trusted and good at her work—and pretty hot, too—but he also had his doubts. They all sat down at the wooden table in their meeting room, and Mark stood in the front, as did Jeanie. Jeanie picked up a black dry-erase marker and started using it.

"That one is dry," Robert told her. "Sorry. These suck."

Jeanie grabbed a green marker this time. "So, Cyber has everything to do with Operation SANDY BEACH. It should be the core ingredient of the op."

She even knows the name? Emily thought. *My, my, the pillow talk is powerful these days.*

"Mark has told me that you have detected EMI from this aircraft. If I understand it correctly, you have fitness trackers, smartphones, GPS navigation off our satellites and theirs, and a live oxygen and carbon dioxide link, or transmission from ChinaSat 2 Charlie. Is that correct?" Jeanie asked.

Everyone shook their head yes. "That's correct, Jeanie," Robert confirmed. "Their coms and data are on our birds as well as theirs, ground-based cell towers, and an aircraft performance app that communicates with their phones and the jet."

Jeanie looked at Mark for acknowledgement. She drew a rudimentary two-line stick figure aircraft on the dry erase board resembling something of an X with a tail. Then she drew out two satellites, which were ovals with some stubby lines coming out, directly over the aircraft. She also drew a little lightning bolt, which looked like communication between the satellites and the jet. Her final stick figure was a second aircraft, above the first one.

"What is all that?" Ford asked, then slowly glanced down at her tan legs. *She has a toe ring?* Emily didn't catch him, but if she did, he'd get a good punch to the arm. *She doesn't look like a government employee,* Ford said to himself silently, smirking.

"Please allow me to show you. OK. So, your jet is in outside communication with a phone or phones, in addition to satellites for navigation. Someone in Chinese-land can see their live data, while flying...while airborne. Yes?"

"Yes," Robert answered. Others in the room nodded.

"I am proposing that I cyber-hijack into both their phones and our GPS satellites while they're on one of their test flights, then get into their flight computers. While airborne. Stay with me, OK? While airborne, we then, remotely, reroute the aircraft and fly the jet to a destination of our choosing. I'm able to see all their avionics and flight instruments, and we should be able to control the aircraft remotely, like flying a flight simulator on a home computer. Or, like we currently fly our Global Hawks and Reapers. And then we land her."

Ford looked white as a ghost. "Come on. Cyber-hijacking? We can do that?"

Mark laughed, adjusting his man bun. "Kid, you didn't learn from Devil Dragon how we can pull something like this off? Come on, man. This is the DIA. We can do anything."

"Huh," Robert had said out loud. "Cyber-hijacking? That sounds pretty intense."

Cyber-hijacking was not something of the future or fictional, but very real. This topic was made popular after the mysterious disappearance of Malaysia Airlines Flight MH370, a Boeing 777, with 239 people aboard. Theories developed after potential vulnerabilities were found in the aircraft software, hardware, and satellite communications, in that a computer or a person shut off the aircraft transponder and rerouted the aircraft. Investigators determined this could have easily been completed remotely from a smartphone, USB stick, or a computer.

What also made it easier for hackers was that in-flight Wi-Fi use for passengers was on the rise. Despite requirements for service providers to acquire certifications by safety regulators, the airlines were installing technology packages by the thousands. The heavy demand by the airlines forced the FAA to approve supplemental type certificates that were needed to install level 2Ku hardware on thousands of airframes. This new 2Ku technology was using high-capacity satellite communications with all sorts of commercial services available. Passengers were happy with the larger bandwidth to stream a movie during a flight, and willing to pay for it, but the excessive risk for hacking was tremendous.

Jeanie explained a bit more. "We have quietly experimented with commercial airliners, with the most recent test on a Boeing 777-200. We were able to penetrate the flight systems using a smartphone and their in-flight entertainment system. Easily using our satellites, too. No question we can do it on your Scorpion aircraft because we already have. Fly-by-wire aircraft already are controlled by electronic signals. We can change communications and navigation, turn systems on and off...fly the entire aircraft."

No one said anything as they all absorbed the information.

Jeanie continued. "We just launched another Delta IV rocket at the cape. It was another of the planned network of Wideband Global SATCOM birds.

Once this WGS-9 satellite vehicle climbs up to her twenty-two-thousand-mile position, she'll join the rest of the constellation above the equator. Plenty of high-capacity communications and signal strength."

The government team was able to extract, decode, and analyze data from nearly any phones, and these two pilot phones were easy targets because the smartphone settings were most likely simple settings. If they weren't, Jeanie would have to remotely load custom firmware upon reboot, or use brute force, which was a methodical guess for their passcodes. The passcodes to unlock the phones remotely and enter into their operating systems meant they were bypassing their security mechanisms. Her work would be done completely by surprise to the owners of the phones and the Chinese military, and no one would know she was even there. This was how she and Mark could generate the plan over the past few days, as her background in information technology and cyber was perfectly suited in this arena.

Jeanie continued the "how" portion with full professional confidence, not normally seen from a younger employee, attempting to dampen any doubters in the room.

"I am able to insert some commands and computer code—you know, lines—and can send a set of processes from our satellites to the aircraft and on-board smartphones. The pilots' phones are in the cockpit, so we'd have double connections. Airplane connection and phone connection. I'll send the signal to upload some bad stuff—you know, malicious software and malware—that I'll install quietly and remotely. At the right time and cuing from you, we can easily send some specific navigation and other instructions."

Emily thought the idea was pretty damn powerful, and part of her was proud that, although young and pretty, a strong woman was telling the men how to do business. Emily liked that she was empowered now, and changed her mind about Jeanie.

"Jeanie, your idea sounds pretty good. I have to say that I am impressed with this cyber-hijacking idea because I wasn't a few minutes ago. Good so far. But the operational side of me has questions. Items like the enormous flight distances...breaks in communications and satellites, aircraft petrol...

right, Ford, petrol? And, of all obstacles, the two, sitting-duck aircrew. The two pilots are still in there, in the cockpit, flying the thing."

"Yes, the pilots. Well. At a location of your choosing, we can...simply eject them."

"Eject them? Oh boy. Jeanie, how are you going to eject them? You have to physically pull the ejection handle from inside the cockpit," Ford said.

"Again, Ford, remotely. I can do it in the cyber world by electronically telling the aircraft to do it. The ejection handle is nothing more than an electrical switch that you're triggering with physical force. It's connected to the essential avionics electrical bus, and connected with simple copper wires. We'd do it over a geographic location of your choosing. Mountains, desert, country, airfield, over the water...whatever you select. We just have to come up with a geo location."

Ejection seats in aircraft have been around since 1910, when compressed air was first used to get the pilot out of the cockpit. The system is designed to get aircrew out in an onboard emergency in a military aircraft. The design is that the aircrew seat gets thrust out of the aircraft by an explosive charge or rocket motor, taking the aircrew member out with the seat. Once a safe distance from the aircraft, the aircrew member separates from the seat and parachutes safely to earth.

Robert loved the idea, too, and was reviewing the discussion. He clucked his tongue a few times and rubbed his hands together. "What's that second aircraft up on the board, Jeanie? The higher one, above Black Scorpion."

Jeanie looked at the whiteboard. "I understand, everyone. Plenty of questions. I'm comfortable with the remote cyber aspect for a certain period of time, but realistically we are not able fly it remotely from China for any lengthy period of time, all the way to the United States. With 100 percent confidence and reliability, that is."

Emily shook her head in agreement, then looked at Mark.

Jeanie took the marker and pointed at the top aircraft. "Yes, Robert, this second aircraft...and this where you come into play, Ford," pointing at Ford with the marker. "You're going to be the pilot flying chase, or a second jet in a formation. Think about it like a chase car, but a chase airplane. You'll be a passenger in the cockpit of a B-2 Spirit, flying above the Black Scorpion. You'll fly in the B-2 jump seat with a specially configured laptop that will enable you to fly the Black Scorpion a short distance once the pilots get ejected out. You'll fly the empty stealth jet without aircrew, just like a flight simulator or one of our Reapers."

"OKaayyyy. Then what happens?" Ford asked, grinning. *Yes, I'm back in the game.*

"You'll land her on a runway in, say South Korea…or Burma, Japan, or, maybe even India. Once on the ground and refueled, crew rested, you get in the jet, along with a copilot, and fly her to the US," replied Jeanie. "No need for the chase plane after that."

"Brilliant. That's one hell of a plan," Emily said, raising her eyebrows.

Ford nodded, but started thinking of the cold temperatures he experienced in the back of the G650ER when exposed to high altitudes and open air. It reminded him of what it would be like in the cockpit without a roof. "Hold up. Hold up."

"Hold what up?" Robert asked.

"You guys are going to literally blow the roof off the jet. Two pilots are going to come shooting out. You know how freaking cold it will be for me once I get in to fly her to the US? You know, at altitude, with me flying to the US for hours on end?" Ford commented, thinking of how much he hated the cold.

"Suck it up, kid. You better get some hand warmers then," Mark humorously told him, as the whole room started laughing.

It wasn't anything to laugh at, though. The cold air temperatures at altitude were professional cold, and the cold-weather gear would have to be of superior quality. Ford's face would be covered by the oxygen mask, and his head covered by his helmet, but any uncovered skin would be an issue.

As an example, a temperature of 0 degrees Fahrenheit, and a simple wind speed of just fifteen miles per hour, would produce a wind chill of -19. In these conditions, exposed skin would freeze in less than thirty minutes. By comparison, an outside air temperature of -35 degrees up at altitude, with a sixty-mile-per-hour wind, was -84 degrees.

"Robert, can you at least acquire two new cockpit seats to sit in, you know, two individual pilot seats, so I can fly her home?" Maybe some good cold-weather gear, like L.L.Bean gear?"

"Consider it done. Can't promise custom sheepskin seat covers but I can get pilot seats. Cold-weather gear as well," Robert answered.

Mark made some more notes on his pad, curious about perhaps flying at a lower and warmer altitude, then looked at his watch quickly. "OK, this is what I want to do. You guys sit here and generate a detailed timeline and take a look at any recent stuff. Again, all ideas on the table to make this happen. I'm going to arrange for the China military brief from upstairs for Burns. Will be back in a few."

Jason then knocked on the door and peeked his head in. "Mark, you have a second?"

"What's up?" Mark looked at him, bothered that he was interrupting.

"Mr. Burns wanted me to come down here and share some news with you guys."

"All right. These guys are all cleared for the mission. You can tell everyone."

"Oh, it's not related to…whatever you're working on. I'm not cleared for it," Jason replied.

Mark looked at Jason strangely. "What is it then?"

Jason cleared his throat, almost nervously. "The undersecretary of the air force just resigned. Mr. Burns is being seriously considered for the position, which means he'll leave DIA. Finding out more information now."

"Christ. We got a real Washington politics and power problem then. No top cover on this mission," Mark said out loud.

Executive Suite, DIA Headquarters, Washington, DC

The secretary of the air force and White House liaison had come in to see Calvin Burns in his office only hours ago, which was unusual, as Calvin usually went to see the secretary on his turf. Air Force Under Secretary Henry A. Parker had resigned, stating that the results of a recent General Accountability Office publication and subsequent Inspector General investigation were a distraction to the president of the United States and the secretary of the air force. The news would be public later today, and he was sending over his messengers to the Hill to inform the Senate Armed Services Committee leadership. The message was that the secretary of defense accepted his resignation, and to respectfully accept Calvin Burns as the acting undersecretary. In addition, the president should respectfully consider Calvin Burns as the permanent nominee.

Calvin was honored for the opportunity to serve in such a leadership capacity, but was taken aback since he was preparing for his pending retirement himself. *What? Under secretary?* he thought. *Need to consider this.*

Calvin had taken a few minutes to comprehend the news and called his wife down in Alexandria, Virginia, and they decided together to take it on. They discussed their adult children and grandchildren, their mortgage payments, retirement accounts, and free time. Traveling together was also discussed, and finally their good health. They came up with the joint decision that he should continue a bit longer in the service of his country. His entire life was being ready for opportunities, and this was yet another time to accept responsibility. *Time to take care of business.*

He made a short list of the items that could kill his nomination, items that the press could use to embarrass the air force and DIA if disclosed by accident. Items that would be a go or no go, items that would crush the air force and himself because they were overlooked. At the top of his list: the Chinese stealth program. Devil Dragon and Black Scorpion were on his mind, and being concerned about this latest aircraft and its future was putting it lightly.

The person he thought of to help him with the management of the committees and elected members of Congress was Michelle Boyd, a DIA foreign missile analyst with former Legislative Affairs experience. Calvin worked with her a few months ago when she was responsible for tampering with his recent testimony to an Intelligence Committee. Michelle essentially owed him for not terminating her, or worse, sending her on orders to Timbuktu or some other undesirable location.

The only way to really sum up Michelle Boyd was to say she was *rough around the edges*. Michelle, in her late twenties with short, brown hair and a thin runner's body, had worked for DIA for the past nine years after graduating from the University of Scranton. Born around Lewisburg, Pennsylvania, her tough blue-collar upbringing in the economically depressed area of central Pennsylvania made her a force to reckon with in white-collar Washington. While others in Washington drank glasses of Chardonnay, Michelle drank cheap, draught beer. When Michelle went out to the bars back at home, she drank Genesee Cream Ale. She watched ESPN fishing shows and *Duck Dynasty*, enjoyed hunting, and played women's soccer. She ran tough mud runs. She had tattoos up and down the inside and outside of her right arm and neck. Best of all, Michelle was successful, empowered, and strong, and she didn't take shit from anyone, especially men.

Rather than stay at home and work at the Susquehanna Valley Mall in Selinsgrove, Pennsylvania, like her girlfriends, she applied for an entry-level government GS-9 position years ago and got it. It was her springboard away from her go-nowhere-fast high school friends, in addition to her unemployed boozed-up mom, alcoholic father, and younger brother—especially her brother, who was constantly in trouble with the Lewisburg Police, or even sometimes, the Department of Public Safety at nearby Bucknell University.

Michelle's upbringing made her a tough cookie, and Calvin saw something special in her. Any employee who had the guts to interfere with the testimony of the deputy director of DIA on Capitol Hill had some real intestinal fortitude, and Calvin recognized that. She was a fighter, and Calvin needed a fighter, for both himself and the air force. The Hill was where business and fights were conducted, and Michelle was Calvin's ticket to success.

"Hello, Michelle. Thank you coming back up," Calvin said, greeting her in the doorway.

"Hey, Mr. Burns. I'm surprised that you called me up here. I swear, I haven't stirred the pot on anything. I haven't breathed a word of our last conversation to a soul, including my supervisor, Mike Klubb."

"I know, I know. Please have a seat. I figured you didn't. Last time we met, I was, indeed, livid, and you know why. But," Calvin shrugged his shoulders, "let's put that behind us, OK?"

"Yes, we can," Michelle answered.

"So, Michelle, I need your help," as he touched his fingertips together. "It's regarding confirmation, or rather potential confirmation, and prep... some Hill work."

"OK. I don't understand. I'm in foreign missiles now, not LA," Michelle answered. LA was Legislative Affairs.

"I understand that. I'm going to share something with you. For the moment, keep it between us."

Michelle nodded her head up and down excessively, like a young girl.

"The undersecretary of the air force has just resigned. Will go public in a bit. I'm going to be acting undersecretary. I need your help working the Senate Armed Services Committee, ensuring that I'm going to be able to lead the Air Staff and air force successfully. Need to know landmines over there, what's hot, who doesn't like who or what, and my chances of getting confirmed. The new administration hasn't asked yet, but they are going through some issues with the new cabinet members coming up for noms."

"I had no...idea. Wait, you have an entire staff here and over at Pentagon's Air Staff for this. Led by a senior executive. I don't get it. What...wait...was the under fired or did he resign?"

"Resigned."

"Huh. Does the committee chairman know? He'd want to know soonest. He'll be pissed off if he hears about it from the news, or even worse, an outside channel. A disaster if it were, say, casually mentioned at the gym. My cousin can tell him if you wanted him to know ASAP."

"See. That's why I'm seeking your help. Its connections and creative thought just like that. A senior executive is too far up the pole. I need a scout with talent, like you. Listen. I'm going to read you into a very time-sensitive op we are running against China, named Operation SANDY BEACH. Very, very sensitive. My biggest potential issue that would cause major problems if disclosed. Have you heard of it?"

Calvin was hoping she hadn't because it was highly compartmentalized and only a few people knew in the world. *Her answer had better be no.*

"No, I haven't heard of that, sir."

"Good, good. I'll read you in right now. This is between us only. I'm telling you so in the event it leaks, you need to be prepared to brief the Hill members on the SASC and intelligence committees in a closed session. So, SANDY BEACH is an op we are running against China. They have developed long-range stealth bombers after stealing our stealth plans using cyber means. We then stole one of their newly built aircraft a few months ago. Looks like we may steal another one from them. We are pretty sure they do not know it is us. And that's it, bottom line. Clear?"

"That's pretty cool. Also, a pretty big deal. Yes, sir. Clear," Michelle answered.

"So, closing this up, I need your help on the Hill. I need your help plowing the way as acting under, prep for confirmation as needed, and prep on SANDY BEACH as required."

Michelle understood everything but needed to know something before she could continue—something the chairman would hunt day and night for, and her cousin would certainly ask. "Yes, sir, I got it," Michelle acknowledged. Her Lewisburg, Pennsylvania, attitude was stirring, and she had to blurt it out, figuring it was now or never. "I gotta ask this. Chairman's gonna ask his people to dig...dig for dirt. I need to know, right now, and you need to tell me so I can do damage control, as needed."

"Go ahead. What?"

"I need to know if you're dirty, and I'm serious. You got any skeletons in the closet?"

Conference Room, DIA Headquarters, Washington, DC

Jason's announcement about Calvin Burns took a moment to sink in. The entire team all looked at each other and smiled, and Mark put his hands up in the air like a touchdown symbol. "Well, hot shit! Good for him."

Ford had a disappointed look on his face. "Crap. Will this change our plans, Mark?"

Mark thought for a second, then shook his head. "Maybe yes. Maybe no. This shouldn't at all. Still a national security issue, and it needs to be solved."

Ford was satisfied with the answer and turned to work with the rest of the team on a timeline. Mark picked up the phone and arranged to go up and talk with the China Military Team to brief Mr. Burns in their conference room. The China team thought that was strange, but they agreed.

Ford was up at the board with a red marker in his hand and drew out a straight line from one end of the white board to the other. It was horizontal, and he made some hash marks. On the far right, he wrote TOT in large capital letters, meaning *time on target*. He also wrote OBJ Area, or *object area*.

"Let's backtrack off the object area. We'd want their jet to be airborne, of course, and we know they only fly at night. Patterns have ranged from 9:00 p.m. to about 3:00 a.m., based upon history. Is that accurate, Robert?"

"Yup. Matches what the acoustics have picked up at the US consulate at Chengdu. Chris Sans's work. Also matches what we know from Wu Lee and Devil Dragon."

"OK, thanks, Robert. So, we would need to ask US Strategic Command and Indo-Pacific Command for a B-2 to be positioned in Guam, or Diego Garcia, to come pick me up, and then get airborne again to do the intercept. Jeanie, is that right?"

"Ford, that's pretty much it. I can take over the avionics bus in a few minutes or less, take over the controls to fly her, and electronically pass them to you for you to fly. We'd then do the ejection at a location of the team's choosing, and then you, Ford, fly her from the laptop inside the B-2 to a landing," Jeanie offered.

Emily pulled down a wall map that was on a scroll. She studied it for a moment, with her fit arms folded. "Bloody hell! Got it!"

"What?" asked Mark.

"Chances are, Black Scorpion will take off again in the next few days over here in mid-China. She goes west, then east as recently shown, to shoot on these ranges here. If you have the B-2 fly in northern Burma, they can do the air-to-air intercept around there. Take her into India!" Emily said, with some excitement.

The Indian government was a true friend of the United States, especially after the secretary of defense just visited for the sixth time in less than a year. Discussions ranged from their newly proposed statue to rupee manipulation to joint military training and agreements. But their government was definitely dysfunctional, as was some of their military. The horizontal chain of command in India meant that certain leaders in specific places owned certain capabilities, like aircraft, bases, and ships. Because the communication was not as solid as it was in other countries, powerful people could make things happen at the local level, without asking for permission to do things. They just…did them.

"India will be a friend of the United States on this one. I'll personally call in a favor to New Delhi for the landing rights at, let me look at the map for a moment. Here, in the south. Bangalore." Emily put her fingers up in quotes when she said "landing rights" and nodded. Both jets, depending on fuel state, can make it to Bangalore, fuel up, and then ferry home. Ford, that's doable? Those flight legs?"

Ford looked at the paper map, looking at distances from the key, rubbing his chin. "Maybe. We'd burn a lot of fuel from Diego Garcia, waiting for an intercept, then ferrying all the way home. No issues on the B-2, as she can take on fuel in the air. It's Black Scorpion that doesn't have air-to-air refueling capability that I am aware of."

"So it's a no-go?" asked Mark.

"No, no, not necessarily. Let's lean forward here for a moment. After landing in Bangalore, let the B-2 return home to Diego solo. I'll take Black Scorpion out, fully refueled from Bangalore, and we land in the far northeast of the US. We'd have to wait it out a day in Bangalore until night came again, rest, then fly and maybe land in Greenland, or St. John's, Newfoundland. If the timing works, continue to, say, Pease Air Force Base in New Hampshire. They have large hangars there for their Air National Guard KC-135s, and we could hide in them until final destination," Ford explained. "I'll also need a copilot."

Pease Air Force Base was home to the New Hampshire Air National Guard's 157th Air Refueling Wing, flying KC-135 tankers. A quick glance at this base, and one might assume that the men and women were from the active component and on full-time status, but actually this was a base bursting with part-timers who had complete, separate full-time civilian careers. From airline pilots to truck drivers to accountants, these citizen airmen had two busy jobs going: a civilian one and a military one.

Robert stepped up to the map. "Mark, my recommendation would be to keep Black Scorpion in the hangar at Pease, and just take her apart there. Put her on trailers right in New Hampshire, and ferry the aircraft on unmarked DoE tractor-trailer trucks to Tonopah."

The trucking system used previously for Devil Dragon ferrying was part of the Department of Energy, the DoE. Energy had an entire fleet of eighteen-wheeler trucks it used to transport nuclear material around the United States. Called the SGT or Safeguards Transporters, since 1975 the Office of Secure Transportation at National Nuclear Security Administration used unmarked tractors and trailers that were special designed to deter and delay adversaries. Trailers built to survive road accidents, fires, and attacks were escorted in convoys with unmarked escort vehicles, along with federal agents authorized to use deadly force. Even without ferrying stealth jets, these trucks logged 4.5 million miles a year.

Mark shook his head in agreement and wrote down plenty of notes for when Mr. Burns came in, especially if the secretary of defense wanted something in writing. Because the mission was so early on and so fluid, documenting the stages on paper was a good step.

"Good point, Robert. Thanks. Ford, a copilot? If you have someone trusted in mind, give me the name. Emily, what do you have?"

Emily had been considering the recent past with China, concerned about the DNA testing they heard from earlier. "The aide whipping up the DNA test is not good. If I were Chen and detected a foreign intelligence issue, I'd send up fighters every time. You know, to escort Black Scorpion like we saw with that Su-35. What are you going to do then?"

"Climb like a bat out of hell!" Ford said laughing. "If that Black Scorpion is anything like Devil Dragon, she can out climb and outrun anything the Chinese have. Those fighters will also run out of fuel, especially if they are running hot, er, fast. An hour, maybe an hour and fifteen of fuel at the most. Plus they are visual the entire time. Their radar will be black...empty. The two bombers won't be detected. At night, that could be an issue if not wearing night vision goggles."

Emily wanted to throw her other issue out there. "I'm also concerned about the ejection. Only a recommendation, but...remotely, can you reduce their oxygen so they are knocked out, or at least in and out of consciousness?

Cause hypoxia?" Emily did a head nod so that the question was directed at Jeanie.

"Totally. Mark showed me the draft schematics for Devil Dragon earlier when we were planning and discussing this. I'm familiar with the new down-link now, and I'm sure the oxygen system is on the electrical bus. If it's there, it won't be a prob."

Mark winked at Jeanie. "That's right."

"For heaven's sake. *Ugh.* Well, again, just a point of reference, but we should fly the black jets due southwest," Emily said, pointing at the paper wall map. "Let's say the pilots are hallucinating, in and out of consciousness. Low on air. And you eject them over the Indian Ocean, where one of our Pacific Fleet ships pick them up for…for…humanitarian assistance." Emily finished her idea with an ear-to-ear grin.

Robert clapped once, with the sound booming, giving one of his rare smiles. "Oh, Emily, that's good. We can do some collection, and at the same time, blame the jet for a below-average oxygen system. Pilots won't know what hit them and will think the jet flew out to sea. Then Chen will think the jet went out to sea. Pilots will return to their leadership with a full story."

Mark looked at the timeline again, with all the hash marks and timing. Ford was busy writing down all the to-do list items on the board. At the top was the China Military Brief, followed by flight simulator time for himself. Ford would need some solid familiarization with flying an aircraft with a joystick from afar, and had only one place in mind to learn the skill.

"Where are you going for some unmanned aerial vehicle flight time?" Jeanie asked, laughing, with her hands on her hips and her low-cut white blouse displaying her fully tanned body even further.

"Where else? Las Vegas! Veeggaassss!" Ford answered, loudly, with a cat-ate-the-canary grin.

Emily raised her eyebrows again. "Oh, shite."

PART 9

VEGAS

Xi'an Xianyang International Airport

The maintenance crews working on Black Scorpion were mostly young men, trained on other People's Liberation Army Air Force aircraft. Many of them came from the Xian H-6K long-range strategic bomber airframe and were trusted to work in this program, endorsed by superiors to keep quiet about things they did, saw, and heard. Their 120 H-6 bombers were upgraded versions of the 1960s Soviet Tupolev Tu-16 Badger and would survive fine without this small group of technicians. With young, aggressive men, some still boys, came horseplay, trouble, attitudes, and always being on the hunt for girls and booze.

For some of the general's actions witnessed by the young men in the hangar, turning wrenches and repairing an airframe, keeping quiet was tough. They would rarely talk verbally because of the oversight of the chief. So, rather than chat about it in person, they took to what the young millennial generation knew best: texting.

All sorts of topics were texted about, easily into the hundreds of thousands, between the maintenance teams of Airframes, Flight Equipment, Avionics, Power Plants, and Ordinance. They were just young men, excited to be able to travel, and drink, and have some camaraderie. The Special Ordinance guys who handled nuclear never got involved because they were too stuck-up to be part of the regular gang. They were, even in their own minds, special.

Unknown to most Americans, the world's largest social networking site, at 806 million users and growing, was Qzone. The young military maintainers were definitely texting and chatting about everything they saw: Chen, his drunkenness, his girlfriends that Chen thought no one talked about or even saw, the bird strike, nearby clubs and bars, and, of course, strip clubs.

What the young millennials did not know was that their phones were leaving specific, detailed digital signatures on a variety of items. Technical audience info, compiled by all telecommunications companies, provided insights into characteristics of their audiences. It usually consisted of behavior, specific technology, active users, lifetime value, cohort analysis, demographics like age and gender, their interests, geography to include language and location, and the brand of their mobile device. Websites visited, length of time, and even their variety of apps, were also stored on the telecommunications company computers.

There was also no way Chen, the definition of a micromanager, would allow phones for any of his aircrew, staff, or mechanics. He even wrote policy about it, explaining how careful they should all be, and flat out denied any of them permission to be on social media or to use a phone while on his team. Which was exactly why everyone had two phones, deceiving Chen: one for work, and one for personal use.

When Chen arrived earlier, knocked over the toolbox, and threw his bloody paper towel, the Qzone texting numbers shot up and off the page. Like a news channel, their phones were full of humor and bitterness, surprise and anger, and certainly nervousness. And tonight, although the pilots were not present in the hangar, they were copied on the texting by the young maintenance team using personal phones because they were well liked. The pilots could read along on their personal phones like a teleprompter without even being physically present.

Aircraft Commander Captain Dai Jian and copilot Captain Chung Kang were still at the bar drinking traditional glasses of sake, staying the night at the Shengjie Hotel at the Xi'an Xianyang International Airport. They were able to pull out their personal phones and laugh at the general's reaction from afar.

It has been said that sake, the alcohol-based rice wine, has been around since before recorded history. Popular in Japan, China, and Okinawa, sake was produced by the parallel fermentation of rice. The rice was polished to remove the proteins and oils from the outside of the rice grain, leaving behind the starch. This polished rice was air dried until it had absorbed enough moisture, preventing cracking when later placed in water. A few more steps perfected over thousands of years, and an enjoyable beverage was made.

Chung raised his clear glass of traditional sake to Dai. "To Chen, the biggest asshole general in all of China." They then clinked glasses and downed the sake together.

DIA Headquarters, Washington, DC

"Is what you're asking…if I am faithful to my wife?" Calvin asked, answering Michelle's question.

"Exactly. Like, if you got a chick on the side. Or some other dirt, like you're a raging drinker, or, …have been stealing money. At night you're bombed and bellied up at the MGM Casino over in National Harbor. Inappropriate pictures. Percs or hillbilly heroin. You know the list." Michelle went ahead and said it, then after what seemed like an eternity, threw on a dose of respect at the end. "Sir."

"What's Percs and hillbilly heroin?" asked Calvin, somewhat naïvely.

"Percocet and oxycodone. Opiates. Largest medical problem in America. Big problem."

Calvin knew she was the right person for this job, and was curious if questions like this would come up. There was no way a senior executive would even think of asking him these questions, especially with her in-your-face tone and attitude. Calvin liked it, though. All business and barely a filter. *Michelle had guts the size of Pittsburgh. She's got balls,* Calvin thought. *I've got to get out more. Percs?*

"I assure you, Michelle, no drugs. I have been faithful to my wife, rarely drink, and have a clean slate. There should be nothing out there except maybe some disgruntled employees who have been fired over the years. For good reason. Clearance interviews are always clean, too," Calvin answered.

"OK, Mr. Burns. I'll do it. I'll come see you every other day, unless it's hot, then I'll see you right away. Good?"

"Perfect. Thank you."

Michelle turned and left the room, and Jason came in. "Pop-up on the schedule. Mark and his team, along with the China Military Team, are prepared to brief you in fifteen minutes in their conference room. You're OK with that?"

"Yes, yes, that's fine. Let's get going then," Calvin replied.

Jason walked with the deputy through the hallways, saying hello to a variety of employees he knew. It was like walking with a small-town mayor because he knew so many employees by name and genuinely liked them. And in turn, the team liked him. He never had to use the word morale, but rather just talked with people to see how they were doing. Genuine concern for others was what he shared with his organization teammates. Now, three decades later, he could be in one of the top leadership positions in the Department of Defense.

The China Military Team had just arrived to the conference room, their slides already parked on the shared drive and ready for the brief. Mark's team did their introductions to the two briefers, and vice versa.

Attending today from the China Military Team were Paul Daily, a senior executive, and a GS-15, Martha O'Connor. They were both civilians, both previously stationed overseas at embassies and consulates in the Far East, Asia, and Europe. In addition, they completed joint tours as students in the Foreign Service School at Arlington, and Paul over at the Eisenhower School at National Defense University. While Martha was a graduate of the Defense Language Institute and studied Chinese, Paul learned his Chinese and Thai while stationed abroad. They were intimately familiar with the structure and status of China's military, which is what Calvin was interested in. They were DIA's best.

Everyone stood straighter upon his arrival in the cramped room, with one empty seat on the side of the table left open for Mr. Burns.

"Hello, everybody. Hello. Please take your seats. Thank you."

"Hello, sir," the room replied back.

Calvin went over and shook everyone's hand to make it personal. He also called out everyone by name, a special touch he often used to make the other person feel important.

Mark said quietly to Calvin when they shook hands, "Sir, Jason told us the good news. Fantastic. Congratulations."

"Thank you," he quietly whispered back. "Let's talk."

Paul cleared his throat and jumped right into the brief. "Good morning, sir, and welcome to this morning's brief on the Chinese military. My name is Paul and..." He went through his introduction.

This guy is pretty smooth, Ford immediately thought and shot a glance and a smirk to Emily. He nodded with approval. She shot a wink back at him, then looked down at the ground so she wouldn't laugh.

Martha began her portion. "Good morning. Good to see you again. The purpose of this morning's brief is to give you a current overview and status of the Chinese military forces. The briefing was compiled from a variety of sources, including open source."

She's good, too, Ford said to himself. *Where do they find this talent?*

"Nice to see both of you again, thank you," Calvin acknowledged. "Paul, I know Eisenhower School. Go Tigers!"

Paul nodded. "Yes, sir, go Tigers. As you may recall, we have always felt it is difficult to fully grasp China's military structure and strategy without us first considering the Chinese attitude and their culture of warfare. This is very thought provoking from afar because their overall media system is completely controlled by the state. Even Google is blocked out. The end result is that the items we see are not always valid, but they do give some insight into facilities, equipment, capabilities, photographs of weapons systems, and their parades, as examples. More on that during the brief."

The DIA team was impressed with both subject matter experts and gravitated toward Paul. His briefing style was one of authority, but not the in-your-face kind. It was more like an esteemed college professor with a casual style that helped inform the students, not ridicule them for skipping a reading.

They liked him, and their body language was a big indicator that they were paying attention.

"This slide depicts a simple chart that shows how the US might view Chinese aggression, and the right side of the slide shows how the Chinese might view our US aggression. You can see that the Chinese view it as one item. The cyber portion is the same during wartime and peacetime. You know it as cyber stealing, or cyber espionage."

Mr. Burns raised his hand up and pointed. "The same?"

"Yes, sir. They steal our secrets and information, as well as from other countries and companies, because…well, because…they can. Simple." Paul had his arms folded for a moment, then raised his hand to gesture. "Yes, yes, sir. Because we estimate them to now have a population of 1.3 billion, they have the manpower to do a lot of things. That is four times the population of the United States. China has over 2.3 million on active duty, with an additional 1.1 million as reservists."

The other briefer, Martha, jumped in. "Our approximation is that the People's Liberation Army has actually gotten smaller over the past twenty years or so, down from three million on active duty. And Mark, you were interested in their army air forces?"

Mark was checking out Jeanie and frankly was distracted. He attempted to say out loud, "Yes," but it wasn't very convincing.

"We estimate the army air forces to be at 398,000 strong. They also still section off the country up into Theater Commands, with simple names such as North, West, and so on. They modeled it off our United States Combatant Command system. It's post-1986 Goldwater-Nichols Act, which I've heard is ready to change with new proposals in the Senate Armed Services Committee, but that's another brief."

Ford's ears perked up when the numbers sank in. "Hey, Martha. I'm Ford Stevens. What are they doing toward modernization? New stuff. Next-generation aircraft or subs, systems like that?"

"Next slide, please, Robert. Thank you. Hi Ford, yes, you can see that here," Martha pointed at the screen. "Their navy is doing well with getting updated, pouring money into new subs. The army air force, at about 30 percent modernization, is on the right track over the past five years or so. Their newer aircraft in the fourth-generation Su-27, Su-30, and Su-35, are top of the line. I'm talking new-Cadillac aircraft. New-car smell. RAND Corporation, *Jane's*, and CSIS, which is where some of these numbers are from, have been publishing for a while that the Chinese are on a spending spree. Even their J-11 is past fourth generation. Since about 2002 or so, they have been purchasing new, modern fighters by the hundreds. Probably half their force is now updated. Naval aircraft numbers are on the rise, too."

Ford raised his eyebrows in amazement. *I thought the yuan was in trouble? Where are they getting all this money?* he asked himself. He was surprised at their ability to purchase such new and modern equipment for a fleet of aircraft, not just a few stealth planes.

"Hello Martha, I'm Robert. You mentioned naval. Can you elaborate some more on that?"

"Ha. Plenty going on there. Yup. Their defensive boundary is in complete sight for the world to see throughout the artificial islands in the South China Sea. Their vessels are on the upgrade track, especially their antiship cruise missiles. Ford, like you asked before, they are pouring money into this area as well. We understand them, as does the Congressional Research Service, to be yanking up their submarine fleet from…sixty-two to about seventy-eight by the year 2020. They are also jamming out additional aircraft carriers and using the *Liaoning* for training. We know this data from—Paul…next slide, please. No, next one. Sorry. There it is. We know this data from testimony from an expert on China's navy before Congress back in July 2015. Complete open source."

"Wow. Thanks, Martha. Air force. Anything else to add that you may have missed from earlier?" Robert asked.

"Sure. Those flyer guys. No question, they are speedily catching up or bypassing western air forces across a broad scale of capabilities. These guys have it together on both defense *and* offense. But we do have the huge advantage over their pilots due to our quality training and simulators. Ours and coalition forces are really top notch, no matter how you view it. Can't be beat," Martha said.

Paul began nodding. "Can't forget that we have plenty of issues, though. Postwar, reducing budgets and sequestration, our US flight time and spare parts stink. Take a look at Marine Corps air. High mishaps lately, terrible readiness, guys not flying enough. Struggling to offer pilot bonuses, and when they do, not much of a take rate. Also, look at the gigantic reduction in US Air Force pilots to the major airlines. Major, major problem at the Pentagon," Paul said.

Ford spoke up. "Agree. Airlines are grabbing guys from all the airframes. No deployments or nonflying work there with pretty good salaries. Even larger cash bonuses weren't keeping some pilots in the military cockpit." There was silence in the room. It was tough for the others to comprehend because they didn't fly, but Ford felt good mentioning it.

The elephant in the room, though, was that no one was asking about stealth. Mark just couldn't wait any longer. "How about stealth? What do they have?" Mark said.

"Yes to fighters, which we discussed already. Rumors are they built bombers. Titled...what, Paul, an H-18 and H-20? And an H-18 stealth jet, but no one has seen it. There is no evidence it was built, test flown, or is operational. So, to answer your question, nothing confirmed."

Calvin continued to listen and remained silent. Paul stood with full confidence, as he was taught years ago at West Point, awaiting additional questions from one of the most powerful men in the organization.

"And, sir, the ground force. They are still the largest in the world, but have many mobility problems," he said, speaking with authority. "They don't have enough helicopter transportation and rely on diesel trains to get around their country. Ground focus is still to deter border countries," Paul said.

Mr. Burns was now making some notes on the legal pad in his leather portfolio, writing down the name Mike Klubb with a question mark. "How about rockets...cyber...and let's see here. Space? Anything there?"

Martha gently nodded her head in agreement. "Yes, I believe Mike Klubb can really drill down for you on this, but we do know they are developing and testing some new classes and versions of offensive missiles. They are also forming other missile units, updating older missile systems, and developing some tactics to counter ballistic missile defenses. You may remember all too well that China has very operational intercontinental ballistic missiles, which of course, can carry nuclear payloads. We think China is a nuclear triad power."

"Sure, sure. What are the open-source analysts saying? Future?" Calvin asked.

"Yes, sir." Now Martha cleared her throat. "We, along with the Congressional Research Service, think that the PLA's Rocket Force is their bread and butter to the PLA's emerging capacity...to support freedom-of-sea operations in the Asia-Pacific region, but also threaten all the regional powers."

"Well, that's reassuring, Martha," Mr. Burns commented. "The Spratly Islands."

"Again, Mike Klubb can come over and give you specifics on that. In answering the latter part of your question, I can tell you that on the space front, there is nothing new you haven't heard before. Status of their space forces still show seventy satellites. Usual uses, like communications, navigation, positioning and timing, meteorology, and electronic and signals intelligence. Best of all, and in our favor, China still uses our GPS technology regularly." Martha nodded to her partner. "And finally, Paul, next slide. Here it is, they still have directed-energy weapons, satellite jammers, and antisatellite missiles."

Ford was always bothered with China and cyber, and he figured Martha and Paul were saving the best for last, so to speak. After all, Ford did spend years there as a kid, and his best friend Wu Lee was from China, but it left him uneasy. He always felt cyber was a true intrusion into his personal space and liberties because computers kept personal items. Emails with family, video chat with Emily, surfing the net to look at new options on cars, and reading the news. He hated that the Chinese may be able to see everything he was doing. And everything the US was doing. "How about cyber? You left that out."

Paul perked up. "Oh, no, Ford. We have that. Super Bowl Halftime Show status. Last slides in the deck. This is a hot topic. As you know, the president and secretary of defense are making decisions on expanding US Cyber

Command and a Space Force. Cyber is just too big to keep it as is. Too many cyber roles between the interagency."

Martha, ever so high on emotional intelligence, began her wrap-up. "There are still big disagreements among the agencies on cyber, sir. DHS, Treasury, FBI, DoD…all the players in cyber. No one gets along, and everyone thinks they are in charge at the same time. Well, we do know that China has three types of cyber forces. Their first one is a dedicated military network warfare force in the PLA. You know, the uniformed guys. The second one is a PLA-authorized team of network warfare specialists in government organizations. That's most likely civilian government workers. And the third is a nongovernmental force that may be mobilized for network warfare operations, like some smart college students."

"All right. We've felt some of their work over the years. What capabilities do they have? What can they do?" Ford asked, eager to hear, especially since this latest mission involved cyber.

Martha hesitated. "Hands down, they could access some of our networks, and even deny foreign nations access to their own networks. Bottom line, Mr. Burns, is…really, anything they wanted, they can pursue. That doesn't mean they will always get through."

You think? We've already seen that, Ford thought.

Martha then asked for the next slide, which was labeled "Wrap-Up," and she gave her conclusions. "So, to help you with building your situational awareness, just know that China can influence all tools in the tool box on their national power. Yes, the threats and capabilities are real, but only, for the most part, in Asia. Allow me to tee up AI, or artificial intelligence, now while I can. Between the US and China, one of us will win, so to speak, by the year 2035. Whoever gets the AI win first wins strategically. While we in the US will have an advantage in fighting, they already have the advantage in cyber."

Calvin was still curious about their overall strategy and figured that if they were wrapping things up, he'd better ask now. He leaned over to Mark and spoke in a hushed tone. "They have the time, the capability to steal cyberwise, the ways and means…and we already know the execution. What do you think?"

"They are already…past us. We're stuck with bureaucracies, they less so. Like our F-35 Joint Strike Fighter from bureaucracy hell. New Air Force One being dragged through Twitter and the news. China seems to be pouring funding in and flying and making things happen. We're short on spare parts and pilots and flight time. We just…huff. We have to get Black Scorpion," Mark quietly replied.

Cal Burns moved his eyes from Mark's face, up to his slicked back hair and down to his shirt. It was suddenly a distraction, one that Calvin Burns had not noticed previously until this moment. "Is that a Hawaiian shirt you're wearing?"

Mark laughed out loud, and the rest of the room stopped and looked. Here, the number-two man was getting a brief on China, and he's asking about a Hawaiian shirt. Mark found it hysterical.

"I'm sorry, Martha. Thank you," Calvin Burns told her. "Mark thinks the modernization plan and their navy is amusing."

Xi'an Xianyang International Airport

Chen sat at his desk drinking tea, attempting to sober up and waiting impatiently for the jet to be fixed. He ruffled through the stack of papers on his desk located in his makeshift office inside the aircraft hangar. It was somewhat Spartan for a general of his level, consisting of nothing more than a few seats, a gray metal desk, and a small table with a pot warmer. His chin injury was not covered and was airing out with a light scab beginning to form.

Embedded in the desk paperwork but prominently displayed on top was the DNA report, which Chen started reading. This was the info he was waiting for on the two pilots picked up months ago connected to the Devil Dragon loss. It was only a few pages thick, and it looked to provide the information he was hunting for.

Human DNA was about 99.5 percent identical from person to person. Nevertheless, there were minor variants that made each person unique. Since our DNA was handed down from our parents, and their parents, there was always a reliable connection to the bloodline. Deviations could be connected to certain diseases, ancestry groups, and people, but Chen only cared about the people connection. This report compared the results of individuals to other sources, and while they could be used for medical use, Chen was only interested in the genealogical information.

The DNA report tested three samples from each of the pilot's bodies, specifically blood, mouth, and hair follicles. Chen asked members of the PLAAF to retrieve samples from their apartments and residences, specifically toothbrushes and combs. In Liu's case, a hair sample from his child. This method of DNA forensics would show Chen the number he was waiting for.

He scanned, then slowed down to read the conclusion at the end. He read it slowly, then read it again. Chen looked up, staring at the blank, white wall. His face became flushed. The damning line read: "There is a 0 percent chance that the two pilots' bodies are the Devil Dragon flight crew."

"Zero percent? Zero percent?" Chen said loudly to himself, rapidly sober. "Who are these two bastards then? Where are the real pilots, and where is my aircraft?" Chen slammed his hand down on the metal desk, and the booming sound reverberated throughout the hangar. Maintainers looked in the office direction once again but kept repairing Black Scorpion's left wing.

Chen was fuming and wanted answers. He stood from his desk and slowly walked to the back of the office and stared out the back window at the airport. He had his arms crossed and folded and was lost in thought. Tapping his index finger on his forearm once every second, he had the infamous thousand-yard stare. There was no way now to locate his aircraft or its crew. Going on a wild-goose chase this late would jeopardize his fourth star, producing a waste of time. He had no other evidence that something related to espionage took place, and since the DNA report was for his eyes only, neither the Party leadership nor senior general officers in the PLAAF would know of these latest details. After careful consideration, he decided to keep these results quiet.

Chen walked over to his doorway and told his aide, Bai, to get the chiefs of maintenance and engineering into his office. After only three minutes, they walked in together.

Chen stared at both of them, and no words were spoken. His piercing eyes seemed to drill through both their skulls, all without Chen blinking.

"Where are you on Black Scorpion repair?" Chen asked. "I want us flying tonight."

"That's impossible. General, we need at least three days of repairs, at a minimum," replied the chief of engineering.

"What about you, Maintenance?"

"I am in agreement, General. There was extensive damage to the leading edge of the wing, which affected the anti-ice and deice systems, in addition to the bleed air systems. If not repaired properly, it would lead to catastrophic damage and loss of both the aircrew and aircraft. Air could seep into the hole in the wing if we rushed."

"Show me. Now," Chen barked.

The three of them walked out from the office and onto the hangar floor. Chen walked behind, arms in back and hands folded, as both chiefs explained the delicate repair job taking place. It was no easy effort on such an advanced jet that did not readily have parts available, as so much of the repair work was done from fabrication on the premises.

All Chen would reply back with was "Hmmmm" as the chiefs went on. At the end of the presentation and walk-around, Chen used his single index finger to call each of the chiefs closer to him. It was amusing to the young maintenance guys stealing glances to see two grown men get called over like kindergarteners.

They physically got closer to Chen, and barely above a whisper, he said to them, "Get it done. Fast. You understand?" Chen had his eyebrows raised as high at the ceiling.

Both men, visibly nervous standing in front of the unpredictable general, both replied to him favorably.

They walked away as Chen stood alone, staring at the nose of Black Scorpion, cracking each knuckle on his hands, one by one. He then blew his nose, forcing out the mucus without a tissue and onto the pristine hangar floor, as was popular in Asia. Chen then spit on the hangar floor. *I have that same feeling again*, Chen said quietly, to himself.

DIA Headquarters, Washington, DC

Paul and Martha both received a DIA Deputy Director Challenge Coin and a grateful handshake from Calvin. They were appreciative to brief the boss, and left the room, leaving only Mark's team behind.

"Well, what'd you think?" asked Calvin.

Mark Savona spoke up first. "Nothing we didn't really know already, but always good to get a refresher. Would have been nice to specifically ask about General Chen, but then we'd be tipping our hands. Not surprised about the mention of the H-18 and H-20, but no firm data that's widespread."

Calvin bowed his head, looking at his notes. "Concur. Who else?"

No one said anything. Only head bobs among the team.

"Bathroom break, and then I'd like to hear what you guys have for a plan," Calvin announced.

A bit caught off guard, Mark jumped right in to reply. "We're only in the idea phase, sir."

"That's OK. Let's talk through it. At a minimum, Ford, let's get you to Vegas. I'll think about briefing the director and see if we should brief SecDef."

Everyone got up from the room, and Robert grabbed Emily. "Hey, let's check on those phones again. You got a sec?" They all sat together and looked at the timeline a bit closer.

Robert sat down in his cubicle to work the large monitor as everyone else eventually crowded behind. They scanned websites, and nothing was catching their eye until they found their "hidden diamond." The data on the screen was a combination of social media sites like Qzone, Sina Weibo, Facebook, and Instagram, all geo located at and around the Xi'an Xianyang Airport.

Overlooked by many, Qzone had over 850 million users and Sina Weibo, known as Chinese Twitter, was close behind at 415-plus million users. To put this in perspective, that would be every single American using Weibo, plus an additional 95 million users. Leading the pack was Facebook at 2.1 billion users. If Facebook were a country, it would be the largest one on earth.

"Hey, well look at this," Robert said to Emily.

"What is that? A phone map?"

"Exactly. Shows all the phones near our two pilot phones. If we click here, like this, we can get all sorts of data right off the phone."

"Like what? Show me," Emily said back to Robert.

"Geotags on certain posts contained metadata, which indicated where and when messages were sent. This map shows how they can be searched and plotted on a map. Look. I can click here on a marker, and we can see when and where the messages were sent, as well as their images and words," Robert said.

"This is cool. Show me these phones here…no, not those. Scroll in. Right there. They seem to be inside the hangar," Emily asked.

Different commercial firms across the world had the technology and were contracted to defense, humanitarian assistance, and intelligence community organizations for a variety of reasons. The geospatial software technology, made recently popular since the Syrian conflict had increased, allowed experts to follow the increasing numbers of displaced civilians flowing into countries like Turkey and Greece. As an example, at a Syrian refugee camp in Turkey, 87 percent of the young refugees owned mobile phones, and 82 percent owned personal SIM cards. This was the perfect opportunity to follow, watch patterns, and if you were in certain agencies in the federal government such as the US State Department or USAID, and working global health engagement, to then aid more efficiently. Today, though, Emily and Robert were just looking, able to watch and read.

"Shite. Look at all these texts! These people are discussing a drunk general with an injury. You think they are talking about General Chen in that hangar?" Emily said, excitedly.

Immediate Office of the Secretary of Defense, Pentagon, Washington, DC
Newly sworn-in Secretary of Defense Samuel Price was reading the *Early Bird News* when his new junior military assistant came in to discuss the upcoming travel to the west coast.

"Morning, Mr. Secretary. Here's the Trip Book for Nellis, Los Angeles, and San Diego," said Rear Admiral Chuck "Rocko" Cooper, US Navy, carrying a white three-ring binder with colored divider tabs. Rocko, a Surface Warfare Officer, was the former commanding officer, USS *Gettysburg*. Not by coincidence, he was selected for both promotion and this junior military assistant position for working the location of the Devil Dragon aircraft off Okinawa.

"Thank you, Rocko. Standard Andrews jet, et cetera?"

The secretary of defense had his choice from a variety of VIP air force aircraft from Andrews Air Force Base in Maryland. From the large Boeing E-4 Advanced Airborne Command Post, call sign Nightwatch, to the smaller C-37A, a Gulfstream V, the SecDef had speed and comms on his side.

"Yes, sir. Speechwriters and the advance team have you at each facility thanking military families, meeting two mayors, one group of Team Rubicon, another from the Headstrong Project, and some returning injured at Balboa Naval Hospital," replied Rocko. "Also have a request from Mr. Burns at DIA. Wants to talk with you regarding the undersecretary position at air force, and, what he phrased as a special topic. Asked to chat in person for about an hour."

"An hour? I don't have an hour," barked the SecDef, looking back down at the *Early Bird*. "Rocko, just put him and a few of his guys on our jet to the west coast. We can chat on the plane."

"Will do."

Creech Air Force Base, Nevada

Ford Stevens was already in Nevada for the past few days, getting oriented to Creech and its remotely piloted aircraft (RPA) systems and missions. Creech Air Force Base, located north of Nellis Air Force Base in the Las Vegas area, had paved runways and sprawling buildings and was the home a variety of flying squadrons. Also located on the desert base was the air force's Unmanned Aerial Vehicle Battlelab.

Creech, specifically located in Indian Springs, Nevada, was the home of the 732nd Operations Group, flying remotely piloted aircraft around the world for its mission. This unit trained airmen to provide special capabilities and developed new technology for operations requiring remotely piloted aircraft. This was a unique Air Reserve Component mission, consisting of members from both Air Force Reserve and the Nevada Air National Guard. Because they were reservists, Ford felt right at home.

Ford was attending a modified RPA orientation course for pilots in the 17th Reconnaissance Squadron, hoping to gain the minimum orientation experience to fly the Black Scorpion from a laptop. The hushed plan was still in play for him to sit in a B-2 jump seat with a specially configured laptop and fly the jet to touchdown after a remote ejection. While the cyber portion may have been discussed, the practical, hands-on pilot stuff needed some work.

The regular RPA training program in the US Air Force is six months in length for RPA pilots and six weeks for sensor operators. Sensor operators controlled the cameras and weapon systems on the remotely piloted aircraft, and air force RPA crews consisted of one pilot and one sensor operator. Air force training for aircrews was as follows: attend a screening course at Pueblo, Colorado, then a qualification course at Randolph AFB, Texas, followed by the RPA fundamentals course. For this SANDY mission, though, Ford would only be provided a few days' orientation without a sensor operator. He had, though, selected a copilot.

Ford sat in the weakly lit, air-conditioned trailer, eyes glued to bright video and data screens, while his hands were on the small stick and throttle. Next to him was his old friend and B-1 copilot, Tiffany "Pinky" Pinkerton, invited, screened, and completely read in to the operation.

Pinky, small, petite, and athletic, wearing a short brown bob and an aura of confidence, could handle her own in a mostly male aviation world. An Air Force Academy graduate recruited for women's soccer, she received her top choice of "pilot" upon graduation. Her personality was as a perfectionist, self-critical but bold in her actions. She had good decision-making skills, was smart and sharp, and was a rule follower. And attractive, too, earning the Miss Black America beauty contest title a few years ago at nineteen years old.

Pinky was also a fighter for equality, fighting for her right to be considered for leadership positions throughout her career. Racist critics were always making comments just outside earshot of her, constantly wondering if she was accepted to the academy or a coveted pilot position due her race. All she ever asked for was the opportunity to compete equally and fairly, as Pinky was just as clever, ambitious, and gifted as anyone else at the academy or in the air force. Her top performance as a mathematics major at the academy demonstrated her capabilities, and she graduated from the Colorado Springs school with honors and a smile. Her parents taught her well and were proud.

Because of her strong pilot performance, Ford selected her to accompany him to India to fly the Black Scorpion out of Asia and into America. She wouldn't be with him in the B-2, but it was important they train together as a crew for the actual flight. Just yards away, many aircrews were doing real-world missions, but today Ford and Pinky were just learning the ropes on an RPA simulator.

The technical challenge Ford had was that he would have only one instrument panel screen to view on his laptop, one without a camera available, where normally one would be in use to see outside the cockpit. In comparison, RPA pilots had six screens to use to fly the MQ-1 Predator, RQ-4 Global Hawk, or MQ-9 Reaper drones between two aircrew. The newer RQ-170 Sentinel (Wraith) was next in their lineup.

One thing in their favor was the standard layout of flight instruments located in the cockpit. Every cockpit in the world, even the NASA space shuttle fleet, had a standard flight instrument panel layout. This standardization allowed all pilots to fly globally in a variety of cockpits with only some basic familiarization of flight instruments. The attitude indicator was always in the center, the altimeter was always on the top right, and so on. These flight instruments provided the pilots with information about the aircraft, such as altitude, airspeed, and direction. Ford, once getting the laptop up and running, would immediately recognize all the Black Scorpion instruments and gauges. These instruments would allow them to fly the aircraft in all attitudes and altitudes, takeoffs and landings, turns and level flight, and if needed, without a visible horizon.

Located in the standard instruments were an airspeed indicator, an altimeter, a compass, an artificial horizon, rate-of-turn indicator, a slip-skid indicator, and a clock. Some advanced aircraft cockpits, like the Gulfstream 650ER have four glass screens called electronic flight instrument systems, which was similar to what Devil Dragon had installed.

The contracted instructor, retired Master Sergeant Bill Myers, USAF, was standing behind Ford and moved the headset mic closer to his mouth. All Bill knew about Ford and Pinky was that they needed a few days orientation training on an RPA, with no other information provided.

Sporting his trademark muscular tattooed arms and handlebar mustache, he provided encouragement to Ford in the trailer. In his gruff voice, he coached the pilots. "Ford, you're doing fine here. Don't forget that you won't have a need for shooting a Hellfire, or constant video surveillance over mountains, deserts, and oceans," said Bill. "Fly the basics here. Keep your scan going. Basic instrument scan. Pinky, back him up. Use your own IFR scan, too. Make sure you tune up your NAVAIDs all the time."

IFR was the acronym for instrument flight rules, or flying by instruments only and not looking outside visually. NAVAIDs was the nickname for navigational aids, signals coming from the ground or GPS satellite providing navigational guidance to aircraft.

Ford kept up his instrument scan and flew precisely on the route instructed. "Thanks, Bill. Can you share with us anything on the downlink? How do these aircraft communicate?" Ford asked, looking to gain more information since his classroom brief.

This was complicated, so Bill paused the simulation. "You mean how does a flight crew here at Creech control an RPA halfway around the world?"

Both Ford and Pinky replied back with a yes.

"Both easy and difficult to explain. Here it is as simple as I can make it. Fiber optics to Europe, then a satellite uplink, then to a Pred or whatever RPA you got. Pred video is from Pred to satellite to here in reverse. Launch and Recovery is similar, but, as you know, requires folks on scene to help. On the ground. Does that answer your question?" Pred was the nickname for Predator, a US Air Force unmanned aircraft.

"I guess so. Get more technical. I want to hear more," Ford answered, being a smart ass. Bill was crusty, but he didn't get Ford's humor. Ford didn't want to hear any more.

It actually was way more complicated than Bill was making it out to be, but he answered anyway. "OK, Ford. You asked. There're videos, full-motion videos, secure comms, satcoms, and chats to deal with. The complex system that the Defense Information Systems Agency had set up uses difficult-to-comprehend Asynchronous Transfer Mode transmission technology. It's enough to make anyone's head spin. This ATM cell relay, or fixed-sized cells, is internet protocol for variable-sized packets and frames. I learned about it on Google because the manuals are too technical. This switching method used by the commercial telecommunication networks uses asynchronous time-division multiplexing to encode the data into small, fixed-sized cells and..."

"Hold up, Bill. Hang on. I had enough. Google or not. I have no idea what you're talking about," Ford replied, zoning out and thinking about hitting the casino floors with a drink in a few hours.

"Jeez. OK. Let's get back to the mission then. Unpausing the sim," Bill said, laughing, shaking his head.

Xi'an Xianyang International Airport

The airframes technicians from the Black Scorpion team were finishing the ducting work on the left wing and were about ready for a maintenance inspection. The light stands were all huddled about one area, ensuring the men could see their precise work. One buckle of the airframe at high speeds could rip the wing off, and a small buckle would ruin their stealth capability.

"You done? You done?" asked the chief of maintenance to the men, attempting to hurry them along. What he wanted was a rush job, but as safe as possible.

"A few more long hours. Ready two nights from now, yes? Two nights. Two nights," answered the shift supervisor.

The duct work in the wing was where hot air from the engines flowed internally to keep ice from building up in flight. The weather up at altitude was from cold, moist atmospheric environments that could lead to ice on the fuselage, wing, or engine inlets. No matter where ice ended up on an aircraft, it was bad news, so it was important that heat was used properly in all aircraft to prevent icing conditions. Not only did it change the aerodynamics of the wing, but added extra, unnecessary weight. Even unheated and exposed fuel lines to the engines that contained water in them could cause catastrophic failure. Ice meant internal blockage of fuel, working like a plug in the bottom of a bathtub.

The conditions for icing on the outside of the aircraft existed when the air had in it droplets of supercooled liquid water. The perfect combination of droplet size, air temperature and water resulted in ice on an aircraft. In the aviation community, three main types can be found: clear ice, rime ice, and mixed ice.

Clear ice was clear and smooth, similar to freezing rain normally seen on the ground. Rime ice was opaque and rough. Lastly, mixed ice was a mishmash of both. Depending on the atmospheric temperature, which at high altitudes is easily below thirty-two degrees Fahrenheit, it would be not be an overstatement to say that any water found on the exterior of the aircraft would freeze to the airframe in mere seconds.

The chief waived his hand around. "Get it done. Get it done right. Bad duct work means icing, means this jet doesn't make it home. One night. Keep going," the chief told them, walking away.

The men, looking on and not turning wrenches, took to texting, faces down and thumbs moving.

DIA Headquarters, Washington, DC

Calvin had his office desk phone up to his ear. "Thanks, Rocko. Copy all. The team and I will be there. Will be good to see you again as well. Bye," Calvin said, then hung up the phone.

Jason saw he was off the line, snickered, and told the gang near him in the waiting room that Calvin would yell in to him. "Watch this. One-one thousand, two-one thousand, and three…"

"Hey, Jason, have those guys come in here!" Calvin yelled out, like clockwork.

Mark, Jeanie, Robert, and Emily walked in, smiling from Jason's antics. Arms full of folders, they stood in front of the table.

"Please, have a seat. Just hung up with our old friend, Rocko Cooper. Working these days as the new junior military assistant for SecDef. The secretary invited me, and you guys, to fly out to Las Vegas with him on his jet so we can brief him up on SANDY BEACH. I'll be able to chat with him about the undersecretary position, too. Good?"

Smiles came across everyone at the table. Mark spoke first, "Yes, sir. That sounds terrific. We've never met him. What are you expecting our role to be?"

Calvin tiled his head down and looked over his glasses. "Tell him the truth. Keep nothing back. Standard brief of what we know, when we knew it, and what your recommendations are, if any. Me, too, actually. What do you have for today? Please, sit."

Mark nodded in agreement. "Will do. We want to bring you up so speed on BEACH. Robert, you start."

"Sir, Emily and I have been tracking some Black Scorpion maintenance crew social media texts from the hangar. We can read everything they are saying. Pretty funny, actually. If this wasn't so real, it would be on a television show because it reads like a drama. Bottom line, most of the men hate Chen. They make fun of his drinking and girlfriends, and his weight. Some of the young airmen are friends with the two pilots, so they are involved in passing info on social media. Plenty of talk of girls and their travels. At times, the smartphone app What's App is used to prevent outsiders from seeing their texts…but we can see it all. Weibo and Qzone are their most popular."

"Like a reality TV show over there, eh?" Calvin said, smiling.

Emily was happy. "It is. Gossipy. Luckily, we can detect their flight schedule now. Seems the jet is delayed a bit. Sustained some engine damage from a bird strike, as well as the left wing. Looking at another two days' delay, then take her airborne for more night flying for a functional check flight, which is standard, according to Mark. Of note, Chen is becoming more impatient with the chiefs of maintenance and engineering at the delay."

There was a pause, then Mark started. "Here's our plan; it will sound far out in left field, but here we go. We arranged with US Strategic Command to have Ford fly in a B-2 cockpit jump seat with a specially loaded laptop. The B-2, piloted with its usual US Air Force aircrew, will fly in Indian airspace in a holding pattern. At the appropriate time, we will *cyber-hijack* the jet remotely, and Ford will fly her to a landing in India."

"What is that? Cyber-hijacking? No. No way," Calvin told them. "That leaves a trace. You can forget that plan."

Paris Las Vegas Hotel, Las Vegas, Nevada
Pinky knocked a third time on Ford's hotel room door with the palm of her hand, but there was no answer still. Concerned he overslept, she continued to ring the doorbell, but nothing stirred inside. Pinky then took out her phone and dialed and listened. She could hear the phone ring inside the room, but no Ford.

All Pinky could think about was Ford being drunk last night at the poker and pai gow tables, even trying to kiss her on two different occasions. *At the same time, he was telling me about how he loved his girlfriend, Emily. Get it together, Ford!* she said to herself. "Pai gow, Chinese dominos, eh? He's just got to be passed out in there."

Pinky briskly walked down the hotel hallway to the end, and saw a young woman in her thirties standing in front of a housekeeping cart. Pinky looked at her nametag and saw her hometown was Colorado Springs, the same city that the Air Force Academy was located in. After a minute of small talk, Pinky asked for a favor in opening Ford's door.

"Thank you so much," Pinky told the housekeeper. "Yes, go Falcons!"

Pinky got into the doorway, looked inside, and leaned in to check the bathroom first. Nothing. Looked at the two beds, but no Ford. She put her purse on the table in the room and walked over to the window.

"Hey, what are you doing here?" Ford asked Pinky, startling her. Ford was wearing a tee shirt and running clothes, walking in from the hallway.

"Oh, sorry, Ford. I…I thought you might have overslept," Pinky said, her oval face turning beet red. "You were pretty drunk last night. Like, you drank a lot. We need to get going. I'm sorry I came in here."

DIA Headquarters, Washington, DC

"Yes, sir. Cyber-hijacking. We can elaborate," answered Mark. Mark took out a paper PowerPoint slide he had previously made with upgraded stick diagrams. "The B-2 will fly in loose formation with the Black Scorpion after we eject the crew. From the laptop, Ford will remotely land her in Bangalore, India. The B-2 will then land and drop off Ford."

"Hmm. I don't know. First cyber-jacking. Now eject the crew? Wow, OK, got it. Heavy stuff. OK, keep going," Calvin said, taking his glasses off. "Willing to listen."

Jeanie smiled. "Sir, I'll already have installed some malware to remotely cyber-hijack the aircraft, fly her using the autopilot, and navigate her to someplace like the Bay of Bengal for pilot ejection. I'll lower the Chinese pilots' oxygen levels to give them hypoxia, so they won't follow what's going on.

Then, transfer the controls to Ford in the B-2, and Ford flies the jet remotely to landing at Yelahanka Air Force Station, Bangalore."

The team still wanted to induce hypoxia in the Chinese Air Force pilots. If there was not enough oxygen in the aircraft system, as Jeanie would do when she lessoned the flow electronically, the pilots would not have enough of the vital air in their lungs and blood stream, and their brains would be temporally impaired.

The result would be dazed pilots who would feel off-balance and light-headed, not thinking clearly, and the drowsy feeling would be uncontrollable. The dizziness would be overwhelming, they would perhaps get a headache, and their lips and fingertips would turn blue. In this condition, the ejection timing would be perfect.

"Cyber. Reminds me of the newspaper clips from the missing Malaysian flight. And Mark, you and the team coordinated landing two large foreign stealth aircraft in India?" Calvin asked.

"We did, sir. The B-2 will have landing rights to drop Ford off. Copilot Pinky will catch up and rendezvous with Robert in Bangalore to receive and park Black Scorpion in one of their Indian Air Force transport jet hangars. Pinky is short for Tiffany 'Pinky' Pinkerton, who has been cleared as the copilot."

Right away, Calvin was thinking of diplomatic issues and who in the Indian government and air force knew. "So, do I want to know how you co-ordinated all this with Bengaluru—you know, Bangalore?"

"That was me, sir," Emily answered. "I phoned my college roommate, whose father is the current Indian deputy defence minister, Charan Pranav Ahuja," Emily said with a grin. "I talked with the deputy personally and ar-ranged the specifics. He only awaits our timeline."

The Indian armed forces were busy these days, with their navy leading the way at 135 warships and submarines, and nearly 230 air platforms, all supporting the gigantic Indian Ocean Region. Of concern to them was re-cent info right out of the newspapers. Chinese naval assets deploying along Pakistan's naval assets—to include a port in Whadar, Pakistan, financed and constructed by China—took up some of their time. To this day, India keeps an eye on Chinese military operations.

The secretary of defense's relationship had grown with the Indian defence minister, discussing regional issues, US defense partnerships, and Asia-Pacific topics important to both of them. Calvin was a fan of India and knew the strengthening of the defense cooperation between the two countries. Both the secretary and the defence minister had been discussing India's commitment to a healthy, strategic partnership with America, so this latest decision by his team was aligned.

"Very impressive. Very good. I think the secretary will be impressed with this, considering his multitude of visits there. You know, their deepening of the security and political ties. I would expect Ford and, what is her name, Pinky? They would need some rest and take off the next night, right?" Calvin asked, making a note on his pad.

"Yes, that is correct," Robert answered. "Ford, Pinky Pinkerton, Emily, and I will be over at the Ritz-Carlton Bangalore to sleep, then they take off next evening. Risky having the jet there for any more than twenty-four hours, as we may not keep it a secret after that. Jeanie will conduct the cyber ops from here in DC."

The Ritz-Carlton in Bangalore would be perfect for them to rest. Beautiful in every aspect, safe, high end with good food, the impressive luxury hotel would be the perfect spot to recover and work from. Not to mention the impressive and attentive staff on hand to serve hotel guests.

Mark flipped over his sheet. "Last step is for Ford and Pinky to fly north from Bangalore, cross the Middle East, Europe, and the North Atlantic, and stop in New Hampshire for fuel. One plan we have is to cut her up in New Hampshire and transport via tractor-trailer truck. Energy will help with that again perhaps. Another idea was Robert's, to cut her up, truck to the Maine shipyard, and transport via US Navy to the West Coast. Still working on that idea."

"Let's wrap this up then. Let me know on the trip out to Vegas what the plan is once you get Black Scorpion stateside. I would consider keeping her flyable, as you never know what the future will hold. I'll leave it up to you to decide. So, we're done here today. Any questions of me before we leave?" Calvin paused, and no questions were asked. "OK, none. Andrews VIP Terminal, 11:00 p.m. tomorrow then."

Emily's face turned red. "Sir, Ford is out in Vegas getting his RPA training. Staying at the Paris Hotel. Perhaps we can have him meet the SecDef, too? When we fly there tomorrow night? He's out at Creech, but it's not far from Nellis."

"That's a great idea, Emily. The secretary would be impressed by meeting Ford and Pinky. Yes, let's arrange a meeting with them, as I know the secretary would want to shake hands."

"Thank you," Emily replied. *That's interesting; Ford hasn't called in a while. What's he up to out there?* she thought.

Ford Stevens' Hotel Room, Paris Hotel Las Vegas, Las Vegas, Nevada

"Pinky, I was out on a morning run. It's OK. And I wasn't that drunk, was I? You sound like Emily. I don't drink excessively or whatever you're thinking. Anyway, I'll jump in the shower and meet you in the lobby?"

Pinky lefty his room, and immediately thought he was in denial, because he was pretty bombed. Ford could barely walk, and she had to help him to his room. *How could he not remember?* she thought, taking the elevator down to the lobby. She also left her purse behind in his room by mistake, but figured Ford would bring it down.

Ford picked up his smartphone and dialed Emily to say hello, verifying he was in the green on the Peanut.

"Hey, girl, how you doing?"

"Hello, love. What time is it?" Emily said, glancing at the clock, then her Peanut light. "Ford, it's 7:00 a.m. here."

"I know, Emily. Good morning. I can't take my phone with me out there, so I have to talk now. You doing good? Miss you."

"Yes, miss you, too. Things coming along at work. I'm coming to see you. We're coming to see you. Flying out with the team and the big boss."

Ford made a face. "That's awesome. What big boss?"

"The secretary."

"The secretary? Of defense?"

"Yes, Ford."

"Cool! On his jet? Into Nellis? That's going to be great, Emily. I'm out here and waiting for you." Ford's eyes were wide open in excitement. His type-A personality and commitment were in full force.

"Yes, will be in your lobby tomorrow morning. He wants to meet you after we land. Be in your Paris lobby to say hello tomorrow at 6:00 a.m., love."

"Me? The secretary wants to meet me?" Ford asked, surprised.

"Yes, why not?"

Ford figured this was also as good a time as any, so here he went.

"OK, I'll be there. Emily, I want to talk about us when you get here. You and me. I want us to be more serious. Just planting the seed for us to talk when you get here," Ford told her.

Bullocks. He wants to get married. Emily rapidly sat straight up in bed.

"Me, too, Ford. I want to be more serious, too. I love you."

"I love you, too. Can't wait to see you. The view of the Las Vegas strip and the mountains in the desert are striking. It's breathtaking."

DIA Headquarters, Washington, DC

Since Calvin was potentially moving to another position in government, Jason Cohen figured he would apply for and take another job at DIA in order to compete for a promotion. He was ready for another directorate with different hours than the one he worked now, and he looked forward to the change.

"Michelle, thanks for coming back up here. You may not know, but Jason is no longer with me," Calvin explained.

"Yes, I noticed he isn't up front," Michelle Boyd said. "What's up with that?"

Calvin smiled at her tactless way of asking where Jason was. "He received an opportunity in another office and took it. I encouraged him. That's what we do for good people. Groom them to take more responsibility. Good for him,"

"Guess so," Michelle replied, rather monotone.

Calvin wasn't happy with her enthusiasm level but knew she could be groomed a bit. "The reason I asked you up here, besides an update, is to ask if you would be my new executive assistant. Stay with me here at DIA, and then over to the Pentagon as undersecretary of the air force, if I get the confirmation."

Michelle was taken aback. "I would be honored. Thank you. Thank you for the opportunity," Michelle said, smiling.

"Phenomenal. Thank you for working with me. Now tell me, what's the Hill up to with my confirmation date? What are you hearing?"

Inbound to the Paris Las Vegas Hotel, Las Vegas, Nevada

The hotel lights look beautiful in the dark, thought the secretary as he rode from Nellis to the Paris Hotel, seeing the Venetian, Bellagio, MGM Grand, and all the others. "Cal, I'm good with your brief on BEACH from the flight. Go for it. I'll brief the president once you're mission complete, OK?"

"Yes, Mr. Secretary. I'll make myself available should any questions arise."

"I know you will, Cal. You have a great team back there. Looking forward to meeting Ford Stevens. Reservist, too. Here at the hotel, right?"

"Yes. Ford is here. Thank you, and yes, a great team."

"Good. And we're all pulling for you with air force. Let me know if you want me to call the new chairman. I know him from Goldman Sachs. Anyway, you'll do great."

The motorcade of four black Chevy Tahoes pulled up the wide half-moon driveway under the dark skies, made bright from the famous lights of the Vegas Strip. Looking up at the replica of the Eiffel Tower and a blue-and-yellow hot-air balloon, the crowd of pedestrians looked around in awe. Red-and-blue grill lights flashed on and off in the Tahoes, as the four SUVs followed a Las Vegas Police Department marked car to the Paris Hotel front doors.

The personal protective detail got out first, looked around, and made eye contact with the advance detail that was already there awaiting their arrival. All the doors opened now from the Tahoes, as the detail held the secretary's door open with two hands. The secretary of defense and Calvin walked inside the hotel, following him were his military assistants, chief of staff, and public affairs and protocol staff. Mark, Emily, and Robert were there, too.

The security detail led the entourage in trail to the hotel lobby area, passing the tables, slot machine noise, and loud music. The Paris Hotel was beautifully decorated, from large glass chandeliers and gold paint in the ceiling to intricate tiles and colorful carpeting on the floor. The courteous staff was always ready to host VIP guests, and this morning was no different with the arrival of the secretary of defense.

"Hey, where is Ford?" Mark asked Emily quietly.

"I was just thinking the same thing. He didn't answer his texts or phones yet. Weird, ya?" Emily replied as they looked around the large Paris lobby.

Emily went to the front desk, used her blonde charm and accent on the young male clerk, and got Ford's room key. *Still got it,* Emily thought. She and Mark took the elevator up, walked down the long hallway, and knocked. No answer.

"Ford!" Mark yelled, putting his face close to the door. "Wake up in there, kid." He placed a bit of emphasis on "wake up," knowing full well the secretary was waiting on his arrival.

Emily used the key to unlock the door handle and deadbolt and soon discovered the bar lock was closed from the inside. Ford had locked himself in the room, which was normal practice if you were sleeping and didn't want anyone coming in.

"Well, he's in there, but we're locked out," Mark said, announcing the obvious. "And the secretary is here waiting."

"Please, Mark. You may be locked out, but I'm not locked out. Watch this," Emily told him.

The inside bar lock on Ford's hotel door looked to be secure and had the appearance of protection, but it was actually very weak. Emily took her rubber hair band from her pony tail and held it.

"Mark, this bar lock will only open internally about three inches. I can squeeze my forearm through and create an auto-unlock device with this rubber hair band," then looking down at his black wheeled suitcase. "You have your shave kit in your luggage bag there?"

Thinking quickly if he did, he said, "Right here."

"Get me a nail clipper or, a…pointy nail file. I know you have one of those for your girlish hands."

Mark smirked at Emily, but he did what he was asked and gave it to her. "Here."

Emily tied her hair band into a girth hitch loop and attached it to the bar. She stretched the other end of the rubber hair band toward the wall and away from the door. Emily took Mark's nail clippers, opened them, and fastened the rubber hair band to the wall by shoving the clippers into the band and soft sheetrock wall like a thumb tack. It was now anchored in the sheetrock and set.

Mark watched with intense curiosity. "Where you'd learn this, Harrods of London?" Mark asked. "How do you know how to break into a hotel room?" Emily didn't answer.

As Emily closed the door a bit, the tension and pressure of the rubber band yanked the bar away to the unlocked position. Ford's door was free to open.

"That was easy," Mark announced, walking in. "Ford, you in here?" The lights were on, the shades were open, and the bed was slept in.

Emily immediately saw a woman's purse on the table, then saw the bed was messed up and slept in, as well. Her emotions were now off the charts, and the ground on which she was standing on fell out. *No, Ford, no,* she thought to herself.

They both opened the bathroom door.

"Aw, man! Dude! Call 911!" Mark said loudly, as Emily gasped.

Naval Support Facility, Diego Garcia

The two B-52s and three B-2s were being taking care of by the flight line team, all air force airmen, and preparing the aircraft for local flight operations.

Diego Garcia was an atoll island near the equator in the central Indian Ocean. It is the largest of some sixty small islands covering the Chagos Archipelago, founded by the French in the 1790s. Today, the United States had a large naval and military base on the island, and the only inhabited island in the region, populated with military personnel and contractors.

The US Strategic Command had deployed B-2 Spirits from Whiteman Air Force Base, Missouri, to the island to integrate and conduct training with allies and partner air forces. This area of the world was busy for US Strategic

Command due to the heightened tensions with the Chinese government over the South China Sea dispute.

Overlapping this geographic area was also US Indo-Pacific Command. Their full plate just got larger with the recent arrival of the US Navy carrier USS *John C. Stennis*, three destroyers, a cruiser, and the 7th Fleet flagship, just sailing into the area earlier this week.

"Dey want us ta do what?" said Colonel Zeke Ziehmann, the Diego Garcia B-2 Detachment Commander from Whiteman. It was hard to tell Zeke's humor with his Chicago accent and tone, as sometimes he was funnier than hell, and sometimes he was all business. Today, though, ol' Zeke was being funny.

Zeke was a former fighter pilot turned bomber pilot, accepting the transition years ago to fly what the Air Force told him would be a career enhancer—a special project, of course, now known to all as the B-2—leaving his wife, son, and daughter back in Spangdahlem Air Base, Germany. It worked for him, and he climbed the career ladder to full-bird colonel.

Zeke, having plenty of wisdom and seeing just about everything through the years, was pretty crusty among the junior pilots. His legendary tough attitude in the face of rules made the young guys laugh. Hard. Often seen in the hangar on the catwalk checking out the mechanics turning wrenches, he'd have a cigarette in his mouth in an area full of fuel. Zeke knew the flashpoint was so high that he'd never start a fire, so he routinely ignored the "No Smoking" signs. Once done, he'd put it out and light up another one. A lit cigarette hung on his mouth, off his lip, down low, and was able to stay in his mouth even while talking. Some of the older pilots say he used to fly while smoking, but no one could ever catch him doing so with a photo. They also knew he had a Distinguished Flying Cross, a DFC, which added to his mystique. Zeke was as old-school crusty as you could find and loved by all the aircrew.

"Yes, sir. This mission is real. Highly classified, of course. The pilot is on his way here tomorrow, and the other pilot will meet him in India," replied Lt. Col. Steve "Smitty" Montoya.

"Thoughts, Smitty? I mean, who da heck is dis guy?" Zeke asked. Then, controlling his sarcasm, he said, "OK, OK. I'm thinking a no-brainer here, we'll support dis for sure. Has a liddle DC written all over it. Put you and me on da flight schedule. Have Chief Hernandez ready some birds up...let me see here," said Zeke, looking over the maintenance schedule of available aircraft. He lit up a cigarette, and positioned it perfectly on the end of his lip while he talked.

AV-9	88-0330	*Spirit of CALIFORNIA*
AV-10	88-0331	*Spirit of S. CAROLINA*
AV-11	88-0332	*Spirit of WASHINGTON*

Smitty laughed at Zeke, then looked at his copy of their tail numbers. "*WASHINGTON* is down for corrosion. Perhaps put *SOUTH CAROLINA* on the schedule, with *CALIFORNIA* as a back-up, sir?" Smitty told him.

"Yep, good idea. Do it," ordered Zeke. "Who's da the pilot coming here to ride shotgun?"

Smitty open his clipboard. "A captain. Name is...Ford Stevens. Air Force Reserve. Flies B-1s over at Ellsworth."

"Say the name is Stephens? I went to Southern Illinois with a kid named Stephens. Wait, a reservist?"

"Yes. Ford Stevens. S-T-E-V-E-N-S."

"Nah, not him. Never heard of da guy."

Woody Island Air Base, South China Sea

Chen talked over some plans for the Black Scorpion to fly over the South China Sea region at his meeting with the intention of giving a workout to the radar controllers.

Receiving an aerial helicopter tour on a Z-8S Super Frelon of the newly built-up islands in the middle of nowhere, he was impressed with the massive runway, buildings, fuel farm, and aircraft parking. Even the space for his brothers in the navy had ample parking for their ships. This project was massive and moving along well ahead of schedule.

"All three islets, Fiery Cross, Mischief, and Subi, have hangar space?" Chen asked General Bao Bing. Gray hair, looking like a wise grandfather, he looked and sounded the part of the elder statesman.

"Yes, He, space for twenty-four fighters, plus four larger planes. All built on the reef. Operational very soon," replied General Bing. The general referred to He Chen by his first name, a rare occurrence. It also reflected the closeness of their relationship.

"I'm bringing Black Scorpion here soon, General. Time for the bomber community to shine in our nation's military. A true show of force to our men. Yes?" Chen said, leaning forward, telling and asking his superior at the same time. It was not lost on the senior general.

"He, I appreciate your aggressiveness," General Bing said, then paused dramatically. "Just be sure," he paused again, then pointed at Chen, "you have your house in order before you start extending your reach. Understand what I am saying, He?"

General Bao Bing was referring to Chen losing Devil Dragon without really saying it, insinuating that he may be moving too fast on such an expensive and secret program.

"He," Bing began, then paused. "You had better have your business aligned with the senior military and the party before you start taking her from the mainland to down here. All eyes are upon us, especially their allies. If you're ready, yes, come down. But know if you are not, and something happens, you will retire." Bing looked outside at the clear water down below, then directly at Chen. "Immediately. Understand?"

Chen looked down at the floorboards of the Z-8S, then into the eyes of General Bing. "General Bing, sir, I will be successful."

Paris Hotel Las Vegas, Las Vegas, Nevada

"Ford! Come on, Bro! What the hell?" Mark said.

Wearing only his blue checkerboard boxer shorts and no shirt, Ford was passed out on the bathroom floor next to the toilet. He had vomited and had peed his shorts and was lying in the wet mess.

Emily turned around to ensure the room door was shut, then came back in. She carefully stepped through the chaos, over Ford, and turned on the shower.

"Bro, get up. Come on, man," Mark told him, his patience thinning, checking his pulse on his neck.

Emily leaned in to check his pulse on his wrist. "He's bloody pissed. Plastered," Emily said sternly.

Emily looked at Ford, then walked with a purpose over to the bed area. "I'm ringing Old Man Burns."

She waited with her one hand on her hip, and one toe pointed out at a forty-five-degree angle. "Mr. Burns, we found Ford in his room, and he isn't feeling well this morning. The chap is out and won't be down to meet the secretary, unfortunately," she told him, which was true. No reason to say what caused it, as she looked over at the empty green bottle of Irish Whiskey on the room table near the purse.

"Ford, snap out of it. Come on," Mark told him again in a hushed voice. Mark was crouched down and sure not to step in the nasty vomit.

Emily came back into the bathroom. "Just called Mr. Burns and said Ford wasn't feeling well," she announced calmly, but rapidly raised her voice. "He's *rat arsed*! A tad sick, are ya?"

"Fuck yes, I'd say yes he's sick. Emily, what the hell is this? One-night party or does this have legs? He's a mess. A much bigger problem I don't know about?" Mark was livid.

Emily didn't answer and got some of the fancy hotel towels off the rack and laid them on the floor. *Geez, Ford,* Emily thought quietly. *Really? I'm bloody hell pissed off.* "Ford, you were arse over tit," she told him, huffing. Emily then became concerned about his welfare. "Blimey. Are you OK?" she finally asked out loud.

According to emotional intelligence experts, women had more empathy than men. Despite this fact, Emily felt far from providing empathy and was really torn. Her emotions were right on the edge of bursting, and seeing the purse in the room added to the rise.

Ford was starting to come out of his funk, but was very slow to come to full consciousness. He had a small cut on his ear, most likely from where he tried to prevent himself from falling on the toilet as he came in to throw up.

Mark shook his head and was downright irritated still. He had a stern look on his face and felt deceived, as if Emily was keeping this from him. Thoughts flew through his mind, especially since both Calvin and the secretary of defense were downstairs waiting. "Goddamn it. Emily, is this much bigger than a night? I need to know because we have a whole mission coming and riding on Ford. You know this. You need to tell me if we have a problem. Do we?" Mark asked her, unsympathetically.

Calvin Burns's Hotel Room, Paris Las Vegas, Las Vegas, Nevada

Calvin checked in and was getting settled into his room, and he picked up his phone for a quick check. He had a text from his college roommate, Reggie Bryant of Gulfstream, a few from his daughters, and one from his wife.

Scanning emails, he saw Michelle was checking in as well. Nothing hot, so he lay down for some much-needed rest. He was never told of Ford's true condition.

Ford Stevens's Hotel Room, Paris Las Vegas, Las Vegas, Nevada

"Mark. Yes, Ford has been drinking more since Devil Dragon, but I've never seen him this bad," Emily answered.

Mark stood up and looked around at the mess. He wasn't sure if he should be concerned or laugh, because the painted picture here was that he went out boozing in Vegas and was now paying the price—a typical night in this town for many.

"You would tell me if this was an issue, right?" Mark asked her.

"Yes, Mark, this is not an issue. I don't think. But he has been drinking way more than usual. Let's get him cleaned up."

Ford got up on all fours, and it was becoming clearer to him who was in the room now.

"Good morning, guys. Hi Em...I had a hell of a night downstairs and..."

There was a quiet and soft knock at the door. Emily tilted her head sideways, curious who could possibly be knocking now.

"Get in the shower, Ford. Now," Emily told him, angrily, and she walked over to answer the door.

It was Pinky, wearing her olive flight suit, face full of makeup and ready to start the day.

"Wonderful. A cutie here wearing a tight flight suit. Who the bloody hell are you?" Emily said sarcastically.

"Hi. I'm Pinky Pinkerton. Um, isn't...this Ford's room?" asked Pinky, looking past Emily, leaning to the right and spotting her purse. "Oh, yes, it is, I can see my purse I left here."

"Oh really, that's your purse, doll face? Why is your purse in my boy-friend's room?"

Air Force Station (AFS) Yelahanka, Bangalore, India

"Ravi, we are expecting the Americans here in the coming days. We need to be ready," said Air Commodore Vivhan Priya to Group Captain Ravi Rahul, both flying pilots and leaders at Yelahanka.

"We are ready, Commodore. Hangar number two will be clear for their jet remaining overnight. Will be fueled up and ready for a nineteen-hour turnaround. Second jet will take on fuel and immediately takeoff again. Will not remain here. Is that accurate, sir?" Ravi asked.

The Indian Air Force flew training aircraft at this base for ramping up transport pilots, but also conducted navigator training, too. Yelahanka, four-letter code VOYK, had a main asphalt runway due east/west, runway 09/27, at 9,858 feet.

"Concur, Ravi. Put your best men on this. No camera phones. Silent at what they see and hear. Full security police on the exterior of the building, as well as the interior. Deadly force authorized. Orders directly from the deputy prime minster," ordered Air Commodore Priya.

AFS Yelahanka was home to about forty thousand flying hours per year and was known as the busiest airport in the region. New pilots were trained on the Antonov-32 Cline twin-engine turboprop, Dornier, and Mi-8 here.

Hangar Two, one of four airplane hangars and three helicopter hangars, was modern and strong enough to house something C-130 size, which was the expected size of Black Scorpion. She would be fueled and locked up upon arrival, as Ravi Rahul would not let his superior down, nor his country.

"I take much pride in my work, sir, and will see to it that a superb job is completed on this issue," Ravi answered.

Ford Stevens's Hotel Room, Paris Las Vegas, Las Vegas, Nevada

Pinky had no idea why this British girl had such an attitude problem, or why she was in Ford's room, but she kept her cool and continued to stand there.

"Yes, that's my purse, right there. I am Ford's copilot, Pinky Pinkerton. I left my purse here yesterday by accident when we met up to do our pilot training. I'm sorry if I am troubling you this early. And Ford. Is he…ready for our last day of training today?"

Emily was about to lose her marbles. "You miserable git. Did you shag him? Did you?" Emily was in Pinky's face, pushing her back against the wall with her arm.

"Shag? What? No…"

"Listen to me. Hope you kept your fanny in your tight little flight suit."

From inside the bathroom they heard Ford stirring. "No…no, Emily, nothing happened."

"Shut up in there, you bastard," Emily replied with full venom. Eying Pinky now, they stared at each other.

Mark poked his head out of the bathroom sideways, leaving Ford to see what kind of a fight was developing in the room.

"Get back in there, wanker; this is of no concern to you."

Mark raised his eyebrows and did an immediate about face into the bathroom. Emily turned back to Pinky, and could tell after years of operations work that her body language and voice suggested she was telling the truth. Indeed, it looked like nothing had truly happened.

Emily waived both her hands and stepped back. "No, I am sorry, Pinky. My apologies, I thought you and Ford spent the night here together. Your purse. Please stay,"

Pinky nodded and was somewhat shocked at the pit bull inside Emily. "Oh, OK. Is he…all right in there?"

"Yes, Ford is getting cleaned up. Got sick, and our friend Mark is helping him in there," Emily replied. She walked over and handed Pinky the purse.

"Thank you. I guess you're the girlfriend I've heard so much about? I am jealous. You're so skinny…and pretty. He really loves you," Pinky told her.

Emily was even more disarmed now and felt good that Ford was talking positively about her. "Yes, I am Emily Livingston. It's a pleasure to meet you," she said, extending her hand. "I'm from London and working with our upcoming task, the one Robert read you in on and why you're here at training."

Pinky understood the full connection now. "Oh, yes, I understand. I also believe you and I are going to India together, as Ford heads on to Diego Garcia?"

They heard coughing from inside the bathroom, as if someone was throwing up. Then came moaning.

They both looked at each other and made a face, thankful it was not them throwing up. "Yes, that's our plan for India. At least it was, until this morning in here."

Secure Room, US Air Force Warfare Center, Nellis Air Force Base, Nevada

The brief had just ended, and the teleconference equipment was shut down. This was the first time in a few days that they could all be together, with the exception of Jeanie, who was on the video screen from DIA, as well as the Diego Garcia Group Commander, Colonel Zeke Ziehmann.

"Thank you again for the brief. Ford, I'm happy you have recovered from your sickness. Obviously, the secretary understood and did invite you to see him in his office at the Pentagon. So, let's go around the room and see if there are any closing questions for us locally. Anyone?" Calvin said, ensuring his team was prepared.

Ford agreed and piped up. "Thank you, sir. First thing I'll do when I get back to DC is pay him a visit. Team, thank you again for your professionalism in working together on this mission. I feel very lucky to have been part of this, two times now. I am still saddened by our loss of Wu but look forward to the future. And the future is bright. We can get this mission done. Go Air Force Reserve and Jojo Rising." As he said this brightly, he glanced over at Emily, and she blushed.

The team went over the specifics one last time in private, and it was no different than when they discussed it in planning. This final aircrew walkthrough was a high priority for a mission with so many moving pieces.

Ford would hitch a ride via a C-17 to Diego Garcia from Nellis. Pinky, Mark, Emily, and Robert would head to Bangalore directly to receive the Black Scorpion upon landing. Finally, Jeanie would work her cyber-hijacking magic from Washington.

Mark got the team together for hand shaking and hugging and a few good-byes. They gelled well as a team, and Mark was proud of their work.

"Fly her straight, kid. No aircraft carriers this time. Should be easy. Plus, no bad Chinese copilots to fight. Just take her to India, then the US…good to go?" Mark told Ford, acting like a sports coach. He then gave him a hug.

"Take care, Mark. I'm good. I'm good. I got it covered. Kid!" Ford replied, pointing at him jokingly.

Ford and Emily separated from the group and went back alone to the Paris, spending their last night together for a few days. They got into the room, and Ford sat down in the chair by the window to take his flight boots off.

"Ford, look, before we talk about anything…I have to bring up something delicate. Something sensitive. I must know. Please share with me, love. What happened last night…with you in the bathroom?" Emily asked.

Naval Support Detachment, Diego Garcia

Lt. Col. Steve "Smitty" Montoya, B-2 Spirit pilot, read the message traffic from Washington, double checking when this Captain Ford Stevens was going to arrive at Diego Garcia. *Looks like tomorrow afternoon. Right on schedule,* he thought.

"Hey, Steve. Our det. intel. officer just gave me a heads-up. Seems like you and the boss have a package here from Washington," said a fellow officer.

Steve went from his office to the outer office shared with others in the group and shook hands with someone wearing casual clothing who had the title of courier. Steve had a quick chat. "Thank you. Please wait here," he told him, then Steve walked a few offices down to Zeke's office.

"Sir, excuse me. This laptop arrived for you via courier from Washington's DIA Headquarters. Was hand delivered to me out there to give to you. Courier wants to ensure you received it and needs to see your ID," Steve told Colonel Zeke Ziehmann.

"Sure. Send 'em in," replied Zeke.

The courier dropped off the paperwork after checking credentials.

"Dat here's for Captain Ford Stevens, eh?" Zeke said out loud.

Ford Stevens's hotel room, Paris Hotel Las Vegas, Las Vegas, Nevada

"Emily, all I did was go down to the casino floor and take advantage of the free drinks at the tables. Came back up here and had a few nightcaps. Before you know it, I stumbled into the bathroom and got sick. I think I was leaning on the toilet rim…and slipped, and my ear hit the toilet. My head. I don't know. Then, I didn't realize how liquored up I was, and I peed all over myself," Ford answered.

She looked him in the eye. "Do you realize now how your drinking affects more than just you? It's a family disease. What I mean is that your drinking now affects you, me, Mark Savona, Mr. Burns. Even the secretary of defense."

Ford remained silent.

"You need help, Ford. This is rock bottom. Lying in your urine and throw-up and missing a meeting with the secretary is bottom of the barrel, chap. Seek help. You need to dry out. You need in-residence rehab help if you can't control your drinking, Ford."

Ford shook his head no. "Emily, I can deal with this on my own. I don't need help. I promise I'll cut it down. OK?"

Emily held his hand. "This cannot turn out well. When does this end?"

"Em, let me do this mission first, and I will cut back big time when I get back. Two days, home quick, then a huge reduction in my drinking."

Emily remained silent.

"Let's talk about something more positive, OK? I did want to discuss us, though. You and me. Long term," Ford said quietly.

Emily lit up at those words and had a glow to her face.

"I want to get married…spend the rest of my life with you." *Oh, man. I didn't even ask her parents yet.*

Emily's heart melted. She was so in love with him and wanted the same long-term relationship that he sought. Together, forever. "Yes, I want that, too. I am in love with you, too, Ford."

"You know I haven't asked your parents yet, but we both know. Why don't we go downstairs to Le Boulevard, just to look around? Take a look at all the jewelry stores. Try on some engagement rings for size?" Ford offered.

Emily bear hugged Ford.

"Emily, Emily. I said try them on for size, not purchase one."

"I know. I'm just so excited we'll be engaged soon! I can't wait to tell my family!"

They went down to the stores in the Paris village on the hotel compound, and walked around hand in hand at all the shopping options. They looked into each other's eyes with young love, committed to the other for life.

Ford's mind started to race with nervousness, too, thinking of the articles he previously read on choosing diamonds. Purity, clearness, and rarity were his goal, and it was important to focus on workmanship but not get absorbed with marketing. He also was attracted to the romance part of the hunt, especially since it made Emily blissful. He was definitely in unchartered waters and felt anxious.

Staring in the window, Emily had her eye on a beautiful princess-cut ring, a one-carat stone, with fourteen-karat white gold. They went inside and tried it on, and she was as happy as she had ever been.

Days Later, Air Force Station (AFS) Yelahanka, Bangalore, India

"Hello, Ravi, my name is Mark Savona, and this is Emily, Robert, and Pinky. It is a pleasure to meet you," Mark said, wiping the sweat from his brow.

"Namaste. So happy to meet you. We were expecting you and your team. We are ready to support you, sir!" Group Captain Ravi Rahul told them. "Please allow me to introduce my superior officer, Air Commodore Vivhan Priya, base commander of Yelahanka."

The team exchanged greetings and sought a hangar tour of where the Black Scorpion was to be parked. The Indian accent was thick and distinguished, and the hospitality of the Indian military officers was superior to much of what they had experienced in the past with other countries. There was no place like India in the world, with such top-notch, down-to-earth friendship and respect.

Robert, a man of action and usually of few words, was always on the lookout and checking his surroundings, always trying the simplest of things, talking on a variety of topics with people just to see who was doing what and where.

"Hello, I am Robert, and thank you again, Ravi. A few questions while we walk around the hangar. You have security both inside and out?"

"Yes, Robert. My pleasure to help. We have our security forces inside the hangar and outside the hangar, in addition to our perimeter fence that keeps out the street animals and people by razor-wire fence. Not a problem, sir," Ravi answered.

Robert was full of questions, so he continued. "Ravi, just want to make sure, but...your hangar doors work? You have power? And if not, a manual override?"

Ravi answered nonverbally, giving Robert the famous Indian head bobble. The head bobble was a moving his head from side to side, a usual custom in this area of India, a simultaneous shake and nod. It meant "sure," "OK," and "I hear you" all in one. In western countries, it would be a nod of acknowledgement.

"Fuel. You have working fuel trucks?" Robert asked.

"Yes, of course," he said, answering verbally and with a bobble. "We truck it in from the fuel farm in Bangalore, and before that, it comes from the refinery," Ravi answered.

Mark looked around, too. "Thank you, Ravi. I know we are asking a lot of questions, but do you have a cart? A...an APU to get our aircraft started for the next night?"

"Yes, sir, we have that, too, sir. Full air. Variety of amps available."

Robert looked in his pocket-sized notebook and didn't see anything else in his notes to check. "Ravi, we are staying over at the Ritz-Carlton Bangalore during our stay here. Here is my hotel card. Please call me if something should develop. We will all be back here to receive the jet. Thank you, and see you then," Robert told him.

Ravi smiled at everyone. "It is my pleasure to work with the US government. Thank you for the opportunity, Mr. Mark."

Emily was as quiet as ever and only talked as they were walking away and alone from Ravi. "Robert, did you see that old ass fuel truck? Dripping fuel… muddy tires? Looks like they use the same tank to haul all sorts of liquid, for heaven's sake."

Robert smiled. "Did I ever. I went over and looked at it. Mud on an airfield? It was a 1946 International Harvester. Still runs. Driver admits he uses it out in town when not refueling airplanes to haul water. I've made specific arrangements to be sure he cleans it out first."

Inbound to Woody Island, South China Sea

"Let's perform the cruise checklist, do some functional check flight test card items for the left wing before we go any further," aircraft commander Captain Dai Jian told copilot Captain Chung Kang.

Chung ran the checklist items for bleed air tests, running hot air from all the engines inside both wings. He visually inspected from his windows as much as he could, and there were no signs of anything abnormal. The test card had them doing some slow-speed maneuvers while heading to the southeast and over the South China Sea.

"This jet is good to go. Continuing to Woody. I'm scanning the island from here and can see the radar energy and EMI coming off the southern end. We are also not getting lit up, so we continue to be invisible. Good for flight test on the wing, in addition to our flight test for the radar controllers," Dai announced.

Chen set up the radar controllers on the island to be ready for the unexpected, as in, anything could happen. On the ground, the radar was empty, including the off-shore live weapons range. The controllers kept their eyes open, but nothing was there.

"Hey, Chung, rather than squirt the laser, let's just do a low pass, past the radar controllers and air traffic controllers in the tower. Right across the whole airport and island. Will scare the hell out of them because they can't see us. Don't even know we are coming."

Chung started laughing.

"Descent checklist," Dai ordered. "Take us down to one thousand feet above sea level. I'll get us in lower as we get closer."

Dai started his descent about fifty miles out, heading southeast, and feet wet over the dark water. Their airspace was clear, and not a soul was expecting their high-speed, low-level arrival.

DIA Headquarters, Washington, DC

Jeanie was monitoring China on her monitors and screens while everyone else on the team was traveling to their locations on the globe. She checked some of the telecommunications companies and verified from the text chatter that the Black Scorpion was now airborne. Jeanie also scanned SOSUS, the navy's sound surveillance system, or underwater listening posts, and it turned up nothing. At least she had some previous firm data to work with so far.

Jeanie then started looking at the data traffic on ChinaSat 2 C and was able to see that the jet was in contact with the satellites for the oxygen systems. As predicted, she thought, the maintenance team was monitoring Black Scorpion live.

She moved the mouse with her right hand and was in a flurry of typing with her left. Searching for GPS satellite NAVSTAR 76 USA 266 was easy, but writing the last lines of malicious code was the difficult part. Some hundreds of lines of her malware code had to be specifically placed into millions of lines of the aircraft code, ensuring the malware would be hidden forever and do its job. Completing the placement of the malware in the jet's source code was the crème de la crème for Jeanie. She was excited.

Next step was to just wait and watch on the screen, as she executed the command with one click. Her code immediately traveled along the undersea internet cables. Watching the live Submarine Cable Map from Global Bandwidth Research, Jeanie could visually watch the signal rapidly move across from Washington, DC, to Los Angeles, over the Pacific on cable EAC-2C2 and into landing point Tseung Kwan O in Hong Kong. In separate routing, it also went to the US-China cable across the Pacific Ocean floor, and simultaneously to Guam's Asia-America Gateway undersea cable and landing point as a backup. To think that for a person, a trip like this took months only a mere fifty years ago was mesmerizing, as today it only took mere seconds.

Waiting the few seconds, Jeanie glanced up at the article pinned in her cubicle, looking forward to the day she could use Google's "Faster" cable, which moved info at sixty terabits per second. The article mentioned that it was the fastest undersea submarine cable ever built at ten million times faster than a cable modem, at the cost of $300 million. It was posted next to her bikini picture with Mark, which made her smile.

"Adios, mischievous code. Now we wait," Jeanie announced, sending and uploading the code to both the jet and the two pilots' phones. *Done,* she happily told herself.

With near-immediate turnaround time, her screen already displayed the aircraft flight instrument system, a software depiction that she made based upon the ones and zeros being received into her office. Her software interpreted the numbers into pictorial form, displaying all the cockpit instruments live. She could also see an electrical bus on a second screen, allowing her to monitor and control all electrical systems as needed. Black Scorpion was flying and airborne, and she could see everything as if she was behind the controls or in a simulator.

The same system was also set up for Ford's laptop in Diego Garcia. When turned on, it would display the same information and allow either of them to make changes remotely on the Black Scorpion without either Dai or Chung knowing what was going on.

Jeanie looked across her monitor, confirming what she was expecting from an aviation data sheet on generic aircraft. "Hydraulics, oxygen, weapons, voltmeter, ammeter, fuel, fuel flow, exhaust gas temperature, navigational aids, radios, compass, attitude, radar, oil, and pressurization. Even circuit breakers…list goes on. Got them. Bingo."

Miller Residence, Hudson Street, Hawley, Pennsylvania

Michael and Rex were in their basement again after Michael had just completed his Social Committee shift at the Woodloch Pines Resort. "Rex, you don't have to say anything and can just listen. It's OK. Watch me," Michael told Rex.

Young Rex leaned forward, then glanced at his wall map of the world, wondering where they were going to hear from first.

"W99ZNX, this is W87YYT, over," Michael transmitted, his mouth close to the microphone.

Static came over the radio, and Michael was able to adjust the digits on the two-meter radio to get the right band and frequency to listen clearly.

"This is W99ZNX in Nova Scotia, Canada. Go ahead," came a reply.

A huge smile came across the ten-year-old's face. "Dad, this is awesome. That guy lives way up here," Rex said, pointing at North America, and Nova Scotia, Canada, specifically.

"Loud and clear, my friend. We live in central Pennsylvania, USA, near Scranton. How goes the weather up there?" Michael asked his new amateur-radio friend, waiting for a reply.

The voice signal traveled from the microphone in the Miller basement to the coaxial cable connected to the rear of the transceiver. From there, his voice traveled up the cable that was stapled-gunned to the wooden two-by-fours in the basement, through the first floor hugging the chimney, and up into the attic antenna. The signal then transmitted through the atmosphere, hitting the ionosphere, then ricocheting back to earth. It repeated this pattern many times, up and down, as the radio waves spread out over earth.

Sitting in the attic was their "stealth antenna," named as such because there was no way Michael Miller's neighbors or the Town of Hawley, Pennsylvania, was going to allow him to erect an enormous metal ham radio tower antenna. The Miller makeshift polarized 144 MHz antenna was designed to fit in the sixty-foot-length attic. Michael and a friend from Woodloch Pines built a ground plane antenna and a vertical dipole antenna, doing some back-of-the-napkin math regarding power ratios, transmitter power, and signal loss to coax cable. Michael chuckled at how complicated his friend made it, and told him all he wanted was just for it to work.

"Weather is stormy up here in Canada, eh. Something we are used to. Another one and half to two meters of snow coming tonight and tomorrow."

Rex couldn't believe he could talk with someone that far away.

Naval Support Detachment, Diego Garcia

"And from there, you'll taxi to park at Hangar Two at Bangalore, refuel, and RTB," Ford told Zeke and Smitty, his two pilots. Ford had just completed the brief in Diego Garcia, and tomorrow night would be their goal for launch.

"OK, so how do we know your, what's dat jet again, Black Scorpion? How do we know Black Scorpion will even be airborne tomorrow night?"

"Sir, the team back in DC has ways of monitoring that. These guys have all sorts of capabilities that I don't even understand. I trust them completely, so if they tell me she's airborne, the jet is airborne."

Zeke agreed and looked at Smitty, then up at the flat panel on the wall in his office. "Ford, we're on board with yer plan and can take you there for sure. You see up there on da flight schedule, we have a primary jet and a backup if we go down in the chocks? We'll be all right. Get some rest over at da quarters, and we'll pre-brief tomorrow at 1600 for an 1800 takeoff. Questions?"

Ford shook his head no, as he was barely listening now, admitting to himself that he was thinking about Emily more than normal. The engagement ring he secretly bought back in Vegas, without Emily knowing, was burning a hole in his flight-suit pocket. Ford checked his chest pocket so often that he thought the box would leave a mark on his flight suit.

"Hey, Stevens. What happens if your laptop doesn't work?" asked Smitty, with a deadpan tone.

Inbound to Woody Island, South China Sea

Dai and Chung ensured all their external lights were off, including their infrared lights, known as IR. IRs were invisible to the naked human eye because their wavelength was just greater than the red end of the visible light spectrum, but less than microwaves. IRs had a wavelength of about 800 nm to 1 mm, and unless someone on the island was using an infrared camera, goggles, or binoculars, the flyover would be fast and invisible.

"Autopilot off," Dai announced as he took manual control of the jet and placed his hands on the stick and throttle. "Put the altitude bug on fifty feet. We're going low."

"Roger, fifty feet," Chung acknowledged. *Wow, we are going to be really low,* Chung thought.

"I'm looking for 750 knots at about a hundred feet. I want the sonic boom right over the island. We'll come across the island from north to south, then again east to west, and depart the area to the west for Sanya," Dai told him.

The radar controllers were told by senior officers of the PLAAF to keep their eyes open. The radar dishes were sweeping the sea surface, as well as the airspace, and nothing was being painted with radar energy.

Out the windshield, both pilots looked out at the black ocean and only saw the reflection of the stars off the dark sea. The faint lights of the island were coming into view low on their canopy and fast.

"Got you at 575 knots at two hundred feet. Airspace clear. No other aircraft in the vicinity," Chung shared.

From the left seat, Dai pushed his right hand on the four throttles a bit further to get just a few knots of airspeed, while adjusting the nose slightly with his left hand. The airspeed jolt was felt for just a few knots, but the airspeed indicator climbed rapidly.

"Over the island in five seconds, four seconds, three, two, feet dry. Now. Go ahead, punch it," Chung announced.

BOOOOOOMMMM!

The sound wave cracked from the Black Scorpion and penetrated every building and rolled across the surface of all the islands in the area rapidly. Breaking the speed of sound at that altitude scared the heck out of everyone there, especially the controllers who knew something might be coming. With no mountains or land to absorb the energy, it was quite a jolt. Multiple windows were broken on buildings, and a few car alarms on government sedans were set off.

"That was fun, Dai. You're clear for the turn," said Chung, as Dai turned left out over the water for a few miles.

He came at the island again after a long and large turn, this time from east to west. As they looked down below, all sorts of people were outside now, looking around and up in the sky. They had no idea what was going on.

VVVVRRRRRWWHHOOOSSHHHHHHHHH! The intense sound of the Black Scorpion going over was felt inside everyone's internal organs. As fast as they came in was as fast as they left.

"Chung, you have the controls. Take us to Sanya. I'll mark the kneeboard card. Success," Dai said, recording the air temps, altitude, and simulated attacks on the island for the debrief upon landing.

Inside the radar controller building, it was complete pandemonium. "What do you have on the radar?" asked the PLAAF radar supervisor, a major. His glass monitor had a huge crack in it now.

"Major, nothing. There is nothing on the screen. Whatever that was, we did not see it," answered the young lieutenant. He ran his hand down the glass screen.

Onboard the USS *Buffalo*, Submarine Squadron 1, Pacific Ocean, Two Miles off Woody Island, South China Sea

"What the fuck was that on the surface?" asked Commander Reginald Mack, commanding officer of the USS *Buffalo*. "Battlestations torpedo!"

The loud sound and vibration of something on the surface traveled through the water. The officer of the deck and others were scrambling, as the dim lighting inside the submarine flashed in various shades of red. They were in shallow water, and the sound wave pierced their hull as if there was an explosion on the surface near their vessel. Anyone in their racks sleeping was out now and awake, life vests and helmets on, and the sailors were moving with a purpose.

"Officer of the deck, what do you have? Sonar contacts?" asked the commander.

"Negative, sir. Zero targets tracking. Alone out here."

"Officer of the conn, anything?"

"Negative, sir."

Commander Mack thought for a moment. "Midnight Cowboy, I'm thinking of surfacing. Shit, we're nearly on top of the water right now. I need to see what's going on up there. I mean, what makes a sound like that? What do you think?"

"Surface, sir," replied the Midnight Cowboy. It was an affectionate term from the captain of the ship for his most trusted young, junior officer standing watch. It also came with a lot of additional responsibility. "Go, sir. Unusual sound for sure."

The USS *Buffalo*, hull number SSN 715 with a crew of 150 sailors, was known as one of the fastest and stealthiest submarines in the Indo-Pacific

Fleet. *Buffalo* routinely conducted forward-deployed operations for extended periods of time out of Pearl Harbor, Hawaii, and was forward leaning for a variety of undersea missions. From Singapore to Hawaii and more, she and her crew ensured America's right of entry to maritime trade routes and delivered credible defense against unfriendly maritime forces.

The US Navy had three classes of nuclear-powered submarines in their fleet. *Buffalo*, a Los Angeles–class submarine on her last voyage before retiring to the scrapyard, was known and favored by the sailors, along with thirty-nine same-class sister vessels sailing the world's oceans. Thirty of them were equipped with twelve Vertical Launch System tubes for firing Tomahawk cruise missiles.

"Concur. Hold your horses. Hang on a sec. Sonar, what's SOSUS picking up? How about Echo Voyager?" asked Commander Mack.

SOSUS, the navy's sound surveillance system of underwater listening posts, was the same system Jeanie checked earlier, this time with results. Echo Voyager was a fifty-one-foot hybrid diesel submarine that was an autonomous robot. It had the ability to raise a mast, turn on the generator, recharge the battery, or submerge to eleven thousand feet, all without a manned crew.

"Jammed with noise, sir. Charts are showing a low-altitude multiengine aircraft breaking the sound barrier, but…this is much louder than anything we've seen. More than one jet engine…and the computer does not recognize her signature," replied the sonar operator.

"Well, for Christ sake. Isn't that grand? Doesn't recognize. XO, thoughts? I don't want us to breach for no reason, show our asses. Go up top and take a peek with the periscope or what?" commented Commander Mack.

"Yes, sir."

There was a fine line between toxic leadership and tough leadership, and this sub captain rode the line regularly. His mouth hadn't gotten him into trouble yet, but one day it might. He was one of the navy's best submarine commanders, and he couldn't let something like this go without taking a full look.

"Sir, surface?" asked the XO.

"Huff. Now the Chinese are doing Mach-whatever flybys over their little airport? Fuck them." Commander Mack grabbed the handheld microphone. *Asshole pilots,* he said under his breath. "Officer of the deck, Captain, clear baffles and bring the ship to periscope depth."

Sanya Phoenix International Airport, Sanya, Hainan Island, China

As usual, the airspace was cleared, and no aircraft were taking off or landing this time of night. Black Scorpion landed on Runway 26, an eleven-thousand-foot concrete runway. Sanya Phoenix International Airport was much like many of the airports Chen and his team found to hide Black Scorpion each night.

Sanya Phoenix Airport was on the island of Hainan in the southernmost province of China and was located about nine miles northwest of the city. Chen liked it because located on the northwest side of the airport was, yet again, a large, secluded hangar to hide Black Scorpion in during the day.

Dai taxied the jet to the ramp out front, lights out, and the area they were in was secluded and dark.

"Engine shutdown checklist," Dai announced.

"Throttles, idle..." Chung read, as the engines sat for cool down.

Dai and Chung could see a figure already on the ramp but could not make out for sure who it was. From the side and based on the walking gait, it looked like Chen.

"Power, off, APU, connect. Helmets off," Chung announced, the final step in their checklist.

Thumps were heard below the floor hatch in the cockpit, which meant someone was coming up from the ground and climbing the ladder near the nose landing gear. It was Chen himself.

"Dai, Chung, I have already received word of your flyby at Woody. Aggressive, broke some windows. You did not appear on any radar, and if this attack had been real, you would have been successful. You did nice work."

It was the first time the pilots had ever seen General Chen not be angry at them. Even though the crew damaged some government infrastructure down on the ground, Chen was happy, smiling, and making a compliment. Both pilots sat in their seats while Chen stood in the cockpit.

"Thank you, General. We did two passes to simulate an attack: one from the north and a second one from the east. We visually saw people down below, but no radar energy detection. We also thought about using the laser on the range, but with no targets, it would have been a waste to just hit the sea surface," Dai explained.

"You did a good job. Tomorrow, we do low-level in the mountains, high-altitude speed work, then range testing. Up again tomorrow night. You understand?" Chen asked, but was telling them.

Dai was more surprised with the compliment than anything. So was Chung.

"Thank you, General."

The ground maintainer connecting the tug gear to pull Black Scorpion into the hangar was also listening. He heard Chen from the nose tire area down below because Chen's voice was so booming. Immediately, the maintenance crew started texting about flying tomorrow night.

Ritz-Carlton, Bangalore, India, Mark Savona's Room

"And how do you know this, Jeanie?" asked Mark, huddling around his speaker on his smartphone. Also in his hotel room was Robert, Emily, and Pinky, with Ford connected in Diego Garcia. Calvin Burns was dialed in as well.

"Texts. I can see all of them from what still looks like the maintenance folks. Plan is for tomorrow night, your time, to do a low-level route, speed work, and hit the range for weapons testing," Jeanie explained.

"We're on!" announced Ford, excited. "Easy mission!"

Jeanie also gave the details of her connection into the Black Scorpion flight management system and did a virtual test with Ford's laptop. Everything was working as planned.

"Not done yet, Ford. So far, so good. Be ready for anything," Calvin told him, using a fatherly tone, with a touch of apprehension.

Mark's critical thinking skills came around. "This is too easy. I feel like we are forgetting something. What are we missing?"

"The laptop password! I'll pass it to you at the end of the call. Don't let me forget," Jeanie told him. "Mark tells me you'll recognize it from you and Wu."

When they pulled off Devil Dragon, they ran into all sorts of issues along the way. Wu's health complicated things a bit, as did the covert infiltration using someone else's Gulfstream jet. In comparison, cyber, to Mark, was simple.

It was Pinky's first meeting with the whole team, including the gang on speaker, and she was pleased to be part of such an operation. Her beaming smile was contagious. "Hello, Ford. I'm ready! Seems like things are coming together."

"B-2 all fired up from here. We're a go out here."

Pinky gave a thumbs-up. "We got this."

Next Night, 180 Miles Southeast of Long Chau Island, Vietnam

"Climb checklist," said Dai as he scanned the instruments, then looked out into the dark, overcast sky.

Black Scorpion had just taken off moments before, and they were off for another late night of testing. Their test card was full for a low-level, nap-of-the-earth navigation route with timing and a high-altitude speed run, followed by some weapons range testing.

"Roger. Throttle setting…" Chung replied as he read off each step to be completed.

Air Force Station (AFS) Yelahanka, Bangalore, India

"Mark, Mark, listen to me," Jeanie said, talking very quickly. "They are airborne right now, way earlier than I expected. I can see their route of flight. If you want me to eject them over water, it has to be soon. Minutes," Jeanie told excitedly Mark on the phone. Mark was standing on the military ramp at the airport with Ravi in Bangalore. *Crap, we're not ready, and Ford's still on B-2 on strip alert.*

"Wait. Where does their flight plan take them?" Mark asked. "Calm down."

Jeanie rattled off their overflight of checkpoints, naming cities Mark had heard of, but had no clue as to where they were on a map.

"OK, OK. Hang on," Mark told her, covering the phone. "Ravi, we need a map of China. Right away. Do you have one inside?"

"Yes, Mr. Mark. Come. Right this way," Ravi told him.

Mark and Ravi ran inside the hangar to the student pilot lounge. There were couches and televisions all over the place, in addition to white marker boards and wall charts.

"Let's look here," Ravi said, but there was nothing. There were only aviation charts of India and their coastal regions.

"Hang on, Jeanie," Mark told her.

"You had better hurry. Two minutes and three seconds left until they hit mainland. Speed is increasing," she replied.

Ravi was running around the room now, checking out other rooms connected to the pilot lounge. He found something and came back running to Mark. "Will this work?"

Ravi was holding up an old issue of National Geographic, and inside the issue was a folded paper map of China.

"Open it up. Hurry, open it," Mark told him.

The two of them opened up the map and spread it on a table in the room. It was big enough because it was designed for pilots to plan their flights on.

"Holy crap. Jeanie, go ahead with your aircraft routing. I'm putting you on speaker," Mark told her excitedly. He forgot to check if they were in the green on the Peanut app. "Hooey, are we green light, Jeanie?"

"Less than one minute. Yes, in green. Hurry."

Robert, Emily, and Pinky walked in, looking at Mark in his frenzy.

"Shut up. No one say anything," Mark told them.

"Come on, come on. Here's their route to the west…" She said the coordinates out loud.

Mark drew with a marker with a line, looking like a kid's connect-the-dots puzzle. The black grease pencil made lines across the map easily, and it was clear where the Black Scorpion intended to go.

"Nineteen seconds! Hurry!"

"Come on, Jeanie, if you eject them now, can you fly it until Ford is closer?" Mark asked. "Did Ford even take off yet?"

Emily scanned the map and listened in on the conversation as best she could. She looked at the map and immediately saw what was happening.

In a near panic, Emily turned to Robert and started talking fast. "What do you think, Robert? Chen will know something is amiss if they get ejected here over the water, and then we turn them way over here toward Kunming for the Ford intercept."

Pink and Emily nodded their heads rapidly in agreement.

"Thirteen seconds," Jeanie announced. "You want Ford in the air early?"

Robert had to weigh in. "Mark, Mark, let them fly. Jeanie, Robert here. Let them go. If they are flying on that route, eject them over toward Kunming. We won't be able to interview them anymore, so it's a deviation from the plan. So be it. Dump their oxygen soon, let the crew be in and out of hypoxia. Make the turn for Ford over Burma and the Bay of Bengal. We need to confirm Ford is ready and taking off."

"Jeanie, have Ford take off early!" Mark yelled.

"OK on Ford. Six seconds, Mark. Need a decision right now...four... three..."

North of Naval Support Detachment, Diego Garcia
Runway 13 at Diego Garcia was twelve thousand feet in length, made of concrete, and could handle any jet in the US military or commercial inventory. It was complete with standard approach lighting checked by the FAA and maintained by the US Navy. The pilots enjoyed the challenge of flying there, especially at night.

What was deceiving on takeoff and landing was the darkness. Most airports had some type of city lights, which provided plenty of illumination to aid pilots and help with building their situational awareness. From the air at Diego Garcia, there was blackness, with a tiny strip of lit runway hidden in the vast ocean. To compensate, the pilots relied on instruments in the cockpit to get them to the touchdown zone on the runway. At only thirteen feet above sea level, and next to the sea, errors were normally unforgiveable.

Receiving the early takeoff message from Jeanie, Zeke, Smitty, and Ford were airborne in their B-2, *Spirit of South Carolina*, and heading zero-one-zero northbound. Zeke came up on the headset to talk with Steve and Ford.

"Fellas, looks like here we are a few hundred miles to a general area of intercept. Less if out of the bay. Assuming our average speed of 435 knots or so, and depending on winds, not too much further," Zeke told them, sipping on some Bulletproof Coffee previously sent to the island. "We'll tank in a few minutes over da Bay of Bengal and get some fuel so we can press on to Bangalore. And if you guys don't mind, I'm going to sit up here and have a smoke."

Smitty turned to see Ford from his copilot right seat, checking to see if Ford was in on the smoking joke. "Yeah, Ford. You have a comfy cot back there, a blanket, a toilet, so make yourself comfortable. We'll wake you as we get closer."

Ford thanked them, but was nowhere near close to going to bed. All excited and ready for what he was about to do, he whipped out his laptop and fired it up. The normal Microsoft start screen came on, then something Ford had not seen before...a login with his common access card, his CAC, and a password. Ford closed his eyes in complete frustration, and shook his head from side to side slowly.

"This is horseshit," he announced over the intercom.

"What is it? You need coffee?" asked Zeke.

Silence.

"You OK back there?" asked Smitty from the right seat, turning around to see Ford sitting his cot.

Ford looked up from the laptop screen, then closed his eyes in frustration. "I don't have a password for this thing."

Air Force Station (AFS) Yelahanka, Bangalore, India

"Let them fly," Mark announced. "It's OK, Jeanie. Let them go."

Jeanie looked at her screen and moving map, and the Black Scorpion just flew over the mainland.

"Goddamn...thank you. Jet is flying its planned route. So far, an ops-normal flight. They are climbing up to altitude on autopilot, heading three-three-zero, looking for twenty thousand feet," Jeanie announced.

Sighs were heard in the room.

"Well, that was interesting. Bollocks," Emily announced.

Ravi kept quiet the entire time and did not share his opinion around out of respect. He smiled warmly and observed as his friends from the United States worked out their details.

"All good now, sir?" Ravi asked Mark.

Mark nodded yes. "Yes, Ravi, all good now. That was a close one. This mission was well planned, but sometimes over time zones and distances things come up. You know how that goes," Mark shared with him. "Thanks."

"My pleasure, sir. Hangar is ready, as is my security detail and fuel truck. Please, come. Let us eat. Traditional Bangalore vegetarian."

DIA Headquarters, Washington, DC

"Sir, Hannah Davis, Air Force–White House liaison on the phone," Michelle Boyd said from the doorway of his office.

"No, no, can't take it. The operation I told you about earlier, BEACH... whatever the name is, is ready to happen." *Why can't I remember the name?* he quietly thought. "Well, it's happening. SANDY BEACH. That's the name."

Michelle looked at the deputy. "Sir, this is White House liaison calling. Are you sure?"

"Michelle, she can wait. White House liaison is just that, a liaison. If the president calls, put him through. But Hannah can get a scheduled appointment," Calvin told her.

Calvin was getting nervous, which he normally didn't do.

Two Hundred and Twelve Miles North of Diego Garcia, Pacific Ocean

"Are you bustin' argh balls, Stevens?" Zeke said over the intercom.

Ford was able to get into the computer easily with his CAC and PIN but had no idea how to open the secure software program for the Black Scorpion. In fact, he never remembered receiving it. *Is that the alcohol?*

"I wish I was. Would be a pretty good prank, but I'm for real. Give me a minute," Ford answered. *Jeanie said at the meeting that Mark told her it was something from Wu. That only means one thing.*

He typed it out with both hands, as his high school keyboard instructor taught him. J-O-J-O_R-I-S-I-N-G.

"Access denied" was displayed on the screen.

"What, access denied? What the hell?" Ford said over the headset, then yelled as loud as he could without transmitting over the intercom. He looked up at the B-2 moving map over the Pacific, and saw they were in the middle of nowhere. Ford felt like that, too.

He tapped on his keyboard with his index finger, then started typing. J-o-j-o-R-i-s-i-n-g, a combination of both lower- and uppercase letters.

"Access granted" was displayed on the screen.

Ford felt relieved, and a smile came across his face. "Yes!" Ford said, "Hey, I'm in. I'm in. All good now."

Both pilots looked at each other up front.

"Well, no kidding, Stevens," Zeke announced with a chuckle, taking another sip of coffee.

DIA Headquarters, Washington, DC

Jeanie was monitoring the flight on her screen and could see that the Black Scorpion was flying the purple line on their moving map display with the autopilot. They would soon be approaching the only southwestern portion of the night's flight, which meant this was her new window for hypoxia and ejection.

The Black Scorpion was in level flight, twenty thousand feet mean sea level, and was near six hundred knots inbound to the range. She wasn't aware of what was being said in the cockpit, but she knew things were going to change rapidly.

Jeanie looked at the screen and verified she had the connection still, which she did, and moved her mouse around. She lowered the pilot's oxygen levels to give them the hypoxia feelings as briefed. Jeanie figured this was good for about ten minutes or so, then ejection.

The next step was a slow reduction in their airspeed, remotely. Jeanie again maneuvered her mouse to the autopilot portion of the screen and remotely reduced the airspeed to 590 knots. Her plan was to reduce it by just a few knots for the next ten minutes, then down to 190 knots for the ejection.

Jeanie also masked the transmission of the oxygen data outside the aircraft, making it more erratic than it truly was for maintenance. Ford had written out a cheat sheet for Jeanie describing the types of airspeed that would be optimum for aircrew ejection. Some in the aviation community had discussed rumors of SR-71 pilots ejecting at over seventy thousand feet and 1,800 miles per hour, and with the thinner altitude at that height, maybe it was possible.

What would be impossible to determine is what Dai and Chung were wearing on this flight, so Ford recommended lower and slower. Without getting into ground speed and all the other technical airspeed stuff for pilots, Ford made it simple.

Now at 430 knots, the jet was slowing down nicely, and nothing else in the cockpit was touched, according to her screen. Perfect.

Miller Residence, Hudson Street, Hawley, Pennsylvania

Rex had a headset on and sat in front of the table, listening to ham radio operators talking from Asia, Europe, South America, and even Antarctica. His father did not allow him to talk without him being there, but Rex's hobby of placing pins on their basement wall map was fun.

Looking at the five-by-seven-foot National Geographic world map on the basement wall, he must have had eighty or ninety colored pins sticking out. It was colorful and impressive to see, and no one was more impressed than Rex that he could hear people talk from all over the world while sitting in his basement in Hawley, Pennsylvania, population 1,178.

Rex made a mark in his logbook that he was missing ham radio operators from the Middle East, and over to the east in places such as Korea and Japan. He would bring it up to his dad later.

One Hundred and Twenty-Four Miles South-Southwest of Dianchi Pool, Yunnan, China

"Dai, Dai, I feel weird…I am…out…of breath…" Chung said to Dai, attempting to take in deep breaths. Chung then looked over to Dai, and his head was down with his chin buried in his chest.

Chung looked outside the aircraft at the slight curvature of the earth on the horizon, the sun ready to rise soon, and mountainous terrain below.

The airspeed indicator slowly rolled back, but it wasn't registering in Chung's brain that it was not supposed to happen. His lack of oxygen was lowering his attention to detail and decision making, and his cockpit scan was no longer valid.

Dai woke up and looked at Chung, then started laughing. He took off his flight gloves and saw that the tips of his fingers under his fingernails were purple, but he was so out of it consciously that he didn't do anything about it. No decision to flip the oxygen lever to 100 percent, which would not work anyway even if he tried, nor an attempt to grab air from the emergency canister embedded in his survival vest.

Airspeed indicator was now reading 250 knots, as orchestrated by Jeanie.

This was it, her moment to shine. Jeanie remotely sent the electronic signal to the aircraft, starting a unique sequence. Without warning in the cockpit, the combined electric signal and chemical process of combustion releasing light and heat had begun.

PEEEROO, PEEEROO was heard and felt inside Black Scorpion. Two small explosives that attached to the roof of the aircraft were heard and felt as the hatch was blown off vertically and clear of the aircraft. This allowed glacial, cold air to enter the cockpit. Then, a delay of 0.6 seconds, when another set of actions occurred.

From her Washington, DC, position, mouse and keyboard at the ready, Jeanie transmitted the signal, which took only one breath to reach the Black Scorpion. In sequence, the roof hatch directly above the two pilot's heads was blown clear of the jet and fell into the Yunnan Mountains down below.

Next, the signal sent down from the satellite to the electrical bus transmitted to the electrical switch a simple "on" command. Upon receiving the signal, the seat motors launched each seat out at twelve G's, or G-force. SHH-HHEEEEEEEFFF was heard inside the cockpit, then a small delay of 0.4 seconds, and another SHHHHEEEEEEEEFFF: the two sounds were both pilots' ejection seat rockets being fired, throwing both pilots from the aircraft. There were many factors that went into the calculation, such as temperature and the body mass of the pilots, but since the aircraft was not in a high-G maneuver or out-of-control flight, it was as normal an ejection as one could get.

Each seat model performed differently since technology kept improving, and the Black Scorpion was no different. Chen's pursuit of the famous Russian ejection seat K-36D used in the Su-27 and MiG-29 allowed him to improve upon them. This new seat and ejection would provide enough separation between the aircraft and the pilots so they would hopefully never collide. The pilots would come out of the jet sitting in the seat, but would eventually be separated by their parachute deployment. This drag of the chute filling up with air yanked each pilot out of the seat. Dai and Chung landed near each other in a valley down below, along with their ejection seat full of survival gear.

DIA Headquarters, Washington, DC

Jeanie immediately cut off all electronic ties between the Black Scorpion and ground maintenance crews, who were now receiving zero data on all their accounts. Nothing transmitted off the jet except to US government assets.

She moved the mouse again, increasing the airspeed on the empty jet to six hundred knots and made a left-hand turn to the south to one-nine-zero. Jeanie expanded the rings of distance of the flight display map a bit and made the jet's destination to a waypoint over the water for the B-2 intercept.

She started typing now, sending a Peanut message to the rest of the team over their secure satellite communications link:

BOTH PILOTS EJECTED. REROUTED TO THE SOUTHWEST FOR AERIAL INTERCEPT.

FORD, AT DESIGNATED WAYPOINT, I WILL TRANSFER CONTROLS TO YOU. STAND-BY FOR WAYPOINT INFORMATION AND DESTINATION WEATHER. LANDING TO THE WEST AT BANGALORE. REPLY WHEN RECEIVED.

Jeanie continued to scan the FAA document labeled "Pacific Resource Guide for US Operators" to ensure she flew the jet to the right locations. All the data was apparently checked quarterly, so she shrugged her shoulders, hoping that data was accurate.

Mark wrote: "RECEIVED. NICE WORK."

About thirty seconds later, Ford came up on line: "TRACKING ALL. GOOD COMMS AND WATCHING ON LAPTOP. BEAUTIFUL."

Jeanie located the NAVAID information she was looking for and found it was better located than the original plan of Burma.

Located in Bangladesh, the Shah Amanat International Airport, airport identifier VGEG, was on the coast in Chittagong and would be a good area to have an airborne rendezvous. While both aircraft involved in the linkup had radar, internal navigation systems and GPS from satellites, it was important to provide backup NAVAID data.

She cut and pasted the info for a successful rendezvous so that Ford could give it to his B-2 pilots:

VGEG Airport Location in emergency:

Latitude:	22-14-58.558N (22.249599)
Longitude:	091-48-47.8839E (91.813301)
Elevation:	12 feet MSL (4 m MSL)
Time Zone:	UTC +6.0 (Standard Time)
	UTC +6.0 (Daylight Savings Time)
From City:	0 N.M. of Chittagong, Chittagong Division

VGEG Airport Runways

Longest Runway:	05/23 is 9646 ft (2940 m) long

Then she typed the location.

RENDEZVOUS INFO AS FOLLOWS:

NAVAID: CHITTAGONG 113.4 CTG 81.
RADIAL 278 ON W-174, 25 MILES WEST FEET WET.
DAKID WAYPOINT.

YELANHANKA AIR FORCE STATION, BANGALORE, WEATHER:

METAR text:	VOYK 241000Z 07010KT CAVOK 28/12 Q1016
Conditions at:	VOYK (BANGALORE ARP, IN) observed 2200L
Temperature:	28.0°C (82°F)
Dewpoint:	12.0°C (54°F) [RH = 37%]
Pressure (altimeter):	30.00 inches Hg (1016.0 mb)
Winds:	from the ENE (70 degrees) at 12 MPH (10 knots; 5.2 m/s)

Visibility:	6 or more miles (10+ km)
Ceiling:	ceiling and visibility are OK
Clouds:	unknown
Weather:	no significant weather observed at this time

The House of Roosevelt, 27 Bund, 27 Zhongshan East 1st Road, WaiTan, Huangpu Qu, Shanghai, China

Built at the far end of Shanghai's waterfront strip sat The House of Roosevelt Restaurant and Bar, an impressive building built back in 1920 and originally used for trading. The eight-story granite building housed spectacular eating areas with seating on multiple floors, large bars, and an Old World authentic-looking wine cellar.

Owned by an investment firm controlled by relatives of two American presidents, Theodore and Franklin Roosevelt, it was somewhat of an ironic choice for the PLAAF leadership to meet for briefs and social time that evening. It may have connections to American leadership, but this was the perfect location to discuss and plan their future.

The general officers and Party leadership were meeting in the members-only Roosevelt Club room, which was known as the premium room in the house used for diplomats, celebrities, and distinguished visitors. It was also private enough to discuss the future of the PLAAF along with a few party members.

Different speakers were taking the stage and reviewing a number of events in the coming weeks. A party member had just announced some of the topics that would be covered at their upcoming annual policy meeting, which would consist of three hundred officials in the Central Committee. Their plenum, lasting four days at a Beijing hotel, was going to focus on discipline, with directives to improve loyalty of their party members. The hour wrapped up with a not-so-quick discussion on corruption, the hot topic at the upcoming Politburo Standing Committee.

Next up at the Roosevelt House itinerary came the Central Military Commission discussion, with updates on the transformation of a joint combat force, covering everything from information operations to organizing for combat. Sidebar meetings covered their 4 percent GDP military spending, oil imports through the Indian Ocean, and operations in East Africa. East Africa would be teed up for future discussions, too, as this was where China had a large footprint in oil, gas, railroads, and mining.

A decision being tossed around was a force reduction, taking a page out of the United States' playbook. For some time, China had discussed disbanding five of the PLA's eighteen army corps as part of a large overhaul started by the president. It was focused on converting the world's largest ground force into a more expeditionary, current, and efficient fighting force. The reduction would be music to the air force because some of the two hundred thousand troops might be merged into them and the rocket force.

An older PLAAF general then had the floor for about twenty minutes, their last speaker before dinner and drinks upstairs at the rooftop Sky Bar. "We are making substantial progress in research and development, generals. Our improved military capabilities are catching up to or surpassing the United States in many areas," he briefed. "China has moved her focus and resources to Huayang Jiao, and internal research and development. The navy now has thirteen destroyers, three new advanced cruisers, and all of them have upgraded radar. Missiles? We had military maneuvers recently and had our six-meter missiles going, ready to take on large modern targets. These are the ones with higher trajectory and a range of three hundred kilometers. Makes her deadly…"

Huayang Jiao was Cuarteron Reef in the South China Sea, home to various high-frequency antennas installed recently on the southernmost man-made island, as the *Washington Post* and *Wall Street Journal* had been reporting. It was no secret China was making their presence known on these artificially created islands.

The generals finished up their strategic meeting and rolled to fine dining upstairs on the roof. The Roosevelt Sky Restaurant up on the eighth floor, laughing and drinking Shanghai's best and award-winning wines by the case. The enchanted view of the Bund and Huangpu Rivers, in addition to the Pudong Lujiazui Financial District, allowed conversation to flow for everyone, including Lieutenant General He Chen.

Chen's intent, as always, was to constantly network, always pecking away for that fourth star he was after. Never missing a chance to subtlety insert his accomplishments or the stealth program into conversation, he worked the room as a master. Stomach hanging over his pants, drinking glass in one hand, and back slapping or shaking hands with the other, Chen's motivation was transparent and was seen by many.

"Sir, excuse me; may I talk to you, please?" asked First Lieutenant Keung, Chen's aide-de-camp.

Annoyed, Chen excused himself from talking with the group of four-star general officers he was standing with and walked outside to the balcony. His back was to the water and skyline of tall skyscrapers.

"What is it, Bai?" he answered sternly.

Bai swallowed, paused, and was scared to deliver the news. His stomach was weak and had an uneasy feeling as his hands started to get clammy.

"Bai?" Chen boomed.

"The maintenance chief has called me from Sanya Airport, Hainan Island. They haven't left yet for tonight's destination of Wuhan Tianhe Airport," said Bai.

"So what?" Chen barked back.

In the distance, a waiter dropped a tray of empty glasses and a large shattering of glass was heard in the background. A murmur came over the crowd as everyone looked briefly at the employee.

"Sir, the maintenance chief passes on that they have lost contact with Black Scorpion. Complete contact. No oxygen readouts. Nothing. Nothing is transmitting back to them in the hangar. First time this has happened since installing the link."

Chen stood staring at Bai, double chin with two rolls in full effect, and thought for a moment. The pit in his gut was the size of a grapefruit. He was immediately concerned on the inside, but he maintained his poker face. Internally, he was screaming, as he knew this situation was rare: electronic transmissions don't just stop unless something makes them cease.

Holding in his anger, his face turning a bit red now, he looked out over the river at the people walking on the promenade, secretly worried about his pride and joy, then back at Bai.

Drilling a hole through Bai's head with his eyes, he said nothing and let out a long sigh.

Bai knew if they were at one of their many airports, this would be a disaster of a conversation—more like a one-way conversation where Bai listened and Chen yelled and threw items across the hangar or office, with history repeating itself. He was thankful as a junior officer that they were at the Roosevelt House in a public setting, especially with the rest of China's leadership, which saved his own butt from an ass chewing.

Chen coughed loudly, then spit out his green phlegm onto the ground. It was the size of a quarter and made a wet *splat* sound when it landed on the balcony floor. "I want to know...I want to know when they are due to land. Find out, now. Am I clear?"

Approaching W-174 Intersection, 43 Miles Southwest of DAKID Waypoint, Bay of Bengal

Zeke Ziehmann and Smitty Montoya both had their night-vision goggles down from their flight helmets and spotted the Black Scorpion on the horizon. She was the only jet in that area it seemed, and although the radar didn't show her, the pilots both pointed with their finger.

"Stevens," Zeke said over the B-2 intercom. "Wherr yuh-at, Scorpion? Pretty sure we have your jet. Twelve o'clock at four miles, couple hunnerd above us."

"Wait, I don't even see him yet," Smitty said.

Zeke turned a full ninety degrees to give the stare to Smitty. "By over there, Smitty. Come on. You ain't from Shicago, are ya? Pay attention."

Ford stood up in the cockpit from his cot, placed both hands on the pilots' seats, and leaned down to look out the front window. He wasn't wearing any goggles, so he couldn't see anything in the dark sky. Ford went back to the laptop to verify.

"Yup, that's her. I can see on the map here on the laptop."

"Stevens, yer son of a bitch! Yer made it. Cool. Have yer girl back in DC shut off her IR strobes. Will make it easier for us to intercept, plus verify that's our bird," Zeke told Ford.

Ford started typing a message to Jeanie and replied back verbally. "Wilco."

"Keep the jet's position lights on, though. We want to fly loose formation with the jet, not run inna her," Zeke said, thinking of pilot mishaps he had known throughout his flying career where pilots couldn't see each other.

Aircraft lighting was used for identifying the aircraft from both the air and ground, not necessarily for a pilot to see the ground. There were landing lights to help see the runway in the final phase of flight, but in this cruise phase of flight, only two sets of lights were used: a white strobe light that flashed on and off, and red and green wing-tip lights for position.

Zeke smiled. "Whatta yer know, Stevens? Your bird's external lighting just went out for a few seconds, den came back on. Contact. Get control of her on your liddle laptop and you'll have da lead."

DIA Headquarters, Washington, DC

Jeanie was still flying the stealth jet remotely, as the United States had done for so many millions of flight hours before. Whether it was an F-4 Phantom drone or a General Atomics MQ-9 Reaper or an RQ-4 Global Hawk, the country was getting quite good at unmanned flying from a remote console of some type.

The transfer of flight controls was as simple as Jeanie clicking a button, the same process used for transfer of a Reaper between Creech Air Force Base and someplace on the other side of the world. For Reapers, a pilot did the takeoff and landing/recovery at the local airfield, and the airborne flying stuff was done from Nevada. It was done thousands of times a day, and today was no different.

Jeanie saw the jet approaching the DAKID intersection, the invisible crossing of two airborne highways off W-174 that made a latitude and longitude point on a map.

She glanced down at the Peanut app box and typed: "YOU READY?"

A response came back from Ford immediately: "YES. LET'S DO THIS."

Jeanie uncrossed her legs and crossed them again as she moved the mouse with her right hand, staring at her screens. She saw Ford's laptop computer and clicked on it, and his computer icon was now illuminated.

With that one move, the signal was sent from her computer and across the fiber optics, zooming across the earth, to the satellites, to the B-2. Jeanie let out a breath as her icon turned red and Ford's turned green.

"Good to go. Positive connection," she said out loud.

The green light was satisfying to Jeanie because it meant Ford had the flight controls and there was a positive transfer. He now had 100 percent of the operational capability to do all flight maneuvers remotely from his laptop, and the connection for Jeanie was terminated.

The drawback of the red light on her computer meant that she could no longer see the jet on the map, follow Ford's movements such as direction, attitude, or airspeed, or track to him onto Bangalore. The connection was permanently terminated, a drawback of the system.

"Godspeed, Ford."

Jeanie's cyber work was now complete.

The House of Roosevelt Sky Bar, Rooftop, 27 Zhongshan East 1st Road, WaiTan, Huangpu Qu, Shanghai, China

Bai was on his smartphone listening but could not believe what he was just told. He was having trouble comprehending what he was hearing and stared down at the ground in silence. Standing in the hallway near the bathroom in a daze, he took the phone off his ear and walked briskly inside the men's room. Bai then threw up all over the counter and sink, dinner and stomach acid covering the immaculately clean white marble.

He had salvia and stomach acid hanging on his chin while his dry heaving could be heard by other men in the locked stalls.

"Chief, hang on. Hang on," Bai told him, wiping his mouth with a paper towel. *Holy crap*, he thought. "How sure are you about this, Chief?"

The maintenance chief talked off Bai's ear for a solid three minutes, and all Bai could say was to moan in agreement. Others passed by Bai, now out of the bathroom and standing in the hallway. He turned his body so no Chinese generals would see his face.

"You must tell General Chen at once," announced the maintenance chief.

Inbound to AKAGA Waypoint off Bangalore International Airport for Yelahanka Arrival

"What do you think, Stevens?" Zeke asked from up front in the B-2. "Pretty easy to fly?"

"Control inputs are the same as the sim at Creech. I can see everything pretty well on this screen. Fuel numbers are good, airspeed and power settings check. Moving map has us landing in Bangalore in eighteen minutes. Match with what you're seeing?"

Smitty shook his head up and down and gave a thumbs-up to Zeke from across the cockpit.

"Yup. Ol' Smitty here just gave yer a thumbs-up," replied Zeke.

Ford and the B-2 crew verified the weather, NAVAIDS, and landing data, and briefed up the instrument approach into Yelahanka Bangalore.

"Obviously I can't see out the window for a visual approach, so as planned, shoot the ILS to the west for landing. I'm tuned up back here and have positive ID. I'll continue the lead, and, sir, perhaps you just follow the Black Scorpion in for a low pass. I'll stop her off the taxiway until you land behind me and full stop. Good?"

The B-2 pilots were listening and preparing their own jet to land. Ford was in his old Devil Dragon checklists, too, using the flight manual they took when obtaining that jet not too long ago. It was a risk to take, making an educated guess that the jets were identical, or close to it, but it was all they had.

Ford, sensing a lull in the descent, waved his wings a bit and changed direction a few degrees to fool around, partly to have some fun, and partly to see if the two pilots up front were paying attention. He was quietly laughing.

"Stevens. Nice try. You don't think we see ya doin' your liddle wing-waggle out there?"

Air Force Station (AFS) Yelahanka, Bangalore, India

"Is that sound what I think it is?" Robert asked Mark, then glanced to Emily.

Mark smiled ear to ear. "You bet your ass it is. You can't forget a growl like that one."

He was referring to the unique sound of the Black Scorpion, which definitely sounded like Devil Dragon because of the loud snarl that came off the jet. While the B-2 was quiet, especially when approaching someone on the ground, the Black Scorpion made a pretty impressive presence.

Pinky smiled. "Black Scorpion? Sounds like a rocket."

The four of them stepped outside onto the dark tarmac, along with Ravi, and stood looking out into the starlit sky. Nothing could be seen with the naked eye.

Some of the hangar security team were smoking where they shouldn't have been and were startled by everyone's rapid presence; they put out their cigarettes quickly. They, too, looked to the approach end of the runway.

"That's my Ford!" Emily shrieked with delight. "I knew he could do it. Told you, Mark!"

Both jets landed and were now taxiing in, and Ravi had the ground crew standing by. It was loud and chaotic, with the taxi directors shaking their heads in frustration, attempting to direct Black Scorpion to parking with no one physically present at the controls. Ravi ran over and told the young taxi director kid no one was in there, that it was a robot, and to relax.

The B-2 taxied to its parking spot and shut down, as the newer Jet A fuel trucks pulled up in front of her. Emily stood in front of the B-2 as the engines spooled down, and she was all smiles at Ford's return.

Robert walked under the Black Scorpion first, as he had done on the deck of the USS *Abraham Lincoln* for Devil Dragon not too long ago. He checked out the landing gear, the underside of the fuselage, nose section, and wings. Pinky followed close behind, using a flashlight.

"This looks like damn Devil Dragon's twin sister, except for this flat, embedded glass component right here," Robert said, pointing to what they would soon confirm was a laser weapon.

Mark unlatched the hatch from the nose gear area, lowered the ladder, and climbed up a steep ten feet into the cockpit. Robert followed him, then Pinky.

They were all standing in the cockpit of the newest Chinese stealth jet, freshly cyber hijacked, and they were in awe.

"Well no shit, dumbass. Look at that beauty!" Mark yelled.

The House of Roosevelt Sky Bar, Rooftop, 27 Zhongshan East 1st Road, WaiTan, Huangpu Qu, Shanghai, China

The view on the Bund section of the river continued to be a striking view, with the illuminated skyscrapers extending through the clouds. The neon and white lights reflected off the glistening water as the water taxis and flat barges navigated the river. It resembled Baltimore's LB Skybar and Boston's Lookout at the Envoy Hotel, wrapped into one.

Bai stood on the lower level of the outdoor bar and thought about how he was going to relay this disturbing news to his boss. He formulated a plan in his mind, and passed by the busy wait staff, who were catering to the Chinese leadership's every need just one-story above them. Bai took in a deep breath.

At the top of the Sky Bar was a secluded and private area for about fifty guests, all by-name invitations from the owner, and tonight it was full of the country's leadership. China's political and air force military leadership were all there, drinking, laughing, and taking in the festive atmosphere. Anyone who was someone in China's national security apparatus was present.

Bai walked up the stairs, his feet heavy like cement shoes, making a mental note that he felt like he was moving in slow motion. The foggy mist of the river and cooler air hit him up at the top, as the security detail stopped him a second time to verify that he was allowed to have access.

He navigated through the crowd of executives, aides, politicals, and Generals, finally locating General Chen again. Chen was surrounded by peers and senior officers alike, telling stories in his loud, boisterous voice. Bai could tell he was drinking and close to being drunk.

"Sir, do you have a moment?" Bai asked. Bai swallowed and could hear his saliva make a sound in his throat going down, despite the music and crowd talking. He was trembling now, his knees weak and his hands shaking.

"What? What is it Bai?" Chen said to him.

It was a difficult position for a junior officer to be in, but Bai knew his boss would want to know—had to know. This was the speaking truth to power he learned about in his strategic leadership classes back at PLA Air Force Aviation University in Changchun.

"Sir, I just received a phone call from the chief back at the hangar," Bai started explaining, his voice suddenly cracking and dry, sounding like he was going through puberty a second time.

"What?"

"Sir, I said I just received a call from the chief," Bai said again, this time louder.

Just then some passing officers came by laughing, slapping Chen on the back. It definitely interrupted Bai's message.

"Well? What do you want, Bai? What is it? What did the chief say?" Chen asked again.

Bai's legs just about buckled, and he cleared his throat. "Sir...it's the Black Scorpion."

"They are landing? Good."

Bai paused and swallowed again. "Not exactly, General."

Air Force Station (AFS) Yelahanka, Bangalore, India

The cockpit was as open and large as a C-130, large enough to fit even a navigator or extra crew member. It also had two bunks for sleeping, in addition to a small lavatory and galley for meals.

Robert took a close look at where the seats used to be, even noticing the rocket scarring on the far sides of the cockpit where the seats went upward and out of the jet.

Mark took out his secure phone and dialed directly. "Sir, Mark Savona here. In the green," Mark said to Calvin Burns back in the States.

"Hey Mark, how's things? Oh...green here, too," Calvin said, checking his Peanut traffic light. Calvin had been nervously waiting for the call.

"Terrific, sir. Quick update for you. Black Scorpion landed safely here in Bangalore, and she was just towed into the hangar. India is definitely a friend of the US. I'm standing in the cockpit talking to you right now, looking straight up through the ceiling...and no kidding, Ford was right. These Chinese pilots were ejected out, seats and all, and the top of the cockpit is gone."

Calvin chuckled. "Well, maybe Reggie and the boys from Gulfstream can modify it for us again. Just kidding. Go ahead, Mark, tell me more."

Reggie Bryant was the CEO of Gulfstream in Savannah, Georgia, who helped modify a G650ER business jet on their last mission together with Devil Dragon.

"Sir, no need. We've planned for Ford and Pinky to just fly her out tomorrow evening, as you know, wearing some cold-weather gear. Open cockpit style. No changes from the briefs."

Open cockpits were not out of the ordinary. One of the most popular open-cockpit aircraft flying today was the Pitts Special, but certainly not at the altitude and speeds Black Dragon was capable of.

"Got it. Got it. World War I–style. OK. And how are all the aircrew?" Calvin asked. "And our guys?"

Mark looked around outside the cockpit and down below in the hangar. "All present in India, sir. Robert is with me in the cockpit here, taking a look at the new pilot seats he is going to install. Outside, holding hands of course, are Ford and Emily. Pinky is looking at the jet, too. B-2 getting fueled up for their flight back."

Robert threw him a standard stoic look. "Seats. They won't be new."

Mark shushed him, covered the phone, and laughed. "Shut your mouth and get back to work."

Calvin kept talking. "Sounds solid. Thank you. Keep me informed. I'll also be meeting the jet at Pease in New Hampshire…I want to see this thing. Certainly, to say thanks to Ford and Pinky. I'll be working with Michelle Boyd on the undersecretary position stuff, but I'll let SecDef know your status, too. Otherwise, I'm off to Andrews, then New Hampshire. Call me, OK?"

"Yes, sir. We're all exhausted. Heading over to the Ritz-Carlton next," Mark said, wrapping up. Mark was peeking out the cockpit window, looking down at Ford hugging Zeke and Smitty. Zeke tussled Ford's hair.

"One more thing. And keep this quiet, but Ford Stevens just came out on the major's list. I received a call from the chief of Air Force Reserve," Calvin said.

"That's cool. He'll be excited."

"Did you just say Ritz? They better have a government room rate. We're not made of money."

Bangalore-Hyderabad Highway, due east of Air Base, Bangalore, India
Bangalore, India was the home of one of the best cricket teams in all of India, the Royal Challengers Bangalore, or RCB. Loved by millions of fans, they are one of the original eight teams of the Indian Premier League.

Bangalore was also known to be a home to offices of nearly every major Fortune 500 company in the world, in addition to being a hotbed of information-technology companies. One of the most congested cities in India, it combined both immense wealth and poverty on any given block.

The city was exotic, multicultured, extremely heavy on traffic, and surrounded by huge crowds of bustling people everywhere one looked, and there was no preparation for a visit to this part of the world. Cows, monkeys, rickshaws, and motorcycles were all over the place, squeezing anywhere possible. Hundreds of thousands of people were on the streets, both day and night, at times giving the appearance of doing nothing while so many others were conducting their business of the day. The mysterious sights and smells were unlimited. One direction had mothers with babies on the back of fast motorcycles, while another direction featured animals romping the streets and roaming building rooftops freely. Exotic may be an understatement to describe Bangalore.

It was not out of the ordinary then when the two Chinese intelligence officers returning from a collection mission against a foreign technology company spotted two lights-out aircraft flying over their car in the dark sky. It wasn't that they saw the black jets on a black sky, but it was that they heard them first. They heard Black Scorpion.

The driver, a young twenty-five-year-old male and his intelligence partner, a thirty-one-year-old male, both cyber-espionage experts, thought it was quite strange that two jets like this would be flying over this time of night, especially with no lights on.

The driver turned the car around on the highway, due east of the airport, and stopped on the side of the road. Both men got out, stepped over the rotting fruits and vegetables, and walked over to the metal cyclone fence to peek through.

"That's an interesting sound on an airplane. Why would two black jets like that be here?" the driver asked the passenger. "Do you find that strange? Go get your binoculars out."

The two men continued to look at the far end of the taxiway where the jets were now parked. Holding up the binoculars, they could see the flurry of activity with the ground crew.

"Wait a second. That one jet is an American B-2. The other jet...the other one has...our PLAAF star on it? The tail, that's our jet?"

Black Scorpion had indeed, a black, red, and yellow star on her tail, barely visible.

"Let me see that. Give me your binocs."

The binocs were transferred between the men again.

"I've never seen an airplane like that. What kind of jet is it? Why is our jet flying with an American B-2?"

Both men got in the car, left the fence line, and drove for the main entrance of the air base.

The House of Roosevelt Sky Bar, 27 Zhongshan East 1st Road, WaiTan, Huangpu Qu, Shanghai, China

Bai cleared his throat for the last time as he looked Chen in the face. Chen, growing more impatient by the second, wanted to know why Bai called him over and didn't fully explain fast enough.

Here we go, Bai thought to himself, as he saw Chen red faced, as Bai has seen so many times before.

"Sir, the Black Scorpion pilots ejected from the jet. Only one seat locator beacon was detected by satellite. The locator beacon is coming from the heavy mountains in Yunnan."

"Ejected? What? No...no. How...how do you know these details?" Chen asked, knowing this was deeply troubling.

"Beijing called the maintenance chief directly in the hangar. Everyone knows by now, sir. Message traffic is going out secure any minute to all general officers in a formal situation email."

"No, no, cannot be true. No! Must be a mistake..." Chen said, not wanting to believe the news.

The chief of PLAAF at that moment looked at his secure phone, as did all the other generals and political leadership at the Sky Bar. At nearly the same precise moment, they all read of Chen's blunder, then scanned the crowd to look for him.

"No, Bai. Bai! What has happened to Black Scorpion?"

"Sir, the jet has disappeared. No wreckage has been reported yet, and Beijing has declared the aircraft as missing and presumed crashed. Operations Center has already gone on record saying it is a mishap, and the jet is lost. I'm sorry, sir."

All the generals in the room were staring at Chen now, his fate sealed in that very moment. Losing one jet was a bit much, but now Chen had lost two jets on his watch. Chen was never going to get the extra star to full general or the Politburo or Central Committee position he'd sought for so long. A flying career, a life started by his father in the Chinese army so many years ago, now over by the actions of someone else.

Chen was stunned and slowly turned to see all the generals, his peers and superiors, staring at him with both disdain and disbelief. His whole life, Chen was a trusted teammate of their team, and in an instant, he was now garbage to the seniors.

"No, no, Bai...this cannot be true," Chen said, dropping his glass of baijiu, as ice and glass scattered across the rooftop bar floor loudly. He then grabbed Bai with both hands, shaking him by both shoulders. "No! No!" he yelled loudly.

It was at that moment Chen started to feel the numbness in his right arm, then just as fast, in his left. His body started to feel the immense pressure, the tightening of his chest, his heart feeling the uncontrollable pain. His numbness was now felt down far in both arms, and he stumbled backward as the crowd gasped. His chest felt like a truck was parked on top of him.

"Sir, sir, are you OK?" Bai asked, but it was too late.

Chen's searing pain ran to his back now and hurriedly to his stomach and jaw. Wheezing, Chen stood motionless. Short of breath and in a rapid cold sweat, he stepped back and bumped the waist-high glass wall with his hips. The wall was a clear, see-through rectangular piece of glass that separated the upper private bar roof area from the lower. The entire crowd of Chinese leaders looked and gasped, watching as Chen grabbed his chest with both hands.

General Chen's massive heart attack was in full force, unstoppable and uncontrollable. His heart had stopped beating upon the news of losing Black Scorpion, the blood no longer pumping through his clogged arteries and overweight body, and he would soon be lifeless.

"My jet. No…" Chen struggled to speak as his weight broke the glass wall, shattering two panes of glass. The sound echoed across the restaurant. Chen, gasping, and now unstable, pushed through the Sky Bar glass wall and his lifeless body fell to the rooftop bar below.

Chen was dead.

Ritz-Carlton, Bangalore, India, Eighth Floor

Ford and Emily had just showered in the room and were ready to meet the rest of the team upstairs to celebrate the landing at the Ritz Carlton's The Bang Rooftop Bar. He used the hotel shave kit since he forgot his, and they went into the bedroom together.

"Ford, I am so proud of you," Emily told him, resting her head on his bare chest. He ran his hand through her blond hair.

"Thanks. I couldn't have done it without you, without the rest of the team. I also can't wait until we get home, start talking more about the wedding. Us, together. Bachelor party at The Skull Creek Boathouse on Hilton Head. New home. Kids," Ford said, now with excitement.

"Ford, why won't you propose? Do it now. Right now," Emily said laughing, practically begging him. "Then we can go on holiday after we're done here."

"Easy, come on, now. I haven't talked to your dad yet. Two days or so. I will call him after I land," Ford replied, full knowing he had the ring already purchased and in his flight-suit pocket.

"Why put it off, love?" she said with a sexy grin, showing her beautiful white teeth.

Ford thought about it, but he really was a man of tradition regarding family. He knew his own family would be disappointed if he did not go the traditional route, and including her parents in the excitement was the only option for him. He loved her and wanted to do things right.

"Emmy, I love you, but it's worth the short wait. We both know I'll do it soon. Not being cold or anything, but…I want to ask your father for his permission. OK, Em?"

She lifted her head up to look at him and nodded. "Yes, love, I understand. I don't like waiting, though," she said, slapping him playfully on the chest.

"I know you don't want to wait, but that's my decision. Wait, our decision. We have our whole lives together."

Emily put her hand on his face now, leaning up to kiss him. "Yes, I agree. My dad will be excited. Even bigger, so will my mum."

Emily walked over and poured herself a cup of chai, the legendary Indian tea. Though it was usually consumed and enjoyed at a chai stand that doubles as a social center, she drank it in private while nibbling on some Indian snacks of samosas, pakoras, and aloo tikki. "Quite good, really."

Ford sat up now, taking a drink of wine from the night stand. Actually, he gulped it like it was water.

"Easy, Ford, you have to fly tomorrow."

Ford thought about it, bit into a jalebi sweet, and agreed. "One more drink. Then I'll stop."

Miller Residence, Hudson Street, Hawley, Pennsylvania

Michael and Rex were playing with the radio again, and Rex was learning a tremendous amount all by himself. Getting books from the Main Avenue Library near the Lackawaxen River on subjects such as ham radios and geography got him super excited in the hobby.

"Rex, that station transmitting was from Stratford, New Zealand. Check that out on your map," Michael told him.

Michael had just finished organizing another weekly session of the Family Olympic Games at Woodloch Pines and made it home to help Rex push a blue pin into the map.

Rex then looked in his guide book for some more frequency bands that might be in Asia or other Pacific Rim countries. He paged through the chapters.

Both Millers listened in closely after an agreed-upon frequency was found. Rex sometimes enjoyed just listening locally to Wayne County fire, police, and ambulance calls, attempting to see if something exciting was happening around sparsely populated Hawley. His daydreaming was normal for a ten-year-old boy, just hoping for some local excitement. They listened in again, this time from someplace else on earth.

"Yes, talk to you next time. This is VU2XY, signing off."

"VU2XY? Where is that, Dad?" Rex asked.

"Don't know. Here you go, Rex. Look it up again."

Rex looked through the book one more time, checking on the call letters in the beginning of the call signs. *VU. VU. Where is that? And his accent?* Rex thought as he looked in the thick guide book.

"Dad, that was Navi Mumbai, India!"

Michael nodded. "OK, Rex. Pretty exciting, son. Put it in your logbook and map."

Ritz-Carlton, Bangalore, India, The Bang Rooftop Bar

Located at the Ritz-Carlton in Bangalore was the city's highest rooftop bar, complete with panoramic views of the city, visits from celebrity DJs, creative cocktails, and comfy outdoor furniture with pergolas.

Sitting around the fire pit and listening were Robert, Pinky, and Mark, telling stories, drinking, and laughing. The Bang was beginning to get crowded, and the beat of the music was heavy, as was the sunset and haze, but the bar was open until the wee hours of the morning for the guests.

"There he is!" Mark yelled, as Ford and Emily walked in, arm in arm. "How you doin', kid?" He sipped his trademark scotch.

Ford looked at Mark's clothing, smiling. "I bet this is the first time India has seen an outfit like that," he said, busting Mark's chops for wearing red wrestling shoes, a man-bun, and a cutoff Washington Nationals jersey.

"Easy, Mr. Pilot," Mark told him, as he reached for his vibrating smartphone.

Ford and Emily sat down around the fire pit as the waiter came over to take their order.

Mark felt his phone vibrate again, looked, and put the phone to his ear. "Go ahead, Ravi, I can barely hear you, but go ahead."

Mark looked out over the city, then looked up, and finally at Robert and Emily. He nodded a few times, only said a few words, and then ended the call.

He turned to the team. "We got problems. Big-ass problems."

Emily looked the most concerned, using her strong emotional intelligence skill set to see what was the matter. "Mark, sit. Here. What is it?"

"That was Ravi over at the air base. Seems two Chinese men got into a firefight at the hangar with his security detail. Somehow, they were able to get on base and get near the hangar, and were poking around. Ravi's security forces team had deadly force orders and engaged them in a firefight. Both men were killed. Guys had pistols, QSZ-92s. No phones on them, and none in the car they had."

"You bet your ass we have problems. Standard issue weapons for Chinese intel," Robert commented. "Better get Jeanie to start digging around, see if they were sent, or just stumbled up the hangar from the landing. Either way, not good."

Ford raised his eyebrows. "How in the hell did they know we were here? Is there a tracking device on the aircraft we don't know about?"

"No, none that I know of. I dug all over Devil Dragon after we got her and went through this jet the same way. Checked all the same places. Nearly identical. No smartphones by our Chinese pilots left behind either. Bird is clean," Robert responded.

"I agree with Robert, we'd better get Jeanie on it. This mission is in jeopardy now," Emily added.

Mark's phone rang again, vibrating in his pocket. "Well, speak of the devil. She's calling now."

Ford started laughing. "Mark's girlfriend. Who knew he had a girlfriend?"

"Shut it, Ford. This is serious," Robert told him, reflecting on his past. "Two Chinese were killed tonight. We have no idea where the hell they were from…what they were doing."

Ford took another swig, then held Emily's hand, as they all waited for Mark to quickly finish his call.

"Well, I relayed the info to her, and nothing has been transmitted that she has found. Zero. Could be unrelated, but nothing is showing in their systems for Bangalore aircraft," Mark shared with the team.

Emily was relieved and was somewhat selfish at this point. She wanted a quiet night and to be with Ford tomorrow, and the last thing she wanted to do was do was an escape-and-evade mission through the city of Bangalore.

"That's cool. OK, what do we do then?" Ford asked.

"Hang on, that's not all. She and Mr. Burns have something big. Remember our friend General Chen?"

"What about him?" Emily asked, looking at Mark with a smirk.

"Well, he's…dead. Jeanie just got done briefing Mr. Burns. She picked up the social media on Weibo by the maintenance crew in the hangar. Seems he had a heart attack in Shanghai after he was told the jet was missing due to the emitting ejection seat locators. Beijing got the seat signals, sent out a worldwide email to all general and flag officers."

"Wow! Dead, huh?" Robert asked.

"Dead?" Ford asked, smiling. "Based upon what Wu told us, the second missing jet must have crushed him."

"Yup. Dead," Mark answered.

Emily smiled and raised her glass. "To Wu Lee."

"To Wu," they all said in unison, clinking glasses and toasting.

Pinky took a sip of her Merlot, then spoke up. "Who is General Chen?" she asked.

The entire team broke out laughing.

Air Force Station (AFS) Yelahanka, Bangalore, India

The old, rusted-out post–World War II fuel truck they saw earlier was back, fueling up the Black Scorpion on the dark ramp. It was sometimes used for water, sometimes used for jet fuel: the local Bangalore people were innovative in their business dealings. Ravi's ground crew, along with Robert, did everything they could for an ops-normal launch of the peculiar aircraft.

Robert's installation of the seats seemed to fit in nicely and allowed the seat positions to be adjusted back and forth on the vertical portion, as well as forward and rearward for reaching the rudder pedals. The only thing they were missing were ejection seat rockets and survival kits with beacons, but it was a mitigated risk they took for a one-hop administrative flight home.

Pinky and Ford were in the flight planning room discussing their route of flight to the US, based upon winds, weather, and destination.

"Ford, I'm ready for a quick brief. Route is complete. You ready?"

"Shoot."

"OK, out of Bangalore to the north past New Delhi; northwest bound to Middle East Balad, Iraq, then Incirlik, Turkey; across Europe to Scotland; across the North Atlantic to St. Johns, Newfoundland; down to Pease Air National Guard Base in New Hampshire. I've got the route calculated at all sorts of airspeeds, so it depends on the missing roof and the noise I would guess. I'll put into it the flight management software."

Ford smiled, thinking it was similar to a B-1 flight, with long legs, fuel in the air, and tight cockpits.

Pinky waived her hands around at the wrist. "Lastly, no flight plan filed. Not talking to anyone, no radar, no flight following, and no lights. Black. Right?"

"Yes. Yes, Mark?" Ford answered, then asked Mark to confirm. "Right?"

Mark nodded his head. "Absolutely. Can't talk to a soul. Don't let anyone see you. Silent."

"Weeiiirrddd," Pinky told them in a high-pitched voice.

Ravi, Mark, Emily, and Robert all sat in the couch area listening in and barely said anything during their flight-related discussions.

"Based upon the performance of Devil Dragon, we can fly pretty fast. Total flight is about 8,100 miles. I'd say about six to nine hours total flight time. We can talk airspeeds while we're inbound. Should beat these guys home," Ford replied, smirking, pointing with his thumb to the motley crew on the couch.

Walking out to Black Scorpion now, Ford shook hands with Ravi and thanked him, and said good-byes to the team with some hugs. In front of the aircraft on the line, Ford squeezed and kissed Emily privately. He handed her his cell phone and wallet.

Ford whispered in her ear. "Soon, you'll be Mrs. Ford Stevens. We'll be engaged. I love you. See you tomorrow."

Ford was immediately quiet. He was scared shitless again, as the jet reminded him of his flight on Devil Dragon and Wu's passing. He teared up thinking of it, squeezing Emily hard. He had flown thousands of flight hours, yet this flight felt different.

"Are you OK? You scared, Ford?" Emily asked him warmly. "It's all right, Ford. I'm here."

"Yes. Yes, I am. But I can do this. I'll focus, and I'll get through it. I can do it."

Ford did his special breathing. *In through my nose for a four count, out my mouth,* he said to himself. *I can do this. I can do this.*

A tear ran down Emily's cheek. "Fly safe, Ford. I love you, too," she whispered into his ear.

He pulled away from her, smiling. Ford turned to talk away a few steps and stopped. "Emily."

She looked up at him, eyes glassy and red. "Yes?"

"We get engaged. Tomorrow. OK?"

She nodded.

Ford climbed in, joining Pinky, who was already strapped into the cockpit. Robert was up there too, helping and observing, just to see if they needed anything. Wearing full cold-weather gear and oxygen masks, and carrying paper flight charts as a backup, they were ready for takeoff.

Ravi and Robert stashed two backpack bags of prepared food for their meals while airborne, along with some water and toilet paper and an extra set of hand warmers. They also had their overnight bags from the hotel full of dirty laundry, complete with the complimentary Ritz-Carlton shave kit.

The glass cockpit came alive from the ground power cart, and her two outboard engines were quickly started. Stunning glass components, all computer generated, appeared on the displays. The primary flight instruments were state of the art and modern, displaying everything from oil pressures to the attitude indicators to airspeed and navigational aids. It was an attractive cockpit and layout, impressive to any pilot.

"Ford, I'm not up on my Chinese. I took French at the academy. But I can see in these Devil Dragon checklists where you translated it into English. Just keep me honest here," Pinky told him, laughing.

"You got it, Pinky. Pre-taxi checklist next," Ford replied.

The two engines were loud to both ground observers, as well as inside the cockpit, and Robert ensured he used double hearing protection. The remaining two engines would be auto ignited after getting some air down the intakes.

Robert tapped Ford on the shoulder, since he had no way of talking with him, and shook his hand. Robert did the same for Pinky, and they said their good-byes.

Ford and Pinky ran through their checklists as best they could, with most components being in the same location as Devil Dragon. The standard instruments were in the same location, and they were able to pull up all the navigational aids for departure.

"Ford, confirm for me internal nav position," Pinky asked.

"Yup, good to go. What, no satellites?"

"Not yet. I'll get a good sweep airborne. I'll figure it out once we level off," Pinky replied. "Wait, we can't do that. Internal Nav System only. Operational security, right? No transmitting of data, Mark told us…"

The ground crew, along with the entire DIA team, stood on the far side of the flight line as Ford taxied the Chinese jet for departure. Everyone saluted, and Ford flashed the landing light one time. Ford and Pinky then saw everyone wave.

Ford got one last glance at Emily. *Bye, babe. See you soon*, he said silently.

"Pinky, takeoff checklist," announced Ford.

PART 10

MOUNTAINS

302 Miles Northeast of New Delhi, Climbing through 33,250 feet

The clear, dark sky at this altitude only showed the stars and moon, while down below was mostly obscure black. Nearly zero flickers of illuminated light lay ahead, signifying the approach of the Himalayan Mountains with very limited urban areas or people. Every so often they would get a glisten of the bright moonlight off a tall, snow-covered peak, but most times there was nothing for light to reflect off of.

The Himalayan Mountains, some of the most rugged terrain anywhere in the world, bordered India, Nepal, Tibet, Pakistan, and China. Snow covered this "Wonder of the World" area at the high altitudes, black and gray in color in the daytime and full of hard granite rock. Only the most daring and professional climbers attempted to conquer them. It had the ten highest peaks in the world, with five of the main ones somewhat near Ford and Pinky: K2, Mount Everest, Kanchenjunga, Annapurna, and Nanga Parbat Peak. The most popular mountain, Mount Everest, generally located in Nepal and Tibet, was just over twenty-nine thousand feet. This was just one of thirty Himalayan peaks that rose to over twenty-four thousand feet in height.

Straight ahead to the north, Ford could see the overcast skies down below from the cloud layer, and based upon cold weather and infamous history, a likely snow storm.

"This is some jet, Ford. Very nice. Smooth. I can't imagine what weapons this thing can deliver, especially in congested airspace and territories. Undetected on radar, too," Pinky commented.

Ford kept up his instrument scan, although the jet was on autopilot at the moment. He looked at the moving map display, fuel flow, and levels, then the outside air temperature. He was surprised it was only -23 degrees Fahrenheit. "Hey, not too cold up here. Good gear from Robert, huh? Not too cold at all."

Wearing multiple layers of cold weather gear, they were both much larger in body size: polypropylene underwear, then insulated flight suits, two layers of flight gloves, a baklava, and parkas to round it off.

"Yup, I'm not that cold either. But this oxygen mask will hurt for another five hours, sucking on the air," Pinky replied, laughing.

"From your earlier comment. Now we know why we grabbed another one. Another jet, that is. I mean, you know, they stole our cyber technology and used our US smarts, so…we're only taking back what's ours. Right?" Ford said with a chuckle.

"When does it end, Ford? I mean, they take from us, we take from them," Pinky asked, reflecting on the smoke-and-mirrors game.

"Pinky, this stuff has been going on between humans and their countries for two thousand years. It will never change. The players will, but defending one's nation and people will remain the same for our kids and our kids' kids. What complicates it now is cyber."

They sat alone, looking at the dark below them for another minute, taking in the jet and the dark below them.

"So, Ford. Speaking of kids one day. What's up with you and Emily? Are you going to get engaged and—"

Suddenly, out of nowhere, the intercom between them went dead. The Black Scorpion, pushing out thrust and slicing through the sky with ease, instantaneously went silent and dark. The whoosh of the air coming from the missing cockpit roof was now the only thing heard. From behind them, they could hear and feel the turbines winding down. No intercom between the pilots, no cockpit lights, no flight instruments—a complete electrical and four-engine failure in an instant. All engines were completely dead and were providing zero thrust.

"Christ," Ford said in his mask. *What the fuck is this?* Ford said silently. *Class-one emergency brewing.*

"Pinky! Hey, can you hear me!" Ford yelled as loud as he could. "Air start! Air start!" No intercom between them meant they couldn't talk internally or externally. Not even a mayday to the outside world if they tried.

He moved the throttles immediately to what he thought may be the air start position and struggled to find the ignition switches in the dark. He used his small flashlight in an attempt to find the switches, looking around and fumbling in this strange cockpit. Ford found and toggled the ignition switches multiple times, but nothing happened, as the jet remained dead and silent.

Ford looked around the dark cockpit, not a lick of light illuminating from anywhere. He went from a cockpit lit up like a bright Christmas tree to a dark alley in a nanosecond. *This is a hell of a time to have an electrical failure*, Ford said quietly. *We got a major shit show boiling here.*

The powerless glider they were riding in was now lifeless, and they were paying the price for the actions of others. Ford and Pinky were suffering from three issues outside of their grasp.

First, the outdated 1946 International Harvester fuel truck that provided them fuel was, unfortunately, filled with both Jet A fuel and water, not fully cleaned out from the driver's last use hours ago. This meant that the fuel tank on the truck pumped an overwhelming mix of water, along with Jet A fuel, into the Black Scorpion's fuel tanks.

Second, the torrid, freezing air at altitude seeped into the small, unseen left-wing openings from where the bird strikes occurred recently, causing super cold air to surround the wing fuel tanks and lines. The chief of maintenance and the chief of engineering patched it up, but the wing was never the same. At twenty-three degrees below zero, the water ice crystals multiplied at an alarming rate, causing ice to form inside the fuel tank and lines. From the tank, the ice continued to form into the main fuel lines and jammed up the fuel pumps. With no fuel pumping into the engines due to blockage, fuel starvation occurred. No engines meant no generators to produce electricity for the avionics.

Lastly, the fuel lines all joined behind the first one-third of the fuselage so sharing of the fuel tanks could take place for aircraft weight and balance. With the freezing air being plunged in from the missing roof, the interior and exterior of the entire jet was cold soaked. Heated fuel from the engines, which was the normal process in many modern aircraft, could not keep up with the frigid air. The laws of physics were just not on their side.

Pinky kept looking around and had no idea what to say or do, especially since she couldn't hear Ford. This wasn't her jet, and although Pinky was a stellar pilot, she wasn't trained in any memorized procedures for emergencies in this make and model of aircraft.

Ford knew right away they were descending, gliding, and attempted to move the flight controls. First the stick, then rudder pedals. Nothing happened to the attitude of the jet, as Black Scorpion continued with her nose low, dropping out of the sky.

"Pinky! Air start didn't work! Try moving your controls!" he yelled again, but she could not hear him. Ford leaned over to her stick and moved it cross-cockpit, but nothing happened. No control inputs from her side either.

Immediately Ford started thinking of glide ratios and lift-to-drag math formulas from aerodynamics and how far this jet could go without engines. They were heavy, and it definitely would affect how far they could glide.

In his mind, he recalled Air Canada Flight 143, a Boeing 767 that in 1983 had to glide eighty miles due to fuel starvation. It was known in the aviation community as the "Gimli Glider." The pilots glided the aircraft down to a racetrack at a closed air force base and landed there. The Boeing aircraft flew with conventional manual flight controls using cables and pulleys, but today Black Scorpion was a modern, fly-by-wire system, with a complete electronic interface. No power meant no moveable flight control surfaces. After a few seconds of thought, Ford also didn't give a crap because they couldn't turn the jet, even if he wanted.

Pinky tried to locate a page in the flight checklists, a section for ram air turbines—something they could extend into the slipstream air to turn and generate power, but she could not read Chinese. The sections Ford translated to English were clearly marked, but no area labeled ram air that she could find. This definitely complicated their situation. Pinky looked out the window on the right side and could now see they were below the mountain ridges on her side.

"Ford! Ford! What do you want to do?" she yelled.

The altitude to lose would have been a lot longer time wise if they had to glide from altitude to, for example, the low terrain of Kansas, Texas, or the Atlantic Ocean shoreline. In northern India, though, it would just take a matter of a few short minutes before they hit terrain.

"Hey, hey, Pinky! Lock your harness, Pinky!" Ford yelled again, tapping her on the shoulder, then pointing to the lever. "We're going down! Lock your harness!"

Ford ensured his was locked, wishing they had ejection seats now, reflecting on how ironic it was that the only piece of equipment they needed was the only one they were missing. They both sat patiently and waited for what would be the shock of their young lives.

Oh my God. My parents. My brother and sister. I'm not ready. He closed his eyes. *Emily…we never got engaged. Why did I wait? And all my stupid-ass drinking. God, I am so sorry for everything I did. Forgive me.*

"Pinky, we are doing down! Brace for impact!" Ford yelled with his mask off now, pointing. He placed his hands on the dashboard and looked ahead as they penetrated in and out through the sky of snow. The jet rocked back and forth in the wind, most likely from the gusts the mature mountains produced. He looked to his left and could barely see the mountains passing by the jet's left side in the steep and fast descent. Ford then looked ahead, and his previously snowy view disappeared. As in a dark gloomy bedroom after the lights were out, they could now see nothing out the front windows: no mountains, no snow, no moon or stars as they glided down to earth like a heavy brick.

Heading north into the Indian Himalayas at night, without a mayday call, in a jet without a flight plan, on no one's radar, their dreadful fate was sealed.

East of Rishikesh, India, 17,322 feet near Nepal border, Himalayans

BBBOOOOOMMMM. BBBOOOOOMMMM.

The impact of both wings being ripped off by tough granite was the most ferocious jolt Ford and Pinky had ever felt. The wings ripped off at their root where they connected to the fuselage, along with the rear stabilizer and elevator. The wings, tail, and elevators immediately fell a short distance and sat visible on top of the snow but were soon to be covered in the storm. Because of the ice in their tanks and the frigid weather, there was no flash, no fire, and the small sparks were short lived.

Holy shit, holy shit…save me. I don't want to die, Ford kept thinking as they scraped the jagged mountains.

Ford had never been so scared in his life, taking short breaths and holding on to the dashboard for dear life. Pinky's teeth were chattering, and her arms were shaking, as the cockpit and fuselage spun around 360 degrees like a helicopter's rotor blades.

Both pilots yelled as they were jerked into their harnesses with a purpose, as the front portion of the jet slammed down hard onto a small but firm angled plateau of snow, ice, and rock. The fuselage continued to slide downward for hundreds of feet at a high rate of speed, like a dragster at a race. The jet was at a steep descent rate, not to a flat runway, but a sloping piece of terrain.

The cockpit and fuselage began a violent roll, right over left eight different times, top to bottom, top to bottom, unforgiving to both the components and people inside. The aircraft composites were no match for the toughness of Mother Nature, and the barren mountain crushed the cockpit on the co-pilot's side directly into Pinky's body. The beautiful glass screens that just moments ago displayed maps and flight instruments all the home way to America were heard cracking and breaking. Finally landing upright and at a downward forty-five-degree angle, the carcass came to an intense halt. The brutally damaged aircraft stopped hard in a cavernous crack angled downward in the ice—a crevasse—and in complete darkness.

Ford's legs were nearly crushed by the dashboard, getting him stuck between the temporary seat and the front console. The impact had crumpled the space between the pilots' seats like an accordion. Cold now had just about covered his back from behind, flowing into the cockpit from the open gash where the ceiling and fuselage used to be. Despite wearing a helmet, Ford slammed the front of his head on the front console in such a way that his brain bounced in its cerebrospinal fluid, causing a concussion. He sat forward, hanging in his harness, completely unconscious.

Pinky's severe head injury was as a result of the side of the aircraft caving in on her from the right side during the fuselage rolls. Her traumatic brain injury had rattled her brain so badly that her body shut down completely. The awful blow to her skull, even though she was wearing her helmet, was just too violent and forceful for any human. The gray brain matter was external to her skull now, hidden on the right side of her flight helmet. Her blood splatter had sprayed along the frame where the window used to be. Even though it was pitch black, she sat with her eyes wide open, motionless and at peace. Pinky did not make it.

Base Operations Building, Pease Air Force Base, New Hampshire

The door opened to the C-20, and the team of Mark, Robert, and Emily climbed out from their long flight to the United States. They walked toward the Base Operations Building smiling and laughing, looking forward to getting into the hangar to see Ford and Pinky.

Calvin Burns stood at the edge of the flight line, stern faced, wearing a black trench coat; he did not look happy.

"Hi, sir. What's going on? How'd they make out, good?" Mark asked.

"I don't know. Been here for hours waiting. Was hoping you would tell me," Calvin replied sternly, looking at the three of them.

"They're not here?" Emily asked, turning her head and pointing toward the large hangar. "Bloody hell. Where did they land?"

"All I know is that they were supposed to be here hours ago, and there is no sign of them. Been chatting with your Department of Energy truck crew over there," Calvin said, pointing with his thumb. "Talked to the Air National Guard guys, telling them what I am doing visiting their base, and… certainly that's throwing off the base commander. Let's go inside."

THE BLACK SCORPION PILOT

Robert, the stoic, was already running though the what-ifs. His eyes moved up and left, brain going through the motions of what could have happened, from mishap to additional fuel to sabotage and maintenance issues.

They got into the Base Operations meeting room and closed the door to be alone. Robert spoke up first. "Sir, we had an issue with Chinese intelligence before we left. Two agents saw the jets land, or were dispatched to Bangalore, and had a shootout with Indian security forces. Indian forces killed both."

"OK, that's pretty significant," Calvin replied.

"Robert, you think Chinese intelligence affected their flight somehow? Sabotage?" Mark asked.

"No. No. Not necessarily, but just a fact to put on the table," Robert answered.

Emily walked over to the enormous world map and looked at the route of flight. She picked up a black grease pencil and drew out their waypoints on the plexiglass. "This was where they were planning on flying."

"Well, we'd be hearing some pretty strange calls by now if they landed for an emergency or fuel, right? They'd call our Operations and get a hold of one of us," Calvin said. "I hope that's what they did and that jet is parked for the daylight hours." Calvin was still cool as a cucumber, but his tone was different, a touch of tension not seen before. "I want to know where those pilots are."

Robert nodded at Calvin with a grim face. "Sir, we'll get a plan together right away and see what we can come up with. I'll get the base directories out and make calls to see if they landed anywhere close to their route. Some airfield has to have them."

"Get on it." Calvin then turned to Mark. "Mark, I'll need talking points right away. I'm going to have to recommend to the SecDef that he brief the president."

Mark nodded his head yes and immediately looked at Emily. He didn't say anything. They both knew what the end result could be for an overdue aircraft, especially one that wasn't being tracked on radar or a flight plan. Words didn't need to be said for the pending disastrous outcome. She stared back at him, and tears welled up in her eyes. She closed them slowly, tilting her head down to the floor a bit, as two tears streamed down both cheeks.

"I'm sorry, Emily. We'll find them," Mark told her, giving her a hug.

E Ring, Office of the Secretary of Defense, the Pentagon, Washington, DC

"Yes, Mr. Secretary, that is correct. Missing. Both the jet and her pilots," Calvin told the secretary.

"I see. How the hell did that happen? What the hell?" Secretary Price replied. No reply from Calvin yet. "OK, what are you doing about it? Pilots OK?" asked the SecDef, not fully comprehending the details.

"Unknown reason for their delay, sir, and again, unknown status of pilots. My guys are quietly calling every base along the route of flight and inquiring if they landed. You may recall that the jet is undetectable on radar. We also flew this without a flight plan and without diplomatic clearances. I hate to say this, but they could be anywhere."

"Wonderful. Well, this is real fine situation you got us in here, Cal. POTUS will love this one," the SecDef said, taking off his cheater reading glasses and tossing them on his desk. "Why don't we have search parties out? Use the full gamut of our assets?"

"Sir, I don't recommend we do that. Remember, we stole this jet. No one knows except a small circle of people. We launch search parties all over the earth, the Combatant Commands, and we tip our hands. Despite the origin of the stealth plans coming from the US, we can't exactly broadcast what we did," Calvin explained.

The secretary waived over his military assistant, Rear Admiral Rocko Cooper, and pointed at the other extension in the office. Rocko picked up the extension phone and listened.

"Cal, I have Rocko on the line now. I want you two to discuss options. I want options, OK? Briefing POTUS, calling prime ministers, Hill scenario, whatever. This will screw the pooch on the cybersecurity bill if this gets out. Or worse for any number of items for the president...new health care bill, immigration, budgets, elections. Hell. List goes on. Got it?"

Both men agreed and said they would have a plan in two hours. They both silently didn't like that potential legislation and politics were somehow more of a concern than the lives of the pilots.

West of Chal, East of Leelam, India, near Nanda Devi Mountain, Himalayas

Ford opened his eyes, still leaning forward in his seat, and was colder than he'd ever felt before in his life. He swallowed, but barely any saliva came into his dry mouth. Nausea, confusion, and dizziness were in full swing as he closed his eyes again. Ford raised his arms out, and they immediately bumped up against something in the dark.

"Pinky? You there?" he asked. "Hell of a touchdown, huh? Man, I feel awful. Tired."

Ford took off his gloves and slowly reached up to the flashlight on his helmet, hand shivering, and turned it on. The damaged cockpit was in utter shambles, resembling something that would be found at an impound yard. The dashboard was not more than a foot in front of him, along with plenty of snow.

"How are you doing over there?" He turned his head to shine the light on his copilot. He squinted a moment to focus.

There was no response.

"Pinky? Hey, Pinky. Pinky!" Ford was yelling now, seeing her hanging in her seat harness, body stiff, frozen blood on her face, with her eyes open and her skin pale. Ford knew immediately what happened.

"Aw, come on. No, no, Pinky. Pinky…no! Oh, come on. God." Ford closed his eyes. "Pinky. I'm so sorry."

Ford closed his eyes and couldn't believe he'd lost her. *Fuck*, he said to himself, shaking his head slowly from side to side.

He looked around the crumpled cockpit as best he could and was surrounded by damaged components and snow. Ford looked down at his legs and saw they were jammed from the knee below, but not seriously injured. Hanging still in his harness, he knew he would fall out and into the dashboard, so he released it with one hand and held up his body weight with the other.

CLLLISP was heard as he rotated the circular seat harness to release himself. THUMP.

Ford was out of his seat now, tugging and lifting up on both his legs, pulling to break free of the small space that held his legs and boots between the seat and front dashboard. After about a minute of pulling and pushing up and down on each leg, he broke free.

He immediately crawled over the snow to Pinky to verify what he thought, confirming that she was dead. Ford touched her cold body on the neck, could not verify a pulse, and closed her eyes. "I'm sorry, Pinky. God bless."

Ford let out a sigh and took a long breath. He only moved around a few feet in the cockpit, but right away he could tell from his breathing that he must be pretty high up in altitude. He looked at his digital watch, and that glance told him two important things.

One, that he'd lain unconscious for about ten hours, telling him his head injury was serious. There was no way to verify this, but he knew the unprotected part of his forehead below his helmet had taken a heavy hit. The blunt-force trauma knocked him out, and Ford knew he was recovering from something, most likely a contrecoup head injury. His nausea, headache, and dizziness also clued him in.

Second, the altitude he was currently at was 13,320 feet above sea level, according to the altimeter part of his watch. Altitudes of zero (at sea level) to 10,000 feet were about the range in which a person could really think clearly and function successfully with normal oxygen. Above 10,000 feet, the human body acted differently. High altitude or acute mountain sickness included headache, dry cough, weakness, nausea, loss of appetite, and disturbed sleep.

The altitudes for mountain climbers were usually divided up into the following scale: 8,000–12,000 feet was High, 12,000–18,000 feet was Very High, and above 18,000 feet was Extremely High. The percentage of oxygen at sea level was about 21 percent. As altitude increased, the percentage was equal, but the number of oxygen molecules per breath was reduced. At Ford's altitude of just over 12,000 feet, there were about 40 percent fewer oxygen molecules for every breath. This explained why Ford felt the way he did.

Ford's body was undergoing changes that would take time. He was already feeling the depth of his breathing increasing. The pressure in his heart's arteries was increased, which forced his blood into sections of his lungs which were not normally used at lower altitudes. His body was also producing more red blood cells to carry oxygen.

OK. I'm high in the Himalayas without a phone or flight plan, off radar, with limited food. I have ice, but that won't work long term for water. Need to start assessing my situation here. Starts with food in my backpack under all this snow. And Pinky's backpack…

One Day Later, Base Operations Building, Pease Air Force Base, New Hampshire

"And so, sir, our recommendation is to move this Operations Center back home to DC. We feel that they are not coming here, and waiting twenty-four hours was a stretch, but worth it," Mark told Calvin.

Calvin rubbed his facial growth with his right hand, drinking a cup of Battle Grounds Coffee from nearby Haverhill that the base ops guys brought him.

Robert was sitting on some news that would be difficult for Emily to hear, but it had to come out now.

"Yes, I agree. We're all exhausted. Practically living in the same clothes. Let's pack it up."

Robert cleared his throat. "Sir, there is one more thing. I have talked to the chief of staff of Air Force Reserve, Lieutenant General Maria Ruiz. We have to discuss their casualty status."

"Their what?" Emily said with a stern voice.

Robert had a grim look on his face. "Their casualty status. The air force, and frankly all the services, have classifications for service members. Ford and Pinky would have to be declared dead, wounded, diseased, detained, captured or missing."

"Bugger me. Really? Piss off, Robert. We have to give them a title?" Emily said, throwing her arm down and slamming it on the table surface.

Calvin's fatherly and generous touch on her hand made Emily feel more comfortable. *Blimey. I still can't believe this is happening to me. Where are you, bloke? Why can't we find you?* Emily said to herself.

"Emily. Listen to me. We will continue to look for them. We'll be on the hunt and will never stop. It will be OK. We'll find them," Calvin reassured her.

Robert waited a few seconds. "Sir, General Ruiz also said we had to notify their next of kin, and...neither of them was...married...so..."

Emily had tears in her eyes now, with one tear streaming down a cheek. She turned to look out the window. *Married*, Emily thought.

"I am so sorry, Emily. And...so...sir, Air Force Reserve wants to send a casualty team to see the Stevens and the Pinkertons."

Calvin closed his eyes. "I know Marion and Chad Stevens very well, Ford's parents, as you know. I'll go in person. Today. Ask Maria to make plans for Pinky's parents with Headquarters Air Force. I'll facilitate Ford's notification. Missing status, right?"

Mark nodded, then took out his phone. "Sir, we can get you some fresh clothing at the Fox Run Mall over in Portsmouth, fly you down to Hilton Head at 1400, land at 1600. Would that work?"

Calvin nodded.

West of Chal, East of Leelam, India, near Nanda Devi Mountain, Himalayas

Ford used the dim flashlight on his helmet to see as he moved the snow around in the cockpit, resting often, searching for their backpacks. Wearing the gloves Robert had gotten for him, he slowly dug in the rear of the cockpit, exhausted at just moving his body around in the small, dark space.

Finally locating both backpacks, he took a few long sips from the water bottles. He found food that would last a few days or more, dirty clothes, Pinky's make-up kit, and his partial shave kit. Dehydrated, he located all the bottles of water in the backpacks and laid them out so he could see what he was dealing with. He'd have to figure out his water plan soon in order to survive.

Ford also sat for a moment thinking about Pinky's clothing. He was considering using her cold-weather gear in some capacity, too, although he wasn't sure for what use just yet. He was creeped out by the idea of taking her clothing. *She's gone, so she doesn't need it. Kinda weird to take it from her, but she would want me to have it to live.*

Sitting on his knees, Ford looked around a bit at the bleak wreckage he was in. The cockpit was still angled at about forty-five degrees, nose low, and where the windows used to be was complete snow and darkness. The rear of the cockpit was gone, exposing jagged and sharp composite fibers and hundreds, if not, thousands of broken colored wires. It was exposed to the night sky at the top, almost like the opening of a cave.

Ford climbed on his hands and knees inside the cockpit the eight to ten feet of distance to the surface of the earth and immediately felt the forceful wind and wind-chill temperature change. Down in the crevasse where the cockpit was located between ice and the earth, he was concealed and protected from the mountain's elements, and it was warmer. Not up here. On the surface of the earth, Ford looked around like a ground hog searching for his shadow and was now fully exposed to the dismal elements.

The only illumination was the brilliant starlight on the clear night, and no city or suburban lights could be seen. He moved his head and body around in a full circle, searching, and realized there was absolutely nothing to see—no aircraft wreckage, no path of aircraft destruction to where he was presently, no fire, and no civilization. Just snow on the ground everywhere he looked, some blowing, with massive mountains and peaks in the distance. Ford felt the strong wind rip through his thick clothing and past his exposed skin.

Goddamn. Where the hell am I? he thought. *There is nothing here.* Breathing heavily, he closed his eyes, swallowed, then looked up to the heavens. Ford sighed and stayed another few minutes, staring and thinking. *There is nothing here. How the hell are they going to find us if there is no wreckage? The snow covered everything up…and no emergency locator transmitter telling them where we are. No survival vest or radio.* "Fuck," Ford said quietly, shaking his head.

Not spending more than two minutes in total, he slowly crawled back down into the cockpit to evaluate his position. One leg on the back of his pilot seat, and other on the snow-covered floor, he stood quietly, looking at his breath. Immediately, he knew the situation was much, much worse than he originally thought.

"Well, Pinky. They have no clue where we are. Nothing. We're solo up here," Ford told her, angered and disgusted at the situation he was facing.

Green Wing Teal Road, Sea Pines, Hilton Head Island, South Carolina

Calvin, Robert, Emily, an air force chaplain, and a casualty assistance officer, a pilot, from the Georgia Air National Guard Base at Savannah, stood on the doorstep of the Stevens' home, waiting for the door to open. No one answered, and the men remained quiet.

An older retired couple walking their golden retriever passed in front of the house, inbound to the nearby ocean. No words were said as strange glances were exchanged.

An uncomfortable minute passed before a white Mercedes sedan then pulled up in the driveway, parked, and shut down. Marion and Chad got out of the car and walked slowly up to where the group was standing.

"Cal? What? What are you doing here?" Marion asked.

Chad knew better, as his years at DIA and in the military all came to a head in one moment. He sighed, letting out a long breath. "My gosh. Did we lose Ford? Did we lose him?"

"No, no, please let me explain," Calvin replied, attempting to calm things down.

"No, I need to know about my baby. Tell me, Cal," Marion said, raising her voice and ready to burst out crying.

"Marion, he said no. Let's just go inside," Chad said, putting his arm around her.

"God. What's going on with Ford, Cal? Tell me," Marion said, becoming very upset.

Chad and Marion gave Emily a hug, and she warmly hugged back, her eyes welling up.

Everyone walked inside the home, beautifully decorated in a nautical beach theme with complete open windows to backyard pool and Atlantic Ocean. It was a gorgeous sight to see.

"Cal, tell me right now. This isn't the old days. This is our boy," Marion told him with the tone of an experienced DIA wife with years of deployment under her belt.

"Please, everyone, come in. Sit," Chad told them.

Calvin thought about ten different ways to tell them the details, but not everyone there had a clearance. And certainly the program was not open source for everyone to discuss, so it would be a challenge to explain.

"Marion, Chad, as you know, or may not know, we called back Ford for some work. A mission," Cal explained, then paused. "He and his copilot were due to land a few days ago, and they are overdue."

"What does that mean? Days ago? You don't know where he is?" Marion asked. "Emily, he hasn't contacted you?"

Calvin sat on the white couch, looking out at the waves. "That's correct, Marion. He was flying an aircraft, was supposed to land during a set window that was previously coordinated, and they never showed."

"Well, what did their flight plan say?" Chad asked.

Calvin sat stone cold.

"Let me guess, no flight plan." Chad continued, reflecting on a lifetime of covert activity at DIA. Chad Stevens was a retired DIA officer, and was connecting the dots immediately.

Calvin did not answer.

"Well, why not track them on...radar of some kind? Their equipment that sends the signal, whatever that thing is called. Transponder. Whatever. That?" Marion said, asking questions to see what Calvin knew.

Calvin slowly nodded his head from left to right.

Chad rapidly went through scenarios based upon his career and combined Cal's nonverbals with his knowledge of flying. "Cal, Ford was flying off the grid? Let me guess. You snatched a bird from someplace, and he was ferrying it for you and the agency?" Chad asked, figuring out what Cal was up to.

Emily wiped her nose with a tissue.

West of Chal, East of Leelam, India, near Nanda Devi Mountain, Himalayas

It really had not sunk in to his conscious mind yet that he was in this quandary. What Ford had, minus the latest setback with Wu, was mental toughness. Ford was always fascinated with the tests that life threw at people, some when people were young, and others old—times when life just wasn't fair, but these people rebounded and learned from the adversity. Some caved in because life was hard or dealt them a bad hand of cards. Ford was compulsive at finding out the things that made people successful and modeled them. His readings led him to one thing: never quit. And he never did. Because quitting to Ford meant it was permanent, rather than some short-term pain. Ford wanted to be successful and would never quit, no matter what. Jojo Rising was the saying he and Wu used to describe maxing out on life, and he would need that special something today.

The top of the cockpit that was exposed to the sky was bright with sunlight, and it woke Ford up. Sleeping with his back on the pilot seat, but sitting in the snow, made the cold run thru his body like a live electrical wire. No matter what he tried, sleep was uncomfortable, cold, and wet, and he was not restful.

The light from the morning sky allowed him to see a bit better. He realized how lucky he was to be alive after seeing how the mountain tore up the aircraft, crushing it like a thin soda can.

Ford decided to climb back up to the top to look around again. He squinted at the intense sunlight coming from both the sky and the snow, and it reminded him of stories of snow blindness. Ford pulled down his tinted helmet visor, giving him the eye protection he needed.

The morning sun illuminated the surrounding area, and Ford was able to look around at the beautiful landscape. The snow and mountains were breathtaking, majestic, and intimidating, all at the same time. Ford scanned the horizon all around for a few minutes and saw no signs of life—no birds, no wildlife, no aircraft contrails. One side of the sky was gray toward the largest mountain peak, and seemed to look like a storm. He determined his cardinal directions, figuring out his bearing from the sun, then went back down into the cockpit.

Eating a granola bar and drinking some water he kept from freezing by keeping it close to his warm body, he sat wondering what to do next. Recalling his route of flight and his flight time, he knew he was in northern India, but the electronic aviation charts were not to scale to provide city or town locations and names. Certainly on a visual flight rules chart, or VFR, they were well labeled, but not on a digital instrument flight rules version.

Ford threw his wrapper off to the side and determined that there was no way he would be located if he sat there. His mind also wandered to Emily and his family, everything from his engagement to drinking. *Get it together already.*

"Pinky, I've been doing some thinking, and I'm going to have to leave you. I just don't think anyone will find us sitting down here in this hole. I'll die, too, and there is no way that is happening."

Ford knew from Survival School that one of the most important things he could ever do at this moment is have the will to survive. The history books were full of stories of people who had the will to make it and live, and as a result of this mind-set, did so. Stories shared by the Survival School instructors were very popular regarding servicemen who were isolated during World War II, Korea, and Vietnam, and attributed their survival to the mental psychology game. The most important thing he could do was concentrate on living and being positive. The positive psychology research was overwhelming in Ford's favor: be an optimist.

Certainly, there was no way that Ford could prepare ahead of time mentally to overcome this specific obstacle, but because he had strong mental toughness in his life prior to takeoff, his chances of living were above average. One of Ford's favorite books was *Man's Search for Meaning* by Dr. Viktor Frankel, which discussed surviving through World War II concentration camps. As a result of this book and his air force training, Ford knew that the body's demands from food sources for energy can be reduced to nearly zero.

Because Ford also did not have the proper survival kit in the jet, he knew immediately it would a tough go in such environmental conditions. He questioned why he and the team did not prepare ahead of time, but this remote possibility never crossed anyone's mind on an administrative flight. Ford was stranded, and he now wished he had some type of a survival manual with him. He also remembered that the top item on the list was not to panic. Fear was definitely in his mind and enhanced his senses, but he certainly did not panic.

Think, think. OK. Review SURVIVAL.

Ford had a surge of adrenaline still going, but he had to channel his emotions so that there was no energy wasted. He thought about Survival School and remembered the word survival as S-U-R-V-I-V-A-L, using it as a memory device.

The letter S meant that he was to *size up the situation*, considering any injuries and first aid. Ford reviewed what he had experienced to date, thinking about what he perceived as altitude sickness and a concussion. Other than that, he was healthy. He also checked again on his week's or so worth of food and some limited water, but felt OK with the bountiful snow and ice available. The weather was definitely going to be an issue, and he had not even left his little survival cockpit shelter.

The U in survival was *undue haste makes waste*. Ford had no clue as to what else was out there and really wasn't aware of what was at stake outside. He did not want to waste precious time and energy on things that were not important, so focusing on a route to hike out would be first. *These are no foothills.* Conserving energy to do it would also come into play, and luckily, he had not wasted any physical activity just yet, so that was good.

The R in survival was *remember where you are*, which an issue was already. He did have paper aviation charts somewhere in the cockpit as a backup to the digital maps on the screens, but they were not the right scale.

The V in survival meant *vanquish fear and panic*, which would always give him a solid attitude check. *I'm good there so far.*

The I in survival was *improvise*, which is something he would have to do. No climbing gear was the elephant in the room. *Perhaps get down to a lower attitude sooner rather than later for oxygen. Catch food? I cannot imagine there are any animals living at this altitude.*

The V in survival was *value living*, which was Ford's will to survive in extreme conditions. *That shouldn't be an issue, but I sure as heck miss her. Why did I not propose earlier?* He would have to limit his self-talk on Emily but use her as the motivation to get out of this mess. *OK, mitigate all the risks in order to survive.*

The A in survival was *act like the natives*. For the mountain people of India, anything could happen. *Perhaps that is the only way I can get out of here.* Ford had no clue as to who lived in this region, other than watching the History Channel on cable.

Finally, the L in survival meant to *learn basic skills*. *Got the basics, need the advanced here,* Ford said to himself, putting on his two backpacks and preparing to exit the cockpit.

Grabbing Pinky's jacket in a delicate manner off her body, he tied it to his waist, placed her gloves in his pockets, and crawled out.

Days Later at Headquarters Air Force, Pentagon, Washington, DC

"Team, a few days have gone by, and I understand nothing has turned up still. I am hesitant to say this, but I need you guys to stay on top of this. Get on it. Tier-one forces, all assets available. You know I can't be on this 100 percent because the Hill will want to know what the hell I'm up to. So, I'm going to have to progress with my nomination and hearing. Again, I want you guys to press on with your search. Just let me know what you need, OK?" Cal told them.

Sitting at the long wooden table in the undersecretary's conference room at the Pentagon were Emily, Robert, Jeanie, and Mark, all suffering from the loss of the two pilots, as well as the aircraft. Michelle Boyd, now Cal's assistant, was in the room and off to the side.

Emily was suffering the most, and rightfully so. She was feeling a variety of emotions, and while physically present, was not present emotionally. Emily was still in shock and sad and was numb to the business side of this recovery.

"Emily, how are you doing?" asked Cal.

Staring down at the floor, Emily didn't hear Cal.

"Emily?" he asked again, quietly.

Startled, she looked up. "What? I'm sorry. Were you talking to me?"

"Yes, Emily, how are you doing? I know this must be tough on you. What can I do to help?" Cal asked.

Cal was a wonderful leader, and in a time like this, he connected with people of all ranks and titles and demonstrated his high emotional intelligence. He walked over to her and grabbed her hand. She stood, and they hugged while she cried uncontrollably in his arms. It was very nonbusiness like and demonstrated the closeness of a solid team who loved each other.

They sat, and the room remained quiet for a brief moment. Mark stood up and grabbed the white binder by the doorway table.

"Sir, this is where we are. We have all the satellites scanning the route of flight, as we know it from the verbal plan discussed back in Bangalore. Robert has arranged for RPV's from PACOM and EUCOM to fly the route, and that is already underway as of 2200 Zulu," Mark shared.

Robert turned the page in his binder. "I've got us office space in the basement for an Ops Center, with enough phones and computers to rival Best Buy. Keeps us out of the rest of the intel community. Your phone calls to the combatant commanders have already helped, sir, because I've taken plenty of flak from guys asking what we are doing. Kind of tough to tell the guys monitoring the feeds what to look for."

"Let me know if you run into trouble. I'll call Admiral McDevitt at Indo-Pacific Command again if I need to," Cal replied. "Thank you."

"Mr. Burns, I have also refragged four C-130s to fly the entire route again. Air Force Reserve tasked Niagara's 914th Air Wing as their last mission before converting to KC-135 tankers and are already in Bangalore as of yesterday."

"Last mission? Another political decision for western New York?"

"Guess so. They take off our tonight, their tomorrow morning—ten and a half hours ahead of us on the time zone," Mark shared.

Emily turned her page. "I'm sorry, sir. Thank you for your support. I'm going to use my connections from MI6 at home to see if anything is turning up. Chatter. We have found it difficult, as you can imagine, to talk openly about this. Trying to find a secret aircraft that doesn't exist, and still not tell anyone what we are looking for this week is just bloody tough."

"Understand, Emily. You're very welcome. Please tell Sir John Young at MI6 I said hello, and pass on my thanks for his assistance. He will understand if you tell him it is country-sensitive and specific to me."

Emily swallowed. "Thank you, sir."

"Anything else?" asked Cal.

Jeanie smiled. "Yes, there is. The Chinese had their funeral for Lieutenant General He Chen yesterday."

Robert, puzzled, looked at Jeanie. "Why are you smiling?"

"Chatter from the texts. Seems hardly anyone attended."

Two Miles South of Black Scorpion Cockpit Wreckage, West of Chal, East of Leelam, India, near Nanda Devi Mountain, Himalayas

Weeks passed, and the snow was knee deep. Each step required Ford to lift his legs up much higher than normal. His lungs were burning from the lack of oxygen, and he felt tired, thirsty, and hungry after only hiking a short amount of time.

On the horizon, the blowing snow blended in with the ground and mountains, and it was nearly impossible to see anything. From up above, he could see the peaks of mountains, moving clouds, and a strong sun. *This place is just so desolate.* The other item that Ford was attempting to ignore was the forceful wind-chill temperature. The combined cold air and wind on his body was intense and accelerated the loss of his body heat. *I am so freaking cold.*

Looking up through the tinted visor on his helmet and into the blowing snow, he finally spotted something ahead of him. He noticed it was a different color black from the granite he was used to seeing. Ford made that his next checkpoint, walking slowly.

Ford wasn't sure if the high altitude was playing games with him or not, but all he could think about through his headache was the loss of his best friend, Wu Lee. Ford took a rest due to his severe shortness of breath, taking the opportunity to laugh at himself. For some reason he felt like Wu was with him. Wu wasn't talking to him, but Ford sure felt he was hiking just in front of him. Ford's dry, irritating cough was now producing a pink and frothy sputum, another sure sign of high-altitude sickness. As he started to throw up, Ford knew he'd have to get lower in altitude.

Arriving an hour later, Ford got to the object he had seen earlier. Sticking up out of feet of snow was the Black Scorpion vertical stabilizer, the tail, lying on its side. Connected to it and severely damaged, was a portion of the fuselage and right wing. He walked around it slowly, falling multiple times, inspecting the area where the terrain had ripped the aircraft structure with violence. *Well, China doesn't have their aircraft anymore. Neither do we.*

It was completely covered in snow now, camouflaged to any overhead aircraft or satellites. Ford took a breather and looked at his watch. Nearly nine hours had gone by just to get to this point, and Ford was already tired, windburned, and severely dehydrated. He made his way completely around the aircraft structure finally and saw that the right wing he'd just inspected would make a good makeshift shelter for the night. Seeing a small space that would easily fit him and protect him from the elements, he made his decision. Exhausted and breathing heavily, he crawled under the wing to stay for the night. *Crap. I feel like I'm hungover. What I'd do for a warm bed.*

Weeks Later, Basement Ops Center, Pentagon, Washington, DC

"No wreckage is weird, but not uncommon. Through the years, we've lost plenty of airframes and pilots. Amelia Earhart. Bermuda Triangle. Right?" Mark said to the team.

"Yes, understand, Mark, but in this day and age, to have nothing sent up the chain is pretty odd," Robert replied.

"Yep. But the seas are huge, so are the oceans, and so are the mountains and deserts. It could take years to locate wreckage," said Mark.

"Who said anything about wreckage?" Emily sternly commented.

"I'm sorry, Emily. Aircraft," Mark replied, realizing his comment.

"No. I'm sorry for snapping at you. This loss is tremendous. To be involved professionally and personally is very tough. My parents are coming in tonight from Heathrow to be with me. That will help."

Jeanie scanned the data and passed on that nothing was seen from any of their sources. Robert looked at his computer while talking on the phone to EUCOM Operations, and he, too, had nothing.

"Where are they?" Mark quietly said to himself, standing with his arms folded, looking at a wall map of the earth.

Seventeen Miles East of Chal, 12,480 Feet, near Nanda Devi Mountain, Himalayas

Nearly a month had gone by now, and Ford had managed to make his limited food supply last until now. Still tucked away in the mountains, with a face full of facial hair, he struggled to make his movements count in the steep terrain.

Nearly eighteen pounds lighter due to the high-altitude calorie burn and lack of food, his energy level was at an all-time low. Sunburned from the snow glare, lips severely chapped and fully cracked from being forced to suck on snow and ice for water, he was suffering intensely.

His mind was also clogged with thinking of a variety of items from his entire life. One moment he was thinking of when he used to play with Thomas the Train, naming all his friends like Percy, Sir Topham Hatt, and Gordon the Big Engine, all on the island of Sodor. Minutes later, he was back on the football team at Notre Dame, humming the Fighting Irish fight song. At other times, he was thinking of the Skull Creek Boathouse on Hilton Head, then his fond memories of there would fade away. Most of the time, his thoughts turned to Emily and their future together. The isolation played tricks on his mind, but he continued to stay as strong as he could.

Ford's long uncut fingernails were now caked with grime and dirt, as was his soiled clothing. His trench-foot toes, frostbitten and constantly wet, were on the verge of being lost. His head and ears were protected from the elements, but his much-longer-than-usual hair was knotted, dirty, and oily. Ford's crotch was chaffed and painful and felt like his skin was rotting. His anus was on fire, and he sure missed the comfort of a toilet seat and paper.

Because of the prolonged exposure to the cold, and that his feet stayed wet in dirty socks and boots, the frostbite was most likely permanent. He checked his feet often because he could not feel his toes. Early on, his toes were red, then turned waxy white, and now had blisters. Because of the condition of his feet, he was clumsy in his walking.

Pinky's backpack was empty of food, too, but he still used it to carry her cold-weather jacket, which he laid down every night for a ground cover. Ford learned swiftly that after sundown, the mountain was a nightmare weather wise. Each night, he hunkered down in a spot close to large rocks that would block the wind a bit. He would use Pinky's jacket as something to sleep on top of.

One desolate snow-covered mountain looked the same as the other, and he kept following an invisible path to the west, descending in altitude slowly as he went down in what he saw as valleys. There was still no sight of the terrain leveling off, or where the snowline would turn to exposed brown dirt, green plants, and wildlife.

Lying up against a granite rock, looking out to the horizon, he loved and hated his scenery at the same time. While it was breathtaking to view during the day and at night, he'd had enough. His breaking point was near, and the pain and loneliness were overwhelming.

"God! Help me!" Ford yelled out into the lonely night sky. "Help me get out of this mess! I'm sorry for everything I did. I'll never drink again," he said out loud. He broke down and cried.

The wind continued to blow, making it noisy, the whooshing sound still being heard though his helmet. Ford had never felt such intense cold in his life. Although he did not have a thermometer, he knew the temperature couldn't have been over zero degrees. The snow started to pick up again, rapidly changing from a clear sky to gray. The sudden pickup of wind, as well as its turn of direction, told Ford another storm was coming.

Ford's time in the mountains was taking a toll on him physically, but he vowed to never, ever, give up while he had the chance. He would do everything he could to survive. "You can't beat me, mountain! You can't do it! I will win!" he yelled so loud he became hoarse.

Sporting a thousand-yard stare, the once dynamic Ford Stevens sang out loud the lyrics to the Notre Dame fight song to keep himself occupied. "Rally, sons of Notre Dame...her glory and sound her fame..." *How I respond to this will either kill me or save me*, Ford thought silently as he closed his eyes.

Senate Armed Services Committee, Room SD-G50, Dirksen Senate Office Building, Washington, DC

"For the record, Mr. Burns, thank you," Senator Juan replied, as the room erupted in phony laughs.

Cal Burns sat at the confirmation hearing table, along with some other nominees, microphones on, ready for the political theater he had seen so many times.

Behind him were a variety of uniformed air force officers, from colonel to major general, sitting up proudly at their inbound undersecretary of the air force.

"Thank you again, Senator Juan, for the opportunity today. As I said in my earlier opening statement, and in my written testimony, the following subjects are for your review: Reshaping the air force, single-service-member military family readiness programs, the situation in Afghanistan, future air force budgets, and current readiness of the air force," said Cal.

"Yes, thank you, Mr. Burns. And for the record again, you will come back for closed hearings on…" said Senator Juan, motioning his staff for the list with his hand. "For closed sessions on antiaccess area denial challenges in Europe, long-term defense strategies, and cyber threats. Is that correct?"

"Yes, sir. At your invitation."

"Final thoughts on the South China Sea before we depart today, Mr. Burns?"

"I do have a few brief statements, Senator. I think we will continue to have overflights and ship operations in and near the disputed waters of the South China Sea. International airspace for the aircraft and ships as part of maritime routine operations," Cal answered, staying pretty neutral in his answer. "The Chinese enjoy trade with the world, including the United States. They will not jeopardize their economic position."

Michelle Boyd, sitting directly behind Cal, knew this was the final bout of questions, based upon the script previously decided on. She closed her notebook, as she had done countless times before, proud of her witness. Michelle took pride in grooming Cal Burns for this position, and if she played her cards right, would continue to stay on his staff in the E Ring.

"Thank you for your time today, Mr. Burns. The committee appreciates your time. This committee is adjourned."

Cal shut off his microphone, closed his black binder, and smiled. *Thank God no China stealth questions.*

Basement Ops Center, Pentagon, Washington, DC

Mark stood with his arms folded, looking at a wall full of printouts, magazine articles, newspapers and maps. The world map they had up had all sorts of push pins in it, from India, across Europe, across the North Atlantic, down northern Canada, and into the northeastern United States.

"What do you think, Robert?" Mark whispered to Robert.

"I think your new beard, wrestling shoes, and plaid printed shorts suck," Robert replied back.

"No. No, dumbass. Not my clothing. This. This. Everything here," Mark replied, waving his arms around at the room. "Emily isn't here. We need to have a serious discussion. It's been two months now, and not a clue of them. They are gone. Done."

Emotionless Robert shifted his body weight, looked down at the floor, then across at the digital clocks. He glanced at the same wall Mark was just referring to. "What are you thinking?"

"Shut it down," Mark told him. "I'm thinking that we are well past search and rescue, well past recovery. We can't just keep the Ops Center here open with no leads. We have nothing. These guys disappeared. What else can we do?"

"I'm thinking we have to plan on a funeral. Burial at Arlington for both of them. Close this down."

"Agree. Let's go see Mr. Burns," Robert said, as they head for the door.

"OK. We have to tell Emily first," Mark announced.

Emily's Apartment, Overlooking the Potomac River above Iwo Jima Memorial, Rosslyn, Virginia

Country music artist Kenny Chesney's "I Want to Know What Love Is" was playing in the background as Emily sat alone on her couch. Her knees up and near her chin, only wearing a long sleeve T-shirt, pink underwear, and socks, she sat and cried, mourning the loss of Ford. Her black lab, Daisy, was sleeping in the corner.

Emily's pain from the loss was intense, as she felt the pit in her stomach ache day and night. More tears streamed down her cheeks as she cried and cried. She felt as alone, as her loss was difficult to comprehend, and if she had to have closure on this, it wasn't happening any time soon. Emily wanted her mum there, or her sister, even her close girlfriends in London. But she was a career woman, and at the moment, her position assigned her 3,674 miles to the west of the UK. Wiping her mascara on her white sleeve, Emily looked out at the Iwo Jima Memorial outside her apartment window, then out across the Lincoln Memorial on the Mall. She sipped more Chardonnay as more doubt crept in.

How am I going to make it? How I can I go on without him? I am so numb to… work…life…my heart hurts…

Emily had not eaten for the last two days, only moving off her couch or bed to use the bathroom. She had bottomed out in anguish and sorrow.

PART 11

WATER

Foothills of Chal, 11,300 Feet, near Nanda Devi Mountain, Himalayas

The United Nations in 2011 stated that "any imposition of solitary confinement beyond fifteen days constitutes torture." Even as far back as 1842, Charles Dickens wrote that isolation was something very few men were capable of handling. He once wrote about isolation that "I hold this slow and daily tampering with the mysteries of the brain, to be immeasurably worse than any torture of the body."

His mind continued to fight him as he was constantly attempting to keep it busy. Sometimes he conducted math problems in his head, like adding multiple numbers or calculating compound interest, return-on-investments, and one-person debates on index funds versus real estate. He even remembered specific plays at the Notre Dame versus Michigan football game he played in years ago, replaying movements from the field in his mind. At other times, he wondered if the mishap was his fault, perhaps something he missed in the cockpit. He felt abandoned and lost and was embarrassed thinking that he may have been partly responsible for Pinky's death. The reflection on his life was constant, and he made note many times that the happiness in his life was in living for others, helping others. He had to live.

Physically, Ford barely had an ounce of fat on him and may have looked chiseled at an outward glance, but he was thirty-three pounds lighter over the past nine weeks of isolation.

Reaching a bit lower in the mountains that were dirt covered and full of wildlife, Ford was able to make a variety of animal and fish traps to aid in sustaining himself. During one capture, he made trail snares with his boot-laces and ate rabbit. Using his survival knife from his backpack, he was able to clean the rabbit somewhat, cook it up on a fire, and eat like he hadn't eaten before. But it was temporary, and he didn't capture anything else for a while.

Ford was also able to capture some fish in the icy streams he came across by making a hook from Pinky's jacket zipper. By twisting a portion of her jacket fibers, he made a line. Because he could not find a suitable worm as bait, he used Emily's engagement ring after breaking the band with a rock. With the flashy metal of the ring, he was able to make a fish hook to catch the fish's attention. *Not sure if I will tell her this one*, he said to himself. *But she'll find out.*

He was also able to find plenty of edible plants, from wild onion to nut grass to bark. The wild onion was especially tasty if he cooked it, and to Ford, it tasted like just like old-school onion. He also noticed more moss, Indian tortoiseshell butterflies, and purple Himalayan primrose in bloom, all good signs that he was descending in altitude.

What Ford did not expect for the past week was his severe case of the diarrhea caused by all the wild food and unclean water he was drinking. The water looked clean and fresh, but it definitely was not.

At first, he would go, then have to wipe himself with any leaves he could find. Then it was a few times an hour. Now, it was nearly uncontrollable. His body was full of viruses, bacteria, and parasites, and the intense agony he was feeling had him buckled over and holding his gut. Ford was having so much pain and diarrhea that it left him severely dehydrated, weak, and destitute.

If Ford were able to get a blood test, we would see that his white blood cells were on the hunt for the viruses, bacteria, and fungi. His white blood cells, or leukocytes, knew enough to destroy the aggressive foreign bodies before they caused him harm. Some white blood cells directly attack the foreign bugs, while others go after cells that are infected by viruses. Either way, his body could not keep up with the infections.

"God, I made it this far out of the mountains. Don't take me this way. I can...I can...I want to live," he slowly said out loud, struggling to talk coherently.

Drinking tainted water was the downfall of millions of the earth's people. Ford drank contaminated, dirty water. The World Bank had estimated that 21 percent of communicable diseases in India were water related. Diarrhea alone killed over seven hundred thousand people in India each year, with the highest mortality under the age of five. Ford was feeling every one of the bad organisms eating away at his immune system, and it wasn't promising. He looked and felt absolutely awful.

Ford's very unhygienic water collection and zero hand washing added to the transmission of his diarrhea-causing germs. His infection was riding the highways of his body and spreading through his tissues and lowering his blood pressure, leaving him at the beginning of shock. His body's organs, specifically his lungs, liver, and kidneys, were at the early stages of shutdown.

Ford was going to die.

Miller Residence, Hudson Street, Hawley, Pennsylvania

"Hi Aunt Michelle, this is Rex," said a young Rex Miller into the telephone.

"Rex who?" replied Michelle Boyd, clearly teasing her nephew.

Rex was silent and didn't know how to answer, and he looked at his Dad standing next to him.

"I'm just kidding, Rexy! How are you, buddy? Doing well?" Michelle replied.

"Doing good. We saw you on TV. You were on C-SPAN channel where the people talk all the time. Daddy showed me you sitting in back of the man at the table. You were next to the women in the blue uniform."

Michelle warmly smiled at hearing this for a few reasons. One, it proved to others back in her economically depressed areas of Pennsylvania that she had a real job in DC. Two, it provided a goal for young Rex to study hard. Lastly, it was cool to be seen on television.

"Yes, that was me! I'm so happy you got to see Auntie Michelle at work! Thank you for watching."

"You looked pretty."

Michelle continued to smile. "Thanks, Rexy. Tell me...what are you up to these days?"

"Um, well, Daddy and I have been using his ham radio in the basement. We can talk to people all over the world, and then I put the location on our map."

She nodded and was impressed. "Wow, your dad has you doing that?"

"Yup. Sometimes I listen all by myself, too. It's kind of cool," Rex replied, proud of himself.

Headquarters Air Force, Pentagon, Washington, DC

Emily sat at the table talking to Cal. "Yes, sir, I am in agreement with Mark. He and Robert talked to me about it the other day, and it seems like the best move is to shut down the Ops Center. We are approaching weeks and weeks of them gone, and, although I love him and want him back, it is the right move. Life has to go on," Emily told him. "I'm also aware of the pending funeral at Arlington, with burial next to Captain Wu Lee."

Cal was prebriefed by Mark and knew she was going to say that, but he was still sympathetic to her for the loss of Ford and Pinky. "Yes, I understand, Emily. I do know this is tough. I wish we could get them back, too. I really do," Cal replied.

"Me, too, sir. I wanted to share with you that I'm leaving the United States and the team. I'm due to return back to London next week. My choice. It's time to go back and do some work at home."

This threw Cal off guard. "Oh, really? I wasn't aware. Of course, Emily. Whatever we can do to facilitate this, let me know," Cal said, then turned to Mark. "Like, Mark, hey. How about a party for Emily? Let's celebrate her work and time with us, yes?"

"Yes, sir, of course. Robert and I were already talking about that. We'll take care of it," Mark replied, with the atmosphere changing for the better in the room.

"You weren't thinking of that. Please," Emily said, cracking up at Mark and Robert.

They all started laughing. "We forgot," Mark replied.

Foothills of Chal, 9,100 Feet, near Nanda Devi Mountain, Himalayas

Flight suit around his ankles yet again, Ford finished his bodily fluid business and slowly zipped up. Moving in slow motion, he stumbled away from his makeshift bathroom site, still in intense pain and agony from the organisms eating away inside of him. When he wasn't having diarrhea, he was throwing up. *I'm not going to make it.*

Ford sat on the ground in the brown dirt, legs extended out, his left shoulder leaning on the side of tree, and curled up. His helmet was off, filthy hair matted and long, with a full beard covering his face and neck, completely exhausted. Ford was a complete wreck. Soiled, smelly, and downright nasty-looking, he closed his eyes slowly. He was physically and mentally beat and in a terrible state, at the end of his life.

Ford slowly opened his eyes a few minutes later after hearing snorts. Squinting a bit through the mountain mist, he saw on the clearing near the stream in front of him someone walking. A man appeared to be walking with a large yak, bell around his neck clinking, along with a handful of brown and red tahr goats.

Ford moved his head slowly off the tree to see the tahr eating their grass and other vegetation. "Hey," he said quietly, not able to gain any real sound coming from his vocal cords. He swallowed again, barely any saliva going down his throat. "Hey," Ford said again, but it was barely audible. Ford struggled to raise his arm to wave, wanting to ensure the man saw him.

The wild tahr wandered over to where he was leaning on the tree and sniffed around. The man brought over the yak, and Ford was surrounded by animals. The man got down on all fours to look into Ford's eyes. Ford squinted, and it was the first human he had seen alive in three months. In a raspy voice, Ford spoke. "Need help. Need help. Please."

The man, Aayush, helped Ford up on his feet and slung him over on the Yak's back for the ride into his village, named Chal.

Gordon Biersch Restaurant, 2nd Floor, 9th and F Streets NW, Washington, DC

"And we are so grateful that you could work with us these past three years, Emily, and on behalf of the team here, thank you very, very much," Mark told Emily and the rest of the crew at her farewell dinner. There was a round of applause as Robert yelled out, "Speech! Speech!"

Emily blushed as she stood next to Mark, looking out at Robert, Jeanie, Michelle, and Cal Burns. They had a private room on the second floor of Gordon Biersch just for them, and it was the perfect setting to say good-bye to their cherished partner and close friend from the UK.

"I am so thankful to have each of you in my life," Emily began, tears streaming down face. "I am forever grateful to have participated in such important and moving events during my time here, and to play a role in your personal and professional lives. I am also deeply humbled and appreciative that you could help me through the most difficult time of my life in losing him. For that, thank you, friends. I love each of you so much. Cheerio."

Village of Chal, India, 8,200 Feet, Himalayas

The village of Chal consisted of about thirty homes, constructed closely together from flimsy wood, thatched and sheet metal roofs, and mud. The village was well established and had existed for hundreds of years as a farming and livestock community with no access to civilizations from any paved roads. They had no electricity and no running water this far north and deep into the mountains.

Because India had about four hundred languages and dialects, there was no way for Ford to understand the Hindi language being spoken by Aayush. Hindi, one of the most common languages spoken in India, had been a delicate political subject since independence sixty years ago. What did help Ford was that both Hindi and English were the most widely used languages in India.

Aayush brought Ford directly to the village sadhu or holy person, named Vivaan. Vivaan was sitting alone and singing in Hindi, playing a hand-hewn instrument, reflecting and meditating. His lyrics surrounding Indian folk music were about yellow mustard flowers, his children, and the desert earth; his music provided him with a soothing pastime. His horsehair strings and bow were of fine craftsmanship, and he put them both down quickly in a flurry at the unannounced visitor. In English, the men spoke. "Aayush, who is this? Who is this man?"

"Vivaan, this man needs help. Please help me inside with him. I found him near the stream. He, he is very sick."

Ford was delirious and needed dire assistance going into the village building by both Aayush and Vivaan, each man taking an arm. Ford dragged his nasty boots and feet. They got him into the bedroom onto an elevated charpoy, a rope-strung bed, careful not to step on the children playing on the dirt floor. They took off his grimy olive-colored cold weather jacket.

Ford was woozy and not following what was going on in the dark room with the limited outside lighting. "Need...need help. I am an American," he told them, breathing heavily. Slowly he said, "Name is Ford Stevens, a United States...Air Force Reserve pilot. My airplane crashed in the mountains. Contact my US embassy. Ford...Stevens."

Ford used every ounce of his energy to relay the message, then passed out.

Gordon Biersch Restaurant, 2nd Floor, 9th and F Streets NW, Washington, DC

"It was our pleasure working with you, Emily. Thank you very much for your service," Cal told her, standing up to give her a hug. "You are a true professional."

"Thank you" Emily replied, wiping her tears. "And congrats to you, sir, for your new position. Happy times to you."

The speech time had come to an end with a round of applause, along with some tears of good-bye. Michelle came over with a Chardonnay wine, and the group all mingled and talked.

"I cannot imagine how tough this has been. I am sorry, but I do hope that time will heal some of this for you," Michelle said to Emily.

"Yes, thank you, Michelle. I'm not over him, but I guess...with time, I may meet someone else...get back into my work in London. I start a new staff job in a few weeks, so that will be a change," Emily replied.

Jeanie came over and was listening, too. "You'll be missed, Emily. Everyone loves you here. We're just a secure phone call away."

"Thanks, Jeanie. I think I will see my sister, then my parents, maybe take holiday down to Italy and get some quiet beach time. Just to think things through."

Emily was being somewhat standoffish at the Ford comments. For months, she had been in a fog, a haze of losing someone she fancied so much. To have him disappear without closure was torture to her, and there would be no other group of people on earth that would ever understand her unfathomable loss and pain.

Village of Chal, India, 8,200 Feet, Himalayas
"Ford Stevens. OK, Ford Stevens, we can help you," Vivaan told him. Ford never heard the reply.

Vivaan motioned for three females from the home to come over, pointed at Ford, saying something in Hindu as he waved his hands and arms. They females began to wash his hands as best they could and wipe his face with a cloth. They were not doctors by any stretch, but they knew he was not well, and they all discussed it.

"Vivaan, he is warm, almost hot, to the touch. This man is sick with the fever. Perhaps you get Dr. Dennis to come see him?" asked Vivaan's wife. His two adult daughters were also there, heating up some more water on the kitchen fire.

Dr. Dennis Jenkins was a volunteer with Doctors Without Borders based out of New Delhi, India, but his full-time job was working in a Detroit hospital. Doctors Without Borders was helping India on improving their treatment and diagnosis of diseases such as tuberculosis, HIV, and visceral leishmaniasis for citizens unable to access healthcare in India.

Basic medical care was not available for much of India's population due to poverty, social exclusion, and their small government health service, so Doctors Without Borders volunteered their time to help with mobile clinics in the villages. To date, more than fifty-seven thousand consultations were carried out and over fourteen thousand patients were treated for malaria.

"Yes, yes. I will," Vivaan replied. Vivaan and Aayush walked through the village paths to the building that housed a small car battery and radio.

Aayush turned on the power as Vivaan sat down on the floor and grabbed the microphone. Loud static came thru the speakers. He turned the dial on the seventy-five-watt system, donated by Dr. Dennis so the village could communicate for treatment and medicine as needed.

Not touching the frequency numbers because Vivaan could not read, he knew enough to just press the button and talk on the system. He looked at Aayush, and they nodded.

"Dr. Dennis, this is Vivaan in Chal," he said on the radio. No answer. "Dr. Dennis, this is Vivaan in Chal. Dr. Dennis, Dr. Dennis."

"This is Doctors Without Borders in New Delhi. Say again, over."

"Yes, hello, hello, sir. This is Vivaan in Chal. Dr. Dennis is our village doctor. We need help."

"Hello, Vivaan. You have reached Doctors Without Borders in New Delhi, but Dr. Dennis is not here at the moment. He is with Team Rubicon Global in Nepal. Can we help? What is the nature of your request, over?"

Eyes wide open, Aayush was pleased that they had reached the doctor organization.

"Yes, hello. We have an American here who is sick. He needs Dr. Dennis. He is hot with fever and not talking. Very sick, sir."

"That is unfortunate. We understand. What is his background? You say an American. What is the issue at hand, Vivaan, over?" came the reply from New Delhi.

"Yes. This man. He said he is a pilot from an airplane. From air force in America. His plane landed in the mountains," answered Vivaan.

"OK, understand. We are looking at the map now. We are not aware of any airplanes or runways in your area." There was a long pause as the staff looked at the availability and distances that would have to be traveled. "We think we can have someone to you in three days. Maybe four. What is the American's name?"

"Ford. Stevens. His name is Ford Stevens."

Miller Residence, Hudson Street, Hawley, Pennsylvania

"Dad, Dad. Did you hear that? They talked about Team Rubicon. And they have a pilot who is sick who landed in the mountains? That is soooo cool!" Rex said to his father.

"That is kind of strange. An American air force pilot in Chal...India? Look it up, Rex. Where is that?" Michael told him. "Won't be on your wall map, I don't think. Use the computer."

Rex used Google Maps to find Chal, along with satellite images of the village and snow-filled mountains. "Here it is Dad, check this out."

Michael looked at it closely, then thought about the conversation. "Rex, no one just lands in these mountains. They are big. Like, really big, in fact, they are massive. These aren't the Pocono Mountains; we're talking Mount Everest."

"Dad. Like this?" Rex showed him on the monitor.

"Yep, just like that. Gigantic. No one lands in there. You crash. That guy, whatever his name was, may have...survived."

Rex looked at his logbook. "His name was Ford Stevens. I wrote it down. The town name is Chal. I just looked up the coordinates, too, Dad. They are 33° 16' 30" North, 74° 9' 0" East."

Michael followed the grid lines on the wall map with his finger. "Hmm. Right here on the India-Nepal border. Weird. Terrain couldn't be any steeper or colder on earth."

Rex sat in silence thinking about what his dad just said.

"Something isn't right here, Rex. I have an idea."

"What is it?"

"Get me my phone, please."

Michael looked at his smartphone, found the number, and hit the button.

"Who are you calling, Dad? The state police in Honesdale?" Rex asked.

Michael waived his hand. "No, no. Listen in with me."

The person on the other end of the phone answered. "Hi, Michael."

"Hi, Michelle. Do you have a minute?" Michael asked.

"Actually, no, I am at a going-away party for a coworker at a restaurant. Can it wait till tomorrow? I'll just call you at lunch."

Michael hesitated for a minute, and Rex shook his head no two or three times.

"No, Michelle, this will only take a second. Rex and I were listening to the ham radio in the basement just now, and we were listening in to a conversation in India."

Michelle had to excuse herself and walk to the far side of their private room at Gordon Biersch due to the noise.

"I'm sorry, Michael, can you say that again? Can we talk at lunch tomorrow? I had to move myself from the dinner."

"Michelle. I mean no. Ol' Rexy and I were listening to the ham radio just now in the basement, and we were listening in to a conversation in India."

"OK," Michelle replied, but she was wondering why it couldn't wait. "Can we...just talk tomorrow about it?"

"Well, it was from a man located in a tiny village in India, talking to a Doctors Without Borders doctor."

PART 12

TATTOO

Gordon Biersch Restaurant, 2nd Floor, 9th and F Streets NW, Washington, DC

"India? OK, keep going, Michael," Michelle answered, rolling her eyes and wondering why her brother was bothering her about India.

"It was an interesting conversation. The villager, named Vivaan, said he found an American air force pilot that landed in the mountains. He's apparently very sick, hot with a fever they said. And I know you work for the air force, and maybe wanted to know, since it sounded kinda weird."

Michelle plugged her other ear with her finger and bent down awkwardly somewhat to shield the noise. Her eyes were wide open. "Michael, did you just say they had a sick air force pilot that landed in the mountains? Did they give a name over the radio?"

Michael turned to look at Rex's logbook. "Yeah, air force pilot. Hang on, Rexy is locating it now."

Michelle waited with the most patience she ever had shown.

"Yeah, Michelle, we have his name. Ah, Ford. Ford Stevens."

Michelle shivered and spun around rapidly like a ballerina to look at the rest of the team in the room. Her eyes locked on Emily Livingston. "Michael, understand his name is Ford Stevens?"

"Rex, that's his name, right? Ford Stevens?"

"Yeah," replied Rex. "Like the car, Dad."

"Michelle, Rex wrote it down. Yup, Ford Stevens."

Michelle was in complete disbelief and couldn't believe what she was hearing.

"Shut the front door! Michael, this is an emergency. Write everything down and email it to me ASAP. Keep listening to that conversation, and I need everything you got. Frequency, names, times, everything. I'll call you right back."

"Oh, OK, Michelle. Wait, we're in the basement and not near the front door, but we'll…"

Michelle hung up on them in midsentence and immediately walked over to the group. "Geez. Holy shit!" Michelle loudly said to the team.

"What is it, Michelle? Is everything OK?"

Michelle swallowed and stared at everyone. "He is alive. Ford is alive. Ford is alive!"

Emily dropped her glass of wine, shattering the glass all over the wooden floor. She had to lean on Robert for a moment, nearly fainting. "He is? Ford. My gosh…"

"Goddamn!" Mark said, taking his red Nationals baseball hat off and turning it around backward. "Goddamn right he is! Let's get to work."

Six Hours Later, Basement Ops Center, Pentagon, Washington, DC
"I've already talked with the SecDef twice, and he is very interested in this, so tell me the latest, Mark," Cal told him.

The entire team was in their basement Ops Center, and the flat monitors had digital imagery and maps up of northern India. Another had weather on half a screen, and a feed from J-2 Operations Cell over at PACOM. Another panel had up the logo for the 11th Marine Expeditionary Unit and looked to be a secure communications link with the USS *Makin Island*.

"Sir, this is truly unbelievable. We've established good comms via the MARS radio link up on the fifth floor. We are actually talking with the village elder in Chal, India, who has Ford in his village," replied Mark.

MARS was the Military Auxiliary Radio Station network, established in 1925, and was built for amateur radio operators. Still in use today, the

Defense Department–sponsored program was a civilian auxiliary consisting of citizens interested in assisting the military with communications on a local, national, and international basis as an adjunct to normal communications. MARS has a long history of providing worldwide auxiliary emergency communications during times of need and has a volunteer force of over three thousand amateur radio operators.

"What's his health condition?" Cal asked.

"Not sure. All we can get is that he is burning up hot, no injuries that he can see, but Robert talked with the gentleman for a while. Any other details, Robert?"

"It's him. Village elder Vivaan says he was wearing a one-piece outfit, green, with black foot gear. Has a beard. Smelly. Was completely out of it when they picked him up," Robert added.

"They must have crashed somehow, and he has been living in the mountains for the last...what, almost four months?" Cal commented. "No mention of Pinky?"

Emily shook her head. "Unknown, sir."

"Got it. OK. What are we doing about it? Plan generated yet?" Cal asked.

Mark nodded. "You betcha. A few options. We have a few MH-60 Seahawks available from HSM-73 Battlecats on the *Roosevelt* with Carrier Air Wing-17."

Smiling, "Nope. I know their Skipper Bick and love Seahawks, but they won't have the speed for that distance. What else?" Cal said.

"We figured you'd say that so...earlier, we selected the Marine Corps option. Makin Island Amphibious Ready Group and her embarked 11th Marine Expeditionary Unit. They are in the US 5th Fleet area of operations in the Indian Ocean. They already had two MV-22 Ospreys doing an embassy milk-and-cookies run," Mark said. "You know, sir, delivering the mail and admin stuff." He pointed to the map on the screen. "They were already at the New Delhi airport getting fuel with both Marines and navy corpsmen onboard. They are now waiting for Mr. Lance Monterey from State Department to arrive. Lance is their interpreter for Hindi, plus he'll be dressed like a local instead of a cammied up Marine," explained Mark.

"Good. V-22's are good."

The United States Marine Corps had been deploying forces around the world since the year 1775. Today, their forces were organized into a Marine Air Ground Task Force, which is a team of air, ground, and support assets located on a US Navy ship. Sometimes the units were established for specific missions, while others hoped they could lend a hand to project the United States' national security interests. Priding themselves on time-sensitive missions, the combined US Navy and US Marine Corps team was able to provide a dominant and effective force on exceptionally short notice.

"An air force C-17 is inbound to New Delhi from Qatar, rerouted in the air from their previous mission. We expect Ford to be back to New Delhi soon, and then on the C-17 to Germany in no more than three hours," Mark said. "I've also called over to the hospital in Ramstein and Walter Reed at Bethesda to give both a heads-up. Once he's stable at Ramstein, he's off to the States. Expecting him in both intensive care units," Robert shared.

"Excellent. Thank you, Mark. And we can watch here on the video feed?"

Jeanie nodded her head. "Hi, sir, yes, we can. I'll pull it up live from the 11th MEU gear. Helmet cams. No issues at all."

Village of Chal, India, 8,200 Feet, Himalayas

The two V-22 pilots, Captain Mike Zimmerman and Major Terry Haines, zoomed over the landing zone at about five hundred feet above ground level. Happy to be out of the heavy smog and pollution, the Marine pilots were pleased with the visibility to the northeast. The MV-22 was loud, and the mountain valleys made their engine and propeller noise even louder, their blades slapping the wind as they rotated to produce lift.

The MV-22 was a radical tilt-rotor aircraft that had a single three-bladed turboprop engine nacelle on each wingtip. For her takeoff and landing, the pilots could move the nacelles vertical to move like a helicopter. For in-flight operations, the nacelles on the wings could move ninety degrees forward in just seconds, making it fly like a fuel efficient, fast airplane. The Marine Corps version of the aircraft could fly over 2,100 miles, and her operational range was 1,100 miles.

The loud sounds startled the villagers of Chal, as they had never seen an airplane up close. The aircraft circled the village now at about 250 feet above ground level, ensuring the area was clear of obstacles below, especially people and animals.

Major Haines selected her landing area and started a descent for a relatively flat piece of terrain near the stream. The aircraft bucked and moved through the disturbed airflow on the way down, looking to the locals like something from another planet. The kids in the village kept pointing while their parents held them from running.

The aircraft landed safely, and Lance Monterey got out with two Marines dressed in camouflage, as well as two corpsmen who were experts in medical care. The live feed was being transmitted to the Pentagon off the Marines' battlefield operations kit.

The kit consisted of a small tactical computer, a helmet-mounted camera, a mini weather sensor, a wearable antenna with secure GPS, a pocket range finder, satellite communications, a PRC-152A radio, tactical ROVER-e and tactical ROVER-p, and a digital close-air support system.

"Namaste. Welcome to Chal village. Please. Come. You come and eat chaat with us. I will show you your American, too," Vivaan told them. Chaat were hot, sour, and spicy snacks known in Northern India, and Vivaan had more than twenty-five different seasonings available for them.

Lance was surprised he spoke English, as he was expecting perhaps Hindustani, which was a combo of Hindi and Urdu. When spoken together, they have some scripts the same, but different words that mean different things. Muslims are associated with Urdu, while Hindus are associated with Hindi. There are fifteen main languages in India, and half of India's 1.32 billion people understand both of these languages.

"Namaste. Sir, that is very kind of you. My name is Lance Monterey, and I am a foreign service officer with the US Department of State, from the US embassy in New Delhi. Please know we are grateful for your gracious hospitality with our American citizen Ford Stevens. On behalf of our deputy chief of mission, Daniel Lewis, we have some gifts for your village as a show of our appreciation. May we see him?" Lance explained.

"Yes, yes, come, this way. My wife and daughters have been caring for him. He has been asleep since arriving. Aayush had found him just past where you just were. Back there toward the creek. Here. Sir. Please, have something to eat and drink."

When foods were concerned, each state in India was proud of their specific specialty. Some of the best good in India was not found in restaurants of a large city, but in villages full of talented cooks, serving everything from dried turnip rings with sun-dried tomatoes to tasty rice cakes.

"Understand, sir. Thank you." Lance replied, as they entered into his home to see Ford. "Thank you so much for your generous hospitality, Vivaan. But I think we should attend to your guest first, if that is OK."

Lance and the two navy corpsmen took a look at Ford while the two Marines watched on. One corpsman had his eyebrows raised and slipped his hands into medical gloves with a snap. "Awful. Just an awful, nasty smell. He's filthy." One corpsman opened each eye and shone a pen light in it. "Let's get an IV in him. Nasty. This critter is beat down hard."

One corpsman cut open Ford's sleeves on his thick flight suit with scissors and saw that his body was riddled with sores and red rashes. He was able to wipe his arm clean with an alcohol swab and find his vein nearly immediately. Ford received a saline solution of sodium and chlorine to begin replacing lost fluids, attempting to correct his electrolyte imbalances.

The other corpsman started cutting off his side of the flight suit, and the smell was overwhelming. Ford had defecated in his rotted boxer shorts and flight suit and was lying in his own filth. He was covered in urine and feces and infested with gruesome maggots.

"Temp is 105.7," he said as he raised his eyebrows. "He's got a severe infection here. That's, like, danger fever. Chief, throw in some levofloxacin in his IV for me. This cat is burning up," he said, placing his stethoscope on his chest. "Lungs sound like total crap. Wheezing...wind tunnel...full of fluid. Bet he has pneumonia, too."

A medical professional can hear wheezing in a patient's lungs, which usually means spasm and inflammation are present in the bronchial tubes.

The Pentagon group watched in horror as the corpsmen feverishly moved around him.

THE BLACK SCORPION PILOT

"I'm going to get his blood pressure, oxygen saturation, and pulse readings," the second corpsman said, and in what seemed like seconds, he didn't like what he saw. "Mr. Monterey, we have to move him stat," he said to Lance. "Your guy ain't gonna make it if he stays any longer. Grizzly Adams here is going to die, like real soon, if we don't fly his ass out."

Basement Ops Center, Pentagon, Washington, DC

The secretary of defense, along with Undersecretary Cal Burns, were in the room, as well as the entire team of Mark, Emily, Robert, Michelle, and Jeanie.

"Hold up, Mr. Monterey. Lance. Hold up. Can you hear me from the Pentagon?"

Lance turned to the Marines holding the comm gear. He could hear him over the clear satellite feed, but not see him.

"Yes, Mark, loud and clear. I can't see you, but I can hear you."

"OK, we can see you and the team there in India. We've been watching on a live feed and didn't want to interrupt. Hey, have the Marine with the camera go over to Ford closer. The one with the camera. That doesn't look like him to me. Are you sure that is Captain Ford Stevens?"

The Marine went over to Ford as instructed.

"No way that's him," Robert said. "Nowhere close."

"You think?" Mark asked. "Hey, Marine. The flight suit on the ground. Pick it up and put it on camera. Read his cloth name tag." He put it on camera.

"Yup, that's his name tag," Robert said, master of the obvious, reading Ford Stevens out loud to the team standing there.

"We can read," Mark snapped humorously at Robert.

Emily sat silently, taking it all in. She didn't know what to think.

Mark wanted the camera much closer on his face. "Lance, go much closer with that camera. Hey, Marine, I want to see his face. Closer."

The Marine with the helmet camera and Lance walked around from the pile of Ford's gear and jacket to the other side of the makeshift rope bed. They got the camera right on Ford's face for the room to see.

"Fuck. That's Ford?" Mark said out loud. "No way that's him. This wiry guy is a disheveled mess. That looks nothing like him. Are you sure? If it is, he looks hideous."

Robert was now curious. "Lance, any identifiable birthmarks on this guy? We can check his medical records, but do you see anything, like a scar? Last time we saw him he was about 190 pounds, maybe 200. No facial hair, a former Division I football player."

The navy corpsman were laughing out loud. "Well, this guy is no husky grizzly bear. Looks like a little Division III gymnast, not a football player."

Lance wasn't sure now himself. "Huh. Let me check," as he searched. "Nothing I can see on his arms." The Marine helped him look at his neck and chest. "Nothing. No scars or tattoos that I can see. Beard is pretty grown in and scraggly."

Emily shook her head with a blissful aura on her face. "Hey. Hey, Lance Monterey."

"Yeah?"

"Check his arse."

"Check his what? I'm not checking his ass," Lance replied. "I don't even have gloves on."

"Listen to me. Listen to me closely. Check his arse. Pull his trousers down and roll him. Does he have a tattoo of a leprechaun on his arse cheek? The Fighting Irish logo from Notre Dame?"

The secretary chuckled and let out a smirk, then glanced at Cal. Cal shrugged his shoulders. Everyone in the room shot glances at each other.

The corpsmen both heard the request and took their latex-gloved hands to roll him over to check. Their eyes rolled back at the smell and sight.

"Aw. The smell," the corpsman said looking. He shot a look at the others in the room, and a smirk.

"Confirmed, Washington. This is your guy," replied Lance over the satellite feed. "Luck of the Irish on his ass."

All eyes in the room went to Emily as she sat smiling ear to ear.

"That's interesting, Emily, that you…knew that," Robert told her, attempting to hold back his rare smile and laughter.

"Belt up and shut it," Emily replied back, winking at him.

THE END

EPILOGUE

Walter Reed National Military Medical Center, Bethesda, Maryland

Mark handed him the velvet engagement ring box, and Ford slipped it under the white bed sheets out of sight. "We nearly lost you twice, kid," Mark told Ford.

"I feel very blessed to be here. Downright lucky. If there is anything I learned up there in the mountains, it's priorities on the important things in life. First, that I'm done drinking. Acted like a cleansing program up there. I don't know, maybe like AA. You know, Alcoholics Anonymous. Second thing was about family and doing things now, rather than waiting," giving him a head nod. "Thanks for fixing the diamond."

Ford's trip through the mountains, both mentally and physically, was as close to the Greek mythology "katabasis" as someone could get. Katabasis, meaning a journey of "going down" and returning stronger after the event, was one of textbook resilience. With no distractions and plenty of time to think things through, Ford had the opportunity to work out his demons and place true importance on things in his life. The crash provided his own twelve-step program. He was able to get rid of baggage and any thoughts of overinflated ego, leaving him isolated in the wild with himself, the real and raw Ford Stevens.

"I'm sure it did feel like a dry-out. Plenty of time to think about life and decisions. You know, your future…" Mark quietly shared with him. Mark took off his bowling shirt, revealing a purple camouflaged T-shirt.

Psychologists have talked about behavior change in this manner and many agree that it's hard to do. Replacing old habits with new ones made substantial changes in Ford's brain, allowing him to do something with his time on the mountain instead of drinking: reflecting on life to date, singing songs from his Notre Dame days and thinking about his future.

"Jeez, nice purple shirt, Mark." A few seconds passed. "I'm sorry I missed Pinky's funeral. Glad you guys could find her, get her remains. I'm sure her parents were upset, but hopefully just a little bit satisfied about the closure," Ford told him.

"We all attended. Not a dry eye in the place. Her family knows you did your best."

"Any indications of what caused it? The rollback and shutdown?"

"We'd have to ask Robert. He just got back from a collection and destruction mission to see what he could find in the wreckage. I do know you climbed plenty of terrain without a lick of climbing gear. Really impressive, Ford. Robert will be here soon, and we can ask him."

Ford nodded. "Thanks," he relied quietly, feeling fortunate to have lived.

"Got to get you back up flying!" Mark told him, with a tone of sarcasm.

Ford lay in his hospital bed, recovering slowly, having lost nearly thirty-five pounds, a toe, and the tip of an ear; nearly died from kidney failure; and suffered the loss of a crew mate. His maggots were so bad that his groin and rectum had to be packed with ground beef to lure them away, a rare but real medical procedure.

"Mark. I know. Need a break from flying to just sit here and recover. Drinking this blue Pedialyte here. What do ya think?" Ford asked.

"I think we can arrange that, Major," Emily told him as she walked in from the hall with her gigantic smile. "How are you doing, Ford? Better today, love?"

"Hey, Em. Yup, doctors think I can start physical therapy across the street next week. Kidneys and blood work looking much better, too."

Ford's parasites, or worms, were the one of the last items he was having trouble getting rid of. Discovered in his stool sample, and picked up by unwashed food and undercooked meat, they took some time to get rid of from his body.

A few seconds passed, then, walking into the room and surprising Emily were her parents, along with Ford's parents. "Hello, Emily. Hi, Ford," the parents said, greeting everyone in unison.

Emily was shocked. "Hi, what…what's going on? Everyone is here?"

"Emily," Ford said, clearing his throat. His sunken face displayed a slight look of embarrassment.

"Yes…why are you acting weird?" Emily asked.

"Emily, we both love each other. And I wished I had done this earlier, but was distracted by Wu's passing," Ford explained. He took out a box from under the sheets.

"I want to spend my whole life with you. Your parents blessed what I am about to ask you. And if I could get out of bed and down on a knee without this IV in my arm, I would," Ford told Emily, taking the box from its hiding place. "Em, will you marry me?"

Emily blushed, and her eyes were full of tears of joy. "Yes, mate, I will marry you. Yes."

The Bethesda hospital room erupted in cheers and clapping. Little did they see that Cal Burns had walked in, too, smiling and happy he was able to see his team smiling again.

After all the congratulations went by, Cal went over to Ford.

"How's my favorite Air Force Reserve pilot?"

"Hi Mr. Burns. Recovering slowly, but I'll make it. Medicines make me feel dopey at times, but I'll recover."

"Good to hear, Ford. Well, when you're ready, I'd like you to come to the Pentagon and work with me. When you're fully recovered. Be my military assistant, OK? At Headquarters Air Force. That's if you want to do it."

"I would be honored Mr. Secretary, but Air Force Reserve just offered me command of a squadron. Tankers at Niagara flying KC-135s." Ford replied. "But thank you."

"Buffalo Niagara Falls area?" Cal said, nodding his head. "Great people, excellent unit to lead. Good for you, Ford. I'm happy for you," he said, placing his hand on Ford's shoulder.

"Thank you, Mr. Burns. We'd like to settle down. Considering living on the Niagara River, north of the falls. Perhaps Lewiston or Youngstown, New York."

"Can't forget the Bills. Jim Kelly territory."

"Since this has happened, it's allowed me to think a bit. My brother Charlie will be getting his pilot wings soon, assigned to Niagara to fly as a lieutenant, so it's a good fit for us all."

Cal understood, shook hands, said his good-byes, and nodded twice to Mark that he wanted to talk to him in the hallway. Standing in front of infamous orange fluorescent sign of the Navy SEAL Lt. Jason Redman hanging in the hallway, the two men looked at each other.

"Mark, need you do something for me. I know you're at DIA still, but I need you. A few things," Calvin said, hesitating.

"Me? OK. What is it?"

Calvin pushed out a long breath. "Does he know?" asking, with his demeanor and tone changing. He was as serious as a heart attack now.

"Know what?"

Calvin just stared at him, drilling a bore through his eyes.

"You know what I'm referring to."

"No, sir, Ford doesn't know yet. Still med'd up. I'll tell him once he recovers more and the reason why. No one knows actually."

Calvin nodded a bit. "All right, all right. Just tell him once he settles up there at Niagara. Next item. Write up a memo for me, make it effective today," Cal told him.

"Memo?"

Cal waited for two nurses to pass by, then said it quietly. His personal protective detail was looking strangely at him from down the hall. "Look, Operation SANDY BEACH is over. Effectively immediately, get rid of all our freaking stealth jets from the museums. The black jets from Air Force Wright-Patt, like the damn SR-71, stealth fighter, and bomber, and U-2 and all of it. All gone. Done. Get rid of those freaking things in the memo, and I'll facilitate the political fallout. Got it?"

"Yes, Mr. Secretary," replied Mark, holding his trademark Hawaiian shirt in his hand, laughing.

"And don't get someone else do to it, like Mike Klubb. You, you do it."

"Wouldn't even think of Klubby," replied Mark, grinning, and looking at his watch. "He already home drinking his hot chocolate."

"Last thing, Savona. I know you call me the 'Old Man.' Cut it out," Cal told him sternly, his face slowly growing into a huge smile.

Much later on that evening, Ford lay awake in his hospital bed alone, reading Ric Edelman's new book *The Truth about Your Future*. Ford had been a Ric Edelman fan for years, reading and following the famous financial planner with the national radio show since his dad had introduced Ford to him over twenty years ago.

Ford sat up a bit in his hospital bed, with IV pumping meds into his body still, trying to concentrate over the beeps, tones, and alarms of the hospital floor. He was alone in his private room now and switched his attention between the book, the flurry of nurses walking up and down the hallway outside, and the routine news messages appearing on his smartphone screen.

The vibration from a text message on his phone startled him, unexpected this late at night.

Private caller: i am glad your OK
Who is this at 1:30 a.m.? Ford thought. *Grammar is awful.*
Ford: Thank you. Who is this?
Private: I watched wille Wonka movie. went to Wegmans and Hersey Park mue zeem

Willie Wonka? Ford whispered to himself. *Wegmans Grocery Store?*

Ford: Who is this?
Private: u were rite about Netflix. You really can watch anything u want

No response from the private caller on text. A few seconds went by, so Ford continued with his texting.

> Ford: Who is this? I don't know you. You must have the wrong number.

Ten seconds went by, and no further messages appeared, so Ford continued with reading Ric Edelman. A nurse on her rounds stopped in to look at the screen and made a note for the chart at the foot of Ford's bed.

> Private: you looked really sick coming in, but much better now. Coloring back.
> *This person must know me. Who is it?*
> Ford: Your name comes up as private caller. Who is this?
> Private: it is me. got to watch new star Wars
> Ford: Who is me?
> Private: I got to see who won President. I ate a hot dog earlier today. Went to Nationals Cubs game. Got to do all my kick the bucket stuff we talked about.

Ford looked up from his phone and displayed the thousand-yard stare of horror, laser focused at his bathroom doorknob in front of his bed. His expressionless face was frozen, his breathing calm, his mouth gaping open, and his head titled sideways a bit. *Is this my medicine?* Ford squinted his eyes. The room was quiet, and now the hallway. *Only one guy has ever mentioned Wegmans or Willy Wonka to me in my entire life.*

> Private: like the old days, Ford.
> Ford: Look, I'm getting annoyed. I don't know who this is. You had better stop texting me ASAP.
> Private: Ford.
> Ford: What??!!?? What the hell do you want?

Another few seconds of silence. The phone vibrated yet again.

Private: Ford.

Geez. This freaking guy. Then Ford noticed strangely his Peanut light was in the green, which meant whoever this was had the encryption software on their own phone.

Ford: Last time, guy. Then I block you. Stop.
Private: Jojo Rising, my friend.
"Jojo Rising?" Ford mouthed the words quietly.

Just then, a man in his thirties walked into the hospital room and closed the door behind him. Ford could not see who it was at first because his back was turned, as the hospital night-lighting was set on the hospital floor and made it hard to see.

Ford's eyes squinted and then got bigger by the second. *No way. It can't be.*

The man walked over with his face down, limping from a bad leg or knee, and grabbed Ford's left hand. The Chinese man looked up and smiled at Ford.

Slowly, Ford began to recognize who was in front of him. Ford mumbled slowly, "Oh my, God, Wu. You...you're...alive?" Ford said quietly and in shock. His eyes welled up.

Ford's best friend, previously thought dead and buried at Arlington National Cemetery, stood in front of him and held his hand. Captain Wu Lee was, indeed, alive.

APPENDIX

**Sign outside Navy SEAL Lt. Jason Redman's Door at Walter Reed
National Military Hospital, Bethesda, Maryland**

Attention to all who enter here. If you are coming into this room with
sorrow or to feel sorry for my wounds, go elsewhere. The wounds I
received I got in a job I love, doing it for people I love, supporting
the freedom of a country I deeply love. I am incredibly tough and
will make a full recovery. What is full? That is the absolute utmost
physically my body has the ability to recover. Then I will push that
about 20 percent farther through sheer mental tenacity. This room
you are about to enter is a room of fun, optimism, and intense rapid
regrowth. If you are not prepared for that, go elsewhere.

—SEAL Lt. Jason Redman, USN, Retired

Personal Note

Wu Lee's health condition was based off my close friend, John, a retired C-130 Delaware Air National Guard pilot and United Airlines pilot.

He was misdiagnosed multiple times, both in Europe and in the United States, and later passed away after fighting terminal pancreatic cancer for only six short months.

I appreciate the tremendous outpouring of support from readers who have related to Wu's condition since writing *The Devil Dragon Pilot*. From kids sharing stories about their parents to coworkers sharing stories about their friends, I am happy to have helped bring a smile on your face and aid in celebrating their lives.

If you enjoyed *The Black Scorpion Pilot*, it would mean a tremendous amount to me if you were to leave a positive review on Amazon.com.

Thank you.

All the best,
Cheese Colby

ABOUT THE AUTHOR

Lawrence A. Colby's first novel, *The Devil Dragon Pilot*, part of the Ford Stevens Military-Aviation Thriller Series, has been a worldwide bestseller in the United States, India, Canada, United Kingdom, and Australia and is published in twelve countries.

Writing with full authenticity from being part of a small group of pilots who completed both US Navy and US Air Force Undergraduate Pilot Training Programs, he includes real-world action from his experiences. He has flown six different types of civilian aircraft and ten different types of military aircraft from two different services. Known in the squadrons by the call sign "Cheese," he is qualified in jets, propeller aircraft, and helicopters, and has completed multiple worldwide deployments. Cheese is also an FAA commercial pilot. His number of takeoffs match his number of landings.

Cheese is working on book three, titled *Buffalo Rules*. He and his family live in the Washington, DC, area.

www.ColbyAviationThrillers.com
Facebook/Twitter/Instagram: @ColbyThrillers

ACKNOWLEDGMENTS

A warm and sincere thank-you to the following individuals for their expertise, encouragement, and research.

One of the best things about this job is the interviews, getting to understand a different culture, traveling to a different country, and talking to people with different perspectives than my own. For all of the people that graciously gave me their time, I am grateful.

To Jodi, for your continued love and patience, thank you for everything you've done to take care of us. To Gavin and Brennan, for your positive attitude and story ideas, allowing me to provide stories highlighting our great teams. To the Russo family, you guys are the best, thank you. To George M., thank you for all of your strong encouragement and ideas. To Ginny and Ed, thank you for years of love and support. To Cliff S., thanks for making it happen so many years ago and overriding my 'no.' To Brian Smith and Lisa Ziehmann, thank you for your kind support to veterans, especially your generous financial donations to Team Rubicon Global. To All Civil Air Patrol Cadets, with encouragement that you can do it, too. To Andrew R., Sonny H., Bill Y., Sean M., Jerry T., Brian S., and Neal B., for the edits and technical aspects of the stories—simply, "wow." To Marine Corps Officers at The Basic School, Quantico, Virginia, thanks for reading it in the Q. To Uniformed Officers and Special Agents of the US Secret Service, thank you for reading The Devil Dragon Pilot at the White House. To Special Agents of the Federal Bureau of Investigation at WFO, keep up the great work and thanks for being fans. To The men and women of the 914th at Niagara- you guys are one heck of a team, and I was proud to fly with you. To USAF and USN Flight Students, thanks for being fans and providing your years of photos on Instagram- remember, never give up. To Rocko B. Cooper, thank you for years of friendship from the top. To Owen and Debbie S., Buffalo, thanks for the support and ideas – keep them flowing- come at me bro. To Lindsey and the Skull Creek Boathouse Restaurant Team, Hilton Head Island, South Carolina, thanks for the early opportunity and giving me a chance. To Mark M. at The Eisenhower School, National Defense University, thanks for the book reading! To Chris and Megan P, you guys are terrific friends- thank you. To Janice, General Aviation News, thank you for your article years ago and the assistance. To Management Team at Clyde's Restaurant, Georgetown, Washington, DC, for allowing fans to take photos of the Ford and Emily table up front. To Ric Edelman, Edelman Financial, Fairfax, Virginia, thanks for mentioning The Devil Dragon Pilot on the air- BIG! To Peter at Navy League. To Bigfoot, Joint Forces Quarterly. To Hilton Head Monthly Magazine, thanks for putting me up there with the big dogs. To Danny, 45 Bistro in Savannah, Georgia for your kind support, as well as putting a copy of The Devil Dragon Pilot on display at the bar. To Jeff, Reserve Officers Association for your support in stressing the constant importance of our Reserve and National Guard heroes! To Team Rubicon Global and the Headstrong Project for continuing to support our great veterans, long after they return home. To Superfans Vern S and Marshall K., thanks for being the best. To Todd, Steven F. Udvar-Hazy Center, Smithsonian National Air and Space Museum, Washington Dulles International Airport, for allowing me to contact you for weeks with a smile. To Thomas and Jean, Barnes and Noble, thank you for the Meet and Greet support. To Jenny, and her professional editing team at Elite Editing, thanks for the fantastic work. To Alphonse R., for working to bring The Devil Dragon Pilot to the big screen! To Bick, for my final flight, as it was one for the history books. To Mom and Dad, for everything.

Thanks for reading!

Join our mailing list and get regular updates on *The Ford Stevens Military-Aviation Thriller Series*!

Stay in touch to see what Ford Stevens will be up to next in *Buffalo Orders: Book 3*!

www.ColbyAviationThrillers.com
Facebook/Twitter/Instagram: @ColbyThrillers

CPSIA information can be obtained
at www.ICGtesting.com
Printed in the USA
LVHW091255170519
618237LV00001B/38/P

9 781541 285835